'*Harlem Shuffle* is a wildly entertaining romp. But as you might expect with this two-time Pulitzer Prize winner and MacArthur genius, Whitehead also delivers a devastating, historically grounded indictment of the separate and unequal lives of Blacks and whites in mid-20th century New York'

Independent

'Golson Whitehead has a couple of Pulitzers under his belt, along with several other awards celebrating his outstanding novels. *Harlem Shuffle* is a suspenseful crime thriller that's sure to add to the tally – it's a fabulous novel you must read'

NPR

'With *Harlem Shuffle*, Whitehead stakes a claim to be the storyteller America needs right now'

Spectator

'Another triumph from Pulitzer-winner Whitehead'

People

FROM THE PULITZER PRIZE-WINNING AUTHOR OF *THE UNDERGROUND RAILROAD*

Colson Whitehead is the author of ten books of fiction and nonfiction, including the Pulitzer Prize-winning novels *The Underground Railroad* and *The Nickel Boys*. A recipient of MacArthur and Guggenheim fellowships, he lives in New York City.

Praise for *Harlem Shuffle*:

'Colson Whitehead's dazzling new thriller . . . In *Harlem Shuffle*, Whitehead flexes his literary muscles further, extending the boundaries and expectations of crime writing. The book is also a social drama interrogating the nature of prejudice and how an environment limits ambition'
Guardian

'Gloriously entertaining . . . a zingy social drama, that combines flights of high comedy with reflections on the nature of black self-help and black empowerment in America. A more purely enjoyable novel is unlikely to emerge this year'
Evening Standard

'Within the morality tale about a good man dragged into the underworld, there lurk still darker accounts of broken lives, which capture the longing for dignity and agency at the heart of the black American experience. It's a red-blooded book full of powerful personalities and worldly wisdom'
Sunday Times

'Whitehead's latest book, *Harlem Shuffle*, finds its centre of gravity in Harlem, New York, transporting readers to the precipice of the civil rights movement in the late 1950s and early 1960s, a moment when Harlem uprisings were remaking the literal and political landscape. From here he crafts a brilliant crime novel that doubles as a meditation on the nature of black geography . . . It is Carney's effort to reconcil[ ] trive for a home [ ] [und]erbelly, that pro[ ]
Financia[l]

90710 000 524 006

'Wildly entertaining ... Whitehead also delivers a devastating, historically grounded indictment of the separate and unequal lives of Blacks and whites in mid-20th century New York'
Daily Mail

'The plot he devised for *Harlem Shuffle* offered a new, high-geared narrative engine to play with, but it also gave him a way to explore ideas about the slippery nature of morality, power (and who holds it), and the social hierarchies of criminal subcultures'
New York Times

'*Harlem Shuffle* is a bravura performance, an immersive, laugh-out-loud, riveting adventure whose narrative energy is boosted by its memorable hero and a highly relevant backdrop of social injustice'
Harvard Review

'A fiendishly clever romp, a heist novel that's also a morality play about respectability politics, a family comedy disguised as a noir ... *Harlem Shuffle* reads like a book whose author had enormous fun writing it. The dialogue crackles and sparks; the zippy heist plot twists itself in one showy misdirection after another. Most impressive of all is lovable family-man Ray, whose relentless ambition drives the plot forward while his glib salesman's patter keeps you guessing about his true intentions. This book is a blast that will make you think, and what could be better than that?'
Vox

'*Harlem Shuffle* is a wildly entertaining romp. But as you might expect with this two-time Pulitzer Prize winner and MacArthur genius, Whitehead also delivers a devastating, historically grounded indictment of the separate and unequal lives of Blacks and whites in mid-20th century New York'
Associated Press

'It's a superlative story, but the most impressive achievement is Whitehead's loving depiction of a Harlem 60 years gone – 'that rustling, keening thing of people and concrete' – which lands as detailed and vivid as Joyce's Dublin. Don't be surprised if this one wins Whitehead another major award'
Publishers Weekly (starred review)

'This riotous, sentimental and brilliant novel feels like another piece of the jigsaw being placed. Or a trump card being laid down'
Scotsman

'*Harlem Shuffle* exudes authorial power and profound insight into the American experiment. In this multi-layered crime narrative, Whitehead presents complex characters who embody the complexity of their social milieu. Like America, Harlem's stratified beauty is symbolic of the constant tension between those who are corrupt and those who are trying to lead a respectable existence'
National Book Review

OTHER BOOKS BY COLSON WHITEHEAD

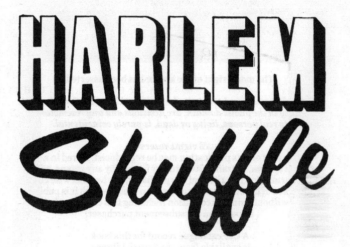

HARLEM Shuffle

COLSON WHITEHEAD

FLEET

2022

FLEET

First published in the United States in 2021 by Doubleday
First published in Great Britain in 2021 by Fleet
This paperback edition published in 2022 by Fleet

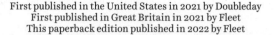

1 3 5 7 9 10 8 6 4 2

The moral right of the author has been asserted.

The protest flyers on pages 288 and 297 are taken from Race Riots
New York 1964 by Fred C. Shapiro and James W. Sullivan.

ISBN 978-0-7088-9947-2

Book design by Pei Loi Koay
Printed and bound in Great Britain by Clays Ltd, Elcograf S.p.A.

Papers used by Fleet are from well-managed forests
and other responsible sources.

Fleet
An imprint of
Little, Brown Book Group
Carmelite House
50 Victoria Embankment
London EC4Y 0DZ

An Hachette UK Company
www.hachette.co.uk

www.littlebrown.co.uk

for Beckett

CONTENTS

THE TRUCK

1959

> "Carney was only slightly
> bent when it came to being
> crooked . . ."

His cousin Freddie brought him on the heist one hot night in early June. Ray Carney was having one of his run-around days—uptown, downtown, zipping across the city. Keeping the machine humming. First up was Radio Row, to unload the final three consoles, two RCAs and a Magnavox, and pick up the TV he left. He'd given up on the radios, hadn't sold one in a year and a half no matter how much he marked them down and begged. Now they took up space in the basement that he needed for the new recliners coming in from Argent next week and whatever he picked up from the dead lady's apartment that afternoon. The radios were top-of-the-line three years ago; now padded blankets hid their slick mahogany cabinets, fastened by leather straps to the truck bed. The pickup bounced in the unholy rut of the West Side Highway.

Just that morning there was another article in the *Tribune* about the city tearing down the elevated highway. Narrow and indifferently cobblestoned, the road was a botch from the start. On the best days it was bumper-to-bumper, a bitter argument of honks and curses, and on rainy days the potholes were treacherous lagoons, one grim slosh. Last week a customer wandered into the store with his head wrapped like a mummy—beaned by a chunk of falling balustrade while walking under the damn thing. Said he was going to sue. Carney said, "You're in your rights." Around Twenty-Third Street the pickup's wheels bit into a crater and he thought one of the RCAs was going to launch from the bed into the Hudson River. He was relieved when he was able to sneak off at Duane Street without incident.

Carney's man on Radio Row was halfway down Cortlandt, off Greenwich, right in the thick. He got a space outside Samuel's Amazing Radio—REPAIR ALL MAKES—and went to check that Aronowitz was in. Twice in the last year he'd come all the way down to find the shop shut in the middle of the day.

A few years ago, walking past the crammed storefronts was like twirling a radio dial—this store blared jazz into the street out of horn loudspeakers, the next store German symphonies, then ragtime, and so on. S & S Electronics, Landy's Top Notch, Steinway the Radio King. Now he was more likely to hear rock and roll, in a desperate lure of the teenage scene, and to find the windows crammed with television sets, the latest wonders from DuMont and Motorola and the rest. Consoles in blond hardwood, the sleek new portable lines, and three-in-one hi-fi combos with picture tube, tuner, and turntable in the same cabinet, smart. What hadn't changed was Carney's meandering sidewalk route around the massive bins and buckets of vacuum tubes, audio transformers, and condensers that drew in tinkerers from all over the tri-state. Any part you need, all makes, all models, reasonable prices.

There was a hole in the air where the Ninth Avenue el used to run. That disappeared thing. His father had taken him here once or twice on one of his mysterious errands, when he was little. Carney still thought he heard the train sometimes, rumbling behind the music and haggling of the street.

Aronowitz hunched over the glass counter, with a loupe screwed into his eye socket, poking one of his gizmos. "Mr. Carney." He coughed.

There weren't many white men who called him mister. Downtown, anyway. The first time Carney came to the Row on business, the white clerks pretended not to see him, attending to hobbyists who came in after him. He cleared his throat, he gestured, and remained a black ghost, store after store, accumulating the standard humiliations, until he climbed the black iron steps to Aronowitz & Sons and the proprietor asked, "Can I help you, sir?" Can I help you as in *Can I help you?* As opposed to *What are you doing here?* Ray Carney, in his years, had a handle on the variations.

That first day, Carney told him he had a radio in need of repair; he had just picked up his sideline in gently used appliances. Aronowitz cut him off when he tried to explain the problem and got to work unscrewing the case. Carney didn't waste his breath on subsequent visits, merely set the radios before the maestro and let him have his way with it. The routine went: weary sighs and grunts as he surveyed the problem, with a jab and flash of silver implements. His Diagnometer tested fuses, resistors; he calibrated voltage, rummaged through unlabeled trays in the steel filing cabinets along the walls of the gloomy shop. If something big was afoot, Aronowitz twirled in his chair and scurried into the workshop in the back, to more grunts. He reminded Carney of a squirrel in the park, darting helter-skelter after lost nuts. Maybe the other squirrels of Radio Row understood this behavior, but it was animal madness to this civilian.

Often Carney went down the street for a ham and cheese to let the man work in peace.

Aronowitz never failed to make the fix, find the part. The new technology vexed the old man, however, and he usually had Carney return the next day for TV sets, or the next week once the new picture tube or valve arrived. Refusing to shame himself by walking down the block to hit up a competitor. That's how Carney ended up there that morning. He'd dropped off the twenty-one-inch Philco last week. If he was lucky, the old man would take the radios off his hands.

Carney carried one of the big RCAs into the shop and went back for the next. "I'd have the boy help you," Aronowitz said, "but I had to cut back on his hours."

The boy Jacob, a surly, pockmarked teenager from a Ludlow Street rookery, hadn't worked there for more than a year as far as Carney could tell. The "& Sons" on the sign had ever been aspirational—Aronowitz's wife had moved back to Jersey to live with her sister long ago—but bluster and bravado were a motif for Radio Row establishments. Top of the City, House of Values, Cannot Be Beaten. Decades before, the electronics boom made the neighborhood into a theater for immigrant ambition. Hang a shingle, deliver your pitch, and climb out of the tenement stew. If things go well, you open a second location, expand into the failed shop next door. Pass the business on to your sons and retire to one of the new Long Island suburbs. If things go well.

Carney thought Aronowitz should drop the Sons thing and go for something more hip: Atomic TV & Radio, Jet Age Electronics. But that'd be a reversal of their relationship, as it was Aronowitz who delivered the advice at this address, one entrepreneur to another, generally of the "physician, heal thyself" variety. Carney didn't need the old man's tips on accounting practices and merchandise placement. His business degree from Queens College hung in his office next to a signed photograph of Lena Horne.

Carney got the three radios inside. Sidewalk traffic on the Row wasn't what it used to be.

"No, they're not broken," Carney said as Aronowitz unfurled his roll of instruments. The roll was green felt, with slots. "I thought you'd want them, maybe."

"Nothing wrong with them?" Like something that worked okay was an alien proposition.

"I figured I was coming down to pick up the TV, I'd see if you were interested." On the one hand, why would a radio man need a radio, but on the other, every businessman had a sideline. He knew this to be true of Aronowitz. "Strip them for parts or something?"

Aronowitz's shoulders dropped. "Parts. I sure don't have customers, Mr. Carney, but I have parts."

"You have me, Aronowitz."

"I have you, Mr. Carney. And you are very reliable." He asked after Carney's wife and daughter. A baby on the way? Mazel tov. He ran a thumb down his black suspenders and considered. Dust squirmed in the light. "I know a guy in Camden," Aronowitz said, "he specializes. Likes RCAs. Maybe he's interested. Or he isn't. You leave them, next time you come in, I'll tell you how it went." There was the matter of the Magnavox. Walnut cabinet, eighteen-inch woofer, Collaro changer. And top-of-the-line three years ago. "Leave that, too, we'll see."

The old man had always been droopy in the face, a jowl overall with saggy lobes and eyelids, and droopy in his wretched posture. As if when he bent over the machines all those hours they were sucking him into themselves. The downward pull had accelerated recently, his submission to the facts of his life. The merchandise had changed, the clientele transformed into new beings, and aspiration wasn't all it was cracked up to be. But he had a few diversions to keep him busy, these twilight days.

"I have your TV," he said. He coughed into a faded yellow handkerchief. Carney followed him into the back.

The name of the store—stark letters in gold paint on the shop window—promised one thing, the shabby front office another, and this room delivered a third thing that was entirely spiritual. The atmosphere was different, murky yet reverential, the Radio Row hubbub hushed. Disassembled receivers, picture tubes in various sizes, guts of machines lay on cluttered metal shelves. In the center of the room, the worktable was spotlit where a blank space in the scarred wood waited for the next patient, tools and boxy measuring instruments arranged neatly around it. Fifty years ago, most of the stuff in the room hadn't existed, was half a notion scurrying at the edge of an inventor's imagination—and suddenly there were rooms like this, where men maintained its secrets.

Until the next thing came along.

There was a collapsible army cot where the boy's desk used to be, a plaid wool blanket curled in an *S* on top. Had he been sleeping there? As the radio man led him, Carney saw that he'd lost still more weight. He thought about asking after his health, but didn't.

Aronowitz kept a dusty display of transistor radios by the front door, but in the back items moved in more constant exchange. Carney's Philco 4242 sat on the floor. Freddie had steered it into Carney's store on a creaky dolly, swore it was in "A-1 condition." Some days Carney felt the need to press his cousin on a lie until it broke and some days his love was such that the slightest quiver of mistrust made him ashamed. When he'd plugged in the TV and turned it on, his reward was a white dot in the middle of the tube and a petulant hum. He didn't ask where Freddie got it. He never asked. The TVs moved quickly out of the gently used section when Carney priced them right.

"Still in the box," Carney said.

"What? Oh, those."

There was a stack of four Silvertone TVs by the bathroom door, blond-wood Lowboy Consoles, all-channel. Sears manufactured them, and Carney's customers revered Sears from childhood, when their parents ordered from catalogs because the white men in their Southern towns wouldn't sell to them, or jacked up the prices.

"A man brought those by yesterday," Aronowitz said. "I was told they fell off a truck."

"Boxes look fine."

"A very short fall, then."

A hundred and eighty-nine retail, let's say another twenty with the Harlem tax from a white store; overcharging was not limited to south of the Mason-Dixon. Carney said, "I could probably sell one to a customer in the market." A hundred fifty on installments, they'd sprout feet and march out the door singing "The Star-Spangled Banner."

"I can part with two. I'll throw in the work on the Philco. It was just a loose lead."

They did a deal for the TVs. On his way out the door, Aronowitz asked, "Can you help me bring your radios into the back? I like to keep the front presentable."

Uptown Carney took Ninth Avenue, not trusting the highway with his new TVs. Down three radios, up three sets—not a bad start to the day. He had Rusty unload the TVs into the store and drove up to the dead lady's house, 141st Street. Lunch was two hot dogs and a coffee at Chock Full o'Nuts.

* * *

3461 Broadway had a busted elevator. The sign had been up for a while. Carney counted the steps to the fourth floor. If he bought something and lugged it out to the truck, he liked to know how many steps to curse on the way down. On the second floor, someone was boiling pigs' feet and on the third, old socks from the smell of it. This had the feel of a wasted trip.

The daughter, Ruby Brown, let him in. The tenement had settled, and as she opened the door to 4G, it scraped the floor.

"Raymond," she said.

He couldn't place her.

"We were at Carver together, I was a few years behind you."

He nodded as if he remembered. "I'm sorry about your loss."

She thanked him and glanced down for a moment. "I came up to take care of things and Timmy James told me to call you."

Didn't know who he was, either. When he first got the pickup and started lending it out, and then buying furniture, he knew everyone. Now he'd been in business long enough that word had spread outside his old circle.

Ruby flicked on the hall light. They passed the galley kitchen and the two bedrooms off the hall. The walls were scuffed, gouged to plaster in spots—the Browns had lived there a long time. A wasted trip. In general when he got a furniture call, people had strange ideas about what he was looking for. Like he'd take any old thing, the saggy couch with springs poking out nappily, the recliner with sweated-into arms. He wasn't the junkman. The good finds were worth it, but he wasted too much time on false leads. If Rusty'd had any sense or taste, Carney could send his assistant on these missions, but he didn't have sense or taste. Come back with something that looked like raccoons nested in the horsehair stuffing.

Carney was wrong this time. The bright front room overlooked Broadway and the sound of an ambulance snuck in through the window. The dinette set in the corner was from the '30s, chipped and discolored, and the faded oval rug revealed traffic patterns, but the sofa and armchair were in factory condition. Heywood-Wakefield with that champagne finish everybody liked now. And sheathed in transparent vinyl slipcovers.

"I live in D.C. now," Ruby said. "I work in a hospital. But I'd been telling my mother to get rid of the couch for years, it was so old. Two months ago I bought these for her."

"D.C.?" he said. He unzipped the plastic.

"I like it there. There's less of that, you know?" She gestured toward the Broadway chaos below.

"Sure." He ran his hand over the green velvet upholstery: pristine. "It's from Mr. Harold's?" She hadn't bought the sofa from him, and Blumstein's didn't carry the line, so it had to be Mr. Harold's.

"Yes."

"Took good care of them," Carney said.

Work finished, Raymond took another look at Ruby. Dressed in a gray dress, round and plump. Tired in the eyes. She wore her hair in a curly Italian cut now, and then it flickered—Ruby

Brown as a stick-limbed teenager, with two long Indian pony-tails, a light blue blouse with a white Peter Pan collar. She hung out with a clique of studious girls back then. Strict parents, that type.

"Right, Carver High School," he said. He wondered if they'd laid Hazel Brown to rest already, what it was like to attend the funeral of your mother or father, what expression you screwed into your face at such times. The memories that popped up, this small thing or that big thing, what you did with your hands. Both of his parents were gone and he hadn't had that experience, so he wondered. "I'm sorry for your loss," he said again.

"She had a problem with her heart, the doctor told her last year."

He was a senior when she was a sophomore. Eleven years ago, 1948, when he was busy trying to get a handle on things. Spackling himself into something presentable. No one else was moved to help, so he had to do it himself. Learn to cook a meal, pay the bills when late notices arrived, have a spiel when the landlord came around.

There was a gang of younger kids on his case all the time, Ruby's classmates. The rough boys his age left him alone, they knew him from before and let him be because they had played together, but Oliver Handy and his group, they were of that feral breed, street. Oliver Handy, two front teeth knocked out since whenever, never let him pass without starting something.

Oliver and his group made fun of the spots on his clothes, which didn't fit properly and so they made fun of that in addition, they said he smelled like a garbage truck. Who had he been back then? Scrawny and shy, everything out of his mouth half a stammer. He shot up six inches junior year, as if his body knew it better catch up to handle his adult responsibilities. Carney in the old apartment on 127th, no mother, father aprowl or sleeping it off. He left for school in the morning, closed the door on those empty rooms and steeled himself for whatever lay beyond.

But the thing was, when Oliver made fun of him—outside the candy store, in the back stairwell at school—he'd already taught himself how to properly wash out a stain, hem his pants, take a good long shower before school. He made fun of him for who he'd been before he got his shit together.

What put a stop to it was smacking Oliver's face with an iron pipe. Curved in a *U* like it came from under a sink. The pipe had appeared in Carney's hands it seemed, cast out of the empty lot at the corner of Amsterdam and 135th where they surrounded him. His father's voice: That's how you handle a nigger who fucks with you. He felt bad seeing Oliver at school, swole up and slinking. Later he learned that his daddy had ripped off Oliver's daddy on some scam, stolen tires, and maybe that explained the whole thing.

It was the last time he raised his hand. The way he saw it, living taught you that you didn't have to live the way you'd been taught to live. You came from one place but more important was where you decided to go.

Ruby had decided on a new city and Carney chose life in the furniture business. A family. If it looked opposite of what he knew when he was little, it appealed.

He and Ruby talked crap about the old school, the teachers they hated. There was overlap. She had a nice, round face, and when she laughed he got the sense D.C. had been a good choice. No shortage of reasons to get out of Harlem if you could swing it.

"Your father used to work at the garage around the corner," she said.

Miracle Garage was the place his father worked at sometimes, when his main business ran dry. Hourly work, steady. The owner, Pat Baker, had been a running buddy of his father's before he went straight. Straight as in less bent; it cannot be said that every vehicle on the premises had its papers right. The garage had churn, as Carney called it, like Aronowitz's. Like his place. Stuff comes in, it goes out, like the tides.

Pat owed his daddy from back when and gave him work when he needed it. "Sure," Carney said, waiting for the kicker. Usually when someone mentioned his father it was a prelude to a disreputable story. *I saw two policemen haul him away outside Finian's* or *He was beating this sucker with the lid of a garbage can.* Then he had to figure what to make his face look like.

But she didn't share any shabby anecdote. "It closed down a few years ago," Ruby said.

They did a deal for the couch and the matching armchair.

"How about that radio?" she asked. It was next to a small bookcase. Hazel Brown had kept a bunch of artificial flowers in a red vase on top of it.

"I'll have to pass on the radio," he said. He paid the super some bucks to help him carry the sofa down to the truck, he'd send Rusty tomorrow for the armchair. Sixty-four steps.

* * *

Carney's Furniture had been a furniture store before he took over the lease, and a furniture store before that. In sticking around for five years, Carney had outlasted Larry Early, a repellent personality ill-suited for retail, and Gabe Newman, who lit out in the dead of the night, leaving behind a clutch of fuming creditors, his family, two girlfriends, and a basset hound. A superstitious sort might have deemed the location cursed in regards to home goods. The property wasn't much to look at, but it might make a man his fortune. Carney took the previous tenants' busted schemes and failed dreams as a kind of fertilizer that helped his own ambitions prosper, the same way a fallen oak in its decomposition nourishes the acorn.

The rent was reasonable for 125th Street, the store well-situated.

Rusty had the two big fans going on account of the June heat. He had a tiresome habit of comparing the weather in New York City to that of his native Georgia, in his stories a land of monstrous rainfall and punishing heat. "This is nothing." Rusty maintained a small-town sense of time in all things, devoid of urgency. Although not a natural salesman, during his two years in the store he had cultivated a brand of bumpkin charisma that appealed to a subset of Carney's customers. Rusty's newly conked hair, red and lush—courtesy of Charlie's on Lenox—gave him a new confidence that contributed to an uptick in commissions.

Conk or no conk, nothing was happening in the store that Monday. "Not a single soul," Rusty said as they carried Hazel Brown's sofa to the gently used section, his voice a lament, which Carney found endearing. Rusty reacted to routine sales patterns like a farmer scanning the skies for thunderheads.

"It's hot," Carney said. "People have more things on their mind." They gave the Heywood-Wakefield prime placement. The gently used section occupied twenty percent of the showroom floor—Carney calculated to the inch—up from ten percent last year. It had been a slow creep for the used merchandise, once Carney noticed its pull on the bargain hunters, the payday strollers, the just-walking-by types who wandered in. The new goods were top-notch, he was an authorized dealer for Argent and Collins-Hathaway, but the secondhand stuff had durable appeal. It was hard to pass up a deal when faced with choosing a warehouse delivery or walking out that day with a wingback lounge chair. Carney's careful eye meant they were getting nice furniture, and he took the same care with the secondhand lamps, electronics, and rugs.

Carney liked to walk his showroom before opening. That half hour of morning light pouring through the big windows, over the bank across the street. He shifted a couch so it wasn't up against the wall, straightened a SALE sign, made neat a display of manufacturer brochures. His black shoes tapped on wood, were silenced by the plush give of an area rug, resumed their sound. He had a theory about mirrors and their ability to reflect attention to different quadrants of the store; he tested it on his inspection. Then he opened the shop to Harlem. It was all his, his unlikely kingdom, scrabbled together by his wits and industry. His name out front on the sign so everyone knew, even if the burned-out bulbs made it look so lonesome at night.

After checking the basement to make sure Rusty had put the TVs where he'd asked, he retreated to his office. Carney liked to keep up a professional appearance, wear a jacket, but it was too hot. He wore a white short-sleeve shirt, sharkskin tie tucked between the middle buttons. He stuck it in there when he packed the radios so it wouldn't be in the way.

He ran the day's numbers at his desk: down what he'd paid for the radios years before, down the money for the TVs and the Brown lady's furniture. Cash on hand was not heartening, if the heat kept up and the customers stayed away.

The afternoon dwindled. The numbers didn't fit, they never did. This day or any other. He double-checked who was late on their payments. Too many. He'd been thinking about it for a while and decided to end it: no more installment plans. His customers loved them, sure, but he couldn't afford the lag anymore. Sending collectors wore him down. Like he was some crime boss dispatching muscle. His father had done some work like that, banging on the front door, everybody on the hall looking to see what the fuss was. The occasional follow-through on a threat . . . Carney stopped himself. He had his share of deadbeats and was a soft touch when it came to extensions and second chances. He didn't have the traffic right now to extend himself. Elizabeth would reassure him and not let him feel bad about it.

Then it was almost closing time. In his mind, he was already a block from home when he heard Rusty say, "It's one of our top sellers." He looked through the window over his desk. The first customers of the day were a young couple—pregnant wife, husband nodding earnestly at Rusty's patter. In the market, even if they didn't know it maybe. The wife sat on the new Collins-Hathaway sofa, fanning herself. She was going to drop the baby any day. Looked like she might deliver right there on the stain-resistant cushions.

"Can I get you a glass of water?" Carney asked. "Ray Carney, I'm the owner."

"Yes, please."

"Rusty, can you get the young lady a glass of water?" He removed his tie from between the buttons of his shirt.

He had before him Mr. and Mrs. Williams, new additions to Lenox Avenue.

"If that sofa you're resting on is familiar, Mrs. Williams, that's because it was on *The Donna Reed Show* last month. The scene at the doctor's office? It's really taken off." Carney ran down the attributes of the Melody line. Space-age silhouette, scientifically tested for comfort. Rusty gave Mrs. Williams the glass of water—he'd taken his time, to ease Carney's transition into the sale. She drank from the glass, cocked her head, and listened thoughtfully, to Carney's pitch or the creature in her womb.

"To be honest," the husband said, "it's so hot, sir, Jane needed to sit down for a minute."

"Couches are good for sitting—that's what they're for. What line are you in, Mr. Williams, if I may ask?"

He taught math at the big elementary school on Madison, second year there. Carney lied and said he was never that good at math, and Mr. Williams started talking about how it's important to get kids interested early so they don't get intimidated. Rote, like it came from some new teaching manual. Everybody had their pitch.

Mrs. Williams was due in two weeks with their first. A June baby. Carney tried to come up with a folksy bit about June babies but couldn't pull it off. "My wife and I, we're expecting our second in September," he said. Which was true. He pulled the picture of May from his wallet. "That's her birthday dress."

"Truth is," Mr. Williams said, "it'll be a while before we can afford a new couch."

"No harm in that. Let me take you around," Carney said. Not to feign interest after a glass of water would be impolite.

It was hard to conduct a proper showroom tour with one party anchored in a spot, panting. The husband shrank from the merchandise when he came too close to it, as if proximity plucked money out of his pockets. Carney remembered those days, everything too dear and too necessary at the same time, just him and Elizabeth making their way in the world as newlyweds. He had the store then, paint still fresh; no one thought he'd make a go of it except her. At the end of the day when she propped him up and told him he could do it, he puzzled over these alien things she offered him. Kindness and faith, he didn't know which box to put them in.

"The modular setup makes every inch of your room livable," Carney said. He sold the virtues of Argent's new sectional, which he really did believe in—the new saddle finish and tapered legs made it appear to float in the air, look—as his thoughts ran elsewhere. These kids and their striving. Actors did this every night, he figured, the best of them, delivering their lines while sifting through last night's argument, or suddenly reminded of overdue bills by a man in the fifth row who had the same face as the man at the bank. You'd have to come every night to detect an error in the performance. Or be another member of the company, suffering your own distractions and recognitions at the same time. He thought, It's hard to make your start in this city when you have no help—

"Let me see it," Mrs. Williams said. "I just want to see how it feels for a moment."

She'd popped up. The three of them stood before the Argent, the turquoise cushions like cool water beckoning on a hot day.

She had been listening the whole time, sipping. Mrs. Williams took off her shoes and lay across the curved left arm. She closed her eyes and sighed.

They did a deal for a smaller than usual deposit, with a generous installment plan. Ludicrous, the whole thing. Carney locked the door behind them after they finished the paperwork to prevent another lapse in judgment. Argent's Metropolitan line was a sound investment, with its chemically treated bouclé cushions and Airform core, voted most comfortable by four out of five respondents in a blind test. It would last a long time, through one kid and another. He was glad he hadn't told Rusty or Elizabeth about eliminating time payments.

Rusty clocked out and it was just him. Down for the day after all the cash he dropped. He didn't know where the rent was going to come from, but it was still early in the month. You never know. The TVs were smart and they were a nice couple and it was good to do for them what no one did for him when he was young: give a hand. "I may be broke, but I ain't crooked," he said to himself, as he often did at times like this. When he felt this way. Weary and a little desperate, but also high-hearted. He turned off the lights.

TWO

"Oh, Ruby—yes. She was sweet," Elizabeth said. She passed the water pitcher. "We played volleyball together."

In keeping with their history, his wife remembered the dead lady's daughter, but had no high-school recollection of the man she was going to marry. Carney and his wife had biology class together, and civics, and one downpour Thursday he walked her four blocks under his umbrella, out of his way even. "Are you sure?" Elizabeth said. "I thought that was Richie Evans." Her teenage memory rendered him a blank space, like the one left after she cut out a paper doll for May. Carney had yet to devise a comeback to her teasing about his inconspicuous profile back then: "It's not my fault you were you." He'd think of it one day.

Dinner was Caw Caw chicken. The recipe came from *McCall's,* but May pronounced it *caw,* and it stuck. It was bland—the main seasoning appeared to be breadcrumbs—but they were fond of it. "What if the baby doesn't like chicken," Elizabeth asked one night. "Everybody likes chicken," he responded. They had a good thing going, the three of them, wonky plumbing aside. The new arrival might alter the dynamic in the house. For now, they still had their unspoiled delight in Elizabeth's main dish, served tonight with rice and stewed green beans, pale ribbons of bacon adrift in the pot.

May squeezed a green bean to mush. Half went

in her mouth, the rest on her polka-dot bib. Under her high chair, the linoleum was a mottle of stains. May took after her mother, and her grandmother, had those big brown Jones women's eyes that took in everything and gave no more than they decided to permit. She had also inherited their will, mulish and impenetrable. Take a look at those beans.

"Alma go home early?" Carney asked. With Elizabeth on bed rest, her mother came by most days to lend a hand. She was great help with May, if not the kitchen. Even if dinner hadn't been one of his wife's trademark dishes, tipping him off, the food tasted good, which meant Alma hadn't had a hand in it. Elizabeth's mother cooked the way she did most things, with a healthy sprinkling of spite. In the kitchen it manifested on the tongue.

"I told her we didn't need her today," Elizabeth said. A euphemism for Alma meddling too much, necessitating a cooling-off period after Elizabeth lost her temper.

"You didn't do too much?"

"Just to the store. I had to get out."

He wasn't going to make a fuss about it. After she fainted a month ago, Dr. Blair told her to take a break from work, stay off her feet. Let her body devote itself to the job at hand. Stillness went against her character; the more she had on her plate, the happier she was. She had resigned herself to a few months of humdrumery, but it drove her batty. Alma's constant harping made it worse.

He changed the subject. The store was quiet all day except at the end, he said. "They live in Lenox Terrace. He said he thought they still had some three-bedrooms available."

"How much?"

"I don't know, more than what we pay now. I thought I'd take a look."

He hadn't brought up moving in more than two weeks. No harm in taking the temperature. One source of Alma's carping was the size of their apartment, and for once Carney agreed with her. For Elizabeth's mother, their small apartment was another way her daughter had settled for less than she deserved.

Alma used the word *settled* the way the less genteel used *motherfucker,* as a chisel to pry open a particular feeling. Elizabeth had settled for her position at the travel agency, after her parents' careful maneuverings to elevate her, turn her into an upstanding Negro doctor, upstanding Negro lawyer. Booking hotels, airplane flights—it was not what they intended for her.

She'd settled for Carney, that was clear. That family of his. From time to time, Carney still overheard his father-in-law refer to him as "that rug peddler." Elizabeth had brought her parents to the store to show it off, on a day Moroccan Luxury happened to deliver a shipment. The rugs were marvelous specimens, couldn't keep them in stock, but the delivery men that day were disheveled and hungover—they usually were—and on seeing them slide the rugs down the basement chute, Mr. Jones muttered, "What is he, some sort of rug peddler?" Knowing full well the range of home goods Carney sold, all of which were of fine quality. Go into a white store downtown, it was the same stuff, Moroccan Luxury sold all over. Not to mention—what was wrong with selling rugs? It was more honorable than grifting the city out of taxes, Mr. Jones's specialty, no matter how he dressed it up.

And their sweet Elizabeth had settled for a dark apartment with a back window that peered out onto an air shaft and a front window kitty-corner to the elevated 1 train. Weird smells came in one way, trains rumbled in the other, all hours. Surrounded by the very element they'd tried to keep her away from her whole life. Or keep down the block, at least. Strivers' Row, where Alma and Leland Jones had raised her, was one of the most beautiful stretches in Harlem, but it was a little island—all it took was a stroll around the corner to remind its residents that they were among, not above.

You got used to the subway. He said that all the time.

Carney disagreed with Alma's assessment of their neighbors, but yes, Elizabeth—all of them—deserved a nicer place to live. This was too close to what he'd grown up in.

"No need to rush," Elizabeth said.

"They can have their own rooms."

The apartment was hot. In her bed-rest term, she often stayed in her housecoat all day, why not? It was one of the few pleasures left to her. She wore her hair in a bun, but some strands had gotten loose and were plastered to her sweaty forehead. Tired, skin flushed red under brown in her cheeks. She flickered then, as Ruby had that morning, and he saw her as she was on that rainy afternoon under his umbrella: almond-shaped dark eyes under long lashes, delicate in her pink cardigan, edges of her mouth upturned at one of her strange jokes. Unaware of the effect she had on people. On him, all these years later.

"What?" Elizabeth said.

"Nothing."

"Don't look at me like that," she said. "The girls can share." She had decided the baby was a girl. She was right about most things so had a certain bravado with this fifty-fifty proposition.

"Take her Caw Caw and you'll see how much she likes to share." For proof, he reached over and plucked a piece of chicken off May's plate. She howled until he plopped it in her mouth.

"You just finished telling me you had a slow day and now you want to move. We'll be okay. We can wait until we can afford it. Isn't that right, May?"

May smiled, at who knew what. Some Jones girl course of action she'd planned.

When Elizabeth rose to start the girl's bath, Carney said, "I have to step out for a bit."

"Freddie show up?" She had pointed out that he only said *step out* when meeting his cousin. He had tried varying his phrasing, but gave up.

"He left a message with Rusty saying he wanted to see me."

"What's he been doing?"

Freddie had been scarce. Lord knew what he'd gotten his paws into. Carney shrugged and kissed them goodbye. He carried the garbage out, trailing greasy dots all the way to the sidewalk.

* * *

Carney took the long way to Nightbirds. It had been the kind of day that put him in the mood to see the building.

This first hot spell of the year was a rehearsal for the summer to come. Everyone a bit rusty but it was coming back, their parts in the symphony and assigned solos. On the corner, two white cops recapped the fire hydrant, cursing. Kids had been running in and out of the spray for days. Threadbare blankets lined fire escapes. The stoops bustled with men in undershirts drinking beer and jiving over the noise from transistor radios, the DJs piping up between songs like friends with bad advice. Anything to delay the return to sweltering rooms, the busted sinks and clotted flypaper, the accumulated reminders of your place in the order. Unseen on the rooftops, the denizens of tar beaches pointed to the lights of bridges and night planes.

There had been a bunch of muggings lately, an old lady carrying groceries hit on the head, the kind of news Elizabeth fretted over. He took a well-lit route to Riverside Drive. He went around Tiemann Place, and there it was. Carney'd picked 528 Riverside this month, a six-story red brick with fancy white cornices. Stone falcons or hawks on the roofline watching the human figures below. He favored the fourth-floor apartments these days, or higher, after someone pointed out that the higher views cleared the trees of Riverside Park. He hadn't thought of that. So: that fourth-floor unit of 528 Riverside, in his mind a pleasant hive of six rooms, a real dining room, two baths. A landlord who leased to Negro families. With his hands on the sill, he'd look out at the river on nights like this, the city behind him as if it didn't exist. That rustling, keening thing of people and concrete. Or the city did exist but he stood with it heaving against him, Carney holding it all back by sheer force of character. He could take it.

Riverside, where restless Manhattan found itself finally spent, its greedy hands unable to reach past the park and the holy Hudson. One day he'd live on Riverside Drive, on this quiet, inclined stretch. Or twenty blocks north in one of the big new apartment buildings, in a high-letter apartment, J or K. All those families behind those doors between him and the elevator, friendly or not, they live in the same place, no one better or worse, they were all on the same floor. Or maybe south in the Nineties, in one of the stately prewars, or in a limestone fortification around 105th or thereabouts that squat like an ornery old toad. If he hit the jackpot.

Carney prospected in the evening, checking the line of buildings from different angles, strolling across the street and scanning up, speculating about the sunset view, choosing one edifice and then a single apartment inside. The one with the blue window treatments, or the one with the shade half down, its string dangling like an unfinished thought. Casement windows. Under those broad eaves. He wrote the scenes inside: the hissing radiator, the water spot on the ceiling where the rummy upstairs let the bath run and the landlord won't do a thing about it but it's fine. It's nice. He deserves it. Until he tired of the place and resumed his hunt for the next apartment worthy of his attentions, up or down the avenue.

One day, when he had the money.

The atmosphere in Nightbirds was ever five minutes after a big argument and no one telling you what happened. Everyone in their neutral corners replaying KO's and low blows and devising too-late parries. You didn't know what it had been about or who'd won, just that nobody wanted to talk about it, they glance around and knead grudges in their fists. In its heyday, the joint had been a warehouse of mealy human commerce—some species of hustler at that table, their bosses at the next, marks minnowing between. Closing time meant secrets kept. Whenever Carney looked over his shoulder, he frowned at the grubby pageant. Rheingold beer on tap, Rheingold neon on the walls in two or three places, the brewery had been trying to reach the Negro market. The cracks in the red vinyl upholstery of the old banquettes were stiff and sharp enough to cut skin.

Less dodgy with the change in management, Carney had to allow. His father's city disappearing. Last year the new owner, Bert, had the number on the pay phone changed, undermining a host of shady deals and alibis. In the old days broken men hunched over the phone, hangdog, waiting for the ring that changed their luck. Bert put in a new overhead fan and kicked out the hookers. The pimps were okay, they were good tippers. He removed the dart board, this last item an inscrutable renovation until Bert explained that his uncle "had his eye put out in the army." He hung a picture of Martin Luther King Jr. in its place, a grimy halo describing the outline of the former occupant.

Some regulars beat it for the bar up the street, but Bert and Freddie hit it off quickly, Freddie by nature adept at sizing up the conditions on the field and making adjustments. When Carney walked in, his cousin and Bert were talking about the day's races and how they'd gone.

"Ray-Ray," Freddie said, hugging him.

"How you doing, Freddie?"

Bert nodded at them and went deaf and dumb, pretending to check that there was enough rye out front.

Freddie looked healthy, Carney was relieved to see. He wore an orange camp shirt with blue stripes and the black slacks from his short-lived waiter gig a few years back. He'd always been lean, and when he didn't take care of himself quickly got a bad kind of thin. "Look at my two skinny boys," Aunt Millie used to say when they came in from playing in the street. If Carney hadn't seen his cousin, it also meant Freddie'd been staying away from his mother. He still lived with her in his old room. She made sure he didn't forget to eat.

They were cousins, mistaken for brothers by most of the world, but distinguished by many features of personality. Like common sense. Carney had it. Freddie's common sense tended to fall out of a hole in his pocket—he never carried it long. Common sense, for example, told you to not take a numbers job with Peewee Gibson. It also told you that if you took such a job, it was in your interest not to fuck it up. But Freddie had done both of these things and somehow retained his fingers. Luck stepped in for what he lacked otherwise.

Freddie was vague about where he'd been. "A little work, a little shacking up." Work for him was something crooked, shacking up was a woman with a decent job and trusting nature, who was not too much of a detective when it came to clues. "How's the store going?"

"It'll pick up."

Sipping beers. Freddie started in on his enthusiasm for the new soul food place down the block. Carney waited for him to get around to what was on his mind. It took Dave "Baby" Cortez on the jukebox with that damn organ song, loud and manic. Freddie leaned over. "You heard me talk about this nigger every once in a while—Miami Joe?"

"What's he, run numbers?"

"No, he's that dude wears that purple suit. With the hat."

Carney thought he remembered him maybe. It wasn't like purple suits were a rarity in the neighborhood.

Miami Joe wasn't into numbers, he did stickups, Freddie said. Knocked over a truck full of Hoovers in Queens last Christmas. "They say he did that Fisher job, back when."

"What's that?"

"He broke into a safe at Gimbels," Freddie said. Like Carney was supposed to know. Like he subscribed to *Criminal Gazette* or something. Freddie was disappointed but continued to puff up

Miami Joe. He had a big job in mind and he'd approached Freddie about it. Carney frowned. Armed robbery was nuts. In former days his cousin stayed away from stuff that heavy.

"It's going to be cash, and a lot of stones that's got to get taken care of. They asked me if I knew anyone for that and I said, I have just the guy."

"Who?"

Freddie raised his eyebrows.

Carney looked over at Bert. Hang him in a museum—the barman was a potbellied portrait of hear no evil. "You told them my name?"

"Once I said I knew someone, I had to."

"Told them my name. You know I don't deal with that. I sell home goods."

"Brought that TV by last month, I didn't hear no complaints."

"It was gently used. No reason to complain."

"And those other things, not just TVs. You never asked where they came from."

"It's none of my business."

"You never asked all those times—and it's been a lot of times, man—because you know where they come from. Don't act all, 'Gee, officer, that's news to me.'"

Put it like that, an outside observer might get the idea that Carney trafficked quite frequently in stolen goods, but that's not how he saw it. There was a natural flow of goods in and out and through people's lives, from here to there, a churn of property, and Ray Carney facilitated that churn. As a middleman. Legit. Anyone who looked at his books would come to the same conclusion. The state of his books was a prideful matter with Carney, rarely shared with anyone because no one seemed very interested when he talked about his time in business school and the classes he'd excelled in. Like accounting. He told this to his cousin.

"Middleman. Like a fence."

"I sell furniture."

"Nigger, please."

It was true that his cousin did bring a necklace by from time to time. Or a watch or two, top-notch. Or a few rings in a silver box engraved with initials. And it was true that Carney had an associate on Canal Street who helped these items on to the next leg of their journey. From time to time. Now that he added up all those occasions they numbered more than he thought, but that was not the point. "Nothing like what you're talking about now."

"You don't know what you can do, Ray-Ray. You never have. That's why you have me."

A bunch of hoods with pistols and what they got with those pistols was crazy. "This ain't stealing candy from Mr. Nevins, Freddie."

"It's not candy," Freddie said. He smiled. "It's the Hotel Theresa."

Two guys tumbled through the front door, brawling. Bert reached for Jack Lightning, the baseball bat he kept by the register.

Summer had come to Harlem.

THREE

He preferred the street-side booths but Chock Full o'Nuts was busy. Maybe a convention upstairs. Carney hooked his hat on the stand and sat at the counter. Sandra was on patrol with her pot and poured him a cup. "What else can I get you, baby?" she asked. In younger days she'd danced in the top revues, Club Baron and the Savoy, head girl at the Apollo. You'd still think she danced professional from the way she glided on the cheap gray linoleum. Certainly she hadn't quit show business, waitressing being a line of work where you had to play to even the cheapest of seats.

"Just the coffee," he said. "How was your son's visit?" The Hotel Theresa's Chock Full o'Nuts had been part of his morning routine since he opened the store.

She sucked her teeth. "Oh, he came. Not that I saw him. Hanging out with those friends of his the whole time." She let the pot dangle without spilling a drop. "Left me a note."

The hot spell was unbroken, which was unfortunate. The heat from the kitchen made it worse. From his stool, Carney got a view of Seventh Avenue, where the hotel entrance hopped with checkouts. Bellboys blowing whistles, yellow cabs pulling up in staggered approaches.

Most days Carney wouldn't notice the hotel's patterns, but his meeting with Freddie had him twisted. He'd been with his cousin the first time he'd witnessed the sidewalk choreography in front of the Hotel Theresa, during an outing with him and Aunt Millie. Carney must have been ten or eleven, if she was minding him. That unsettled stretch in his life.

"Let's see who it is everybody's fussing over," Aunt Millie had said. She'd taken them for ice-cream sodas at Thomforde's to celebrate, Carney couldn't remember what, and they were walking home. The crowd outside the Hotel Theresa's blue canopy drew her in. Young men in their hotel uniforms corralling gawkers and then the big bus pulling up. They went over to see.

The red carpet outside the Waldorf of Harlem was the theater for daily and sometimes hourly spectacles, whether it was the sight of the heavyweight champ waving to fans as he climbed into a Cadillac, or a wrung-out jazz singer splashing out of a Checker cab at three A.M. with the devil's verses in her mouth. The Theresa desegregated in 1940, after the neighborhood tipped over from Jews and Italians and became the domain of Southern blacks and West Indians. Everyone who came uptown had crossed some variety of violent ocean.

Management had no choice but to open its doors, and well-to-do Negroes had no choice but to stay there if they wanted the luxury treatment. All the famous Negro athletes and movie stars slept there, the top singers and businessmen, taking supper in the Orchid Room on the third floor and throwing soirees in the Skyline Ballroom. From the Skyline's thirteenth-floor windows you could take in the lights of the George Washington Bridge one way, the Triborough another way, and the sentinel Empire State Building to the south. Top of the world. Dinah Washington, Billy Eckstine, and the Ink Spots lived upstairs. So went the lore of the place.

That Thomforde's afternoon with his aunt marked the return of Cab Calloway's orchestra. A public relations firm—or a concierge on tabloid payroll—tipped photographers to ensure an adequate commotion. The bandleader's name flowed across the side of the tour bus in gigantic white letters, stained faintly where crackers had thrown eggs at them in some Podunk, could've been worse. The bystanders screamed when the musicians stepped onto the sidewalk, dapper and cool in their powder blue suits and bug-eye sunglasses. Freddie joined in—flashy dressers impressed him even then. Cab himself arrived later that night. He kept a lady in D.C. who had a knack for down-home breakfasts and other early-morning pleasures, or so it was said.

The band entered the lobby in a hepcat line as if strutting onstage, for this display was as much a gig as any of their nightly concerts, a show of glamour, an affirmation of Negro excellence. Show over, the audience split and the sidewalk was quiet until the next celebrity landed. Aunt Millie liked to read out Theresa items from the gossip columns: *We hear a certain velvet-voiced Lothario kicked up quite a ruckus last week at the fabulous Hotel Theresa with one of the Savoy's beige beauties. Seems his wife decided to surprise him for his birthday and blew out all the candles on that little cake . . .* Carney lived with his aunt and Freddie for a couple of years after his mother passed. He was in the kitchen when Aunt Millie squealed at the *Courier*'s coverage of the Calloway orchestra's arrival, even if the account puzzled her. "I don't think there were hundreds of people there, do you?"

The night Carney signed his lease on the store, the movie studio Twentieth Century-Fox held their premiere party for *Carmen Jones* at the hotel. Three blocks over on Seventh, the massive spotlights tilted and swerved. The traffic down 125th was honking molasses, cops angrily waving at the cars. The white light coming around that corner was so bright it made you think the earth had split open, like some miracle eruption was underway. Carney's new arrangement with Salerno Properties Inc. received less fanfare. It didn't make the papers, but he chose to believe it was momentous in its own way. Like all those bright lights were for him.

The sidewalk action was rare these days. Downtown hotels recognized the profit in opening to black patrons and the years

of sordid carousing, late-night gambling, and gossip-page she-
nanigans diminished the hotel's reputation. At the bar, you
were more likely to find yourself bending elbows with a pimp or
a working girl instead of Joe Louis or a grande dame of Negro
society. The coffee shop where Adam Clayton Powell Jr. used to
charm the waitstaff was bought out by Chock Full o' Nuts. The coffee was better and so was the grub, so Carney figured no big loss.
It was still the Hotel Theresa, headquarters of the Negro world,
and its thirteen floors contained more possibility and majesty
than their parents and grandparents could've dreamed of.

Robbing the Hotel Theresa was like taking a piss on the Statue
of Liberty. It was like slipping Jackie Robinson a Mickey the
night before the World Series.

"Goddamn it, Bill!" Sandra said. Something smoldered in one
of the stoves and gray smoke, heavy with grease, floated through
the window into the dining area.

"I got it, boss!" the cook said, avoiding her eyes.

Sandra knew how to handle herself, whether dealing with the
kitchen staff or the impetuous attentions of customers. Dancing
at the Apollo was a tutorial in the male animal, after all. Consid-
ering the hotel's legend for nighttime fun, men probably bought
her drinks at the bar across from the lobby, everybody hung out
there in those days. Lighting her cigarettes over dreary prom-
ises. Back in the glory days—hers and the hotel's. One time Carney asked why she quit dancing. "Baby," she said, "God tells you
it's time to hang it up, you listen." She took off her high heels and
slipped on a waist apron, but she couldn't quit 125th Street—you
could see the Apollo from the window.

The morning after Freddie's Nightbirds pitch, Carney took
Sandra's words for wisdom about knowing your limitations. To
wit: Even if he were crooked enough for his cousin's proposition, he didn't have the contacts to handle a haul from the Hotel
Theresa. Three hundred rooms, who knows how many guests
locking up valuables and cash in the safe-deposit boxes behind

reception—he wouldn't know what to do with it. Neither would his man Buxbaum down on Canal. Have a coronary if Carney walked in with that kind of weight.

Sandra refilled Carney's cup, he didn't notice. Carney was only slightly bent when it came to being crooked, in practice and ambition. The odd piece of jewelry, the electronic appliances Freddie and then a few other local characters brought by the store, he could justify. Nothing major, nothing that attracted undue attention to his store, the front he put out to the world. If he got a thrill out of transforming these ill-gotten goods into legit merchandise, a zap-charge in his blood like he'd plugged into a socket, he was in control of it and not the other way around. Dizzying and powerful as it was. Everyone had secret corners and alleys that no one else saw—what mattered were your major streets and boulevards, the stuff that showed up on other people's maps of you. The thing inside him that gave a yell or tug or shout now and again was not the same thing his father had. That sickness drawing every moment into its service. The sickness Freddie ministered to, more and more.

Carney had a bent to his personality, how could he not, growing up with a father like that. You had to know your limits as a man and master them.

Two guys in pinstripe suits, probably salesmen in the city hawking insurance schemes, came in from the bar, which separated the coffee shop from the lobby. Sandra told them to sit wherever and when she turned they checked out her legs. She had nice legs. That door. Through the door you passed from the bar and into the lobby. There were three ways into the lobby: the bar, the street, and the clothing boutique. Plus the elevators and fire stairs. Three men at the big front desk, guests coming and going all hours . . . Carney stopped himself. He sipped his coffee. Sometimes he slipped and his mind went thataway.

At Nightbirds, Freddie had made him promise to think about it, knowing that Carney usually came around if he thought too long about one of his cousin's plots. A night of Carney staring at the ceiling was enough to close the deal, the cracks up there like a sketch of the cracks in his self-control. It was part of their Laurel and Hardy routine—Freddie sweet-talks him into an ill-advised scheme and the mismatched duo tries to outrun the consequences. *Here's another fine mess you've gotten me into.* His cousin was a hypnotist—suddenly Carney's on lookout while Freddie shoplifts comics at the five-and-dime, they're cutting class to catch a cowboy double feature at Loew's. Two drinks at Nightbirds, and then dawn's squeaking through the window of Miss Mary's after-hours joint, moonshine rolling in their heads like an iron ball. *There's a necklace I got to get off my hands, can you help me out?*

Whenever Aunt Millie interrogated Freddie over some story the neighbors told her, Carney stepped up with an alibi. No one would ever suspect Carney of telling a lie, of not being on the up-and-up. He liked it that way. For Freddie to give his name to Miami Joe and whatever crew he'd thrown in with, it was unforgivable. Carney's Furniture was in the damn phone book, in the *Amsterdam News* when he could afford to place an ad, and anyone could track him down.

Carney agreed to sleep on it. The next morning he remained unswayed by the ceiling and now he had to figure out what to do about his cousin. It didn't make sense, a hood like Miami Joe bringing small-time Freddie in on the job. And Freddie saying yes, that was bad news.

This wasn't stealing candy, and it wasn't like when they were kids, standing on a cliff a hundred feet over the Hudson River, tip of the island, Freddie daring him to jump into the black water. Did Carney leap? He leapt, hollering all the way down. Now Freddie wanted him to jump into a bunch of concrete.

He paid Sandra. She winked a practiced wink. When Freddie called the office that afternoon, Carney told him it was no-go and cussed him out for his poor judgment. That was that, for two weeks, until the heist went down and Chink Montague's goons came to the store looking for Freddie.

* * *

The robbery was in all the news. He had to ask Rusty what Juneteenth was, and he was right, it was some country thing.

"Juneteenth is when those slaves in Texas found out slavery was over," Rusty said. "My cousins used to throw a party to celebrate."

Finding out you were free six months after the fact didn't seem like something to celebrate. More like it was telling you to read the morning paper. Carney read the *Times,* the *Tribune,* and the *Post* every day to stay informed, bought them from the stand on the corner.

HOTEL THERESA HEIST
BLACK HARLEM STUNNED BY DARING
EARLY MORNING ROBBERY

The cops blocked off the traffic outside the hotel 'til past noon. A different sort of sidewalk performance unfurled outside the hotel—detectives and insurance men running in and out, newspaper men and their shutterbug buddies trying to get the scoop. Carney had to get his morning coffee at the scruffy diner down the street.

Customers carried rumors and theories into the furniture store. *They busted in with machine guns* and *I heard they shot five people* and *The Italian Mafia did it to put us in our place.* This last tidbit put forth by the black nationalists on Lenox Ave, hectoring from their soapboxes. *That's why they picked Juneteenth, to mess with us.*

No one got killed, according to the papers. Scared shitless, sure. Carney called his aunt to make sure his cousin wasn't involved—he'd heard Freddie was back home—but the phone just rang.

The robbery was early Wednesday morning. Chink's men came into his store the next day around noon. Rusty said, "Hey!" when one of them bucked him out of the way. The two men moved in a lumbering prowl, like escapees from the wrestling league who'd strapped themselves into suits. Brown jackets hung over their forearms, ties loose, big sweat circles under their pits. I don't owe any money, was Carney's first thought. The second was, Maybe I do.

He waved Rusty off and closed the door to the office. The man with the handlebar mustache had a scar that dug from his lip to the middle of his cheek, as if he'd wriggled free from a fisherman's hook. He eyed the sofa but didn't sit, as if to do so was to breach protocol, it might get back to a higher-up. The other man had a shaved bullet head beaded with perspiration, and a woman's made-up eyebrows. He did most of the talking.

"You Ray Carney?"

"Welcome to the store. You thinking of a new living-room set? A dinette?"

"Dinette," the bald man repeated. He squinted through the office window, only now registering what kind of store it was. "No." He swabbed his brow with a blue handkerchief. "We work for a man you know. Heard of. Name of Montague?"

"Chink Montague," the man with the scar offered.

"What can I do for you?" Carney asked. Something to do with Freddie, then—his cousin owed money? Was he supposed to pay it or they'd start beating him? He thought of Elizabeth and May, that these men knew where he lived.

"We know you handle stuff sometimes—jewelry, stones?"

Too shaken to play dumb. He checked—Rusty lingered by the front door with his arms crossed, nervous. Carney nodded at the men.

"The robbery yesterday at the Theresa," Baldy said. "Mr. Montague wants the word out that there's something he wants back. A necklace with a big ruby—big. He wants it back so much, that's why we're going around all over talking to people who know about that kind of thing. He says anyone comes across it, he'd like to hear about it, keep him appraised."

It was the wrong word, but here it fit. "I sell furniture, Mr. . . . ?"

The man shook his head. His partner followed suit.

"But if I come across it, I'll tell you," Carney said. "That you can be certain of."

"Certain of," Baldy said.

Carney asked for a phone number. Like he was asking a customer for home information. Baldy said, "You live around here, you know how to get in touch. And I'd recommend you do that."

On their way out, the man with the scar paused by one of the boomerang tables, a low model with a multicolored starburst design hovering in the glass top. Scar checked out the price tag and started to ask something, but thought better of it. It was a nice coffee table and Carney had spent a lot of time on where to put it so you didn't miss it.

Rusty came over. "Who was that?" If he'd been mad about being pushed, he'd crossed over into hick-in-the-big-city wonder.

"Selling flood insurance," Carney said. "I said I already got some." He told the Georgia boy to take a lunch break.

Carney called Aunt Millie again and asked her to have Freddie get in touch. That night he'd hit Nightbirds, go to Cherry's and the Clermont Lounge, all of his cousin's spots until he tracked him down. Freddie in trouble and Carney chasing him down, like they were teenagers again. "Handle stuff sometimes"—nobody knew about his sideline except his cousin. His cousin, and the few guys who came around sometimes with items that had materialized in their vicinity, stuff in fine shape, stuff he'd feel okay about selling to customers. Not merely okay—proud to sell. But just those guys. Plus his man Buxbaum on Canal. Carney'd kept his head down and Freddie put his name out there.

He locked the door at six o'clock and was almost done moping over his ledgers when his cousin knocked. Only Freddie knocked like that, since when they were kids and he knocked on the frame of the bunk bed—*You still up, hey, you still up? I was thinking . . .*

"You got these hooligans coming around my store," Carney said, *hooligans* being an Aunt Millie word for bogeyman. Hooligans defaced the subway entrance, hooligans beat her to the last bottle of milk at the grocers, it was an invasion.

Freddie's voice was a squeak: "They came here? Jesus!"

Carney brought him into the office. Freddie plopped onto the Argent couch and exhaled. He said, "I gotta say, I've been on my feet."

"That was you with the Theresa? You okay?"

Freddie wiggled his eyebrows. Carney cursed himself. He was supposed to be angry at his cousin—not worried about the nigger's health. Still, he was glad Freddie was unscathed, looks of it. His cousin had the face he wore when he got laid or paid. Freddie sat up. "Rusty gone for the day?"

"Tell me what happened."

"I am, I am, but there's something I got to—"

"Don't leave me hanging."

"I'll get to it in a minute—it's just, the guys are coming here."

"Those thugs are coming back here?"

Freddie appeared to probe a sore tooth with his tongue. "No, the guys I pulled the job with," he said. "You know how you said no? I didn't tell them that. They still think you're the man."

Before Miami Joe and the crew arrived at Carney's Furniture, there was time for monologues that ranged in tenor between the condemnation and the harangue. Carney expressed his rage toward, and disappointment in, his cousin, and proceeded to a dissertation on Freddie's stupidity, illustrated with numerous examples, the boys having been born within a month of each other and Freddie's boneheadedness an early-to-emerge character trait. Carney was also moved to share in emphatic terms why he feared for himself and his family, and his regret over the loss of his sideline's anonymity.

There was also time for Freddie to share the tale of the heist.

FOUR

Freddie had never been south of Atlantic City.
Miami was an unimagined land, the customs of
which he filled in with details from his acquaintance with Miami Joe. Miamians dressed well,
for Miami Joe dressed well, his purple suits—
solid, others of pinstripes in different widths—
masterfully tailored, complemented by his
collection of short, fat kipper ties. Pocket squares
jutted like weeds. In Miami, Freddie gathered,
they turned out straight shooters, it was something in the water, or a combination of the sun
and the water. To hear Miami Joe expound on a
subject—whether it was food, the treachery of
females, or the simple eloquence of violence—
was to see the world shorn of its civilized ruses.
The only thing he dressed up nicely was himself;
all else remained as naked and uncomplicated as
God had created it.

Miami Joe operated in New York City for five
years after departing his hometown in the wake of
an escapade. He found work as a collector for Reg-
gie Greene, maiming welshers and shopkeepers
who were miserly with protection money, but he
tired of such easy game and returned to thieving.
At Nightbirds Freddie had recounted to Carney
some of Miami Joe's more recent capers—a trailer
full of vacuum cleaners, snatching the payroll of
a department store. The flashy, efficient scores
were the ones he chose to advertise, alluding to a
host of others kept private.

Freddie and Miami Joe drank together at the Leopard's Spots, the last to leave, the nights unfinished until the duo had been converted into rye-soaked cockroaches scurrying from sunlight and propriety. Freddie never failed to wake with a fear over what he'd revealed about himself. He hoped Miami Joe was too drunk to remember his stories, but Miami Joe did remember—it was more evidence for his unsentimental study of the human condition. The day Miami Joe brought him in, Freddie had recently quit running numbers for Peewee Gibson.

"But you've never done a robbery before," Carney said.

"He said I was going to be the wheelman, that's why I said yes." He shrugged. "What's so hard about that? Two hands and a foot."

The first convocation of the crew was held in a booth at Baby's Best, on the brink of happy hour. In the dressing room the strippers covered their scars with powder; blocks away, their faithful customers waited to punch out of straight jobs. The lights were going, though, spinning and whirring, perhaps they never stopped, even when the place was closed, red and green and orange in restless, garish patrol over surfaces. It was Mars. Miami Joe had his arms spread on the red leather when Freddie walked in. Miami Joe, sipping Canadian Club and twisting his pinkie rings as he mined the dark rock of his thoughts.

Arthur was next to arrive, embarrassed by the meeting place, like he'd never been in this kind of establishment before, or spent his every hour there. Arthur was forty-eight years old, hair corkscrewed with gray. He reminded Freddie of a schoolteacher. The man favored plaid sweater vests and dark slacks, wore bookworm glasses, and had a gentle way of pointing out flaws in aspects of the scheme. "A policeman would spot that phony registration in a second—is there another solution to this problem?" He'd just finished his third stint in prison, thanks to a weakness for venal or otherwise incompetent comrades. Not this time. Arthur was "the Jackie Robinson of safecracking," according to

Miami Joe, having busted the color line when it came to safes and locks and alarms, generally regarded as the domain of white crooks.

Pepper showed up last and they got to business.

"What about this man Pepper?" Carney asked.

"Pepper." Freddie winced. "You'll see."

Cocktails at the Hotel Theresa were a hot ticket, and Miami Joe often installed himself at the long, polished bar with the rest of the neighborhood's criminal class, talking shit. He took out one of the maids every once in a while, a slight, withdrawn girl named Betty. She lived at the Burbank, a once-dignified building on Riverside Drive that had been cut to into single-room accommodations. A lot of new arrivals washed up there. Betty liked to stall before she let Miami Joe into her bed, which meant a lot of talking, and in due course he had enough information to plan the robbery. The job struck him the first time he laid eyes on the hotel. Where others saw sophistication and affirmation, Miami Joe recognized opportunity, for monetary gain, and to bring black Harlem down a notch. These up-North niggers had an attitude about Southern newcomers, he'd noticed, a pervasive condescension that made him boil. *What'd you say? Is that how y'all do it down there?* They thought their hotel was nice? He'd seen nicer. Not that he'd be able to provide an example if challenged on this point. Miami Joe was strictly hot sheet when it came to short-term accommodations.

The hotel bar closed at one A.M., the lobby was dead by four, and the morning shift started at five, when the kitchen staff and laundry workers punched in. Weekends were busier, and on Saturday nights the hotel manager ran gambling rooms for high rollers. Which meant bodyguards and sore losers—too many surly men walking around with guns in their pockets. Tuesday night was Miami Joe's lucky night when it came to jobs, so Tuesday.

He allotted twenty minutes for the takeover of the lobby and the raid of the vault. "Vault?" Freddie asked. It wasn't a real vault, Miami Joe told him, that's what they called the room containing the safe-deposit boxes. Since they were smashing the boxes open, Arthur wouldn't be able to use his expertise, but he was dependable, a scarce quality. He was cool with it. He cleaned his glasses with a monogrammed handkerchief and said, "Sometimes you need a pick, sometimes a crowbar."

Twenty minutes, four men. Baby, the eponymous owner, brought them another round, refusing eye contact and payment. The crew debated the details as the happy-hour trade grabbed stools at the bar and the music cranked up. Pepper kept his mouth shut except to ask about the guns. He focused on his partners' faces, as if around a poker table and not the wobbly Formica of Baby's Best.

Arthur thought five men was better, but Miami Joe preferred the four-way split. At the safecracker's gentle suggestion, they plucked Freddie out of the car and inducted him into the lobby action. It was only a few yards from the street to the hotel lobby, but infinitely closer to peril. Poor Freddie. Purple-and-blue lights sliding all over the place, this gun talk, it was unnerving. He didn't see a way to protest. Pepper glaring like that. The crew picked up on his hesitation, so when Miami Joe said his usual fence had been pinched the week before, Freddie gave up Carney as an offering, although he did not phrase it to his cousin this way in his retelling.

At 3:43 A.M. the night of the job, Freddie parked the Chevy Styleline on Seventh across from the Theresa on the uptown side of the street. As Miami Joe had promised, there were plenty of spots. The traffic at that hour was nothing. King Kong come running down the street, there was no one to see. Through the glass doors, the night guard stood at the bell stand, fiddling with the long antenna of a transistor radio. Freddie couldn't see the front desk, but the clerk was somewhere. The elevator operator sat lethargically on his stool, or was on his feet directing the cab up or down, depending. Miami Joe said that one morning, forty-five minutes went by without an elevator summons.

It spooked Freddie, being in the night man's field of vision like that. He moved the Chevy closer to the corner where the guard couldn't see him. It was the first deviation from Miami Joe's plan.

The knock at the window startled him. Two men got into the backseat and Freddie panicked—then he realized the disguises had thrown him off. "Settle down," Pepper said. Arthur wore a long, conked wig and a pencil mustache that made him look like Little Richard. Shaved twenty years off him, the time he spent in the joint refunded. Pepper was in a Hotel Theresa bellhop uniform, which Betty had stolen from the laundry two months ago. The night she grabbed it, she asked Miami Joe to put it on and say some dialogue before she permitted him to kiss her. It was all in the overhead.

Pepper had the uniform altered. He didn't change his facial appearance. He had gravel eyes that made you stare at your feet. The aluminum toolbox sat on his lap.

Thirty seconds before four A.M., Arthur got out of the car and crossed the median. His tie was loose, jacket rumpled, his stride erratic. A musician calling it a night or an out-of-town insurance salesman after a night in the Big City—in short, a Hotel Theresa guest. The night man saw him and unlocked the front door. Chester Miller was in his late fifties, slim-built except for his belly, which perched on his belt like an egg. A little sleepy. After one o'clock, when the bar closed, hotel policy only permitted registered guests inside.

"Perry? Room 512," Arthur told the night man. They'd booked a room for three nights. The clerk wasn't at the front desk. Arthur hoped Miami Joe had that situation in hand.

The night man flipped through the papers on his clipboard and pulled the brass door wide. Arthur had the gun in the man's rib cage when he turned to lock the door. He told him to take it easy. Freddie and Pepper were on the red carpet outside—the night man let them in and locked the door as directed. Freddie held the three leather valises. A rubber Howdy Doody mask covered his face; the crew had bought two of them at a Brooklyn five-and-dime two weeks earlier. Pepper carried the heavy toolbox.

The door to the fire stairs was open. A crack. They were halfway to the registration desk when Miami Joe opened the door the rest of the way and entered the lobby. He'd been hiding in the stairwell for three hours. The Howdy Doody mask had come on five minutes earlier, but as far as he was concerned he'd been in disguise all night because he wasn't wearing a purple suit. There were no hard feelings about who got masks and who didn't. Some of the crew needed their faces revealed in order to do their jobs, and some didn't.

The arrow above the door indicated the elevator was on the twelfth floor. Then the eleventh.

For most of the day the hotel lobby bustled like Times Square, guests and businessmen crisscrossing the white-and-black tiles, locals meeting for a meal and gossip, their number multiplied by the oversize mirrors on the green-and-beige floral wallpaper. The doors to the phone booths by the elevator folded in and unfolded out, weird gills. At night, the swells congregated in the leather club chairs and sofas and drank cocktails and smoked cigarettes as the door to the bar swung open and shut. Porters ferrying luggage on carts, teams of clerks at registration handling crises big and small, the shoe-shine man insulting people in scuffed shoes and arguing for his services—it was an exuberant and motley chorus.

All that was done now and the cast had shrunk to thieves and captives.

The night man was pliable, as Miami Joe had promised. Miami Joe knew Chester from his nights at the hotel; he would do as he was told. It was one of the reasons Miami Joe covered his face. The mask smelled like piney ointment and pushed his breath back at him, gusting up hot and rotten.

Arthur nodded toward the bell on the desk, a signal for the night man to ding the clerk. When the clerk emerged from the offices, Miami Joe was upon him, one hand over his mouth and the other jabbing the nose of the .38 beneath the man's ear. One school held that the base of the skull was the best spot, the cool metal initiating a physical reaction of fear, but the Miami School, of which Joe was a disciple, liked below the ear. Only tongues went there and metal made it eerie. There was an alarm with a wire to the police station, activated by a button beneath where the guest book rested. Miami Joe stood between the clerk and the button. He motioned for the night man to come around so Pepper could watch him and the clerk.

"Elevator on four," Freddie said.

Miami Joe grunted and went into the back. To the left was the switchboard, where an unexpected visitor waited. Some nights the switchboard operator's friend kept her company. They were eating pea soup.

The weeknight operator was named Anna-Louise. She had worked at the Hotel Theresa for thirty years, since before it was desegregated, routing calls. Her chair swiveled. She liked the night work, joking with and mothering the succession of young desk clerks through the years, and she liked listening to the guests' calls, the arguments and arrangements of assignations, the lonely calls home through the cold, cold wires. The disembodied voices were a radio play, a peculiar one where most of the characters only appeared once. Lulu visited her at the switchboard some nights. They had been lovers since high school and around their building referred to themselves as sisters. The lie made sense when they first moved in, but it was silly now. No one really cares about other people when you get down to it—their own struggles are too close-up. The women screamed, then shut their mouths and put their hands up when Miami Joe aimed the gun. To the right was the manager's office. "Get the key," he said.

Pepper brought the clerk and the night man into the office area. Miami Joe stood by the wall of iron bars that separated the room from the vault, far enough away to cover both the men and the women if they tried anything funny. He didn't think that was going to happen. They were rabbits, quivering and afraid. Miami Joe's voice was level and calm when he spoke to them, not to soothe but because he thought it more sadistic. He felt the erotic rush he always got on jobs, it kicked in when the caper got going and dissipated when it was over and then he didn't remember it until the next job. Never could get ahold of it when he wasn't thieving. It told him his idea for the job and its practical execution were in harmony.

When the elevator door opened, its two occupants saw a lean young man at the desk in a silly mask looking at them. He nodded hello. Arthur swept around, his gun out. He waved the elevator operator and the passenger out of the cab and directed them behind the registration desk. By now Pepper had taken the key to the manager's office from the clerk and was conducting the four other captives into the room.

Rob Reynolds, the manager of the hotel, had arranged a nice refuge for himself. There were no windows, so he created them—tasseled curtains, identical to those in the finest suites upstairs, framed painted Venetian scenes. After the afternoon rush, he liked to think that was him under the hat, steering a gondola down salty boulevards in silence. The overstuffed sofa matched the ones in the lobby, though this one endured less wear and tear; one man's naps and quickie fucks with past-due long-term residents couldn't compete with the weight of hordes. Autographed photos of famous guests and residents covered the walls—Duke Ellington, Richard Wright, Ella Fitzgerald in a ball gown, long white gloves up to her elbows. Rob Reynolds had provided exemplary service over the years, the standard amenities and the secret ones. Late-night smack deliveries, last-minute terminations via the Jamaican abortionist who kept two rooms on the seventh floor. It was no surprise, in some quarters, when the gentleman turned out to not be a doctor at all. In many pictures, Rob Reynolds shook hands with Hotel Theresa's celebrity visitors and grinned.

Miami Joe checked the desk drawer for a gun—it had just occurred to him. He didn't find one. He asked the clerk where they kept the cards that tracked the safe-deposit boxes. The young clerk had gone by Rickie his whole life but now wanted folks to call him Richard. It was a tough haul. His family and those he grew up with were a lost cause. New acquaintances switched to the nickname as if they'd received instructions by telegram. The hotel was the only place they called him Richard. No defections so far. This was his first real job and each time he walked through those front doors he imagined he stepped into himself, the man he wanted to be. Clerk, assistant manager, top dog with this office to call his own. The day after the heist, a porter called him Rickie and it stuck. The robbery cursed him. Rickie pointed to the metal box. It sat on the desk between the phone and Rob Reynolds's nameplate.

Miami Joe directed the captives to the rug between the desk and the couch: Lie there with your eyes closed. Freddie covered them from the doorway. Freddie wasn't a gunman, but Miami Joe figured he was jumpy enough that he'd get off a shot if anyone moved, it didn't matter if he missed if it bought the rest of the crew time to put down an insurrection.

The team hit their marks. They wore thin calfskin gloves. Pepper in his bellhop uniform took up his station at the front desk. Arthur had unlocked the door to the vault and now he and Miami Joe stood before the bank of safe-deposit boxes. The brass-colored boxes were twelve inches tall and eight inches wide and deep enough for jewelry, bundled cash, cheap furs, and unsent suicide notes. Arthur said, "This is all Drummond. You said they were Aitkens."

"That's what I heard."

Aitkens took three or four good whacks before there was enough purchase for a crowbar. Maybe that's why they replaced them with Drummond, Arthur thought, which required six to eight whacks. The take had been cut in half, if they stuck to the timetable. Miami Joe said, "78." Arthur got to work with the sledgehammer. The index cards recorded the box numbers, the name of the guests, the contents, and the day of deposit. The manager had sissy handwriting that was easy to read. Arthur got into box 78 after six blows and started on the next while Miami Joe cleaned it out. The contents matched what was on the card: two diamond necklaces, three rings, and some documents. He put the stones into a black valise and searched the cards for the next box to hit.

If the banging rattled Pepper, he didn't show it. He was at the desk one minute when he concluded that working registration was a lousy job. Most straight jobs were, in Pepper's estimation, which is why he hadn't held one in many years, but this gig was spectacularly bad. What with all the people. The constant yipping and complaints—my room's too cold, my room's too hot, can you send up a newspaper, the street noise is too loud. Fork over thirty bucks and suddenly they're royalty, ruling over a twelve-by-fourteen-foot kingdom. Shared bathroom down the hall unless you pay extra. His father had worked in a hotel kitchen, cooking chops and steaks. He came home stinking every night, in addition to the other worthlessness, but Pepper would take that work over desk duty any day. Talking to these fucking mopes.

Bang bang bang.

Pepper got the first call about the noise five minutes later. The switchboard buzzed and Freddie told the operator to get up and answer it. Anna-Louise put room 313's call through. "Front desk," Pepper said. It was the voice he used when he was telling a joke and making fun of white people. He apologized for the banging and said they were fixing the elevator but they'd be done soon. If you come to the front desk in the morning, we'll give you a voucher for ten percent off breakfast. Negroes do love a voucher. The mezzanine floor was offices and a club room, shut now, and the Orchid Room occupied most of the third, or else they'd be getting a lot more calls. Mr. Goodall in room 313 had a voice like a chipmunk, whiny and entitled. Fry chicken all day in that kitchen heat over this goddamned job.

"Tell her to stay at the switchboard in case there's more," Miami Joe said. Freddie stood in the doorway of the manager's office. He'd sweated through his shirt and into his black suit. The eyeholes in the mask made him think something outside his range of vision was about to clobber him. The men and women on the floor didn't move. He said, "Don't move!" anyway. His mother did that all the time—tell him not to do something right before he was about to do it, like he was made of glass and she could see inside. But so many things lived in his head that she never suspected, he hadn't had that little-boy feeling in a long time. 'Til tonight. He'd jumped off the Hudson cliffs—but instead of hitting the river he kept falling. Freddie wasn't able to pull the trigger, so he hoped the captives did what they were supposed to. At her station, Anna-Louise covered her face with her hands.

Bang bang bang.

The rug was freshly vacuumed, which suited the captives, who had their faces in it. The elevator passenger, the man from the twelfth floor, was named Lancelot St. John. He lived two blocks away and his occupation was sitting at the hotel bar until he lit upon a suitable lady from out of town. If his quarry picked up on his euphemisms, Lancelot straightened out the money before he undressed them; if not, afterward he mentioned a present he wanted to buy for his mother, but he was a little short this week.

In the service industry you shift your approach depending on the customer. Tonight's lady had flown in from Chicago to speak to a real estate lawyer about a brownstone she'd recently inherited. Her mother had passed. Perhaps that explained the tears. He'd walked into robberies before—he'd be in bed soon enough. It was almost time for the Theresa to wake to the day and the criminals had to wrap it up.

The elevator operator had done time for stealing a car, and later that day when questioned by detectives he said he didn't see a goddamned thing.

Arthur smiled. It was good to be out, it was good to be stealing again. Even if a quick glance told him that half the jewelry was paste. Half of it was real, fine-quality stones. He measured his prison time in terms not of years lost but of scores missed. The city! And all its busy people and the sweet things they held dear in safes and vaults, and his delicate talent for seducing these items away. He'd bought farmland in Pennsylvania through a white lawyer and it was waiting for him, this green wonder. Arthur put the pictures the lawyer sent him up in his cell. His cellmate asked him what the hell it was, and he told him it was where he'd grown up. Arthur had grown up in a Bronx tenement fighting off rats every night, but when he finally retired to the nice clapboard house, he'd run through the grass like he was a kid again. Every hammer blow like he was busting through city concrete to the living earth below.

Bang bang bang.

They got two more calls about the banging. It was loud, rebounding on the vault walls, vibrating in the very bones of the building. The excuse about the broken elevator came about after they decided to keep the operator on ice in the office. How many people would call for the elevator between 4:00 and 4:20 A.M.? Maybe none, maybe plenty. How many would take the stairs down and be ushered by Pepper in his gentle way into the office with the other captives? Just one it turned out, at 4:17, a certain

Fernando Gabriel Ruiz, Venezuelan national and distributor of handcrafted crockery, who would never visit this city again, after what happened last time and now this, fuck it. And how many guests knocked on the front door to be let into their rooms? Also one—Pepper unlocked the door and marched Mr. Leonard Gates of Gary, Indiana, currently staying in room 807 with its lumpy bed and the hex from the guy who'd had a heart attack, into the back with the rest. Plenty of room in the manager's office. Stack them like firewood or standing room only if need be.

Given that only two souls had intruded on their scheme, Miami Joe said, "Keep going," when Arthur told him twenty minutes was up.

He wanted to push their luck.

Arthur kept swinging. Freddie became aware of his bladder. Pepper said, "It's time." It wasn't his visceral distaste for the front desk and the interaction it represented. You tell Pepper it's twenty minutes, it's twenty minutes. Arthur kept swinging.

Pepper could take care of himself if it went south. He didn't know about the rest of the crew and he didn't care. When the fourth complaint came in about the noise, he told room 405 that the elevator was being fixed and if they bothered him again he'd come up there and beat them with his belt.

Pepper permitted them to empty four more deposit boxes. He said, "It's time." It was not his white-boy voice.

They'd filled two valises. Miami Joe said, "Now." Arthur packed the toolbox and Miami Joe put the index cards inside, too, to mess up the next day's sorting-out. He almost left the empty valise, then remembered the cops might trace it.

Pepper cut the wire to the police station and Freddie yanked the office phone out of the wall. They weren't neutralizing the switchboard so this didn't change their chances materially, but it was a show of enthusiasm that Freddie hoped would serve his cause in the postmortem. In Baby's Best, Miami Joe might mention it and affirm him. Those melancholy lights roving over him, red and purple. Miami Joe recited the names of the staff—Anna-Louise, the clerk, the night man, the elevator operator—and shared their addresses. If anyone so much as twitched before five minutes was up, he said, it was their job to stop them because he knew where they lived.

The bandits were a mile away when Lancelot St. John sat up and asked, "Now?"

FIVE

The thieves were overdue. Carney had a notion to turn out the lights and hide in the basement. He might fit in the unloved Argent buffet, among the spiders.

"What if one of them tried something?" he said. Referring to the captives.

Freddie shook his head. As if harassed by a fly.

"And what do you expect me to do when they get here?" Carney said. "Check out the stash? Pay them for it?"

Freddie bent over to tie his shoes. "You always want in, in the end," he said. "That's why I gave them your name." But the crew wasn't supposed to meet up until next week, after the heat died down. He didn't know what this was about.

Miami Joe rang the buzzer, longer than any decent person would.

He arrived with Arthur. Tonight Miami Joe's purple suit verged on the zoot, high-waisted with wide lapels. The man was smaller than Carney remembered; Freddie's accounts had magnified him. His handshake, the rings pincering Carney's flesh, brought back the night they met, last winter, however briefly: the Clermont Lounge. One of those spots where his cousin ran into hard men of his acquaintance, who stared Carney down when introduced. Cigar smoke twisting like genies below the green glass shades; sharp, cruel laughter from two drunk ladies at the end of the bar;

and Carney telling his cousin that May had taken her first steps. A good night.

Arthur's demeanor, as Freddie had described, was that of a schoolteacher. Chalk dust under the fingernails. Except for the small lump at his ankle where he wore a pistol. When he was little, Carney and his father played a game where he had to guess whether or not his daddy was wearing his revolver under his pants leg. For a long time he thought it was his father's attempt to get close to him, bleak as it was. Now he was sure his father was merely testing his tailor's competency. A guy on Orchard handled his work-related alterations.

The architect of the Theresa heist and the able safecracker took the office couch. Pepper showed up last, as he had at the Baby's Best meeting. A tactic of his, Carney gathered. He was burly and long-limbed, stooping to hide his true size. Something off about him made you look twice, but his dark gaze made you turn before you could figure it out. He shouldn't be there, but was. A mountain man who'd taken a wrong turn and stayed in the city, or a blown-in weed that'd found purchase in a sidewalk crack: a foreign body that had adapted to its new home.

When Pepper saw there was no place to sit, he picked out the new Headley ottoman from the showroom and set it against the back wall of the office. He hunkered, lips pressed together in an expression equal parts attention and impatience. Faded denim overalls, a dark checkered work shirt, and scuffed horsehide boots. Like the construction truck had just dropped him off on the corner of St. Nicholas after daywork. He could have been any number of Harlem men, outrunning some brand of Southern devil, new to the city and trying to put some grub on the table. Less a disguise than a shared biography.

Nonetheless: something off.

It'd been a long time since Carney had been in the company of such men. Criminal types used to be a regular thing in his life. His father invited cronies to the apartment on 127th; they thumped up the stairs, these mean-eyed rogues with flashy style and smiles as counterfeit as the twenties in their hip pockets. Sent to his room, Carney'd kneel at the bedroom door, puzzling over their shop talk: *pinch, vig. Juggler?* Why did they need a juggler? Not juggler, a jugger—a safecracker. Reminded of their own lost children, the men sometimes gave him toys of unfamiliar make, trinkets with sharp points and hungry edges that broke within minutes.

"Place looks halfway legit," Miami Joe said. He squinted at Carney's college diploma on the wall.

"It is legit," Carney said.

"Some nice stuff," Arthur said. "Good front for an offman. TVs."

Freddie cleared his throat. Pepper looked bemused, reminding Carney of a photo from *National Geographic*—a crocodile raising his lids above the waterline, gliding toward unsuspecting prey.

"Why Juneteenth?" Carney asked.

Miami Joe shrugged. "I didn't know that's what day it was."

"It's some country shit," Pepper said. "They have a party."

According to the *Tribune*'s account, the Brown family, late from Houston, Texas, held a Juneteenth party every year. The Skyline Ballroom soiree the night of the robbery was their twentieth celebration. Honoring the day that the final enslaved men and women received word of emancipation was a tradition worth bringing North, they thought. The bandleader played with Duke Ellington, it was jumping. They had hoped to make the party an annual affair; no more. "This sort of thing doesn't happen back home," Mrs. Brown told the reporter. "Waking up to such a scene!"

"If it pissed people off," Miami Joe said, "good." If it made it look like there was a racial aspect to throw everybody off, so much the better.

"Why don't you tell them why we're here," Pepper said.

They had a Chink Montague problem, Miami Joe said. Everyone north of 110th Street knew the mobster from the papers, from a gossip-page roundup of a big charity ball at the Theresa, or a police blotter item about a shootout in a basement gambling room: *The victim was taken to Harlem Hospital where he was pronounced dead.* If not the news, then from daily routine, if you were the sort to play numbers, and there were many of that sort, or handed over an envelope of protection money to his men once a week, and of these there were many, or needed a loan now and again, and who didn't need a little help now and again.

Miami Joe provided a more detailed résumé to explain the predicament. Chink was a protégé of Bumpy Johnson, he explained, starting off as a bodyguard, then muscle at one of Bumpy's numbers spots. Tradition called for hoods and gangsters to dump bodies in Mount Morris Park; the joke was that Chink had his own reserved spot, like a private parking space. A quick promotion put him in command of one of the plum Lenox Avenue routes. When Bumpy got sent to Alcatraz on drug charges, he entrusted his numbers bank to Chink's care. Hold on to it until he did his time, make sure he got his cut, his wife got paid every Friday. Don't give an inch to the Italians or a local up-and-comer. Keep it safe.

Chink was known for his facility with a straight razor. "Got that knife of his to keep people in line," Freddie said. "His daddy's that knife sharpener from Barbados." As if the Barbados part explained something. Carney made the connection—Chink's father and his sturdy cart were longtime neighborhood characters. The father and the son had made a name for themselves, taking care of elementary needs. T. M. KNIFESMITH, in faded gold paint on wood slats, GRINDING & SHARPENING BLADES SAWS SCISSORS SKATES. The old man steered up and down the Harlem streets, ringing his bell—never know which building might send customers onto the sidewalks with their dull steel. Heaving that cart, ringing the bell, and bellowing, "Sharpening! Sharpening!" Carney had used his services for years, everybody did. T.M. honed and buffed your cutlery, humming an unrecognizable hymn, then wrapped it in pages from *The Crisis* and handed it back solemnly before resuming his route. "Sharpening!"

Carney didn't see how the elder Montague's sharpening skills meant that his son knew how to wield a blade—it just meant he knew proper care of his instruments. Carney's father was crooked, but that didn't make him so. It simply meant that he knew how things worked in that particular line.

"The hotel pays Chink protection—we knew he'd be coming," Miami Joe said. "Can't have niggers sticking up places on his watch. But this is about something else."

"He got a girl," Pepper said.

"He got this woman he's taken up with," Miami Joe said, "Lucinda Cole. Used to dance at Shiney's before it got shut down?"

"High-yellow gal, looks like Fredi Washington," Pepper said.

"Fredi Washington?" Freddie said.

"What I didn't know," Miami Joe continued, "is that he's been trying to get her into pictures. Paying for lessons on how to act, how to talk right, carry herself like so. All that. He's been putting her up at the Theresa that last six months, paying for it. Movie people coming through town, introducing her around like she's going to be the black Ava Gardner."

"Ava Gardner," Freddie said. Her in those sweaters.

"What we didn't know," Arthur said, "is that she kept her jewelry in the Theresa vault. All the stuff he bought her. *Miss Lucinda Cole.* And he says he'll skin the niggers who stole it, in the middle of 125th Street. For fucking with his investment."

Carney sighed, more loudly than he thought.

"I wouldn't worry too much about that," Pepper said. "It takes a special kind of nigger to skin a nigger, and that ain't Chink

Montague." His delivery was such that one believed his expertise in skinning-people matters, and his measure of the mobster's character. "But he's got his blood up, and it's true what they say, he's handy with a razor. All sorts of folks who'd like that reward money. Or like Chink to owe them one."

Pepper tailed Montague's men all day as they pressed the big uptown fences, and the small-timers, and otherwise fringe operators like Carney. He'd been across the street sipping a bottle of cherry cola when Delroy and Yea Big—those were their names—visited Carney's Furniture. "Walking in like a pair of water buffalo." They hit Carney's joint, they called on the Arab, on Lou Parks, and even walked up to the second-floor offices of Saul Stein, self-proclaimed Gem King of Broadway, from the radio. Other members of Chink Montague's organization visited the known stickup men and heisters.

"Come looking for me, I bet," Miami Joe said. "Maybe tomorrow if they can find me."

"They call him Yea Big?" Freddie said.

"On account of his johnson."

"He has to save face because of the girl," Pepper said, "and because he took over Bumpy's business. That's what we got."

"What'd they say to you?" Miami Joe asked Carney.

"Keep on the lookout for a necklace."

"If they knew who we were, we'd know," Arthur said. "If they connected Mr. Carney to us, they wouldn't have left it like that." He crossed his legs and pinched his pants leg so it fell correctly over his ankle. "You can expect a visit from the cops," he told Carney. "Whoever he's got on the payroll at the precinct. Sniff around, see if they can get a rise out of you."

Carney had explanations ready for cops about some of the items in the store, but they wouldn't hold up if they really wanted to put the screws to him. Cross-check the serial number of a Silvertone TV with a list of stolen merchandise. He glared at Freddie.

"None of you said shit?" Miami Joe asked. "No one?"

Silence. Pepper stuck a toothpick in his mouth and a hand in his pocket.

"We'd know if they knew," Arthur repeated.

Miami Joe said, "Who'd you tell about it, Freddie?"

"I didn't tell anybody, Joe," Freddie said. "What about you? The girl from the Theresa who tipped you off? Where's she?"

"I got her out of town to visit her mother. Living at the Burbank, with those niggers running their yaps all day, she had to go." Miami Joe turned his attention to Carney.

Carney shook his head. It was like Arthur said—if anyone had talked, they wouldn't be in his office acting civilized. Semi-civilized. People had been talking on him, not the other way around, the way Carney saw it. One of the crooks who'd brought a gold watch or a Zenith portable into the furniture store had added Carney's name, finally, to the underground roster of middlemen. It had to happen sooner or later.

The last time Carney had this many people in his office was that odd afternoon when he confronted the very laws of physics: how to get the goddamned convertible sleeper out of the basement. The sofa had been left there by Gabe Newman, the previous tenant, before he split town. Obviously Newman had carried the orange sleeper in through the metal grate in the sidewalk, or down the stairs through the trapdoor in the office. Unless he'd used a matter transporter machine, like in that movie *The Fly,* or a voodoo spell, unlikely propositions. But no one could figure out how to get it out, not Carney and not the four Italian men from Argent, who needed the room to finish the spring delivery. They heaved and grunted. The oversize sofa did not break down, it did not yield, it refused to clear both sets of stairs no matter what ancient, time-honored furniture-moving tricks they tried. Profanity provided no solace. The afternoon ground on and Carney got the fire ax and chopped the fucker up. It was an off-model and thoroughly unloved. The whole thing remained a mystery.

Now men had assembled in the office again and it was only a matter of time before they turned their attention to that other thing that didn't fit: Carney. He hoped the ax wouldn't make a return appearance.

A siren approached, crawling east down 125th Street. No one moved until they were sure it was a fire engine and not a cruiser. They were hard men, and then some breeze came along and they got scared their little match might blow out.

Miami Joe loosened his tie. It was hot. The fan wasn't much use. "What I want to know is," talking to Carney again, "can you handle what we got? I never heard of you before Freddie put your name in. Small-time or what—I don't know shit about you."

The man had a point, more than he knew. For Carney was not a fence.

Yes, a percentage of his showroom was stolen. TVs, radios back when he could still unload them, tasteful modern lamps, and other small appliances in perfect condition. He was a wall between the criminal world and the straight world, necessary, bearing the load. But when it came to precious metals and gems, he was more of a broker. Freddie came into his office with stuff, and Carney hoofed it downtown to Canal and his man Buxbaum. Buxbaum pulled out his loupe and scale, appraised the goods, and gave Carney fifty cents on the dollar to give to Freddie. Carney got five percent out of Buxbaum's cut. It allowed the Jew to serve colored clientele without going uptown, without meeting them at all, and it gave Freddie—and the few local characters who came in with gem-encrusted bracelets or silver—another outlet for their goods, away from the Harlem drama.

Carney didn't go into what happened to the rings and necklaces after his cousin brought them in. Freddie never asked, same way Carney never asked where they came from. If he believed Carney had secret supply lines to the midtown and Canal Street diamond districts, so be it. If it took Carney a day to come up with the cash, he was good for it. They were blood.

These men in Carney's office, however, were not blood, and they were not going to hand over hundreds of thousands of dollars in stones to a stranger and trust that their fifty cents on the dollar was "on the way." Plus Buxbaum couldn't carry that weight, far as Carney knew.

The last hour, Carney had been working on how to get out of this mess. He said, "I sell furniture. People come in off the street, look around, decide to buy somewhere else, that's business. If you want to go to someone else, I don't take it personally."

Miami raised an eyebrow.

Arthur said, "Huh."

Pepper looked Carney over. He leaned forward on the ottoman, alert and stiff. As if perched on a crate of moonshine in a backwoods shack, revenue agents barreling up the driveway, and not on a new Headley with sumptuous, space-age fill. He didn't let Carney off the hook. "He knows, he's in."

Freddie said, "He's solid. I told you."

Carney had sounded too indifferent. Folks mistook that for confidence sometimes. In the store, his job was to nudge people into doing what they didn't know they wanted to do—lay down a couple hundred on a new dinette, say. That was a different matter than convincing them to do the opposite. The crew had come here to reassure themselves of their decisions. He made a note to correct his pitch; it would come in handy the next time Elizabeth tut-tutted one of his ideas or May demanded an extra scoop of ice cream. He'd have to satisfy himself with making it through the meeting in one piece.

The safecracker dismissed the class. "We keep our mouths shut," Arthur said, "see how it shakes out. Then divvy it up like we planned." Miami Joe never closed a job unless he was satisfied they were free and clear. Putting off the split was sometimes a problem with the crew, but Arthur was known as a good thief, steady all around, and they trusted him to hold the loot until

Monday. Give Chink Montague some time to get distracted with other business, the cops time to move on to another case to botch.

Four days, unless Chink Montague rooted one of them out and they put Carney's name out there.

Four days for Carney to come up with an angle.

SIX

"See how quiet it is?" Leland said. "The dealer says it has one of those new compressors."

The Westinghouse was bolted into the parlor window. Carney had never seen an air conditioner in someone's house before; according to Leland Jones, theirs was the first on the block, though his father-in-law was a shameless exaggerator. They crowded around the unit's plastic grille, Elizabeth up front flapping her face with her hands. She'd almost fainted that morning and a treatment was in order. May sneezed as the sweat on her body cooled. Carney had to admit it felt good.

The AC was one part of the treatment, Elizabeth's old house another. She'd grown up in the Strivers' Row townhouse, and a visit never failed to fortify her. Her room was as she'd left it, on the second floor overlooking the alley. W. C. Handy used to live across the way and Elizabeth liked to tell the story of watching the Father of the Blues in his study, his hands like doves fluttering in the air to the songs on his Victrola. The artist surveying a kingdom that only he could see. As far as views went, it beat the elevated and its discordant symphony of metal on metal. Her favorite blanket on the bed, the annual marks on the doorframe that tracked her height. Carney held no such nostalgia for the apartment he'd grown up in.

Leland turned the AC's dial to demonstrate. "You should look into one of these," he said, aware that Carney's budget forbade the expense.

"One day," Carney said.

"They have payment plans," Leland said.

Elizabeth grabbed Carney's waist. He put his hand on May's shoulder. He didn't know what she made of today's round of jousting between her father and grandfather, but she sure understood that cool air. She exposed her belly to the contraption and looked off into a dream.

Despite the company, he liked coming up to his in-laws' place on Strivers' Row. As a kid he'd admired the neat yellow brick and white limestone houses, plopped down in the middle of Harlem. Looking over from Eighth Avenue, the sidewalks were always swept, the gutters unclotted, the alleyways between the houses strange domains. What kind of block had its own name? What would they call his old stretch of 127th? *Crooked Way.* Striver versus crook. Strivers grasped for something better— maybe it existed, maybe it didn't—and crooks schemed about how to manipulate the present system. The world as it might be versus the world as it was. But perhaps Carney was being too stark. Plenty of crooks were strivers, and plenty of strivers bent the law.

His father-in-law, for example. Leland Jones was one of black Harlem's premier accountants, squaring the books of the best doctors, lawyers, and politicians, all the big Negro-owned 125th Street businesses. He'd get you off the hook. He bragged about his collection of loopholes and dodges, the fat-envelope bribes passed over in the drawing room of the Dumas Club. Brandy and a cigar: I got you. *Let's keep this between us,* but he didn't care who spoke of it because it was cheap advertising. "I eat audits like cornflakes," Leland liked to say, grinning. "With milk and a spoon." He was a tall man, with a wide, moon face and thick white mustache and muttonchops. His grandfather had been a preacher, and a taste for the lecture had been passed down, the righteous address from the front of the room.

Alma called them to dinner. It smelled good from the kitchen

and looked good on the nice china: a big ham with sweet potatoes and greens. Carney slid May into Elizabeth's old high chair,
courtesy of a defunct mail-order company that the Jones family held in high esteem, from how they cooed and clucked at its
name. It creaked. Leland sat at the head of the table and tucked a
light blue napkin into his shirt. He asked when the baby was due.

The conversation permitted Carney a return to his dilemma.
That morning, Rusty had asked why he wanted the front door
closed on such a hot day. Carney felt exposed with the store open
to the street, not that an unlocked door provided any defense.
He steeled himself each time a customer stepped inside. No
one stayed long—the store was too hot, the owner's twitchy
approaches off-putting. The dead time allowed Carney to run
scenarios, like the ones performed at the end of the month to
find the combinations of sales that'd put him into next month's
rent: *One dinette, three couches . . . one complete Argent living-
room set, five lamps, and a rug . . .*

Scenarios:

Chink Montague discovers the identity of the thieves and
takes his revenge but it doesn't reach Carney. Freddie is killed.

Chink Montague roots out the crew, including tangential party
Ray Carney—is he off the hook if he's merely the fence? Freddie is killed. *Or just maimed,* squeaked an optimistic voice that
sounded like Aunt Millie.

Chink Montague roots out the crew, but there's enough time
for Carney to get out of town. With his family? By himself? Freddie is killed.

Carney goes to Chink Montague himself, tells the mobster he
had no idea what was going on. Carney is taught some variety of
lesson. Freddie is killed. *Or just maimed.*

"What happened to you?"

"Oh, I got maimed a little once."

He closed the store an hour early and stalked Riverside Drive to
calm himself down. This apartment, that apartment, he couldn't

focus. A sedan nearly hit him as he stood in the street looking up. Then he picked up the girls for the trip to 139th Street.

Alma reeled him into the dinner table with a mention of Alexander Oakes.

"Alexander was accepted into the Dumas Club," Alma said. She dabbed at the corner of her mouth. "Your father said it was unanimous."

"It was," Leland said. "He's been doing very well for himself. We've been trying to recruit that younger generation for a long time."

"Good for him," Elizabeth said. "That's the sort of thing he likes." She and Alexander had grown up together. His family lived three doors down and socialized in the same hoity-toity atmosphere. Alexander had gone to a Catholic high school, so Carney didn't know him from those days, but over the years Alma had filled him in. Football team, president of the debate club, then on to Howard where he continued his Talented Tenth scrabbling. His law degree got him a prosecutor's job with the Manhattan district attorney. He'd be one of the city's Negro judges when it all came together, write-up in the *Amsterdam News* with a grainy photo. Shady enough to go into politics. Membership in the Dumas Club meant he'd get help from fellow members—and lend a hand if trouble came someone else's way.

He attended Carney and Elizabeth's wedding. The look in Alexander's eyes when Carney shook his hand on the receiving line: still in love with her. Tough shit, buddy.

"Perhaps one day you'll join, Raymond," Alma said.

"Mommy," Elizabeth said, glaring. The Dumas was a paper bag club, so this was a dig: Carney was too dark for admittance.

"The store keeps me pretty busy," Carney said. "Though Leland makes it sound very enjoyable. From all his stories." A bunch of stuck-up mummies, as far as he was concerned. Even if he had lighter skin, his family story was another barrier. Also his profession. His humble store wouldn't cut it—he'd have to own a whole department store, a black Blumstein's, to join their fraternity.

The Jones family lineage was impeccable. By their own standards, anyway. The preacher grandfather had been one of the Seneca Village elders, ministering to the free Negro community downtown. Carney had never heard of the place before he met the Joneses, but they maintained the legend. Seneca had been a couple of hundred people, mostly colored with a bit of Irish—the mongrels always lived on top of one another. Landowning free black men and women staking out a life in the new city. Three churches, two schools, one cemetery. Nothing like it anywhere else in the country, Mr. Jones said, although Carney knew that wasn't true. He'd read about thriving colored communities back then in *Negro Digest*. Pockets in Boston, Philadelphia. Black people always found a way in the most miserable circumstances. If we didn't, we'd have been exterminated by the white man long ago.

Then someone came up with the idea for a grand park in the middle of Manhattan, an oasis inside the newly teeming metropolis. Various locations were proposed, rejected, reconsidered, until the white leaders decided on a vast, rectangular patch in the heart of the island. People already lived there; no matter. The colored citizens of Seneca were property owners, they voted, they had a voice. Not enough of one. The City of New York seized the land, razed the village, and that was that. The villagers dispersed to different neighborhoods, to different cities where they might start again, and the city got its Central Park.

You'll find the bones. Dig under the playgrounds and meadows and silent groves, Carney supposed, you'll find the bones.

Carney admired the story. Less so the haughty complacency of those who kept it alive. Alma came from similar stock: teachers and doctors for generations, an uncle who was the First Negro to attend this Ivy League college, a cousin who was the First Negro to graduate from that medical school. First this, First that other thing. Race-conscious and proud, up to a point—light enough to pass for white, but a little too eager to remind you that they could pass for white. Carney spooned Gerber baby food into May's mouth, saw his hand against her cheek. She was dark, like him. He wondered if Alma still recoiled when she saw her granddaughter's skin, felt dismayed that she hadn't turned out light like Elizabeth. He saw her flinch in the hospital room after the delivery. All that hard work and then look at what her daughter marries. Did she stare at her daughter's belly and wonder whose blood would win out this time?

"Ray," Elizabeth said. She noticed his mind had drifted. She raised her eyebrows and smiled, tugging him back. Elizabeth had seen straight through him during school, even when he sat next to her or walked her home in the rain, but he was grateful she saw him now. That night at Stacey Miller's rent party, she offered a coy apology for not remembering him when he told her that they'd gone to school together. He'd finished college and had been putting in the hours as a stock boy in Blumstein's furniture department. It was the first party he'd attended in a long time. Freddie tried to coax him out, to a night spot, a get-together, but he'd been too embroiled in his studies—Carver High School hadn't prepared him for the rigors of Queens College—and once he started the department store job, he was too tired. He fell asleep nights to the news station as the whoops and laughter of uptown snuck in the windows.

But the night of the party he'd saved up for a new suit—a brown pinstripe number that fit perfectly off the rack. Freddie took him to the party and introduced him around. It was different than before, being out. The talk and interaction took less out of him; finishing his studies, his industry, had made him more confident. Currents plopped him next to Elizabeth in the line outside Stacey Miller's bathroom. Someone smoking reefer in there. Freddie had told him to piss off the roof. Ignoring his cousin's advice had always been a good policy; that night it placed him next to his future wife. He had not been one of those boys in his grade who'd had a crush on her. Those Alexander Oakeses with their ploys. She was out of his league so he never wasted a thought on it. "Of course!" Elizabeth said that night outside the bathroom, as if she suddenly remembered him. Lying. They spent two hours on the lumpy couch by the fire escape—apartment full, rent met—and he asked her out to dinner.

She had been at Black Star Travel for two months. He liked the earnestness in her voice when she talked about work, the urgency of her mission. Black Star arranged tourist and business trips for black travelers, booking them into black-owned and desegregated hotels in America and abroad, mostly the Caribbean, Cuba, and Puerto Rico. The company provided entertainment options; tips on banks, tailors, and friendly restaurants; pamphlets on which theaters in New Orleans or some other destination provided colored seating and which ones wouldn't let you in the door.

America was big and blighted in gamey spots by racial intolerance and violence. Visiting relatives in Georgia? Here are the safe routes around the sundown towns and cracker territories where you might not make it out alive, the towns and counties to be avoided if you valued your life. Best to stay at the Hanson Motor Lodge, fifty miles away, and hit the road by five P.M. to make it back in one piece. It wasn't medicine or law, like her parents had envisioned, but it was service, practical and meaningful. "I want them to be safe," Elizabeth said. Carney reached across the table and took her hand. They went to the movies the next night, and the night after that.

Carney met her parents. They'd had their ideas about young men from broken homes. "What did your father do?" Leland asked, knowing the answer but wanting to hear how he'd put it. Which was, "Odd jobs." He had to allow that in retrospect, maybe they had a point. After all, he had mobsters chasing him these days.

"Who's going to finish that up?" Alma asked. The ham, of course, would last for days, that's what ham was for, but they'd almost taken care of everything else. A few bites of candied sweet potatoes remained.

"I know you like sweet potatoes," Leland said to Carney. "Right?"

Carney took the bowl and thanked him.

"Didn't you have a story about them, Carney?" his father-in-law asked. He snuck a look at Alma.

"Sorry?"

"It was a Christmas one. With your father on Christmas morning?"

Carney had, over the years, shared anecdotes about his upbringing. About his mother's death when he was nine, his father's disappearances, and how his aunt Millie took him in for a few years. How his father returned, and various hard-knock occasions. Getting bit by rats, deloused by the school nurse, the winters without heat, the time he woke up in Harlem Hospital with pneumonia and had no idea how he got there. He told the stories without self-consciousness; why should he be ashamed to have lived for so long on his own?

It had been hard. Others had it worse.

Over the years, on nights like this around this very table, Carney told them about those times because they were true and a part of him, and now these people were family. Only too late did he realize he was exposing too much of himself, soft places where someone might stick in a piece of steel. His stories were his in-laws' entertainment, a vaudeville act. Yes, there was the story of the time he woke up one Christmas and he and his father had one mealy sweet potato to share between them, they cut it in half and put it on two plates, and he saw his white breath before him because the heat was out again that frigid morning, and his father took off at noon and didn't return for a week. Well, maybe the tale possessed a colorful majesty in retrospect, but maybe also he didn't need to be so free with that part of his life anymore. Mr. and Mrs. Jones smiled slightly and sometimes laughed when he told those stories, and why not, they were funny in a miserable way. Perhaps there was something amusing in his delivery, or so he told himself. It was long ago. These days, what he got out of telling that kind of story—a sense of pride in having survived it—and the delight Leland and Alma received from hearing him tell it were small compared to what he had in his life now. He had Elizabeth and May, and if he got a hankering to enumerate his troubles, he had more pressing ones than a sad Christmas morning years ago.

He declined the invitation. The jester called in sick. He told Leland he didn't know what he was talking about and said he'd seen a lot of posters for *Porgy and Bess* on the subway, which sent his in-laws relating, as he knew it would, how one of Leland's clients got them opening-night tickets for the Broadway revival some years back.

"I'm tired," Elizabeth said. The home treatment had worked, the patient had revived, but it was getting late. "It's time we got May in bed."

For once, the Joneses forwent a comment on his pickup truck. He'd had it painted recently, midnight blue. Leland and Alma waved from the front steps, muttered something to each other that Carney couldn't catch, and returned to their cool bubble.

It was a quick drive but long enough for him to decide. Two phone calls. The first to one of Chink Montague's spots to give them Arthur's name. The second to Arthur to tell him the gangsters were coming. The safecracker would have to leave town—he was sensible. Arthur had time to get the stash from wherever he was hiding it, or not—it didn't matter to Carney. He didn't care if Arthur split the take with the crew later on or whatever arrangement they decided; it was not his concern. Dropping a dime would insulate him, and he figured it was his best chance to keep Freddie's name out of things. He was like Elizabeth—plotting a safe route of travel for his cousin. As he had in the old days, keeping Freddie away from an Aunt Millie hairbrush spanking. He'd sleep on it, work out the kinks, but he suspected that morning would find him resolute.

Freddie was pacing across the street from Carney's apartment when he pulled up. They were surprised to see him—Carney alarmed, Elizabeth delighted.

"Freddie," Elizabeth said. "It's been a while."

"How you doing, lady?" Freddie hugged her, making a jokey show of avoiding her big belly. Carney carried May and Freddie kissed her on the cheek. His niece regarded him under heavy lids.

"Don't want to wake her," Carney said.

Freddie's face went overcast. "I ain't the bogeyman," Freddie said.

"Let me get the girls upstairs," Carney said. As the front door closed, he turned. Freddie was gone. When he came back down his cousin was across the street, on the stoop of the flophouse. There'd been a fire—a junkie smoking in bed—and char haloed the empty windows.

"I saw your lights were out so I waited." Freddie scanned the street and stuck his shaky Zippo to the cigarette.

"What is it?"

"Arthur's dead."

SEVEN

Sometimes the road appeared around the bend in his thoughts: buckling and pocked, scrubbed away by monsoons, the jungle clutching it close in a dark green smother. Disintegrating. Pepper heard the boys sing:

Engineers have hairy ears
They live in caves and ditches
They wipe their ass with broken glass
They're rugged sons of bitches

No one knew why Services of Supply troops called themselves *hairy ears*—he found out later that all engineers used the nickname—but he understood the *rugged sons of bitches* part. Rugged son of a bitchness got him sent to Burma in the first place.

Pepper was born in a gray clapboard house on Hillside Avenue in Newark. Womb-wet and shaking, he belted his mother in the face when she lifted him for a kiss. "First punch," he told her years later, bored of hearing the story. In his line, slugging someone hello was a job requirement, and his apprenticeship started early.

He left school in fifth grade to push a broom at the Celluloid Manufacturing Company. At lunch he'd sit on the loading dock atop a crate of black-and-white keys earmarked for the Ampico piano factory and watch the hustlers come and go outside Hank's Grill, which maintained a well-loved craps game in the back, a couple of slot machines, and a hooker named Betty, known for cooing postcoital nursery rhymes. It was the Great Depression and times were strange and Betty stranger still. She had devotees.

One afternoon Pepper finally crossed the street and lunch-hour visits turned into daywork. A variety of crooks gave him nickels for errands, dispatched him to dilapidated tenements to deliver notes written on butcher paper and envelopes they warned him not to open. As if he gave a shit about their schemes; he did not. He liked the money. Nickels became rolls of bills after puberty shot him up a foot and he turned to bruising. He bounced at the Negro clubs on the Barbary Coast—the Kinney Club and the Alcazar Tavern—and made a name for sucker punches and a dizzying backhand. The owners pleaded with him to dress better, but Pepper stuck to his uniform of dungarees and stiff work shirt. Tucked in if he was feeling fancy.

He did not go to church. He was his own sermon. The fifth time Pepper beat a man unconscious the judge said it was either jail or sign up for the war effort. Boot camp and a berth on the USS *Hermitage*. The judge got a kickback for everyone he steered to war.

On the way over Pepper and the rest of the colored soldiers ate hardtack and beans in the dingy hull while the white boys chowed down on proper rations above. They showered in seawater, and Pepper cursed the whole time, not suspecting he'd long for such a luxury once he got down in the mud and silt. There were Negro soldiers who wanted to kill Nazis and Japs and were angry at their deployment behind the lines. Pepper, for his part, was most comfortable where no one was looking, the in-between places, whether it was an alley that separated the church from a line of juke joints or some map grid nobody'd heard of, like Pangsau Pass in the Patkai Hills. Hard to find a place more in-between than a road that didn't exist yet, hard to find work more dangerous than carving out supply lines from India to China.

It was one thing to believe the world was indifferent and cruel, and another to wake to proof every day in the treacherous mountain slopes, the hungry gorges and ravines, the myriad jungle treachery. Only a lazy God could deliver the meanness of things so unadorned.

None of the black boys had seen anything like it. The SOS was there to reestablish a route to China after the Japanese invasion of Burma, to conjure a road out of nothing, clear airstrips for materiel drops, lay mile upon mile of fuel line. The secondhand equipment was a joke—pickaxes broke in their hands, bulldozers shuddered and shook as the white officers looked on. But the native workers, the Burmese and Chinese coolies, had third-hand equipment, so you thanked your lucky stars. Seven days a week, day and night—whorehouse hours. The road claimed a man a mile, so they said, and when the quota fell behind, the jungle made up for it in spades. Malaria, typhus. At quitting time landslides washed away the day's work and men, too, sometimes. You buried them if you could find the bodies.

The night of the earthquake he thought the Devil was reaching up to claim him, but then he remembered he didn't believe in the Devil or those above, and he went back to sleep.

Back home, Pepper had two dependable enemies: cops and bad luck. In the SOS, he found counterparts for them in command, whose harebrained operations were designed to destroy him, and in the jungle, with its random bloodthirst. Do the work, survive the day: He was used to living like this, and now everybody else had to play catch-up. Work and sleep. There were no brothels, no craps games worth a damn, nobody worth beating senseless. Nothing to do but complain, smoke reefer, and remove leeches from your balls. The leeches were out of myth. "Like being back home," Pepper told his bunkmates as he put a Zippo to an especially large specimen. This was back when Pepper still told jokes. No one laughed because they were miserable or because they thought he was serious. Most of his unit was these dopey country boys.

He didn't see combat, but did his first murder nonetheless. Thirty miles from Mongyu, a new deployment of native workers arrived, hardworking Burmese to replace the ones the jungle chewed up. Mostly they stuck to their own camp at quitting time, but there was one young man with delicate features who slunk around, ever underfoot. He wanted to learn English, he said. This gang of white officers used to taunt and waggle their tongues at him. He was not the first womanish man Pepper had seen—there was a place on Warren Street that catered to johns of that bent. The Burmese man only approached the white soldiers for practice, as if the colored grunts had a different language. (They did and they didn't.) As the weeks went on, those officers kept on his case, lobbing kissy noises and jeers. The man just smiled and did a slow, servile nod, dipping his sad eyes from view.

There was no doubt who had beaten him so. One murky evening at the end of monsoon season Pepper went out to smoke some reefer by the Yard—that's what they called the area for the broken-down bulldozers and cranes, as if it were a proper motor pool. No one around. No one was ever around when Pepper was put to the test, and he was not one to speak about things he said or did so what happened next joined the other items in his grim scrapbook. The man's brains were spilled out in the mud when Pepper found him. Pants around his knees. If there'd been a hospital for native workers, he might have taken the man there. If anyone would've been held accountable, he might have reported it. White soldier calls someone a Jap spy, he can get away with anything.

Red bubbles on the Burmese nostrils wobbled and popped as he gurgled. Pepper fixed a palm to the man's mouth and pinched closed the nose, then put a knee to his chest when he started to buck. Pepper's hands were callused from the road work. He didn't feel the man's skin at all, like he was wearing thick rubber gloves.

You hear people say, "Oh, when our boy came back from the war, he was *changed*." The war didn't change Pepper, it completed him. He'd lose himself in different, darker caves and ditches when he returned to the States and started his career in earnest.

The rain washed the Burmese's blood off his hands. In the barracks, Armed Forces Radio announced the score of the Dodger–Giants game eight thousand miles away. Back among normal people and their diversions. The normal world kept spinning when he was up to no good and he stepped back in like nothing happened. This Houdini trick.

The Dodgers were playing Cincinnati when he heard about Arthur.

He was at Donegal's, up on Broadway. Friday night, three days after the heist. Everyone was hunkered and listening to the game. What kind of deviant rooted for the Dodgers on Giants turf? The Dodgers splitting Brooklyn for Los Angeles was a crime, and to cheer for the lost team meant you were an accomplice, but perpetrators and accomplices made up the majority of Donegal's clientele. A tendency toward moral irregularity made you a regular. Pepper sat on a stool at the mahogany bar with the usual swindlers, thieves, and pimps. Kept his ears open for chatter about the Theresa job.

Banjo, an elderly hustler who claimed to be the first man to steal a car on the "Isle of Manhattan," limped inside and announced that someone had bumped Arthur. The limp was courtesy of the robbery squad, who'd been disappointed that Banjo sicced his dog on them the last time they picked him up. It had been a crowbar-shaped disappointment.

Banjo placed his plaid beret over his heart in tribute to Arthur. The thief was known, with fans of his own among these Dodgers fans. Pour one out for the Jackie Robinson of safecracking. Pepper guzzled his beer and walked down to where the dead man had flopped. Eighth inning, six to one Dodgers.

Outside Arthur's building on 134th, two cop cars had their lights spinning, red and white on the faces of the onlookers. No reason for it—the cops were waiting for the meat wagon—but they liked the show of power. As if white people didn't remind these people of their place all day. At work, at the white bank, at the grocery store as the clerk explained they'd reached the end of their credit. Pepper jostled to the front of the mob. Scenes like this drew a crowd, killed time, especially on hot, listless nights. One of the cops—this beefy-faced peckerwood—noticed Pepper and gave him the once-over. Pepper stared back and the pig turned his attention to his shiny black shoes.

Pepper got the low-down from the wino swaying next to him. You want to know what's going on, you ask the block wino. They see everything and then the booze pickles it, keeps it all fresh for later. The wino told him that a man named Arthur—"looks like a schoolteacher"—had been shot in his bed. The landlady saw the open door and phoned the precinct. "His head blown up like a watermelon fell off a cart." The wino made an evocative *splat* sound. The landlady was a nice woman, he added, always with a warm hello no matter how shaky he was.

"That's a shame," Pepper told the wino. It was too bad, on top of not knowing where his damn money was. He'd liked Arthur, the way the man rubbed his fingertips together when he got to thinking, like he was about to punch out a safe. After the crew went to meet the furniture-store owner last night, he and Arthur went for a drink. The safecracker kept going on about this farm he owned. Out in the country. "I'm going to get a horse, and some chickens." Come Labor Day, Arthur said, when the heat died down, he wanted to return to Carney's Furniture and talk to the man about home furnishings. "We won't say a word about the

Theresa job. Won't even acknowledge that we've ever met. Just a salesman and a man in the market. Just: Is it comfortable? Will it last?" He raised his glass to toast the idea.

Gets himself some land, then he kicks the bucket up here. Bought the farm, then bought the farm. More proof for Pepper's philosophy vis-à-vis making plans. Whoever heard of a crook keeping chickens? Begging for God to smite your uppity ass. Take the road, for instance. Three years to finish, hundreds of men lost, and then the Japanese surrender a month later. It was only good for war and with the war over, the jungle took it back. What was it now? A ribbon of rubble in the mud.

When Pepper woke the next morning the heat was murderous and it was only seven A.M. A nice day for a hunt. Hunting a rat, smoking out a double-crosser—it had been a while. Pepper liked the heat, which flushed out weasels to stoops and shade. Plus today he'd have wheels. He waited outside the furniture store for Carney to show up, and then it was on to the likely hideouts, the fronts and flophouses and fuck pads of this chase.

* * *

The heat made Harlem into a forge. Pepper rode shotgun.

Pepper caught up with Carney as he unlocked the front door of the furniture store, greeting him with "Mr. Businessman." Carney jumped, on alert from Freddie's visit the night before. The keys in his hand a talisman of the lost, normal world. Everybody knew how to find Carney—one of the drawbacks of having his name in two-foot-tall letters on 125th Street. Chink Montague's men, this crook. Freddie had all his addresses and in the last three days had popped up with bad news each time. Carney had never thought overmuch about his accessibility before, but now recognized it as a hazard in the criminal trade.

Miami Joe understood this. He was nowhere to be found. "I want to talk to that nigger," Pepper told Carney after his greeting. "You can drive."

"I can't," Carney said.

"You got that truck, right?"

Carney twisted a thumb at the store.

"That's what your man is for, right?" Pepper said. "You the boss."

Yes, Rusty could open up and handle business. Two minutes later Carney and Pepper were in the Ford pickup.

"Uptown," Pepper said. He put a steel lunch box on the seat next to him. Just another day of work. "Your cousin told you what happened to our friend." Said as a statement of fact.

"Uptown where?" Carney said. As if not acknowledging Arthur's murder might make the man alive for a little more.

"It'll come to me," Pepper said. "This way for now." He rolled down the window for a blast of hot air in his face.

Pepper told him about Donegal's and the scene outside Arthur's flophouse, which broke up when a soda bottle detonated on a prowl car and sent the onlookers for cover. Kids on the roof across the street, taunting the cops. "Used to call that 'giving them the Blitz,'" Pepper said.

"I know," Carney said. He was thirteen during the riots of '43. A white cop shot a Negro soldier who'd intervened in the arrest of a Negro lady who'd had one too many. For two nights Harlem was aboil. His father went out "shopping" and returned with new duds for the two of them. Shopping of the sort where you step over the broken glass of the front window and don't need help from the salesclerk. He wore that porkpie hat until the day he died, chocolate brown with a green feather in the brim that he wicked up whenever he left the house. Carney outgrew the slacks and sweater sooner than that. To this day whenever he walked past T. P. Fox or Nelson's, he wondered if his father had stripped the clothes from their mannequins.

"Good days," Pepper said. Dropping bombs on the cops from above. He chuckled and gazed off wistfully, recalling some caper. Carney recognized the look from his father. "Then your cousin

Freddie showed up," Pepper said. "Was it Chink? Is he onto us, or did Arthur have it coming from some old buddy? I told Freddie to get you and I went to find Miami Joe. But that nigger's trying to be Houdini."

Hence this Saturday-morning excursion. Freddie was probably still sleeping it off after getting his ashes hauled down in the Village. He'd shown up at Carney's place, nervous as all get-out, and then split for the subway after delivering the news about Arthur. Too afraid to go to his mother's—what if they were staking it out? Freddie had this blond chick on Bank Street, a Fordham co-ed he'd picked up one night at the Vanguard. The first time he took her out she asked if he had a tail. Her daddy had told her stories about Negroes and their monkey tails. "I showed her something else, I'll tell you that."

Freddie was safe or not safe, downtown in a different neighborhood and its other perils. Carney had gone back upstairs to the apartment—should he take the girls and leave town? Twice he'd driven up to New Haven for a swap meet and there was this little motel off the highway. Blinking sign. Whenever he saw it, he joked to himself that if he ever had to lam it, that's where he'd go. COLOR TV SWIMMING POOL MAGIC FINGERS. Less funny now, when it involved explaining things to Elizabeth.

Lack of sleep made him foggy at the wheel. Pepper said, "Grady Billiards on 145th Street," and broke down the situation. If it was Chink Montague was onto them, that was one thing. "But if Miami Joe is pulling a cross, that's some other shit," Pepper said. "Who has the loot?" Either way, Carney was part of the crew now and had to pitch in, the way Pepper saw it.

Carney squeezed the steering wheel, let go, squeezed harder. Over years this ritual had stilled the tremors when he got anxious. "Fucking truck is haunted," he said under his breath.

"What's that?"

"Hundred and Forty-Fifth Street," Carney said.

If they wanted a lead on where Miami Joe hung his hat, they

had to talk to some people. Pepper didn't know Miami Joe well, first met him when he came over to him at Baby's Best and said he had a job Pepper didn't want to pass up. "Baby's—you spent time in that place? Anything that starts there ends up in the pigsty." Pepper should have known then that it'd go south, he said. He tapped the lunch box.

First up, a pool room on Amsterdam. Carney had walked the block many times and it was impossible that he'd never seen the joint before, but there it was with sooty windows and an ancient sign: Grady Billiards. Older than him. Pepper had him wait in the car. Carney thought he heard a loud crack, but a round of honking—a green sedan stalled out at the light—covered the noise. Pepper emerged, wiping blood on his dark blue dungarees. He got back in the passenger seat and opened his lunch box. Inside were an egg sandwich in wax paper, a faded thermos, and a pistol. He didn't say anything while he ate half the sandwich and gulped down some coffee. "Three blocks up there's another guy," he said, finally.

Next stop was one of those Puerto Rican grocers. Carney nabbed a spot out front with a view inside. Pepper ignored the guy at the cash register and disappeared past the Employees Only door at the back. He came out nodding a minute later. Neither he nor the guy behind the counter acknowledged each other.

After that was a barbershop—Carney couldn't see from his angle but caught the five customers duck out after Pepper walked in—and another pool room Carney had never noticed before. Places in Pepper's city that were nowhere on his own map.

"We going to Mam Lacey's after-hour's spot," Pepper said. "You know where that is?"

Carney had been there plenty; it had been a Freddie favorite. One of Carney's, too, owing to the gregarious owner Lacey, a big, glad lady who kept track of all her customers' drinks and predilections. Her station was behind the ramshackle bar, which was made out of old oatmeal crates, where she whispered offers too heavy in euphemism for Carney, square that he was, to decipher. Girls in the rooms upstairs, narcotics. He declined with a "No, thank you, ma'am," and she'd wink: *One day, my young man . . .* But the spot had been closed down for years after a shootout. Or a knife fight. There were always new basement joints opening up.

The sickness originated at Mam Lacey's and tendriled out. The residential block had been inviting and tidy in the old days, stickball street with nice plantings. Now Lacey's windows were smashed, the two buildings on either side had the same affliction, boarded up and depopulated, and the two buildings next to those looked sketchy. Carney frowned. "Urban blight" was right; it hopped from place to place like bedbugs.

"You come, too," Pepper said. He waved Carney over as he peered into the dark windows of the basement apartment.

Gun it and split. Get the girls and split.

Pepper'd chase him down even if he was going fifty miles an hour.

Carney removed the key from the ignition.

The front room had smelled rank from cigarette and cigar smoke in the glory days, and from the cheap beer and rotgut soaked into the floorboards, but the stench now was another register of foul. The big fat couch where Carney used to sit with his drink and shake his head over the other patrons' antics was split open and layered with revolting stains, the dark mirrors set into the walls were smashed, and the top of the oatmeal-crate bar was an altar of junkie worship. Blackened spoons, wadded paper, emptied cylinders. Two skinny men slept on the floor, soiled and raggedy. They didn't stir when Pepper turned them over to check their faces.

"I used to come here," Carney said.

"Used to be nice," Pepper said.

Pepper led the way to the garden, past a small room filled with garbage, and the kitchen, where Mam Lacey had fried chicken all night. Only thing cooking in there these days was misery.

Carney put his hands in his pockets so they wouldn't touch anything. He breathed through his mouth and was glad when they stepped into the back, into the light again. The garden was overgrown and creepy. A tall statue of an angel was broken in half. Its legs stuck up out of a clutch of weeds, white wings pointing this way and that. Along the back wall there was a stone bench. A man slept on it, covered with a wool blanket despite the heat.

Pepper slapped the man awake. "Julius."

The man stirred, unsurprised at the intrusion. Carney recognized him—Lacey's son, the teenager who'd bussed the empty glasses and lit ladies' cigarettes. Joyful and eager in the old days, like the customers' kid brother who lived back home and oh-goshed over their city stories. In that near-noon light, he looked older than Carney.

"You wake up, Julius," Pepper said. "I'm looking for your man Miami Joe."

Julius sat up and patted his pockets after something. He squinted around the garden.

"I'm talking to you," Pepper said.

Julius pulled the blanket around his shoulders and scowled. "I'm 'unreliable,' " Julius said. The words were sour in his mouth; he ran his tongue over his teeth to rub away the taste. "He don't let me come along no more."

"I know that," Pepper said. "I want to know where that nigger sleep."

"Miami Joe's too busy to sleep—" Pepper's slap echoed in the backyards of 145th between Eighth and Seventh. A window opened a few buildings over, some bystander. Pepper didn't even look. The window closed.

Carney remembered the boy as he had been not too long ago: gap-toothed and smiling. He said, "Do you have to?"

Pepper gave him a look—cold steel—and returned to Mam Lacey's ne'er-do-well offspring. "Your mother ran a nice joint," he said.

"I should have joined the navy," Julius said.

His mother dies, Carney figured, Julius takes over the place and instead of listening to his customers' tales of crime, he decides to participate. One thing leads to another. What of the rooms upstairs, the girls who used to work up there? What lived in the rooms now?

"Where's he sleep?" Pepper said.

Julius said, "I asked him if he had anything cooking, and Joe said he wouldn't take me along anymore if I was like this. Those were good times . . ." He trailed off. Then the back side of Pepper's hand brought him to. "He's in that flophouse on 136th and Eighth, the one with the old doctor's sign out front. Third floor . . ." With that, he bunched one end of the blanket and made it into a pillow. Carney looked back as he and Pepper stepped back into the building. Julius was unconscious again, nestled into his narcotic hideaway.

Out on the street, Carney turned the ignition. "He was a happy kid."

"Those the ones you have to look out for," Pepper said. "They got a lot to catch up on if they start late."

The old truck bucked as it always did, then they were in the street. Julius had inherited a building and an illicit bar, Carney this Ford truck. He didn't see his father much once he got out of Queens College. Mike Carney had taken up with Gladys in Bed-Stuy and made Brooklyn his hunting ground. Carney was working in Blumstein's furniture department and saving up his money in a sock in a boot under his bed. Saving up for what, he didn't know.

Then the afternoon when Gladys came to the department store to tell him that his father had been killed by the cops. "There's someone here to see you." His father had broken into a pharmacy to steal a box of cough syrup, the strong stuff druggies were into.

"You still work here," Gladys said.

"I'm working my way up," Carney said. Last winter they gave

him a shift in the Santa suit, a mark of Blumstein approval. The long-running Santa had taken to the bottle and they were teaching him a lesson. *Can't have people breathing rotgut on our customers' kids.*

" 'Working your way up'—that's what he said." Gladys was a full-figured Jamaican gal with a thick, honeyed accent. His father had always liked West Indian women. "Manhattan is an island, too, I figure, so we got a lot in common. Even if I don't understand half of what they say."

Carney couldn't bring himself to ask Gladys for details. Cut down by police—it was how he suspected his father would exit this planet. By police or another crook. The day he picked up his father's truck was the last time he saw Gladys. She threw herself wailing over the hood as if it were his coffin. Two guys from down the street had to pry her off.

Carney had the truck a whole year before he ran over a nail on Lenox Avenue. He went to get the spare in back. That's how he found the money. Thirty thousand in cash. Spare-tire bank. If he'd sold the truck, he wouldn't have found it. That was just like his father, to make him earn his down payment. Three months later Carney signed the lease for 125th Street.

* * *

Carney's companion had his face zipped up in contentment, twisting to check the derrieres of neighborhood beauties and narrating their travels down the avenues. "That's a good chicken spot," Pepper said. "You ever eat there?" The blood on his jeans had dried to a dark smudge, oil or grime from a distance. Pepper rode shotgun, but he was in the driver's seat.

Pepper said he wanted to stop for lunch at Jolly Chan's for chop suey. The owner knew Pepper and gave them a table in the corner, by the window. There was a fish tank with greenish water over by the kitchen door. Something moved inside it. Red-and-orange dragons writhed on the wallpaper, roiling like clouds.

They didn't speak much and Carney's stomach was too sour to accept food. Pepper was preoccupied as well and only ate half his plate. He sat so he could watch the street.

"What made you want to sell couches?" Pepper said, poking at his food.

"I'm an entrepreneur."

"Entrepreneur?" Pepper said the last part like *manure*. "That's just a hustler who pays taxes."

Carney explained that he got a tip about a furniture store that was going out of business. The previous tenant had lit out in the middle of the night. The rent was cheap. It was a steal. Carney was nervous, and babbling prevented contemplation of Pepper's stony face. What was in the man's head? Might as well talk to a sidewalk. Carney shared tidbits from his business-school classes about the logistics of taking over a failing venture. Maintaining or severing existing relationships with suppliers, how to avoid the assumption liabilities. The couch in the basement, for example. It was there, this inherited problem, and he'd had to figure out how to deal with it.

Pepper said, "Didn't matter how it got there. What you care about it is how to take care of it. An ax is good. Fire and a match, too."

Carney took a sip of water.

"Though I've been told I am too quick to reach for the gas can sometimes." Pepper gestured for the check and poured ketchup over what he didn't eat. "So Chan can't serve it to the next guy."

Pepper had a different kind of brain.

"Where are you from, man?" Carney asked.

"New Jersey," Pepper said, as if it were the dumbest question he'd ever heard.

The cookies were stale and the fortunes discouraging.

The doctor's sign outside the flophouse was gone; the two metal chains dangled on the metal brace. Carney joined Pepper without being asked. The front door was unlocked. The landlord, a white-haired gnome, swept up the front hallway. He looked away when he got a load of Pepper. By now Carney was accustomed to the effect the man had on people.

"Three," Pepper said. The floors creaked all the way up. Like a giant had given the building a good shake and then set it down again, well-squeezed.

No one answered Pepper's knock the first two times. "Yes?"

"It's Pepper. And Carney."

"Don't know any Pepper. No salt, neither. You get on."

It wasn't Miami Joe's voice. This guy sounded like he'd read a book once.

Pepper ran his finger along the doorframe, testing, then kicked it in.

Residents rented the room furnished, Carney supposed, from the hodgepodge of styles represented. The old Morgan couch from the 1930s, before the company went under for taking the fill from dirty old mattresses; the scuffed-up pine bureau; and the plywood coffee table that looked like it'd topple over if you put an ashtray on it. Flop here for weeks or months and then slide down to the next bleak escapade. Meanwhile the stained furniture circulated from room to room, that'll be an extra two dollars a week for a bed if you need one, and if you want another lamp we can work that out, too.

The man in the room fit the profile, skinny-armed and potbellied, with thick black eyeglasses, at a loss before these strangers in his yellowed undershirt and drawers. "What'd you do that for?" he asked, pointing at the busted door.

"Looking for Miami Joe," Pepper said.

"You got eyes—he ain't here." The man said his name was Jones and that he knew Miami Joe from Florida. He was here on a sales trip and Miami Joe said he could bunk on the floor. He wasn't going to be around much, or so he told Jones.

"Selling what?" Pepper asked.

"If you'd let me show you—" Jones started for the suitcase at the foot of the bed. The bedsheet held the fuzzy, grimed silhouette of the human form.

Pepper had his pistol out. "He can do it."

Carney popped the snaps on the battered blue suitcase. Jones's merchandise was set in cushioned pockets, vials of dark-colored fluids. Carney held one up to the window, dust drifting in the sunlight: VIRILE WATERS.

"Nice, right?" Jones said. He leaned against the beat-up bedside table, the surface of which was covered with brown cigarette burns that looked like a swarm of cockroaches. "I'm a purveyor of certified masculine tonics," Jones continued, "whether your needs lie in the realm of marital duties or growing a beard."

"Shoot, I got my own roots," Pepper said.

Jones turned to Carney. "How about you, sir? I'm sure your wife would appreciate the new spring in your step. You heard of bedroom eyes? These will give you bedroom binoculars."

Before Carney could answer, Jones reached for the top drawer of the bedside table. He reached inside and Pepper kicked it shut on his hand. Carney dropped Virile Waters and the vial bounced on the parquet floor but did not shatter. Only thing that broke were bones in Jones's hand, from the sound of it. He lurched to the floor and howled.

Pepper pressed his boot on the salesman's neck. He told Carney to check the drawer. There was a rusty hunting knife inside and some cards for a gentleman's club in the Bronx.

"I don't know who you niggers are," Jones said. Without his glasses he looked like a mole. "Miami Joe hangs with some crazies."

"When's he coming back?" Carney asked.

"He ain't—he moved out yesterday," Jones said. "The room is paid up until the end of the month."

"Where to?" Pepper said.

"He said he was homesick."

"He went back to Miami?" Carney said.

"They don't call that nigger Chicago Joe, nigger," Jones said.

"What do you think?" Carney asked Pepper when they were back in the truck. There was a lump in his pocket. He'd swiped one of Jones's potions at some point.

"Miami Joe's up to something shady, no doubt," Pepper said. "But did he take out Arthur, or did Chink do Arthur and then Miami Joe? All we know, he's lying in Mount Morris Park."

With his face cut off, Carney added. He didn't care where the money and stones were. He wanted to know how well he was going to sleep that night.

Pepper decided. "No, it's Miami Joe. He killed Arthur and took the money."

"I have to get back," Carney said.

"Sure."

They drove two blocks in silence, then Pepper said, "You still got that thinking look."

"What?"

"We met, way back," Pepper said. "With your father at that old place you guys had on 127th. 'The Montgomery' carved out there on the front of the building. Sounded so fancy. Back then."

They were at a stoplight behind a gasoline truck. "It wasn't fancy," Carney said.

"I said it sounded."

"You knew him?"

"Big Mike Carney? You pulled jobs in Harlem, you knew Mike Carney. We pulled a lot of shit. He was good."

"Good?"

"You kept the truck."

"He left it."

Pepper slapped the dashboard. "Still runs."

Perhaps he'd ask about his father another time. This day he tried to imagine a young Pepper at the old apartment and wondered if he was one of the men who brought him toys, and if the cheap thing broke in his hands after five minutes, or ten.

EIGHT

Rusty was a law-abiding sort but had no love for its mortal representatives: sheriffs and deputies back home, cops and detectives up here. When the Klan burned down his father's grocery store—the store drew a mixed clientele, and thus white business from Myrtle's on Main Street—the sheriff said they might want to think twice about reopening. The sheriff spat tobacco juice into the ashes and looked bored. Probably his hand that splashed the gasoline. Rusty's parents and sister relocated to Decatur, and Rusty picked up stakes to New York City. His mother had nicknamed him "Big Time" when he was a baby and when he stepped on the northbound Greyhound bus she said, "See, I told you." The police 'round here were the same breed, but Harlem was so big and hectic Rusty figured they didn't have time to hassle folks as much as they liked. Had to spread their hassle around, which suited Rusty fine. The detective who stopped in the furniture store that afternoon didn't even have time for a proper bullying. He beat it for the door when Rusty informed him Carney was out.

* * *

"What did he want?" Carney asked. He'd returned to the office after dropping Pepper off and his mood was curdled.

Rusty gave Carney the detective's card. Detective William Munson, 28th Precinct. Arthur had warned Carney that someone on Chink's payroll would pay him a visit. To probe about the Theresa, but this also could have concerned certain merchandise for sale. He had pushed his luck and now luck's opposite pushed back.

"Did Freddie call?"

"No."

Rusty added that he'd made a big sale that afternoon, but Carney didn't hear. Carney closed the door to the office and brooded over his afternoon with Pepper, and other troubles, until closing time.

The apartment door caught on the chain—only Alma latched it when he was out—and he had to knock to be let into his own home. A crook in the morning and this lady at night. He waited. The strange couple next door had left a bag of something foul outside their door and the marks and grime in the hallways stood out more than usual. Sometimes the train rumble moved through steel struts and concrete and into the building and he felt it in his feet, like now. How had he subjected his wife and child to this place for all this time?

Alma regarded him through the crack for longer than he thought necessary, and that was the first thing.

"May fell asleep in your bed," Alma said. Elizabeth bided her time until it was safe to sneak out, or else she'd fallen asleep, too. "I was just cleaning up."

Carney tried to shake off his mood. He joined her in the kitchen and pitched in. Pot roast and peas for dinner. Carney and his mother-in-law stuck to their quadrants in the small kitchen, squeezing past each other and apologizing too much when they got too close. From her silence, Alma had something on her mind and was being uncharacteristically reticent about making it known. That was the second thing. Carney said, "It's cooled off."

"It's so hot," Alma said. She rubbed the big white serving dish with the red-and-white-checkered cloth. The dish was one of her wedding gifts to them. It was notched and chipped now, with black splinter lines.

Carney waited, like he did when a customer acted squirrelly. Everything in the store too expensive, or they'd walked in on a whim and were searching for an excuse to split.

"Elizabeth fainting the other day," Alma said. "That was a scare." It had just been the day before. Why not say *yesterday*?

"Only a few more weeks," Carney said. He slid the silverware into the sink so it didn't clatter.

"Leland and I were thinking," his mother-in-law said, "what if Elizabeth stayed with us until the baby came? With the doctor's orders to stay off her feet, it's been so difficult. The heat." That kind and gentle register in her voice. She'd never tried to sell him something before and was unsure how to go about it. "It's comfortable there, and with you working in your store. I can look after her all the time and take her off your hands."

"That's nice of you to offer, but we're doing okay right now."

"It'd be easier for May, too," she said, "with the spare room. That's how they built them, for cross ventilation."

"May, too? That's the deal here?"

"She wouldn't want to be apart, obviously. At that age. With you at that store all day. It makes sense."

"Sense."

"We think it's reasonable. My mother always said—"

"Did your mother ever tell you to mind your own fucking business?"

"Raymond!"

" 'With me in the store all day.' Did your mother ever tell you to mind your own fucking business?"

"You'll wake May," Alma said.

"She sleeps like a rock. With that train all night? She sleeps like a rock." He had never talked to her like this, but he had been waiting.

She had been waiting as well. Alma dried her hands on the dish towel. Draped it over the sink faucet, perfectly even. She said, "Talk to me like that—who the fuck do you think you are, nigger? I've seen street niggers like you my whole life, hands in your pockets." She slouched in imitation and her voice went low and colored. "*I'm-a just out here trying to make a dollar.* You think I don't know what game you're running? With your whole jive?"

On the one hand, her honesty. On the other hand.

The phone rang in the living room. And once more. Alma straightened her dress and went to answer it. Carney put his hands on the sink. Outside the window, he caught four floors' worth of kitchen windows in the building next door: one dark; another lit up but empty; the next featuring two hands deep in suds; and in the last a thin brown hand tapped cigarette ashes outside. People trying to make it through the day. The 1 train pulled into the 125th Street station, he felt it in his toes. He couldn't see the line of windows in the train cars, the people pour out onto the platform, head down the stairs, but he pictured them scatter to their private dramas. Regular as sunsets and arguments, this movement. People heading home to their private cars, light spilling from the square windows of kitchens. As if they lived in trains stacked on top of one another.

A fence, and also a thief. He had stolen her daughter, after all. She wasn't getting her back.

Alma's passionate account met a friendly ear and he gathered it was Leland on the phone. If their words hadn't wakened Elizabeth, then she was asleep for the night, arms reaching out for May, with that new baby in between. Carney split.

* * *

Out on the street, the first Saturday-night shift was busy. They were loud: jeers, rhythm and blues, disputes on the cusp of fistfights. Carney walked among the couples heading out for a special dinner, or for one at their usual haunts, where they knew what to avoid on the menu. He dodged the dirty kids who should have been in bed, running and screaming themselves sick, and the teenagers wringing out the last bit of the day before they had to return home to pant by the open window next to their beds. In tenements and split-up townhouses, the second shift made preparations for their entrance. Loitering in the bathtub, ironing their best duds, rehearsing alibis, and confirming orders of business: *We'll meet at Knights and take it from there.* Plus the second-shift men and women meeting no one at all, taking one last confirmation in the mirror before they gave themselves to Saturday-night destiny.

And then there were the crooks, who tied their shoes and hummed jumpy songs, for soon the midnight whistle would call them to the factory.

There was no question where he was headed: Riverside Drive. He crossed the street to avoid the street preacher, then crossed the street again to go around the mission church on 128th and its night congregation filing inside. He'd had enough of sales pitches today. *Don't hurt me, I'll talk. Tell me what I want to know or else.* Then Alma with, *Let the girls stay with us.* Give Elizabeth enough time and she'll come around, Alma and Leland must have told each other. Wake up to the poverty of her choices. He was the rat that crept out of the gutter and squeezed under the door.

Alma's proposal made sense, though not for the reasons she gave. Carney had put his family in danger, and that's why he had cursed at her. Left a trail to his door for bad men to follow. One of the crew dead, two others missing . . . but that was wrong. Pepper was right. It was Miami Joe, no doubt. Miami Joe was not missing. He had killed Arthur and taken the money and stones from the Theresa job. Perhaps brought harm to his cousin. And if Miami Joe hadn't split for the South yet, he needed to eliminate the rest of the crew to cut off Chink's payback. Or to prevent them—well, Pepper—from avenging the double-cross. Carney didn't know how this particular region of the crooked world worked. Maybe Miami Joe was in Florida, or maybe he wouldn't leave town until he was sure no one was coming after him.

There was a breeze off the river. Rank but cool. The buzz of the afternoon hunt and his fight with Alma had dissipated. A little dizzy—he hadn't eaten since breakfast. Carney crossed to the west side of the street and looked north, tracing the wall of Riverside Drive, that jagged line of majestic red brick and white limestone. The perimeter of a fort, to protect the good citizens of Harlem. Wrong again—a cage to keep the mad crowd who called those streets home from escaping to the rest of the world. Who knew the havoc and ruin they'd perpetrate if allowed to run free among decent people. Best to keep them all in here, on this island, bought for twenty-seven bucks from the Indians, the story went. Twenty-seven bucks went a lot further in those days.

He'd wandered across from 528 Riverside Drive, his latest prospect. This is what he was working toward. Who wouldn't want to live on Riverside Drive? Come home from the store, open the front door and the smell of Caw Caw chicken drifts from the kitchen. Radio on, big band, and May hugs one of his legs and the new addition—he was a boy in this reverie—hugs the other. Sunset light from the west, even if you had to look at New Jersey, too. A nice place, like no other he'd lived in his whole life. *Street nigger,* she'd said.

A tall woman in a green dress ducked out of the front door, high heels clicking on the concrete. She checked her purse for keys or lipstick or cigarettes and kept walking. Carney stood in a spot diagonal to one of the gargoyles on a cornice of 528—their eyes met. No hint of the beast's stone appraisal. What would his father do? Big Mike Carney. He wouldn't go to his office, not that he had one, wouldn't go home, that's for sure. He would not lay his head down until he hunted down the man who'd double-crossed him. Like Pepper, he'd turn uptown upside down until he shook out his quarry.

Who wouldn't want to live on Riverside Drive? A few blocks

north was the Burbank. Where the finger—Miami Joe's source inside the Theresa—kept a room. It was a short walk.

The SRO's lobby was Saturday-night busy—residents striking out to their drinking spots, running home after work to gussy themselves up for their evening machinations. The disheveled manager perched behind a scratched-up desk, guarding the array of mail slots. A tiny fan blew into his miserable face, two streamers flapping from the grille like tentacles. Carney said he was looking for his friend Betty, couldn't remember the room number.

"Betty who?"

"I work with her at the Theresa. She forgot her purse."

The manager looked down at his paper. "She ain't been around."

"Maybe I could give it to Joe?"

The manager pushed his glasses up on his nose. He waited for his visitor to notice the hole in his scheme. "Where's the purse?"

Carney jerked his hand toward the street. "My truck."

The elevator opened and two ladies with bouffant hairdos levitated into the lobby like queens, gowns shimmering. "I don't know any Joe," the manager said.

Carney rounded the corner and stopped to think. Freddie had mentioned Baby's Best in his account of the robbery. That was on 136th or 137th, off Eighth. He wasn't going to confront the man—Pepper could handle that. But to help the hunt before calling in the roughneck, it was better than pacing around his living room. Alma rarely stayed past ten o'clock. The apartment would be quiet soon. He chose his route to Baby's Best.

*   *   *

Miami Joe was not a law-abiding sort and had no love for its earthly muscle: sheriffs and deputies back home, cops and detectives up here. Had they the misfortune to stop him when he had his pistol in his pocket, he'd cut them down. His disdain for those he robbed was of a different variety, akin to that of a child grinding his shoe on a cockroach. They were insignificant, they were helpless, and they passed from his mind after the job was done, whether the task at hand was a rip-off or a rubout. There was, for example, an empty place in his mind formerly occupied by Arthur. Eventually the next job would fill that vacancy. Until he finished that one, too. Miami Joe vaulted down the fire stairwell after Gibbs, the night manager, rang Betty's room. Clasping his pistol to his leg. If he were quick enough. Miami Joe was surprised to make out the furniture salesman down 140th Street. Pepper would have sensed his approach. Chink would have sent two men. He lucked out. Miami Joe got as close as he could, dropped to his knee, rested the barrel on his forearm to aim, and pulled the trigger.

NINE

His day ended as it started: with men of hard character bracing him under the two-foot-tall letters that spelled out his name.

Like most Harlemites, Carney grew up with broken glass in the playground, the pageant of sidewalk cruelty whenever he stepped outside, and the snap of gunfire. He recognized the sound. Carney crouched and zagged toward the aluminum garbage cans. When he looked back, there was Miami Joe and the zing as his second shot hit the lid of the can next to him. It wasn't too far to the corner—he sprinted for it.

New York was like that sometimes—you turn a corner and end up in an entirely different city, like magic. 140th Street was dark and silent, and Hamilton was a party. The bar two doors down had a line waiting to get in—one of those bebop spots, from the sound—and next to the bar some Spanish guys drank wine and played dominoes in the light cast from a barbershop. The domino players worked in the barbershop; it paid their rent during the day and provided a refuge from their families at night. Carney bumped through the people standing in line, jostling, and sped down the block. A patrol car cruised on the other side of the street. He looked over his shoulder. No sign of Miami Joe. If Carney saw the cops, so did Miami Joe. He ran once the cops got far enough away.

Carney took an eccentric path south, sawing back and forth down avenues and streets. Before he dropped Pepper off that afternoon, the man told him to leave any messages at Donegal's. "Don't matter who's working—that's my answering service." This was definitely more Pepper's field— gun battles and whatnot. The man was like a swami when it came to putting a hurt on somebody. Carney couldn't go home and lead Miami Joe to his family. If Miami Joe went there anyway . . . There were bars full of people; he could hide out in one. Until last call and then what? He headed for the store, that's where his feet took him at any rate. He'd call Pepper from his office and wait.

Morningside and 125th was quiet when he arrived ten min- utes later. All the activity was by the Apollo a few blocks down. He couldn't remember who was playing that night, the name painted on the side of the big tour bus, but the mob and its squeals meant it was somebody big. His hands shook as he put the keys to the front door.

Miami Joe said, "Hurry it up." He stood off the sidewalk between two dark sedans. There hadn't been time to put on his suit jacket; he wore a white shirt open on his chest, damp with sweat, over striped purple pants. He held his pistol on Carney, low, where the cars hid it from view.

The crowd outside the Apollo screamed and passing drivers smacked their horns. The entertainer coming out to greet his fans.

Inside the furniture store, Miami Joe said, "Leave the lights out." They could see. The streetlight on his showroom beauties at night usually sent Carney into a sentimental mood: It was just him and this little place he'd carved out of the city. Miami Joe jabbed the barrel into Carney's back. "Anyone here?"

"We're closed."

"I asked if anyone was here, nigger."

Carney said no. Miami Joe stopped him at the office door to make sure the room was empty. He told Carney to turn on the desk lamp. The door to the basement was open and Miami Joe peered down, leaning back a little.

"What's down there?"

"Basement."

"Anyone down there?"

Carney shook his head.

He let it drop. "Didn't have time to call anyone." He sat on the couch. From his expression, he was surprised at how comfortable the Argent was. Carney resisted the urge to sell him on the Airform core.

Miami Joe waved his pistol: Sit at the desk. Carney did so and noticed the sales record Rusty had left for him by the telephone. He'd sold an entire Collins-Hathaway living-room set that afternoon.

"Look at me," Miami Joe said. He checked to make sure he couldn't be seen from the street. "How'd you get on the Burbank?"

"I remembered the girl."

Miami Joe scowled. "Always," he said. He rubbed his collarbone and relaxed. "You want to know why?"

Carney didn't say anything. He thought of his wife and daughter on their safe bed. That little lifeboat aloft on the dark and churning Harlem sea. He didn't sell bedroom furniture but a guy he knew from around gave him a deal. Carney'd be sleeping there with them, peaceful and quiet, if Alma hadn't started with her shit. It was her fault he was out in the street. But before her, it was Freddie and years of him pushing Carney into dumb business of one kind or another. It was him saying yes. He wondered if his cousin was still alive.

"Once Chink started looking for us," Miami Joe said, "I didn't want to wait until Monday for the split. Then I had to think about which one of you dummies would talk in the meantime. Your idiot cousin. And if I had to shut one nigger up . . ." He rubbed his temple as if shaving down the rough edges of a headache. "You know what? Half those stones was paste—ain't that a bitch? What kind of dumb nigger locks up their fake shit in a safe-deposit box?"

"I have a family," Carney said.

Miami Joe nodded, bored. "I'm sick of it up here anyway," he said. "The winters are cold as hell. And y'all have a stuck-up attitude. I hate stuck-up people who ain't got nothing going on. It's nonsensical. You got to earn your attitude, you ask me. No, you can keep it. I'm descended from African people—I need to be in the sun." He sat up and rubbed his chin with the gun barrel. "I want you to call Pepper at Donegal's—he uses the joint for messages. Call him up and tell him you got a line on me and he has to get his ass down here, toot-sweet. We can wrap this up. You two, then Freddie. I grab the stash at Betty's, then I'm on the next train out of this dump. Where's your cousin at?"

"I don't know."

"You know. And once I take care of that nigger Pepper, I'll get it out of you."

Carney rang the bar as instructed. It was loud, but once he mentioned Pepper's name, the bartender told everybody to shut up. He said he'd deliver the message.

"Where do you keep the money?" Miami Joe asked.

Carney pointed to the bottom drawer of the desk.

"You don't mind, do you?" Miami Joe chuckled. "Family, whew! I had a cousin like that—my cousin Pete. We got into some shit, boy. All kinds of shit. But he was dumb as a donkey and got hooked on that junk. Can't rely on a man once he gets on the needle."

Miami Joe's hand dangled as he remembered, then he trained the gun on Carney again. "I did what I had to do. Buried him at this fishing spot we used to go to. He always liked it there. Sometimes, they see it coming, and they know it's a mercy. Especially when it's family."

Carney had to turn away. He saw the record of Rusty's big

sale again. An entire Collins-Hathaway living-room set. It was enough to put him over on the rent.

They both saw Pepper pop up from the basement at the same moment, but Miami Joe was unable to get off a shot. The first bullet hit him above the heart and the second, his belly. He fell back on the couch, tried to stand, and tumbled onto his face. Pepper climbed the final steps into the office and kicked the man's pistol away. Carney found it a week later when sweeping up.

"I was across the street," Pepper said. He waved the gun smoke away from his face, bothered. "Someone was going to show up," he said. "If it was you or your cousin, I had a spare hand for the hunt. Midnight shift. If it was him, I'd finish it." He tilted his head toward the street. "You're going to need a new lock on that door in the sidewalk."

Miami Joe's blood crept out in a slow tide toward the desk. Carney said, "Christ," and got a towel from the bathroom.

"Make a little dam, that's what I do," Pepper said. He stuck a toothpick in his mouth. "Where's this Betty live?"

Carney made a dam. "At the Burbank," he said, "140th Street."

"What apartment?"

"I don't know."

Pepper shrugged. "Your cousin's okay, sounds like."

"He usually is."

Pepper walked into the showroom.

"Wait," Carney said. "What do I do with him?"

Pepper yawned. "You got a truck, right? You're Mike Carney's son. You'll figure it out."

Carney leaned against the office doorway as Pepper closed the front door. He headed for the river. Two young men passed by the front window going the other way, joking and howling.

The night proceeded down its avenue. It was physics.

His father's truck came in handy. By sunrise he had dumped the body in Mount Morris Park, per the local custom. From the way the newspapers wrote about the park, he thought there might be a line. It was easier than he thought, getting rid of a body, or so he told Freddie when his cousin returned from his vacation down in the Village. Carney was almost caught by two men copulating under a birch tree, a worn-out hooker scouting wee-hour johns, and a man in a priest's collar who cursed at the moon and did not sound like a man of God at all. Plus he was out the money for the Moroccan Luxury rug he rolled the crook up in, but still: easier. If there was one thing he'd learned in recent days, it was that common sense and a practical nature are a great boon in the execution of criminal enterprises. Also that there are hours of the night when other people are less visible, so vivid are one's private ghosts. He cleaned up the blood in the office. He climbed into bed next to Elizabeth and May. Out cold two seconds later.

The story of that Saturday night made Freddie shake his head and sigh. He had a hungry look. Then he asked, "In a rug?"

It ended up being a good month once the heat broke. Customers returned and he and Rusty closed some nice sales. Some of them were repeat. Sell quality goods, and people come back. The two Silvertones found takers one Thursday afternoon, one after the other. More where that came from, Aronowitz told him.

Elizabeth didn't have any more fainting spells, and if her mother told her about the argument that night, there was no sign. That bill would come due in time.

About a month later Carney received a package. He got an odd feeling and closed his office door and drew the blinds to the showroom. Inside the box, wrapped in newspaper like a fish, was Miss Lucinda Cole's necklace. The ruby glared at him, a mean lizard eye. Pepper's handwriting was childish. The note said, "You can split this with your cousin." He didn't. He sat on it for a year to let the heat die down. Buxbaum paid him and Carney put the money away for the apartment. "I may be broke sometimes, but I ain't crooked," he said to himself. Although, he had to admit, perhaps he was.

DORVAY

1961

"An envelope is an envelope.

Disrespect the order and the

whole system breaks down."

ONE

Five hundred dollars, onetime payment. As far as bribes and payoffs went, the onetime nature argued in its favor. Detective Munson came knocking for his weekly envelope, every Friday Delroy and Yea Big came to the store to pick up Chink Montague's—Carney didn't have the heart to calculate how much he'd paid out to those crooks the last two years. Operating expenses. The price of doing business, like rent and insurance and Ma Bell. Squint at it, the five hundred to Duke was an investment.

"It'll pay off down the road." That's how Pierce had pitched membership to Carney, when the lawyer caught his reaction to the words *Dumas Club*. Carney's expression: a braid of disdain and revulsion. "I'm not the right color," Carney said.

"It's not that bad anymore," Pierce said. He grinned. "Look at me."

It was true that Pierce was a blacker variety of berry than the average Dumas member. Certainly the lawyer wasn't as stuffy or stuck-up as, say, Leland Jones.

"That's your father-in-law?"

"Yes," Carney said.

"Sorry, brother."

They first met at the inaugural meeting of the Harlem Small Business Association. Basement of the St. Nicholas AME Zion Church. Terrance

Pierce was on hand to lend his legal expertise, pro bono. "We're not going to rise unless we all rise, right?"

Carney sat in the front row, as he had as a student. Pierce arrived five minutes late and took the only seat left, next to him. Instead of clapping for the speakers, Pierce tapped a Chesterfield on a monogrammed silver cigarette case. He was a tall man, with wavy black hair that focused his features into something eagle-like. His suit was expensive, gray with silvery pinstripes; Carney had been mulling a wardrobe upgrade and later inquired about his tailor.

They got to talking between the plans and appeals of uptown merchants, restaurant owners, and local pols. Hank Diggs, the president of the Diggs Pomade Company and originator of the slogan "Dig This Shine!," took the podium. "With all the brain power we got in this room," he said, "we could light up Times Square!" He spoke in a slow, rumbling voice that evoked his own low wattage and undercut his point. His hair looked great, though. Carney took the cynic's view when it came to groups, specifically groups and results, but Elizabeth had pushed him to show up. It wouldn't hurt to increase his profile, she told him. Even if nothing came of it, it was good to put a face to the name on the sign. The letters on the new sign he'd just paid for tilted upward like a jet taking to the sky.

Adam Clayton Powell Jr. even popped in toward the end to cheer on the crowd. Regal and dapper. Carney admired the man's hustle; one of these days they were going to name a street after him, you watch. "It's a new day in Harlem," the congressman said. "We have President Kennedy down in D.C., promising a New Frontier—why can't we have our own New Frontier in our own backyards, on the streets of Harlem, one the world has never seen before?" He'd used the same analogy last week, at the opening of a supermarket on Ninth. Carney'd read about it in the *Harlem Gazette*. An assistant materialized, whispered in Powell's ear, and he left the merchants to foment economic revolution.

The association fizzled out after the third meeting—the treasurer running around with the vice president's wife—but Pierce and Carney continued to meet for lunch at Chock Full o'Nuts. They were the first in their families to go to college, although Pierce's father was a solid citizen, working the line instead of working people over, busting his ass for forty years at the Anheuser-Busch bottling plant in Newark. Pierce attended to his studies and got a scholarship to NYU, then graduated with honors from St. John's Law School. "I wanted to be the Negro Clarence Darrow," Pierce said, shrugging.

Franklin D. Shepard, the colorful uptown lawyer, gave him a desk. "Once I got in there, I was in there like a tick!" Shepard liked to see his name in the paper, and it turned out the boy from Newark had an affinity for civil rights cases, the kind that made headlines. The NAACP retained Pierce for crusades against discrimination in public housing, union jobs, and lending. He represented the Dyckman Six against the City of New York— brown water in the pipes and gray rats in the hallways—and lost the notorious Samuel Parker police brutality case, though it was "still good advertising." By 1958, when Mayor Wagner announced the city's antibias housing law and unveiled the Commission on Intergroup Relations, Pierce was a familiar sight in the newspapers, standing next to NAACP leadership with his dandy suit and steely smile.

Pierce could have been on the radio, the way he spoke. Over apple pie, Pierce recounted how a high-school English teacher had hipped him to elocution classes. "He told me, 'You want to make it, you need to speak right. None of this Newark shit.' Like Newark was a different language, but I knew what he meant."

Carney nodded—his freshman-year economics professor Mr. Liebman had told him the same thing, substituting *street* for *Newark*. Liebman was a Lower East Side Jew who declaimed from behind the lectern like a Boston WASP and knew whereof he spoke. Carney couldn't afford to take courses—he was on his own and where was he going to get that kind of scratch? Instead he studied CBS News Radio and William Holden double features. Step back and the world is a classroom if need be. He watched his mouth in the mirror as his jaw worked over *white whale.* Hard stop on the *t,* puff of breath on the *w.* Whenever he pronounced "Heywood-Wakefield" on the showroom floor, he saw those old reflections: his tongue pressed against his front teeth as the air-shaft light limped through the opaque glass of the bathroom window.

Unlikely characters: Pierce in the courtroom, and Carney running his store. "Neither us of is supposed to be where we are," Carney told Elizabeth, "from where we came from. That's why we get along." Like Carney, the lawyer was a family man, joy quickening his features when he pulled out photos of his wife and kids. Carney didn't have any pictures to share in turn, and made a note to pick up one of those new cameras. Finally get a few pics of May and John. Capture his son, with his ten-word vocabulary and two teeth, and his daughter, whose dark intelligence intensified behind her brown eyes every day.

Pierce putting him up for membership in the Dumas was a surprise. Guys like them didn't belong to places like that.

Pierce had been in the club for two years, he said. Franklin D. Shepard put him up, despite his color and humble origins, and made a point of telling his fellow members that they lived in a new era. Didn't have to spell out what he meant. For his part, Pierce had been pleased with his Dumas time so far. "Like that Harlem association meeting where we met. Some men only know how to talk about what they want to do—and then there are men who get it done. At the Dumas, these are the men who get shit done."

Carney said no thanks.

His friend was a patient man. "Come to the mixer," Pierce said. "Have a drink at least. You and me, we've been sticking our foot in the door our whole lives, because we know that's the only way to get into the room. But getting in that room is everything. You get in the room and you will run that room."

Carney called his father-in-law to give him a heads-up. Here was the rug peddler, barging in again—first his daughter, now his club. Alma handed Leland the phone and he said, "When Wilfred said you were coming, I told him I was thrilled."

* * *

The Dumas Club, according to the brass plaque on the black gate of the townhouse, was founded in 1925. The names of the founders were familiar to Carney; they'd lectured him in high-school assemblies on the value of good work and moral health, were the masters of ceremonies at Fourth of July picnics and Labor Day dances in Mount Morris Park. The building dated back to 1898, when the neighborhood belonged to Italians and Irish. New blood in, old blood out—this Dumas visit marked Carney's turn as the new guy disturbing the way things are.

Carney wore his new lightweight tan suit. He checked once more to see if he was sweating through it. Judging from this week's torments, it was going to be another punishing summer. At the end of the block, an old man shaved off ice for yelping children, bottles of bright syrup dancing in his hands like juggling pins. A teenager in a black suit and tails waited at the top of the club's steps and beckoned with white gloves.

To the right of the front hall, the parlor room was full of Dumas men running herd over those they'd put up for membership. The piano player at the baby grand in the corner banged out ragtime, the hectic rhythms a nervous commentary on all the glad-handing. Pierce retrieved Carney and introduced him around. Carney knew Abraham Frye from the newspapers—one of the few Negro judges in the city. Was that a city councilman lingering by the bar, pointing at his preferred gin? Carney couldn't remember the last time he voted, but he'd doubtless voted for the man, the way the machine had everything locked up. Dick

Thompson of Thompson TV and Radio, the Lenox Avenue electronics store, traded dirty jokes with Ellis Gray, who ran the biggest Negro-owned construction company in the city. Sable Construction had performed the recent work on Carney's store, so he figured he'd paid for Gray's tie or pocket square at the very least.

Members wore their club rings on their pinkies. With letters that tiny, you had to own one yourself to make out the seal. Or get real, real close—which Carney had. One of the guys, Louie the Turtle, had brought one to the office for him to get rid of, along with a motley bunch of loot. Louie the Turtle grazed inscrutably and showed up with the oddest things. The words on the ring were Latin and Carney had been incurious as to their meaning. He could've gotten something for the gold, but out of spite tossed it back at the Turtle and told him no, too traceable.

Carney shook the hand of Denmark Gibson, whom he recognized as the owner of the oldest funeral home in Harlem. Gibson had cremated his mother and father.

"How's business?" Carney asked.

"Business is always good," Denmark Gibson said.

And Elizabeth's childhood friend Alexander Oakes, of course, experimenting with muttonchops. Oakes nodded from across the room. It was a Strivers' Row crowd, no doubt, and Carney the only representative from 'round Crooked Way. Politicians, insurance men at the big-time colored firms, and more than a few lawyers and bankers, such as Wilfred Duke, whose new venture kept coming up in conversation. He'd been a muckety-muck at Carver Federal Savings, overseeing most of the neighborhood's loans for twenty years. If a Negro wanted to get something going, he had to go through Wilfred Duke sooner or later. It was his new venture that had everybody talking, putting together the charter for a new black-owned bank to compete with his former employer: Liberty National, or simply Liberty, if you were in the know. Mortgages, small-business loans, community development. According to Pierce, half the room was trying to get their mitts in as board members or investors.

"Just water?" the bartender asked.

"And ice if you have it," Carney said.

Someone touched his elbow. It was Leland, with the smile usually reserved for his grandchildren. "It's good to see you, Raymond," he said, and jetted to one of his cronies.

There was an hour of the typical jockeying, appraisals, and brinksmanship, and then Wilfred Duke stood before the windows overlooking 120th Street and addressed the group. He recognized those who'd stepped down from club leadership, as well as their successors. Those who had recently passed, such as Clement Landford, who'd advised four mayors on the Negro point of view. He announced the endowment drive for a scholarship in Landford's name, full ride at Morehouse for a gifted New York City student. Everyone clapped. Pierce tapped a Chesterfield on his cigarette case.

Certainly Carney was not the only one who saw Napoleon. The *Harlem Gazette,* a Duke antagonist going back to some dispute before Carney started reading the paper, had an editorial cartoonist who liked to portray the banker as the famous general, hand inside jacket, propeller beanie on his head in the place of the military chapeau. Bull's-eye. Duke was short and slightly built and spoke in a staccato, dictatorial style. Thirty years ago, he would have been a rare bird in Young Negro Harlem, a harbinger of the changing city, it was not difficult to see how he'd clambered to his place of influence. Or how he'd gathered enemies. The *Gazette* covered Duke's bank plan as a Barnum-style con.

Duke smoothed his pencil mustache, those rat whiskers. He welcomed the prospective members. The club was named after Alexandre Dumas, the banker reminded them, son of a French army officer and a Haitian slave, who rose to the top of the literary world. "If you remember the story of the Count of Monte Cristo—and I realize it's been a long time since some of you were in school"—there was some chuckling—"he was a man who got things done once he decided on a course of action. And that's the spirit we strive for in our fraternity. The bootstrap spirit that delivered our ancestors from bondage, and now inspires all of us as we try to make a better Harlem." Hear, hear.

Duke told everybody to have a drink and he wound his way through the room to commence his inspection of the applicants. Carney was one of the last to be collared. Pierce gave Carney a wink and slinked off.

They were next to the window, which allowed a slight cross ventilation. "Raymond!" Duke said. "It's hard to believe we haven't met before." The hand was clammy and the cologne first-rate. "How's Elizabeth—and you have two children?"

"Great."

"You tell that lady of yours her uncle Willie says hello."

The street caught his attention. "That's terrible." He nodded below, where a disheveled young man staggered and patted his pockets in a grotesque pantomime. The Junkie Shake, that new dance, all the rage. "It's a scourge," Duke said. "Some places, lots where I used to play handball as a kid, I wouldn't walk past at night."

"Wagner's talking about that drug task force," Carney said. He didn't believe it, but it was something to say.

"That fool's looking to get himself reelected. Against those Tammany hacks? He'll say anything."

"It's a mess," Carney said, and reminded himself to call Freddie.

Duke put his back to 120th Street and asked after the furniture store. Carney assumed the banker already knew all he needed to know about him, but he told him about the expansion into the old bakery next door, just completed. His new secretary was working out fine, although he found it hard to give up tasks he'd been doing on his own for so long.

"You say goodbye to old challenges and welcome new ones."

"That's being an entrepreneur," Carney said.

"Giving that old Jew Blumstein a run for his money, I hope." Duke had had plenty of dealings with the big department store over the years, starting back with the protests in '31 over the lack of Negro clerks and cashiers. He was a young man during the Buy Where You Can Work boycott, but even then he knew the importance of the long game. "Blumstein's wasn't going nowhere, and neither were we!" he told Carney. It had the ring of a well-used line.

Duke checked over Carney's shoulder and adopted a tone of confidence. "I'm glad you're here, Raymond. We're trying to broaden our ranks around here—so it's not the same type. We can only accept a few men each year, that's what's hard about it."

Carney got a feeling.

"Being that selective, sometimes a man, if he wants to head to the front of the line, he'll add a sweetener. So he doesn't get overlooked."

"How sweet?"

"That depends on the man and how front of the line. Last year we had a fellow—I won't say his name, I'm discreet, you have to be in banking—arrived at the number five."

After having bona fide criminals put the bite on him—dirty cops, dudes who cut people's faces off—Duke's genteel shakedown almost made him chuckle. Like last week when May got mad because he wouldn't let her jump on the couch and she punched him in the arm—was that supposed to hurt? There was pain and then there was pain. Different magnitudes you could stand or not stand. Wetting your beak and *wetting your beak.*

Carney asked for Duke's card. The banker had leased an office in the Mill Building, on Madison, after he resigned from Carver Federal to start the community bank. The forces in the room changed vector and Duke was carried to another part of the room. To put the bite on someone else. Or were sweeteners only for the sons of crooks?

Five hundred dollars. Crooked world, straight world, same rules—everybody had a hand out for the envelope. A five-hundred-dollar investment in the future of Carney's Furniture if business kept rolling in like it was. A second store, a third? The members of the Dumas Club circulated around him in the room: whiskey in hand, elbows in ribs. They were a collection of chumps, but he'd need these Dumas chumps for permits, loans, to keep the city off his back. To give the okay one day down the line, or as bagmen for kickbacks to inspectors, to men in departments downtown he'd never heard of. Department of Skimming a Little Off the Top, Office of the Occasional Shakedown.

John wasn't even two yet. By the time his son was old enough to help out with the family business—in a real way, not as a stock boy, as Carney'd gotten his start—the seeds of what he planted with the Dumas Club will have blossomed. It was a betrayal of certain principles, sure, a philosophy about achieving success despite—and to spite—men like these. Condescending Leland types, Alexander Oakes and his lapdog buddies. But these were new times. The city is ever-changing, everything and everyone must keep up or fall behind. The Dumas Club had to adapt, and so did Carney.

* * *

When he told Elizabeth about Pierce's invitation, she said, "Hmm." The Dumas was out of character, as any survey of his comments about the club over the years would attest. Part of him thought she'd be pleased. Surely it was a sign of maturity to set aside cherished animosities in the name of pragmatism. To shed some armor. No New Frontier stretched before him, endless and bountiful—that was for white folks—but this new land was a few

HARLEM SHUFFLE | 119

blocks at least and in Harlem a few blocks was everything. A few blocks was the difference between strivers and crooks, between opportunity and the hard scrabble.

She had more to share when Carney returned from the mixer and told her that he was going for one of those rings.

"Why in the world would you do that? Those men are terrible."

"You said raise my profile." He tugged his tie loose. "This is raising."

"Not like that. There are some real SOBs in that club, I've been around them my whole life."

"Like Uncle Willie?"

"He's the worst of those shitheels," she said.

Elizabeth's vocabulary was saltier these days. She'd returned to Black Star Travel six months after John was born and the work had changed in her absence. They still served their old client pool, but now the company handled bookings for civil rights groups, the Student Nonviolent Coordinating Committee and the Congress of Racial Equality, navigating safe travel and lodging for their excursions into the most hostile and backward places. The stakes were different. One of their mainstay hotels in Mississippi had been firebombed. It was a warning—nobody got hurt. But they could have been. Just last month, the Klan stopped a bus of Freedom Riders in Anniston, Alabama, and tried to burn them alive inside. An undercover cop on board waved his gun around and scared the mob off before the gas tanks exploded. The pictures were in the papers, testimony to the pure white madness she'd sent people into. Black Star hadn't set up that Anniston trip, but they'd organized plenty others like it. Yes, she was saltier now. It suited her.

"It'll be good to have some of them in my corner," Carney said.

"Hmm," Elizabeth said. "Should I ask my father to put in a good word? Have you told him?"

"Said he was glad to see me there." He told her she didn't need to bother him with it. Then one of the kids started wailing, and that was that.

At their next Chock Full o'Nuts lunch, Pierce said he hadn't heard of anyone handing over an envelope before. "I'd say it was a test of whether or not you'd do it, but I know that nigger likes money too much." He shrugged. "We've been to the circus enough times to know how people do—even 'Mr. Community' Dukes." Pierce didn't say pay it. And he didn't say not to. They hailed Sandra for another cup of joe.

Carney scraped the money together. Put a dent in the apartment fund, on top of the recent expansion costs, but he'd replenish it. The savings account devoted to the new apartment—no more hiding cash in boots under his bed—waxed and waned. Knocking out the wall between his store and the bakery cost more than the estimate. Every extra dollar extracted by Gray he experienced as a pain. Plus Marie's salary every other Friday. Elizabeth wasn't up to a move when she was pregnant, then John's arrival made it complicated, and things kept coming up. *Maybe wait until Elizabeth gets settled back at work. Maybe best to hold off until construction is done.* Whenever the fund shrank, so did their apartment: The hallway pressed on him, the living room squeezed. Elizabeth thought the kids' room was plenty big, but Carney could barely fit between May's and John's twin beds, stepping over those damn toys. And the bathroom, he felt like a crowbar every time he went take a piss.

The money from the fencing side kicked in when he needed it, though. Business was doing nicely there, with his new contact. More crooked in one direction and more legit in the other— careful you don't split yourself in half, Carney. He tucked the five bills into a manila envelope, wrapped the string around the button, and folded it over three times.

* * *

Carney visited the Mill Building twice that month. The first time was to drop off the envelope, and the second was to get it back.

The Mill, on the corner of Madison and 125th, was where respectable Negro gentlemen hung their shingle these days. Names in gold paint on frosted glass. Doctors had their floor, dentists another, and Duke installed himself in a corridor of lawyers, corner office. Carney had to imagine the view, as he only made it as far as the small reception room. The secretary Candace was a perky young gal in a red-and-white-checked dress, bouffant hairdo like a fourth Supreme. Duke was married—his wife was a bigwig in Negro society, summoning the usual crowd for charity events that got written up in gossip pages—but he had a reputation as a ladies' man. Carney made an assumption.

Candace poked her head into her boss's office. Carney didn't catch the exchange.

"Mr. Duke says you can leave it with me," she said, closing the door as if sneaking out after putting a baby to sleep.

"He did?"

She nodded. Carney understood a predilection for middle-men, being one himself. He gave her the envelope.

A week later, a messenger appeared at the door of Carney's office. Carney recognized him from the mixer, one of the young bartenders, paying dues. He took the envelope and tipped the kid a dollar for his trouble.

Sometimes you order something from a Sears catalog and when it arrives, it's not what you paid for. He had not paid for what he held in his hands: a letter from the Dumas Club expressing regret that they could not extend an offer of admission.

Carney spent the next hour in his office. When the phone rang, Rusty answered it and told him Pierce was on the line. He waved his hand in dismissal.

He walked to the Mill. Candace answered his knock with a "Come on in." They'd finished lunch, sandwiches, empty wax-paper squares open like sunflowers. Duke sat on the corner of Candace's desk, eating jelly candies from a glass jar she kept next to a small brass lamp. He gestured to his mouth—can't talk—and brought Carney along into his office.

Fifth floor, Duke did indeed have a nice view of the Bronx. On the other side of the Harlem River, industrial buildings and warehouses and then sturdy tenements steamed in the heat, poking into the yellowish smog that got worse every year.

Framed on one wall, centered among numerous diplomas and citations and testaments to his character, hung a large drawing of Duke as Napoleon, one too large to have run in the *Gazette*. He must have commissioned it from the newspaper cartoonist himself. Godzilla-sized, George Washington Bridge behind him as he forded the Hudson with one big foot poised to stomp the West Side Highway. French general's hat in its proper place instead of the beanie.

"Sorry I couldn't help you, Raymond," Duke said when they were seated. "In the end, I'm only one voice of many."

"You ripped me off."

"How'd you expect it to turn out, Raymond?"

"For you to respect the terms."

"I said I'd move your name to the front and that's what I did."

"You take a sweetener, it's a guarantee." The yellow smog—it was like you saw everybody's bad thoughts lurking in the air.

"Where you from, man?"

"127th Street."

"One of those places. How'd you think it was going to go?" Duke was practiced in conversations like this. At the bank snatching back loans, foreclosing on hope. Here were passionless statements of fact.

Carney said, "I'll take my money."

"That's crazy."

"Like I said." He stood.

Duke regarded the visitor on the other side of his desk as if peering over the parapet of a castle. His eyes sparkled. Since he left the bank, it was only once or twice a day that the world handed him such opportunities for malice. Three times if he was lucky. He barked at the front office. "Candace, can you call the precinct?"

"Call the police on me?" Carney said.

Candace cracked the door. "Are you all right, Mr. Duke?"

Carney's father was the one you called police on, not him.

Duke stared at Carney and slowly opened the top drawer of his desk. He slipped his hand inside as if a pistol waited. Harlem bankers, they are prepared.

Out on the pavement, Carney could barely see. The people on the street were shadow-shapes moving around him. It was a normal afternoon and he'd been shunted outside it. A cabbie pounded on his horn at an old biddy jaywalking and she cursed him out, dragging a battered green suitcase. One of the street preachers yelled, "I'm saving souls here!" and raised his arms as if parting seas. Down the block, two newsboys from rival papers fought over the turf in front of a cigar store. Their dropped tabloids fanned out on the sidewalk and trembled in the exhaust of a city bus. Carney squinted. Here was every street corner in this city, populated by noisy, furious characters who were all salesmen, delivering dead pitches for bum products to customers who didn't have a fucking nickel anyway. He moved one foot then the other.

Sucker. The mistake was to believe he'd become someone else. That the circumstances that shaped him had been otherwise, or that to outrun those circumstances was as easy as moving to a better building or learning to speak right. *Hard stop on the* t. He knew where he stood now, had always known, even if he'd gotten confused; there was the matter of redress.

His father—how would he have phrased it? "I'll burn that nigger's house down while he sleeps." In more innocent days, Carney preferred to think of that as a figure of speech; it was more than likely that his father had done that thing once or twice. Wilfred Duke lived in a fine and stately eight-story building on Riverside Drive, the Cumberland, and the complexities of burning it down were numerous and varied, even if Carney had arson in his repertoire. Which he did not.

No. Fire was too quick. And Carney by nature was more of the biding type.

TWO

The Big Apple Diner faced a row of four-story brownstones that had been built by the same developer at the end of the previous century. Identical doglegged stoops, leaf brackets and keystones, wood cornices, one after the other from one corner to the next. From across the street, the houses had distinguished themselves from one another over time through the plantings out front, the decorations behind the front-door glass, and window treatments—the accumulated decisions of the residents and modifications by the owners. One misguided soul had painted one of the exteriors a mealy peach color and now it stuck out, the rotten one in the barrel. A single blueprint—funded by speculators, executed by immigrant construction gangs—had summoned this divergent bounty.

Carney imagined beyond the facades; he was looking for something. Inside, the brownstones had remained one-family homes, or been cut up into individual apartments, and their rooms were marked by different choices in terms of furniture, paint color, what had been thrown on the walls, function. Then there were the invisible marks left by the lives within, those durable hauntings. In this room, the oldest son was born on a lumpy canopy bed by the window; in that parlor the old bachelor had proposed to his mail-order bride; here the third floor had been the stage, variously, for slow-to-boil divorces and suicide schemes and suicide attempts. Also undetectable were the impressions of more mundane activities: the satisfying breakfasts and midnight confidences, the making of daydreams and resolutions. Carney imagined himself inside because he was looking for evidence of himself. Was there an Argent wingback chair or Heywood-Wakefield armoire in one of them, over by the window, the proof of a sale he'd closed? It was a new game he played, walking around this unforgiving town: Is my stuff in there?

He was working on an equation: X Number of Items sold to X Number of Customers over X Number of Years. Business was sturdy enough that a couple of times a day, more likely than not, he passed one of his customers' homes. Maybe not this block, but maybe the next one past the light. The stuff from his store had to go somewhere; the customers weren't chaining it to anvils and pitching those sweet beech-armed sofas into the Hudson River. One day, given the distribution of his customers across Harlem, there might be one of his wares on every uptown block. He'd never know when he hit that milestone, but maybe he'd get a tingly feeling, a sense of satisfaction as he walked the streets.

One day.

The Big Apple Diner was on Convent near 141st Street, halfway up the block. Carney had taken one of the window tables. He waited for Freddie. His cousin was late and it was fifty-fifty whether he'd show. At least it wouldn't be a wasted trip.

The diner was a shabby operation, the cracks in the floor caulked by grime, the windows cloudy. The air smelled like burning hair, but it was not hair, it was the food they served. They probably did a nice morning trade and lunch, too, but at three o'clock the place was dead. The waitress was half in the bag, lurching and muttering. When not groaning at his gentle requests, she tipped cigarette ash into a tin ashtray on the counter and waved away the flies. The housefly traffic this time of day was brisk, but Carney doubted it covered the rent.

Carney grabbed two newspapers from the table behind him. It

was his habit to consult the furniture ads to see what kind of specials the competition was offering this week. The Fischer outlet, on Coney Island, was selling patio furniture. Notable in that the company had branched out into manufacturing outdoor furniture; business was good. He didn't sell Fischer products, but it was good to keep tabs on the big players. All-American took out a quarter-page ad—not cheap—to announce a sale on their Argent merchandise. Their sofa was ten bucks cheaper than Carney sold it for, a rare discount for them. All-American was on Lexington, though, and his customers weren't going to make the trip. Go all the way down there and then the white salesman ignores you or treats you like you were nothing. Carney was fine. He was spending more time away from the store, leaving a lot to Rusty, but Rusty was capable. Now that the man was engaged to be married, he was eager for the commissions. And Marie had quickly taught him that he should have hired a secretary long ago.

The A1 page of the *Times* had a couple of columns on Mayor Wagner announcing that he was running for a third term, and tossing Tammany Hall off his back. All that city hall intrigue was over Carney's head. Like shopping when you go into a white store—the rules were different downtown. Uptown, the machine's man was on the ballot and that was that. He didn't have a strong opinion on Wagner. Did the mayor like black people? He wasn't out to get us, that was the important thing. The recent antidrug push was meant to save white people, but its immediate beneficiaries were the good people who were too scared to walk their own neighborhood, who worried over their children when they disappeared past the front stoop. Someone helps you out by accident, it's still help.

Carney had finished his ham and cheese when Freddie finally showed up.

"Ain't you supposed to be at work?" Freddie said.

"Late lunch. Why don't you order something?"

Freddie shook his head. Freddie was in one of his lean periods, belt cinched. Carney was used to his cousin's spells. What was new was Freddie's indifference to his appearance. The rumpled gray polo shirt was borrowed and he needed to get his ass to D's Barbershop. It was possible that he'd just gotten out of bed.

Reading Carney's frown, Freddie said, "Elizabeth told me you'd be in a bad mood."

"What?"

"I saw her on the street. She said you were in one of your moods."

"You work hard every day, sometimes you'll be in a bad mood." He wondered what was on her mind—his mood or his new hours.

"I wouldn't know," Freddie said. They chuckled. The waitress walked over and muttered something. Freddie winked at her, plucked a sandwich crust off Carney's plate, and gobbled it up. When she retreated, Freddie said, "What's on around town?"

That meant gimme dirt, in his lingo. With regards to crooked characters of their mutual acquaintance, Carney told him that Lester and Birdy had been pinched and were currently cooling it in Rikers. Lester lost his head over girls, ever since they were kids. This time he wasn't chasing tail—he'd stabbed his girlfriend's sister at a Memorial Day barbecue in Gravesend for making fun of his pants. "The ambulance took her away and then they went back to eating that chicken."

As for Birdy, he fell off a fire escape while sneaking out of a third-floor apartment, Carney informed his cousin. Dude was out cold on the sidewalk when the police found him, somebody else's wallet sticking out of his pocket.

"Zippo got picked up for kiting checks," Freddie said. "Arrested him at his mom's house." The cousins groaned and grimaced.

"He should stick to the movies," Carney said.

Before Zippo fell on hard times and started bouncing checks, he took boudoir photos, or "glamour shots," he called them, with a sideline selling stag movies to those interested in that sort of thing. Last spring he'd hired this young lady who wanted to make some extra money, and her man caught wind and made a mess. Smashed his equipment, and Zippo's face. That was three months ago and Zippo was still trying to get back on his feet.

"How's business with you?" Freddie asked.

Freddie hadn't been by since the renovation, part of which involved carving out a door in the wall between Carney's office and the street. It allowed Carney to exit onto Morningside between 125th and 126th and bypass the showroom. And have people enter that way, too, after six P.M. when he sent Rusty and Marie home.

"They think I'm a good boss because I never let them work late," Carney said. The cousins laughed again, as if over one of their shared jokes from the old days, like quoting James Cagney from *White Heat*—"Top of the world!"—when some mope did something especially stupid.

He wasn't sure if he should mention it, but he did anyway: Chink Montague had had some falling out with Lou Parks, his longtime fence, and was now referring business Carney's way. For a cut. "So now Chink gets his weekly envelope from me and then a finder's fee on top," Carney said. "He's worse than Uncle Sam."

It was a reversal. Time was, Freddie was the one who had stuff cooking. "Good for you," Freddie said. "If that nigger only knew." They rarely mentioned the Theresa job, the last two years. Freddie still undertook the odd petty theft, but it was jewelry now, bracelets and necklaces, no appliances. He hadn't brought Carney in on a job after that one time, and as far as Carney knew, hadn't worked with a crew since. Until last winter, Freddie had been a runner for Chet Blakely, handling a nice route on Amsterdam in the 130s, with two old-age residences and traffic from the college. But Chet Blakely got clipped on New Year's Day outside the Vets Club, and that was the end of that upstart operation.

Carney didn't know what his cousin had been up to since then. This meeting had only come to pass after he'd left half a dozen messages at Nightbirds, having tried everything else.

"You been taking care of yourself?" Carney asked.

"I should ask you that—you the one working with Chink." Freddie caught on to the purpose of this meeting. He pursed his lips. "My mom's been talking to you."

Carney admitted that was why he'd invited him here. Aunt Millie hadn't seen him in three months. Usually he dropped by sooner than that, for a meal at least.

The front door to a brownstone across the street opened. Two teenage girls in brightly striped shirts skipped down the stoop and turned uptown.

"What are you looking at?" Freddie asked.

Carney shook his head: nothing. "I told Aunt Millie I hadn't seen you for a while." If Freddie wondered why they were meeting at the Big Apple, as opposed to one of their regular joints, he didn't say. "Where you sleeping these days?"

"I've been bunking with my friend Linus. Over on Madison."

"Who's that?"

"You know, he's this cat I met in the Village."

Freddie told the story as if it were a caper. It was at the apartment of some rich white chick at NYU, after an open showcase at a MacDougal Street coffeehouse. "The Magic Bean or the Hairy Toledo or something." Freddie was the only Negro in attendance, and after some conversation ("What's it like, growing up colored?" "My daddy worked on the Scottsboro Boys case"), he got hip that he was there to perform, put on a show of some authentic uptown magic. What was a night in New York City without a trip to the theater?

"I coulda just pulled out my johnson," Freddie said, but the reefer had made him goofy. There was some good reefer floating around the Village that month. He asked if they'd ever heard of three-card monte. The white chick set up a steamer trunk, produced a deck of cards, and lit some votive candles. All those white chicks had those little candles. Freddie did not, in fact, know how to run three-card monte—"You know me, all those cards flying around make me dizzy"—but he was having too much fun. He reeled off some jive he'd heard over the years on 125th Street and tried not to break out in laughter at their gee-whiz excitement.

Then Linus stepped up. Every three-card monte game needs a ringer to set up the rubes, and suddenly here was this shaggy white boy playing along, throwing down dollar bills onto the trunk. He knew what was up—Freddie's role and everybody else's—and covered for Freddie's lapses in technique. It was hard work picking the wrong card time after time, but Linus was diligent. Out on the street, after it was apparent that nobody was getting laid, show or no show, Linus produced a joint and him and Freddie had a good laugh walking around until the sunrise. Freddie even gave him back his money, such was the feeling of bonhomie.

Linus had just got out of a stint in a sanatorium for "inverted tendencies," Freddie said. Linus's family was rich and patient and thought he'd made some progress after the electroshock treatments, even though it was an act on his part. Easier to act normal and cash the checks. "That electroshock? They tie you down and then zap the shit out of you ten times."

"White people." Carney shrugged.

"White people torturing white people—talk about your equal opportunity."

This Linus character sounded like a head case, but on the whole it was a typical Freddie scenario: half-assed but harmless. Carney steered them back. "Aunt Millie says you've been hanging out with Biz Dixon lately," he said.

Biz Dixon's mother, Alice, was in the same church group as Aunt Millie. The women had looked after each other's kids back when they were little, and continued to do so now that those kids had grown into crooked men. The euphemism for Biz these days among that generation was that he was spending time with a "bad element." Another way would have been to say that Biz was a peddler. He'd been to prison twice already for selling junk, and each time he got out he returned to the streets with renewed dedication, chasing criminal renown the way musicians pursued Carnegie Hall: practice, practice, practice. From Freddie's stories over the years, Carney knew that Biz liked to keep his spots at the lower edge of Harlem, near the subway so it was easy for white customers to score. Five minutes and they were back on the platform waiting for the train downtown. Five minutes that felt like five hours if they got that jones.

Biz sold to folks from the neighborhood, too, of course. Guys they grew up with, anyone who needed a taste. More than one of the crooks who came by the furniture store went straight to Biz's after hitting Carney up.

Carney tried to figure out if Freddie's appearance was on account of too many good times, or too many bad.

"Biz is around," Freddie said. "He's always around. So what?"

"He's sloppy," Carney said, "and it'll only be a matter of time before he gets nabbed again. He sells that stuff on the playground." That last part was solid-citizen hokum, but he couldn't help it.

"You're reading too many papers," Freddie said. "Does he try to make a buck? He doesn't try to hide anything. Put on a costume, like you. Suit and tie every day, pretty wife and kids, trying to hide shit. He's out there trying to run a hustle the same as you."

"You working for him?"

"What?"

"Are you working for him?"

"How could you ask me that?"

"Are you?"

"We grab some food at the Chinaman's and hang out. We go out drinking—so what? You know we've always been tight." Freddie turned his face to the street and when he looked back at Carney he'd found his disgust. "I'm pushing for him, sure," Freddie said. "Playgrounds and churches, everywhere. I find a baby, I stick that junk in their puss. I'm shooting up fucking nuns. They lift their skirts and they're hollering for Jesus."

Behind the counter, the waitress hacked up something wet from her lungs and the cook said, "Oh, boy."

Freddie said, "Asking me that."

Carney searched his face. Maybe that was Freddie's lying voice, maybe it wasn't. He wasn't sure. You can change up your lying voice and lying face if you worked at it. "You make it so I have to," Carney said.

"Asking me that," Freddie said. "The fucking nerve. You're the one who should be watching out. I got a little hustle, but you don't see me on 125th Street, got me a big sign up that says, 'Here I am, come and get me.'"

An apparition appeared and banged and smacked on the glass next to them—a lanky white dude with long, greasy blond hair, dressed in a denim vest and trousers. He waggled his fingers at the window and grinned. His teeth were white and perfect.

Freddie gestured for him to wait outside. "That's Linus. I gotta split."

"That's Linus?" Give him some bongos and he'd be a beatnik out of *Life* magazine.

"That's what he looks like," Freddie said. "Everybody gotta look like something." His chair made a noise on the linoleum as he pulled away. He stopped in the doorway and said, "Now you can tell my mom you've seen me." Freddie slapped Linus five and the duo swayed down the street.

The waitress had been staring. She caught Carney looking at her, raised an eyebrow, and wearily resumed refilling a napkin dispenser.

The cousins had diverged. Their mothers were sisters, so they shared some of the same material but had bent their different ways over the years. Like the row of buildings across the street—

other people and the years tugging them away from the original plans. The city took everything into its clutches and sent it every which way. Maybe you had a say in what direction, and maybe you didn't.

Almost four o'clock. This was his third visit to Big Apple. Was he a regular? This was not Chock Full o'Nuts, and the waitress was no Sandra. The staff decided when you were a regular, not you. Perhaps one day, she'd act more friendly. Recognize him, at the very least. Up here, he was not going to run into Pierce. It had been three weeks since he got the envelope from the Dumas Club. He'd pinned their note under the window to the show-room, next to the yellow slips identifying delinquent customers and installment plans gone awry. The paper made an exhibit of money owed him, debts to be honored. Customers, vendors— there's some delinquent money, a hitch in the order, but once you get paid it's back to business as usual. Other times, you get what's yours, and you're done with them.

At one minute before four o'clock, Wilfred Duke stepped out of one of the brownstones, number 288. The banker straightened his tie and patted the pockets of his gray pinstripe pants after his wallet. Some people, they walk out of a place they shouldn't be and they look around to see if anyone has caught them. Slink away. Not Duke. He glanced at his watch and walked south in the direction of his office.

Carney had hired a man to shadow the banker and the infor-mation checked out: Tuesday and Thursday at three P.M., never more than an hour. He paid the check. Carney was a fast walker. He switched over to Amsterdam so he wouldn't overtake the banker on the way downtown. Plus there was that new furniture store on 130th. Never hurt to size up the competition.

No, not a wasted trip at all.

THREE

The last time he was in Times Square, the air-raid siren howled and suddenly the good citizens of Manhattan were cockroaches after God had flicked on the kitchen light. They skittered into the lobbies of buildings and theaters, crouched inside subway entrances, wedged shoulder to shoulder in doorways. Another tedious drill robbing ten precious minutes from their lunch hour. The last civilians off the street were cabbies and truckers and motorists, who squeezed in with the rest after pulling over. Carney thought this last part strange—keeping the roads clear for evacuation. Soviets drop the bomb, Broadway traffic is the least of your hassles.

Then there was just a cop standing in the empty intersection, policing the nothing.

Doomsday rehearsal. At the siren, Carney darted into the Horn & Hardart and took a spot by the window with the rest of the refugees. At least in a bomb shelter, in a skyscraper basement, you could kid yourself you'd have a chance. What protection was plate glass against the Big One? Carney pictured the windows of the high-rises bursting into shards, ripping the air. The Automat's slots were tiny apartments for sandwiches and soup, and he made their windows explode, too, onto the scuffed linoleum. Everybody staring at the street. That's what they did during air raids: stare dumbly into the street. As if this time something might happen. Carney jammed in with white strangers: in elevators, trains, and on doomsday. The old white lady next to him cradled a poodle and said, "I hope they do drop it." The dog stuck out its tongue.

The siren stopped and the massive contraption of the city chugged and shuddered as it resumed operation. Carney proceeded to his appointment with Harvey Moskowitz, and on his way back home he saw Ernest Borgnine on the uptown train eating two hot dogs.

Tonight he was on another Moskowitz rendezvous, but Times Square 'round midnight was a different creature, an incandescent, stupefying bazaar. White bulbs rippled on and off in waves across the bold marquees, thin neon tubes capered and pranced—a pink martini glass, a galloping horse—among a clamor of honks and whistles and big-band brass out of dance halls. The last screening of *A Raisin in the Sun* let out across the street (he'd promised to take Elizabeth but it hadn't worked out yet), next door to *The Guns of Navarone* (which would have been a Ray and Freddie opening-day special, but no more), and their audiences stepped onto the glistening, hosed-down concrete. Some drained to subway platforms and others were only starting the evening pursuit, peeling off to side-street saloons and knock-twice unmarked clubs. High up on Forty-Fourth Street, the big, busted Timex advertisement was working again, the mechanical arm with the space-age watch on its wrist chopping up and down: The Action Watch for Active People. The Great White Way was full of Active People to be sure, theater mavens and gamblers, goons and drunks—and also crooks, crooks aplenty in service to the next big score.

Midnight, rise and shine. He'd been keeping crooked hours since he slipped into dorvay again, after all these years. Carney first heard the word in his financial accounting class, which had been held in a dingy lecture hall in the basement of the Economics Building. One was not assigned this room if one was held in high esteem, Carney gathered, but Professor Simonov was accustomed to indignities from his former life in a never-specified eastern European country. Occasionally the professor shared anecdotes of that period: surveillance, gallows humor in bread lines, a bedridden wife. The secret police were called "The Muntz" or "The Mintz," Carney couldn't be sure. Whenever the radiator clanged in interruption, Simonov halted his lecture until the pipes relented before his murderous gaze. Word had it that he never gave anything less than an A, as if to deliver one constant in the world's capricious order.

One day in October, while impressing the importance of scrupulous vigil over one's accounts, Simonov recommended that they pick one time every day for bookkeeping and stick to it. "It doesn't matter when you do it, but get it done." His father, a textiles merchant back in the old country (Romania? Hungary?), preferred the dorvay, that midnight pasture, for squaring his accounts. "We've forgotten now, but until the advent of the lightbulb, it was common to sleep in two shifts," Simonov said. "The first started soon after dusk, when the day's labor was done—if there were no lights to see, what was the point of staying up? Then we woke around midnight for a few hours before the second phase of sleep, which lasted through the morning. This was the body's natural rhythm, before Thomas Edison let us make our own schedule."

The British called this wakeful interval *the watch,* Professor Simonov explained, and in France it went by *dorvay.* You went over your accounts, whatever they may be—reading, praying, lovemaking, attending to pressing work, or overdue leisure. It was a respite from the normal world and its demands, a hollow of private enterprise carved out of lost hours.

Professor Simonov returned to his lecture and his unique pronunciation of *receivables.* Carney wanted more on the nighttime flights. He spoke up in his classes but not Simonov's—the old man was too imposing. A trip to the library was fruitless until another librarian overheard Carney pestering the reference desk and suggested the French word was spelled thusly: *dor-veille,* from *dormir,* to sleep, and *veiller,* to be awake. Professor Simonov told the truth; the body had kept a different clock in olden times. Medieval scholars chronicled it; Dickens, Homer, and Cervantes made references. Carney hadn't read Homer or Cervantes, but recalled *Great Expectations* (humble beginnings) and *A Christmas Carol* (rueful ghosts) with much fondness. Benjamin Franklin enthused over dorvay in his diaries, using the intermission to walk around the house naked and sketch inventions.

Learned gentlemen aside, Carney knew crime's hours when he saw them—dorvay was crooked heaven, when the straight world slept and the bent got to work. An arena for thieving and scores, break-ins and hijacks, when the con man polishes the bait and the embezzler cooks the books. In-between things: night and day, rest and duty, the no-good and the up-and-up. Pick up a crowbar, you know the in-between is where all the shit goes down. He upheld the misspelling in his thoughts, in keeping with his loyalty to his mistakes.

In his school days, Carney was a young man alone, unencumbered by all but his ambition. He decided to heed the primitive call in his blood and slipped easily into two shifts of sleep. The lost art of dorvay. It recognized him and he, it. The dark hours were the canvas for coursework and haphazard self-improvement. Alley cats and gutter rats scrabbled outside, the pimp upstairs harangued his new recruit, and Carney drew up sample business plans, advertisements for improbable products, and furiously underlined *Richmond's Economic Concepts.* No rent parties, no girlfriends to keep him up late—just him jimmying his future. He put in nine good months advancing his cause: all A's. Every morning Carney rose rested and energized, until his early-bird shift at Blumstein's prohibited those nighttime jaunts and dorvay became a memento of those bygone days of solitary aspiration, before Elizabeth, before the store, the children.

Then three weeks ago he sacked out when he got home from work and was dead until one A.M. He woke alert, humming. His antenna capturing odd transmissions zipping above the rooftops. Elizabeth stirred in bed next to him and asked if something was wrong. Yes and no. He split for the living room, and the next night, too, when he woke, restlessly pacing until he figured out why he'd returned to dorvay. The banker, the offense. He turned the room down the hall into a second office for his second job of revenge. The elevated train clacking uptown and down his only company. He had been summoned to the old hours for a purpose. Where Carney once studied centuries of financial principles, he now went over his notes on Wilfred Duke and wove schemes.

* * *

Harvey Moskowitz's store was in the uptown Diamond District, Forty-Seventh between Fifth and Sixth, second floor. A lonesome stretch this time of night, but the light was on in the jeweler's office. Walk a street like this uptown, you'd be on the lookout for some druggie to jump out and bust your head open, but the epidemic had not transformed downtown yet. Which is not to say that there weren't persons up to no good in this neck of the woods. To wit: Carney hit the buzzer. He was overdue for a visit, neglecting business since he took up the Duke job. Rusty had the sales floor in hand, but there were areas only Carney could take care of.

One of Moskowitz's nephews came down to let him in and scurried into the back room once they got upstairs. Most of the Diamond District establishments had converted to the modern style of sleek steel and glass but Moskowitz's hewed to its traditions, with dark wood paneling and green globe shades. You walked on creaky old planks, not assembly-line white carpet. During shop hours Moskowitz's was brightly illuminated, the rows of jewelry on their velvet beds glittering under the strategic lighting, and stadium-loud with barking and yelling, as Moskowitz's nephews hectored and cursed out one another nonstop, heedless of customers. The bickering was part of a sales pitch, for when Moskowitz caught your gaze and you shared a weary smile over his relatives' antics, you became a regular, one of the family.

The store was a circus during the day but serious and calm late at night, when the real work went down. Time, straight-world rules, what his watch said—it was topsy-turvy now. The temperament and spirit of these hours, what you stuffed into them, mattered more than where they fell on a clock's face.

Moskowitz's office overlooked the street, separated by walls of frosted glass that allowed sunlight into the showroom. Given the volume of illicit business that crossed his desk, and the travel agency on the second floor across the street, Moskowitz had to open and close the blinds several times a day. Whenever Carney walked in, Moskowitz rose to perform his robot ritual, even late at night when every building opposite was a dead, scuttled ship.

"I put it to you," Moskowitz said. An item on his desk was wrapped in a white monogrammed handkerchief.

Their lessons were over, but the jeweler teased and tested Carney from time to time. Carney picked up the loupe and unwrapped the bracelet. It was a nice piece. Pigeon blood rubies and diamonds, alternating, channel-set in platinum. He counted: fifteen oval links. Maybe from the '40s? Light in his hand, but not too dainty—it'd look swell on a society gal's wrist and also on a woman who worked for a living and would never touch its likes her whole life.

It was a fine piece, an indictment of the motley stuff Carney brought by. He took the challenge as a chance to appreciate the craftsmanship, rather than disrespect. "American-made," Carney said. "Raymond Yard? From the design." Moskowitz was a fan of the man's work and had shown Carney a magazine article on Yard's pieces for Rockefeller and Woolworth.

"Don't rush," Moskowitz often said. "It took a million years to make it, the least you can do is take your time." Carney squinted some more, and gave his best guess.

"About right. Ballpark," the jeweler said. "Platinum market now, maybe more." Moskowitz was a thin man in his late fifties, with the pinched features of a fox. His hair had gone gray but his thin mustache was glossy and black, out of fashion but religiously dyed and groomed. He was a strange mix—congenial but reserved in a way that told you being friendly was an act of will.

The jeweler kept a jar of hard-boiled eggs in vinegar on a filing cabinet and removed one with a pair of brass calipers. Carney always demurred—it reminded him of drinking holes his father used to drag him to—so Moskowitz didn't offer him one.

Moskowitz bit the egg and rubbed his front teeth with his tongue. "Got a new fan," he said. "This heat."

"Times Square, everybody's sweating."

"I bet. What have you got?" Moskowitz said.

The Duke job had kept Carney uptown, so his briefcase was heavier than usual. After the Theresa heist, Chink sent his muscle to collect for operating in his territory, but he also started steering thieves to Carney's office. For a cut. Over time what Chink threw his way became steady business, and lucrative. Half of tonight's haul was courtesy of the gangster. Bracelets, some not-too-bad necklaces, and a bunch of men's chronographs and rings, courtesy of Louie the Turtle, who must have knocked over some Captain of Industry. Or robbed someone who had. Some nice pieces. Tomorrow Carney intended to off-load the lesser stuff on the Hunt's Point gentleman.

Moskowitz lit a cigarette and got to his appraisal. He was not overfond of chitchat, another reason Carney didn't miss Buxbaum. Carney disapproved of criminals who bragged about their cleverness, crowed over the stupidity of their marks, whose paranoia stemmed not from caution but from an outsize sense of their importance. "Big mouth, small time," his father used to say. Buxbaum had ripped him off; Carney's ignorance about the trade demanded it. When the jeweler shared his tales of hood-winking this or that associate, Carney knew that he featured in similar stories Buxbaum shared with other shady types.

That was another thing: There were too many shady charac-ters around Top Buy Gold & Jewelry, unshaven pocket-flask white men who smelled like gin, who clammed up when Car-ney walked in. A store—a jewelry store especially—is made for looking. Characters who studiously looked at nothing at all were conspicuous. Eschewing eye contact, checking the street to see if some mistake was catching up with them. Put on a show, for Christ's sake. Too many losers, too much loser traffic with easily loosened tongues.

But Carney had been stuck with Buxbaum, and the man knew it. The Canal Street jewelry district kept shrinking—merchants going under or joining the Forty-Seventh Street gang—so when Buxbaum's store got raided it struck Carney as part of a natu-ral process: This is how the city works. The jeweler ended up in the joint and Carney was shit out of luck. Carney reached out through Buxbaum's lawyer. The name came back: Moskowitz.

Carney was surprised by two things: how much Buxbaum had scammed him, and Moskowitz's refusal to do the same. Perhaps such easy game was beneath the Forty-Seventh Street merchant. The first time Carney showed up with stones—Buxbaum's name vouched, down came the blinds—the jeweler asked what Bux-baum would've offered. Carney said a number.

"You have no idea what any of this is worth, do you?" Mosko-witz said.

The white man's tone pissed Carney off, before he learned it was straight shooting and not condescension.

"Buxbaum wanted to keep you dependent," Moskowitz said. "You schlepp all the way down here, I'm going to deal with you straight."

Yes, Buxbaum had ripped him off, but the new contact and his more favorable rates took the sting out. He quickly made up the shortfall.

One night, Moskowitz asked Carney what kind of cash he had on hand. "Look," he said, "you're letting a lot of money fall out of your pockets." Under the Buxbaum arrangement, Carney was a messenger and got paid like one. He go-betweened with street hoods, put his legit enterprise on the line, ferried the goods and money back and forth—for a measly five percent.

"You go to Buxbaum," Moskowitz said, "and he turns around and kicks up the stuff to the dealers he works with—his gold guy, his precious-gem guy, whatever. Sometimes it's me." If Carney could maintain this volume, and if the furniture salesman was able to front the money to his "associates"—the jeweler's term for Harlem's lowlife element—he should rightly take Buxbaum's cut. "You got that kind of cash?"

"I do."

"I figured. Let's do it like that, then." They shook on it. "And the *khazeray* you know I'll toss back, there's no need to bring it here. It wastes both our time."

Buxbaum had taken everything, even the junk. Moskowitz couldn't be bothered. He delivered a line like "I'm not even touching that, sir," with the scorn that the object deserved.

"I'll pay you to school me," Carney said. "To give me the eye."

"School you?" Moskowitz said.

"I have a degree in business from Queens College," Carney said.

The jeweler's smile was either bemused or flattered. They shook on this as well.

Moving up the supply chain cut into the Carney family apartment fund, but not for long. He was no longer a mere errand boy for uptown crooks but a proper middleman. How had he suffered the old arrangement for that long? Part of moving up in the world is realizing how much shit you used to eat. He got a tip about a guy in Hunt's Point who'd take his junk pieces, the club rings and costume stuff, and another guy who dealt in rare coins. Soon he had outlets for everything Moskowitz turned his nose up at.

The jeweler raked it in, even with Carney's increased share. Most of the illegal side of Moskowitz's operation ended up overseas. A guy from France came in twice a month and took it off his hands. From there it went who knows where. Despite Moskowitz's international concerns, he didn't skimp on the small stuff, like Carney's lessons. For six months, Carney locked up the furniture store, took the downtown 1 train, and endured the smoke from Moskowitz's hand-rolled cigarettes. The jeweler tutored him in color, clarity, and cut. Explained how a bead setting showcased faceted stones, why a bezel lent itself to high-karat gold. Carney had picked up a lot in the last eighteen months without knowing it; Moskowitz gathered all the unmoored lingo and half-formed notions floating in Carney's head and tethered it to solid objects. He had a good sense of the precious and the fake, the worthy and the chintz; Moskowitz encouraged him to trust his instincts. "You got a nose," he told him. "Anyone can train the eye. But a nose? You need a nose." He did not elaborate.

Most of the knowledge he imparted was less ethereal. How to distinguish a Burmese ruby from a Thai ruby, good-quality lapis lazuli from the cheap dyed lapis that was everywhere these days. Then there was the elusive science of culture and fashion that governed how things went in and out of style, the myriad ways in which history left its mark. "The Great Depression," Moskowitz said, "produced a lot of extravagant design, so that your wife's dress could look like a million bucks, even if she'd made it herself." What caused the boom in costume jewelry after the war? "People wanted to show off their money, whether they had it or not. It didn't matter if it was real or fake, it was how it made you feel."

Carney told Elizabeth he was taking a night course in marketing. Sometimes one of Moskowitz's nephews, an apple-cheeked young man named Ari, sat in for his apprenticeship in the crooked side of the family business. Carney'd catch Moskowitz looking at the two of them studying some rock, side by side, the Negro and the Jew, and the jeweler got this queer smile on his face, as if delighting in this turn in his life. Teaching a colored gentleman and his sister's youngest boy the ropes of his illicit trade. Ari and Carney got along fine in class. The boy pretended not to know him if his cousins were around.

"That's all you need to know for your purposes, I think," Moskowitz told him at the end of one meeting. The teacher produced a bottle of sweet sherry. They toasted.

For his purposes. The hoods who came in the side door of Carney's furniture had a station, Moskowitz had one, and Carney had his.

* * *

Moskowitz priced tonight's haul and they did a deal for the stones. Now came Carney's favorite part of a Moskowitz visit, apart from the cash: the ceremonial opening of the Hermann Bros. safe. The Hermann was an imposing tank, a square-door number of black metal that tiptoed on improbably dainty feet. The utilitarian shell hid the luxury inside, the walnut drawers with brass fixtures, the silk-lined compartments. The dial said *click click click click.* Carney felt like the second mate on a grand ship—the combination dial was a compass pointing the route, the five-spoke handle a ship's wheel to steer them to an uncharted continent of money. Land ho!

He had asked after the safe's provenance once and the jeweler told him they didn't make them anymore. Hermann Bros. had been based in San Francisco. Houdini appeared in their advertisements, wearing a sad face as the Hermann product line confounded him. Aitken bought them and then phased out their consumer lines of safes and vaults. Carney was not naturally prone to envy, but each time he saw Moskowitz's safe he got a real hankering.

"If you get a new one," Moskowitz had said, "make sure it's a proper size. A man should have a safe big enough to hold his secrets. Bigger, even, so you have room to grow."

The jeweler removed a brick of cash from the safe and counted the money. Then he lovingly placed Carney's offerings in their designated drawers inside the metal box. The walnut drawers whispered in and out, so elegant it made Carney wince.

"My wife thinks we should see that Sidney Poitier movie," Moskowitz said.

"The reviews are good. The *Times*. He's good in it, they say."

"She knows I don't go to movies, I don't know why she says it."

"What's up?" Carney said.

"Buxbaum got seven years."

"Oh."

"The lawyer, he was not the best."

"Up the river," Carney said.

The two men did not express sympathy or speculate over what information Buxbaum might share. He hadn't ratted yet. They had to satisfy themselves with that.

Moskowitz closed the door to the safe and spun the handle. "My friend from France is coming in, end of the week."

Carney said, "Good." He stood to go.

"You look good," Moskowitz said. "Business is good?"

"Business is good," Carney said. "So I'm good."

When he got to back to Broadway, it was almost one-thirty A.M. The sidewalks nearly dead. Soon it would be news-truck hour, bread-truck hour, night-shift clock-out-and-scatter time. Carney yawned, that dorvay spell wearing off. Time to get back home.

There was a camera store next to the subway. Carney tried the door and chuckled. The store had closed long before—not everyone was keeping his loopy hours. He satisfied himself with window-shopping. Had Pierce mentioned what camera he used for his family photos? Carney couldn't remember, and he wasn't going to ask that slick motherfucker for nothing.

He disapproved of the crowded display. What's the point if no one can see it? But with Times Square foot traffic, the widening market, the various types of camera customers these days, maybe it made sense to cram it in. It was the same in his field, home furnishings—there was too much of everything these days. He scanned the gizmos. The Nikon F featured something called "Automatic Reflex." Whatever the hell that is. "When using Preview Control it is *impossible to cause an accidental exposure.*" He wasn't an aficionado, he wanted something simple.

Two white drunks tottered at the corner. They dashed into Broadway after a Checker cab. Carney carried a lot of cash these days, a briefcase full of stones or gold or cash, what used to be a year's salary, but he didn't want to get to where he stopped being vigilant. Back to the window. Everybody was talking about Polaroid and their instant film, it was the new thing. In the Polaroid Pathfinder display, a white family enjoyed a picnic by a deep blue lake. White folk on picnics were everywhere in ads these days. The Interstate Highway System and where it'd take you. All smiles in the poster in the window, the dad in a striped polo shirt directing his brood.

An instant camera was fine, Carney decided. Pick it up tomorrow during business hours. Normal-people business hours.

Down the street, the Times Square light show blazed, half power at this time of night but still magnificent. He'd never seen it from this angle before, from Forty-Seventh—the light emerging from the bend on Seventh Ave as if cast from some terrible radiant creature lurching into view. He had this constant sense these days of pushing through into somewhere else. Step outside your known streets and different laws apply, crooked logic. His thoughts turned to those kids' stories about toys waking to their true lives once their masters go to sleep, and wondered what silent switcheroos unfolded on those big marquees and billboards when no one was looking.

He descended into the subway, hustling at the wail of the arriving train. Perhaps on the street above, as in a story for children, the big black letters rearranged themselves into new names and words, and ten thousand blinking lights expounded in an unseen, after-hours performance. Spelling out philosophical declarations. Statements of universal truth. Cries for help and understanding. And maybe among them, an affirmation intended for him and him alone: a perfect message of hate, inscribed upon the city itself.

FOUR

Marie's mother liked baked goods. Cakes, cookies, cobbler, seasonal pies redolent of her Alabama youth. Marie obliged her. Ever since she came on as secretary, Carney's Furniture provided a small supply of baked goods for Carney and Rusty, delighted customers, crooks, and the occasional white policeman. Most mornings, Marie left a glass plate on the small table outside her office door, and last night's labor was crumbs by lunchtime. Her specialty was a lemon-orange chiffon cake.

Detective Munson was a fan. When Carney showed up for their meeting that August morning, the cop was already there, trying to ease the recipe out of Marie. In the man's arsenal of interrogation methods, today's was among the most gentle, and of his various investigations, this was certainly the sweetest. Marie didn't crack. "Mostly you pay attention to what you're doing," she told the cop with a tight smile. Carney was on time for the meeting, Munson was early. It was unclear whether the cop was jockeying for position or merely hungry.

The treat supply was not the only improvement to Carney's Furniture in recent months. Sable Construction had delivered an eye-watering bill for their services, but they'd done a splendid job; there was no indication that the showroom had once been half the size. The latest lines from

Argent and Collins-Hathaway, the gazelle-limbed dining chairs and boomerang side tables, posed elegantly in the bakery's former counter and seating area. The ovens, stoves, and various other equipment had been sold to a junk dealer, and the new robin's-egg blue paint job turned out to be a fine complement to this season's palette, which was heavy on pastels. As he led his customers through the space, Carney had started telling them, "If you can't find it, you don't need it," and the reaction—a small smile and an expansion of their stroll through the store—had made him add the line to his newspaper advertisements. At the back of the store, he'd allocated space for Marie and the ever-multiplying file cabinets. Given her love for baking, Marie's hire was almost a tribute to the vanished establishment.

Carney kept his office in the same place, with the addition of the door to Morningside Avenue, that side entrance for special clientele.

They knew to come at night, the thieves, by appointment only, and if they came knocking during store hours Carney cut them out—find another dealer. Any questions Rusty and Marie had regarding Carney's shady visitors, they kept them to themselves. Rusty was preoccupied with his impending marriage and scraping together a proper nest egg for him and his future bride. She was a prim little thing, Beatrice, a soft-spoken hummingbird who'd grown up two towns over from Rusty back in Georgia. They'd discovered each other in the church choir last year while lining up for punch. Their favorite places back home overlapped, and up here they'd found a common melody in the city. She laughed at Rusty's weird hayseed humor and he called her "my pet," out of some movie. Rusty did not complain when Carney asked him to step up at work the last few weeks.

For Marie's part, Carney gathered she was too grateful for the job and too exhausted to be curious. She lived on Nostrand Ave in Brooklyn with her mother and younger sister. One was lame, the other ailing; it was hard to keep track. Marie was the only one bringing home a paycheck. Any tentative picture of her home life came solely from quotes from her mother: "My mother says these cookies can get tricky if you don't use shortening," "My mother says you need to let it rest near an open windowsill, so the breeze can pitch in." Carney recognized her air of rehearsed competency from his own high-school days, after his mother had passed, his father was out slinking, and he was raising himself. That burden of carrying an apartment on your back; you stagger sometimes but you take the weight, what else can you do? Twenty-two young women answered his ad. Marie's diploma from the Executive Typing School on Forty-Fourth Street clinched it. "Training Fingers for Industry." She carried it in a fake leather folder.

Marie was a broad-backed gal with a short torso and skinny legs; the overall effect was a taper, as if she sprouted from the earth like a tree. Given her affable personality, a sturdy tree of dependable shade. She was fast, efficient, and, yes, overlooked the occasional odd creature who came knocking to her boss's office. She adapted to the Pepper system without comment.

See, not long after the Theresa job, Pepper started using the furniture store as an answering service. One November night near closing, the phone rang.

"It's Pepper," he said, although if he'd said nothing Carney would have recognized him. The man harbored a telltale silence.

"Pepper," Carney said.

"You got a message for me?"

"Sorry?"

"You got a message for me?"

Flummoxed. Carney peered out into 125th to see if he was calling from the phone booth across the street. He stammered and Pepper's sigh cut him short.

"They call for me," Pepper said, "you get me the message." He hung up.

The next day Rusty told him that someone had asked after a

Pepper, but it sounded like a drunk up to mischief. After that, Carney kept a yellow legal pad by the phone for Pepper's inscrutable messages. To flatter them with the word *enigmatic* would have been dressing a pig in a tuxedo. They were a ragtag code of times, places, and objects shorn of referents, the recognizable world stripped to a series of grunts. Reduced to the Job.

Tell Pepper eleven o'clock. Bring the case.

It's on at the place. I'll be there half-past.

Make sure Pepper brings the keys. I'll be out back under the thing.

Carney told Rusty, then Marie, that the mysterious recipient was an old friend of his father's, a daffy old coot. No family to speak of, it was sad, really. When Pepper called in a few hours later, he identified himself and repeated the message with his own intonation as if pondering ancient mysteries—"It's on at the *place*"—and then hung up. Months might go by until the next contact.

Detective Munson popped the last corner of a pink cookie into his mouth. "Could eat your cookies all day," he said. If Marie picked up on the innuendo she made no sign.

"Detective," Carney said.

"The man is all business," Munson said, to make Marie a conspirator in her boss's squareness. She shut the door behind them when they entered Carney's office.

There was a Collins-Hathaway sling-back chair for guests, but Munson sat on Carney's Ellsworth safe. It was a modest number, dark gray with a levered handle. Carney didn't have an etiquette book in front of him, but he was sure it was bad manners to sit on a man's safe.

The detective draped his sports jacket over his arm. Carney shut the blinds.

"I should come here for breakfast every day," the cop said. "What do you think?"

"They're for customers."

"You ain't trying to sell me on something? What's up that couldn't wait until Thursday?"

Thursday was when Munson usually picked up his envelope. After the Theresa heist, Chink Montague had broadcast the names of all the uptown fences to get a line on his girlfriend's necklace. It had the effect of listing Carney in the crooked yellow pages, and Munson came calling.

In that first meeting, the detective forgave Carney for not paying tribute earlier. "Perhaps you didn't understand how things work. Now I'm telling you how they work."

"Sure, some of what I sell has been previously owned," Carney had said.

"I know how it is. Sometimes shit shows up on your doorstep. Who knows where it comes from or why. But there it is, like a deadbeat relative, and you got to deal with it."

Carney crossed his arms.

"I'll come by on Thursdays. You here on Thursdays?"

"Every day, like the sign says."

"Thursdays then. Regular. Like church."

Carney didn't go to church. Blasphemers on one side of the family, skeptics on the other, and both sides liked to sleep in. But he understood paying bills on time, and now there was another outstretched hand every week.

Carney had kept Thursday as the container of their transactions. Until today.

Munson slouched and stretched out his legs. He reminded Carney of the mouthy deputy in a Western, cocksure and cracking jokes, and liable to get offed before the final reel. Munson was too smart for such an ignominious exit; when the outlaws came to town, he'd hide in the stables until the gunfire ceased and then step out and check the lay of the land.

Carney's associates had filled him in on Munson's story. He'd worked downtown in Little Italy before getting transferred to Harlem. Working vice was a PhD in Shakedown Sciences. Mafia links, no doubt. In his new post, in addition to clearing the occasional case, he acted as a sort of diplomat for uptown's criminal element, stepping in to cool out turf disputes between gangs and peddlers or to make sure competing numbers routes didn't get tangled up. There was a flow of envelopes, and peace preserved the unimpeded traffic of those envelopes. A man who kept the peace was valuable indeed.

"It's not about your piece," Carney said. "I have some information you could use."

"You. For me."

"You always say, 'If you hear anything.' "

"And you always say you're a humble furniture salesman, trying to make a living."

"Which is true. I have something up your alley. And maybe you could help me out, too."

"Spit it out, Jesus Christ."

It's Biz Dixon, Carney said. He could provide a map for his arrest. "I don't need to sell you on a high-profile bust, do I? Up in Albany, you've got Governor Rockefeller's drug task force trying to make inroads, the state assembly giving millions of dollars for addiction treatment, and nothing happens. It gets worse. Every day in the papers they're talking about all the young kids hooked on junk, the streets too dangerous to walk down—"

"I'm acquainted with the drug scourge, Carney."

"Of course. It's ripping Harlem apart. Like last week, that shootout on Lenox. Broad daylight. People are saying it was Biz Dixon's guys who shot that little girl walking by." He had been making salesman hand gestures, as if trying to close the deal on a dinette set. "What I'm saying is, I know where he operates— where he keeps his stash." *Stash* wasn't in his vocabulary and it showed. "I think it's a raid you'd like to have your name on. Roust. Bust."

"Man, what do you know about what I like and don't like?" Munson sat up. "Who's Dixon to you?"

"I grew up with him. Knew him then, know who he is now."

"And what's your angle?"

Carney gave him the name: Cheap Brucie.

Munson cocked his head. "The pimp? What do you care about him for?"

It was a good question. Carney had been asking that himself lately. A month ago he hadn't even heard of the man. "He's a crook," he said.

"If being a crook were a crime, we'd all be in jail," Munson said. "He's got friends."

"A man's got friends so you don't do your job?"

"It's not my job to pick up a man because a civilian, who I know happens to be bent, asks me to. Your envelope ain't that fat."

"He should be locked up."

"I should be locked up, this loony bin bullshit."

At Carney's expression, the detective took off his hat. He spun it around on his fingertips by the brim.

"It's like this," Munson said. "There is a circulation, a movement of envelopes that keeps the city running. Mr. Jones, he operates a business, he has to spread the love, give an envelope to this person, another person, somebody at the precinct, another place, so everybody gets a taste. Everybody's kicking back or kicking up. Unless you're on top. Low men like us, we don't have to worry about that. Then there's Mr. Smith, who also runs a business, and he's doing the same thing if he is a wise and learned soul and wants to stick around. Spreading the love. The movement of the envelopes. Who is to say which man is more important, Mr. Jones or Mr. Smith? To whom do we give our allegiance? Do we judge a man by the weight of the envelope—or whom he gives it to?"

He seemed to be saying that Dixon paid protection, and that there was another peddler also laying out ice, and that some sort of arbitration had to occur. So where did that leave matters?

Munson stuck his arms into his sports jacket and beat it to his next shakedown. The jacket was a plaid number that made him look like Victor Mature, second feature in a matinee. Had Victor Mature played a mouthy deputy? Carney was sure of it. More than once. "I'll look into it—both things," the detective said. "Ask around if Dixon's up or down these days. Maybe someone's interested in what you got."

On the way out, Munson asked Marie when she was going to make those little snack cakes again, the ones with that stuff on top.

The circulation of envelopes. It reminded Carney of his idea about churn, the movement of merchandise—cabinet TVs, easy chairs, stones, furs, watches—in and out of people's hands and lives, between buyers, dealers, and the next buyer after that. Like an illustration in a *National Geographic* story about the global weather, showing the invisible jet streams and deep-fathom currents that determine the personality of the world. If you took a step back, if you were keyed in, you might observe these secret forces in action, how it all worked. If you were keyed in.

Had it been a dumb play, to make his pitch to the cop? Last night he'd spent the entire stretch between his first and second sleep scrutinizing the setup as if it were something out of Moskowitz's safe, the most precious of stones. Tilting it to and fro, challenging the light to reveal its planes and facets. Checking for color, identifying flaws. He approved. And with that, his midnight plans broke through to his other, daytime life.

* * *

The rest of the day was store business. He summoned Rusty for his opinion on when they should put the rest of the fall line on the floor.

"I'd like to see it out there," Rusty said. "I think they'll be keen on it."

He was confident. It was nice to see. Carney thanked him for picking up the slack the last few weeks.

"Thank you for letting me do more, Ray," Rusty said. "Any time you want to spend more time with family, I'm here."

"It's been nice, seeing them every night." Carney described his routine lately. Hanging out with his family, going to bed early, getting up again. Minus the revenge part.

"So you go to bed at eight? That's a lot of sleep."

"No, I get up and do paperwork. Read. Then I go back to sleep again."

"Why not go to bed later? Do all that stuff before you go to bed."

"It's not like that. It's your body telling you what it wants, and then you do it. That's how we did it in the old days."

"Like how now?" The appearance of a prospective ottoman buyer spared them more discussion. They got a bunch of customers toward the end of the day and before Carney knew it, it was quitting time.

John's wailing greeted him at home. According to May, John had stuck the hand of her Raggedy Ann doll into his mouth so she grabbed it away, and he was overcome by loss. Elizabeth rocked the boy and in a gesture of hubris Carney took him from her arms. Which made him cry more. Which made Carney give him back. He retreated to the hall to hang up his jacket.

Dinner was finishing off last night's roast beef and potatoes. Since he sacked out early these days, he was not staying late at the store, which meant that for most of the summer the four of them had dinner together. It was a pleasant development, and probably why Elizabeth didn't get on his case about his odd sleeping hours. In late July, he realized it was the longest stretch of family dinners he'd ever had. Before his mother's death, his father had rarely been around at meal time, and after that, scarcer still. Dorvay was a period of focused rage; its counterweight was dinnertime, delighting in his wife and kids.

He liked to stare at their faces when he could, and he kept wondering, how can someone you love seem so strange? When John was born, he had Carney's nose and eyes—they say nature plans it that way. So the father knows the baby's his, Certificate of Authenticity. Almost two years on, Carney wasn't so sure anymore if his son looked much like him. May, for her part, still had Elizabeth's graceful features and keen gaze. But John was already going his own way, and he could barely speak. Who will he be twenty years from now, how close or how far from the blueprint? Will there be some of Carney in there? Carney, on the other hand, hewed to Big Mike more and more all the time. No, he wasn't smacking tire irons on kneecaps, but the original foundation held him up, unseen in the dirt.

Putting John and May to bed left Elizabeth depleted, so meals were a chance to catch up before she got too beat. Work was picking up, which suited her fine. Idle hours killed her. Sitting around the office with nothing to do but stick your face in the fan. With the summer travel season winding down, Black Star was in the midst of fall and winter travel, booking a lot of conventions. American Association of Negro Funeral Directors, National Association of Negro Dentists. Puerto Rico was big this year, thanks to the new brochures, followed by Miami. Some of the groups they'd handled last year, the Negro Lawyers, the Negro Accountants, had told their friends. They were getting a lot of word of mouth.

"We should go this year," Elizabeth said, referring to Miami, which she had been lobbying for. "There are some new hotels going after the Negro market."

"We'll see. I'd like to," Carney said. Christmas was busy, with people spending end-of-year money on practical items they'd put off. He was trying out *I'd like to* as a response to put her off, as opposed to the customary *I wish we could.*

Elizabeth took it as a yes and said she'd find the perfect place. "I had to give my father an earful today," she told him.

Leland had been visiting a client near the Black Star office on Broadway and stopped in to say hello. He mentioned, among other things, that he was investing in Liberty National, and compared it to getting a tip on a winning horse. As if he'd do something as common as bet on a horse race. She hadn't brought up the Dumas Club thing with him but he provoked her. "I asked him why he'd give money to the man who had humiliated his son-in-law—"

"I wouldn't say—"

"Treat his family so shabby. And you know what he said? 'The Dumas Club has a reputation.' So I let him have it."

"Okay."

"I kicked him out of the office I was so mad. Mommy called me to smooth it over but I was mad all day."

Carney told his wife it was nice of her to go to bat for him, but he didn't need it. He changed the subject: "It tastes better the next day." He'd allowed that Leland had taken a small delight on hearing of his rug-peddler son-in-law's rejection, but he had refused to admit the obvious—that his wife's father had actively undermined him. To permit that thought was to accept that Leland would never be his father-in-law in any other sense than a legal one.

Elizabeth cleared the table, a signal that she was going to get the kids ready for bed. He told them to hold on a minute: It was time to finally try out the Polaroid.

He'd snuck a peek inside the box a few times and retreated; the instructions were daunting. But he'd put off talking to Munson and that had gone as well as it could, so why not go for a streak? John reached for the Polaroid when Carney set it on the coffee table and he told the boy to stop in a voice so sharp it made them both flinch. It wasn't cheap, the camera.

He opened the back of the Polaroid and slid in the roll of film while his family arranged themselves on the Argent sofa. The upholstery was the color of faded mint, a fine setting for their brown skin, but the camera only took black-and-white photos. John on Elizabeth's lap, May beside them. May didn't know how to smile yet—all instructions to do so summoned an unsettling, gum-heavy display that would not have been out of place on a Bowery bum sleeping it off in a vestibule. "Sit still," Elizabeth said.

"I can ask Rusty to take one of all four of us," Carney said. On 125th Street, with the store behind them, classy. He also wanted one of the store. Get a nice frame for it and put it on the wall of his office. They looked good, the three of them sitting there. A wave of worthlessness sent him sagging. It was good he wasn't going to be in the picture because he didn't deserve them. Aunt Millie had a few of the pictures of his mother, he remembered. Carney didn't have a single one—his father had taken them, who knew where they'd ended up when he died—and lately his mother's face withdrew into shadow in his memory. Next time he was at his aunt's, he'd ask if she could spare one.

What kind of a man didn't have pictures of his family?

The shutter mechanism and lens moved back and forth fluidly on the wheel. It wasn't as fragile as it appeared. "Ready?"

"Before they start fussing," Elizabeth said.

He botched it. There was a red button on the back to start the developing process and according to the instructions you were supposed to wait sixty seconds. He didn't. Next time he'd get it right, but they were done for tonight once John started howling again. Christ, if Carney'd cried like that, his father would have smacked him across the face—and at that thought he felt the blow, reverberating through the years. Ringing in his ears, his cheek pulsing with heat. He shook it off.

Carney tore away the backing and the four of them crowded around the rind of wet film. They waited, but nothing doing. The photograph remained a light brown square with three thin silhouettes where his family should have been. They looked like ghosts.

FIVE

The woman who lived in the third-floor apartment of 288 Convent was not on the lease. The tenant of record was one Thomas Andrew Bruce, known in grubby corners and underlit byways of the city as Cheap Brucie. When the landlord found out what he did for a living and made a fuss, Cheap Brucie threw him an extra fifty bucks a month. That shut him up.

Miss Laura had lived there for three years and considered one-third of the apartment hers fair and square. The front room was for business, as well as the kitchen. The icebox was a desolate hum but the kitchen had a little bar, if you wanted to wet your whistle before you got to it. The small room in the back overlooking the garden was her domain. No one was allowed past its threshold. She slept there, never easily, and dreamed there, and beneath her bed kept a white leather box for tokens of her life before. Over the decades the street side of the apartment had settled in a slant, but her room was level.

Each time Carney came knocking, he hesitated before he stepped into the front room, as if someone crouched behind the door to spook him—the vice squad, or his wife. By then Miss Laura was accustomed to his skittishness. His intent was bent but he was mostly straight, deep down, she could tell. The man was in sales, so he said. Miss Laura was in sales, too, and knew a mark when she saw one. Let him act this way or that, talk out the side of his mouth, but she knew who he was, what he was worth, the avenues of approach.

* * *

She was a hard case. He didn't know how to read her that first day and hadn't worked it out since.

The afternoon he approached her, the lunch rush was over but it was before quitting time, the in-between zone. The only other patron at the Big Apple Diner was an old white man in a yellow windbreaker, dozing with his head on the Formica counter. Carney sat at the window again and looked up at 288 Convent. She lived on the third floor. The pink drapes in the front room allowed the July sun in.

The waitress that day was a tinier version of the usual miserable waitress, in eerie proportion and likeness, as if he were served by Russian dolls—take the top half off one and there's another inside. Carney had one crook who kept coming to his office with tacky shit like those dolls, rhinestone-covered knick-knacks, and whatnot. Finally he had to tell the dum-dum to beat it and not come around anymore. It was one thing for his father-in-law to disparage him as a rug peddler, but for a common hood to think he trafficked in such crap was a true insult. The waitress grimaced at him when he asked for milk for his coffee. What factory made such living monstrosities as her and her doubles? Some place in Jersey.

The waitress and the cook started fighting and their epithets for each other were so ugly and precise that Carney had no choice but to finally cross the street.

She buzzed him up and was unsurprised to see him round the stairs to the landing. Had the door wide open, unafraid of a stranger in the stairwell. He said he was a friend of Wilfred Duke. She let him in.

Miss Laura was prettied up that day, in a red-and-white cocktail dress, small hoop earrings dangling beneath her curly bob.

In uniform, on the clock. She said, "Hello." At first glance he took her for a teenager—she was petite and lean—but the impatience in her every syllable sounded ancient enough to predate civilization.

A Burlington Hall four-poster bed with tasseled mauve curtains dominated the living room, centered on a Heriz rug of lush crimson. Whoever had furnished the joint had hit a white store downtown—there wasn't a Burlington Hall dealer north of Seventy-Second Street. The lacquered armoire, side chairs, and love seat with the chenille upholstery all came from their 1958 catalog—1958 or 1959. In the three portraits on the walls, plump, nude white women reclined on divans while being bathed or adjusted or otherwise attended to by black-skinned servants. "Atmosphere."

Miss Laura offered him a drink and he accepted a can of Rheingold. She opened one for herself and sat on the love seat. "You want some music?" she asked. Next to the armoire was a 1958 Zenith RecordMaster hi-fi console, with a recess and metal dividers for LPs at the bottom.

He shook his head. Time to make his pitch.

He'd considered various approaches in his midnight stretches of industry, between sleeps, in that new time he'd rediscovered. Bring up the money: "How much would it cost for you to . . . ?" She had a price for her customers; perhaps she had a variety of prices. Or make an appeal to her sense of justice: "You might not know it, but Duke is a bad man." On the man's say-so, his bank kicked widows and families out into the street. This one lives and that one dies, like God. Carney had an anecdote in his pocket about a spastic kid who needed an operation, and the poor boy's eviction in the thick of it. Notorious. Verifiable. The *Harlem Gazette* ran two pieces about it. Certainly the offense against Carney didn't rank compared to that, but there was no need to be specific about his own complaint.

If she said no, she didn't know Carney's identity. She could find out, but that would take time, and there were other ways to get at the banker. Carney had a notebook full of stratagems. The first two schemes had not panned out. So this was the next contender.

Sitting in her apartment, searching her narrow brown eyes, he couldn't read her.

In the end, he didn't have to go into a big pitch at all. What you want in his trade, that most perfect thing, is a product that sells itself, an item of such craft and novelty that it renders the salesman superfluous. He had barely begun his spiel when it was clear that Fucking Over Duke, it turned out, sold itself.

"Lay it out like that, all cool," she'd said. "Like you're selling me a couch."

"You in the market for a couch?"

"What's my end?"

"Five hundred dollars."

The number impressed. "Who are you?" she asked.

He didn't say.

"Right. Men come up here," Miss Laura said, "I'll take any name they want to give. Take their money, too." She sipped her beer. "But this is real business, and I need to know the name of my partner. Like how a bank needs to know."

It was like Freddie and the Theresa job—there's being outside in the car, and being in the thick of it. "Raymond Carney. I own that furniture store on 125th—Carney's Furniture?"

"Never heard of it."

In many negotiations, a pause opens up, a silent interval in which both parties consider the next move and its implications. Like the pause before a kiss or before a hand reaches into a wallet.

She said, "I knew you wasn't no friend of Willie's. Know how?"

"How?"

"Willie doesn't like to share."

She smiled at him for the first and last time, to say she saw through him and delighted in her superiority. Her lips curved then, her eyes containing a mean brand of delight, and they did a deal for the Duke job.

* * *

The first sleep was a subway train that dropped him off in different neighborhoods of crooked behavior and the second sleep returned him to normal life with a rumble. The Dorvay Express? That was too fancy, galloping and gleaming in the moonlight. Here was a local: rattling, grimy, and it didn't take you anywhere you hadn't been before.

Carney woke to the first summer night that was more fall than summer, with a breeze that sent you to shut the windows and snap open a musty blanket. Elizabeth didn't stir when he dressed. The children were spread-eagled, with their faces nestled into the crooks of their arms. All the Carneys slept like that, as if still shrinking from some primeval ugliness.

He didn't know Convent at night so he took Amsterdam, in and out of stretches of liveliness and desolation—men drinking beer on aluminum folding chairs, clacking dominoes, and then blocks of cratered emptiness, rowdy night spots next to tenements torched for insurance money—until he got to 141st.

His first encounter with Miss Laura took place in July, and they had met a few times since then. Now it was almost a month later, and she had summoned him. He had an inkling why, and it was nothing good. She buzzed him in quickly. Carney had suggested the diner more than once but she wouldn't meet him during the day. It was near midnight.

Her irritated nod served as a welcome. Miss Laura wore a thin blue robe and her hair was tucked with bobby pins. She was slender, and the robe made her look slighter still, exposing the line of her collarbone and a splash of freckles below her throat.

Out of the Zenith hi-fi shook crazy saxophone stuff from the

Village. Freddie could have identified who was playing, and on what basement bebop nights he'd seen them, but whenever Carney heard those sounds he felt trapped in a room of lunatics. Down the hall, the bathtub was running and his host told him to hold on. She disappeared into the back.

Carney's nose wrinkled at the unctuous aroma that underlay the cigarette smoke. He determined that it came from the purple flowers in the vase on the fireplace. Miss Laura returned and caught him taking a whiff. "My mother kept a garden full of them," Miss Laura said. "Back in Wilmington. The flower place on Amsterdam has them this time of year."

"That's where you're from?"

She rubbed her fingertips together.

After that first meeting, she made him pay for their conversations, even though it was just talk. Business. Sometimes ten bucks, sometimes thirty, he never knew. Carney asked her to explain the variance and she told him that not everything costs the same. Tonight he handed her a twenty, guessing.

The amount was satisfactory. "Wilmington is where I came from," she said. He joined her on the love seat. He usually chose one of the Burlington Hall chairs across the room and immediately regretted tonight's choice. The love seat was a two-seater, made to squeeze a couple close, and here he was a married man in the room of a "working lady," as his father used to say.

"I got out of there," Miss Laura continued. "Figured New York was more my size. My aunt Hazel packed her bags and beat it up here when I was little, and whenever she came back, she had the nicest dresses and hats and all these stories of the Big City. It was the first place that popped into my head—New York City."

Observing his discomfort, she sat up and crossed her legs so the frayed edge of her robe relinquished an inch of thigh.

"It's good to have family," Carney said, "when you come to a new place."

"*Good*'s a word. She didn't know me from Adam when I knocked on her door. Still up from last night, to look at her. But she said I could sleep on her couch for a few days until I found a place. I was there six months." However disheveled Aunt Hazel was in the morning, Miss Laura said, she was the picture of glamour whenever she walked out the door. "You have to have an inside you, she used to say, and an outside you. Ain't nobody's business who you are really, so it's up to you what you gave them."

"She still living here?" Carney asked. Miss Laura had arranged this meeting and he wondered when she'd get to the reason. It occurred to him that Laura was not her real name.

"She was," Miss Laura said. "Now she ain't. She's the one got me working at Mam Lacey's—you know it?"

"Of course," he said.

He squinted, and she said, "I didn't work downstairs." In the bar, she meant.

"Right."

He and Freddie had often joked about *going upstairs,* but they didn't mess with hookers. Well, Freddie was up to all sorts of stuff. They knew plenty of guys who used to go upstairs, or who frequented the other whorehouses people knew about. On Carney's fourteenth birthday, his father had offered to take him to "a place I know," and Carney said no, and it was years before it clicked what Big Mike had been talking about. Had Freddie joked about this or that woman getting off the bus or walking into the drugstore *working for Mam Lacey*? Big ass, too much makeup, some kind of look in her eye. Sure. It was in the realm of his humor, and Carney had doubtless laughed. You get older and the old jokes grow less funny.

Miss Laura said, "I used to lie up there and listen to the music. Everybody having a high old time down there. That music . . . If I got bored, or if I had a rough one, I'd picture me in one of those girl groups. Long dress. Gloves up to here." She stuck another cigarette into her mouth. "Downstairs was one good time, and upstairs was a different kind of time."

"Been closed a while," Carney said.

"Good riddance. Everybody talked so nice about her, it made me so mad."

The last time he'd been to Mam Lacey's, it had been closed for some time, a ruin. He and Pepper had been looking for a lead on the loot from the Theresa heist and ended up there. Mam Lacey had died and her junkie son Julius had turned the place into a shooting gallery. There was a broken statue of a white stone angel in the back garden and Julius was lying on a bench in a drug stupor, the legs of the statue sticking up without a body and the torso and wings erupting next to it out of hardy Harlem weeds. Had the statue been in one piece when Miss Laura looked down from that room? And what broke it in two? He didn't know why he thought of it—him, Julius, and Miss Laura in a triangle at Mam Lacey's and gazing on the statue, each of them with their own view. Look at it from one way, it was not a place for an angel, look at it from another and maybe it was a place that needed an angel. And another view was that if it were beautiful, it wouldn't last long there.

He was going to mention the kid, Julius, then nixed the idea.

Miss Laura said, "You come here to tell me what I want to hear?"

"Not yet," Carney said. There was a holdup.

Last Thursday, the cop Munson had picked up his Thursday envelope. Carney reminded him of his proposal vis-à-vis Biz Dixon. "I said I'd work on it," the detective told him. "Like I said, these people have friends. That in itself is not insurmountable, but it complicates. Everybody has to get pinched now and then, regardless of what they're laying out, to keep things democratic. This is America."

Carney had considered giving Munson something more to

sweeten the deal, but what did he have? Second-story men. Half-assed crooks. What would his father have thought, him feeding shit to the cops? Working on being a full-time rat.

Even if he could explain the delay to Miss Laura, she was not the sympathetic sort. "A 'hold up'?" she said. She mashed her cigarette into an *L* in the ashtray beside her. Lit another. "Then what good are you?"

Bottom line, they had a deal and Carney hadn't delivered. If the windows had been open, the smell of the flowers and her cigarettes would have been less cloying. It's a telegram, he said to himself. A saying of his mother's, about nights like this. She only got telegrams when it was bad news, and so his mother called that chilly night at the end of August a telegram, to warn you summer was over. Rip it up and throw it in the trash but you got the message.

Miss Laura pulled her robe tight around her neck.

"You asked me if my aunt is still in town?" she said. "She left our place one day, two months behind on the rent. Didn't say a word. I didn't have two nickels to rub together. She didn't take me to Mam Lacey herself, but she made it so I had no choice but to go to Mam Lacey. That was the start of it. Now we're here."

She was working up to an ultimatum. Making moves in this midnight time of the watch, like Carney. He imagined that she'd had her first sleep, too, and was getting her accounts done before she lay down for her second. All over the city there were people like them, a whole mean army of schemers and nocturnal masterminds working their rackets. Thousands and thousands toiling and plotting in their apartments and SROs and twenty-four-hour greasy spoons, waiting for the day when they will bring their plans into the daylight.

Miss Laura rose to show him out. "Time goes by," she said, "and a girl's got to wonder if a man like Willie'd like to know that someone's dogging him. He's a fucking miser, but surely that'd be worth something. Right? To know that someone is out to get you."

She called down to him when he put his hand on the door to the street.

"Get it done, Carney. You get it done."

SIX

Marie gave Carney the message that his aunt expected him at four o'clock. Also told him that she and Aunt Millie had ended up talking and now his aunt was visiting the store next week for a sandwich lunch. "When she said she hadn't seen the store since you did all this work, I made her promise." Carney, in turn, hadn't been to his aunt's house in a long time. Most of their interaction these days centered around her panicked calls over Freddie. *Where is he? Have you seen him?* Now she wanted Carney to leave work early, in the middle of preparations for the Labor Day Weekend Savings Bash. What kind of mess was his cousin in now? The last time he'd seen Freddie was in the Big Apple Diner, back in June.

Aunt Millie had lived on 129th since before Carney was born. It was two blocks from where he'd grown up. Back then, the Irving sisters had dinner with the boys most Sundays—their husbands usually who knows where—and usually at Millie's. Big Mike was unpredictable and rarely happy to come home and find people in his kitchen, family or no.

Carney avoided the block he grew up on. He only found himself there if he was preoccupied with the store, or money, and his homing mechanism misfired. Safer to direct nostalgia for those days toward his cousin's place on 129th Street. He knew 129th between their house and Lenox Ave by heart and still considered it his kingdom, even if no one paid him tribute. New neighbors were identified by the different curtains and lamps and Jesus paintings visible through the windows, the emergence of an intrepid plant on a sill, a Puerto Rican flag limping on a fire escape. The landlord of number 134 had finally sprung for some new trash cans. He and Freddie had busted up the old ones with firecrackers July 4, 1941. The cousins had never run so fast and never would.

"Look at you," Aunt Millie said, taking stock in the apartment hallway. She pulled him in and kissed him. "Those little kids rubbing off on you—you look great." She was one to talk. He did the math—if his mother, Nancy, was born in 1907, and her sister was two years older, Aunt Millie was fifty-six. It clicked when he smelled that cake. This wasn't about Freddie. It was his mother's birthday.

"You know the way," she said, meaning the kitchen. Of course he did. For two years, this had been his home. When his mother died, his father tore off on one of his jaunts, only he didn't come back after a day or a week. He dropped Carney off here and didn't resurface for two months. Now that Carney thought about it, he might have been doing some jail time. When he returned, Aunt Millie suggested that Carney stay with them. He didn't protest.

It was fun. Uncle Pedro built a bunk bed for Freddie's room. He was around more then and did fatherlike things, like take them to the park or the pictures. Aunt Millie was a good cook, and Carney didn't have that blessing in his life again until he married Elizabeth. The best part was Freddie and him living like brothers. Freddie'd kick the top bunk to wake him: *Hey, you up? Can you believe the look on his face? I got another idea . . .* They had devised a jokey shorthand and way of looking at the world. When they shared a room it was like that private mythology was carved into stone tablets, by dancing fire, like in *The Ten Commandments.*

Carney cried the day his father came for him and took him those two blocks home. The same building and same apartment layout, but two floors lower. Same crummy everything else.

Carney and Aunt Mille took their old places at the kitchen table. Freddie's seat was piled up with magazines, last week's *Amsterdam News* on top. Aunt Millie wore a simple blue dress and her hair was pulled back in a bun, which meant that Pedro was away. She only fixed herself up when her husband was home for a visit; who else was there to look pretty for? Lately he spent most of the year in Florida, where he had another woman and a young daughter.

Aunt Millie had made a butter cake with a cherry glaze. Carney complimented her energetically.

She asked after the children and he gave her a May and John update. Elizabeth's father had made a demeaning comment at their wedding, and now it was hard to get his aunt and his wife in the same room. The four of them, him and Elizabeth and the kids, had run into Aunt Millie on the street on July 4th, which was nice. "You at the hospital tonight?" he asked.

"Six o'clock." She'd take day shifts for a long stretch, then switch to night shifts. A few years ago she'd been promoted to some supervisory role, but most of her job was still nursing.

"I liked talking to that Marie. She comes in all the way from Brooklyn?"

"Every day."

"Raymond! With employees who take the subway in from Brooklyn!" She told him his mother would be proud—of his education, his store, the way he took care of his family. By implication: as opposed to how his father had conducted his life.

His mother died of pneumonia in '42, and the next year these birthday get-togethers started, at this kitchen table, Millie and the boys. Nothing fancy, nothing long, sometimes they didn't even mention Carney's mother at all. Jawed about movies. Freddie was the first to miss one, four years ago. Last year Carney missed it because of bronchitis. This time he'd forgotten it altogether.

Shamed, he said, "Freddie?" To divert attention to the one who hadn't shown up at all.

"He doesn't call me back," Aunt Millie said. "I'll run into someone, they've seen him at this place, they've seen him at some other place. He doesn't call me back."

"He looked okay when I saw him."

She exhaled. Once they got Freddie out of the way, Carney and his aunt did what relatives and friends do sometimes—pretended that time and circumstance had not sent them down different paths, and that they were as close as they had ever been. The performance was easy for Carney; he was scheming so much these days. For his aunt, it was likely a welcome refuge. She told him that a Puerto Rican had taken over Mickey's Grocery and filled it with these Spanish foods and drinks; Miss Isabel from upstairs had moved into the new public housing complex on 131st, where Maybelle's Beauty used to be; and don't eat at that new place across from the Apollo, Jimmy Ellis had a bad meatloaf there and had to get his stomach pumped.

Things she would've told her husband, her son, her dear little sister, if they were around. But there was just Carney.

To sell his enthusiasm for the annual get-together, he asked to see the photo album. Aunt Millie rummaged but couldn't place it. When she called later that night, he thought it was to tell him she'd found it. Instead she said Freddie had been picked up. The police came for Bismarck Dixon, and he'd been there and mouthed off, you know how he does. So they took Freddie, too.

* * *

Pepper was the first person Carney brought in on the Duke job. Early June, three days after the furniture salesman's unsuccessful attempt to retrieve his five hundred dollars. Pepper occasionally used the store as an answering machine. This time he got a job out of it.

What happened was, Pepper called Carney's Furniture to get rendezvous instructions for his last job, a warehouse rip-off. The job had gone off without a hitch. A rug wholesaler on Atlantic Ave in Brooklyn, Royal Oriental, received a shipment from a particular overseas supplier twice a year. Ship comes into port, sits at customs, they off-load the rugs and carpets and what have you, and Royal Oriental forks over the dough. The night before they pay for all that inventory the warehouse safe is full of cash, foreign rugs being a notorious way to wash money.

Some jobs, it was like Burma again. People whose faces you never saw, who you never talked to, plan the setup and you have to hope they have their shit together. When you know they don't. He never met the bankroller of the Brooklyn robbery, or the finger, the man inside with the info on the wholesaler's cash flow. Pepper's partner was Roper, a lock man he'd worked with a couple of times. Roper had his head screwed on straight; that it went south that one time had been no fault of his. The brains behind the setup brought Roper in, Roper brought Pepper in, and if Pepper didn't get the other names on this job it was fine as long as he got his share.

The moon was full. A breeze huffed out humid air to Jersey. It was a beautiful night to be out in the city and up to no good. Pepper subdued the night man and got him out of the way. Roper punched out the safe. There was a guard dog at some point. The main thing being that nothing went sideways, they were back in the Chevy Bel Air and on the bridge like that and two days later when it was time for Pepper to pick up his cut, he used Carney as an answering machine. Pepper only used the furniture store when things were in the clear. As in the clear as things could be, given his line of work. He didn't want to mess things up for Carney if he could help it. If he couldn't, fuck it, point was he wasn't going out of his way to bring down heat on the man.

Roper had left the address for Pepper's money. Carney delivered the instructions. He cleared his throat. "I'd like to bring you in on a job."

"What, you need to move a couch?"

"No, it's a job."

Pepper said he'd head over. After he picked up the money.

He checked in on the store occasionally. If he was going to go-between Carney from time to time, it behooved him. Plus, it was Big Mike's son.

The expansion looked smart—the furniture side was doing well for Junior. Rusty, the employee, had got himself a gal who looked like she'd snuck out in the back of a potato wagon. Pure country. The new secretary carried a wounded look on the street but put on a smile when she opened the door to the store. Pepper would have done the sign different, though. Make the letters blockier, so you can see it, put some red in there. He read an article that said red was a color favored by nature to make animals take notice, and you had to be part animal to live in New York City. Made sense to use red in signs, Pepper thought. But no one was asking him.

The door Carney put onto Morningside Avenue was handy, providing another exit. He refrained from commenting on the safe.

"That other rug had to go?" Pepper said. Carney most likely rolled up Miami Joe in it and dumped him in Mount Morris. That's what he would have done.

"Yes, it's a new rug," Carney said.

The furniture salesman explained the job. At first, it didn't sound like Carney. But then, Big Mike had tended his crop of grudges like a farmer, inspecting the rows, taking care they got enough water and fertilizer so that they grew big and healthy.

"You want dirt to blackmail him," Pepper said.

"Blackmail is when you try to get something from somebody," Carney answered. "I want to burn his house down."

"But not really torch it. You want to fuck him up."

"Yes, not an actual torching, but a real burning down."

"Didn't know you did it like that."

Carney shrugged.

Like father, like son. They did a deal for the stakeout and the general surveillance.

Pepper had never heard of this Duke character. "Guess we run in different circles," he said to himself. Leaning against the greasy spoon opposite the Mill Building on 125th, he had a clear shot of the banker's office window and the entrance to the building.

His grandpa Alfred had kept a steel-drum smoker out back in Newark, on Clinton Ave. He'd do ribs, brisket, make his own sausage. Grandpa Alfred's father had been a butcher and cook on an indigo plantation in South Carolina and passed down the mysteries. "You throw chops on some coals," Pepper's grandfather said, "that's one way to cook a piece of meat. Few minutes later, you got that black on it, you're done. But barbecue is slow. Put it in that smoke, you got to be ready to wait. That heat and smoke is going to do its work, boy, but you got to wait."

One was fast and one was slow, and it was the same for stickups and stakeouts. Stickups were chops—they cook fast and hot, you're in and out. A stakeout was ribs—fire down low, slow, taking your time.

Pepper was a gourmand in that he liked chops and he liked ribs. He hadn't planned a job in years, with the legwork that entailed: casing the place; clocking passenger and vehicle traffic, and how often the prowl car made the rounds; the schedule of the staff, managers, and security guards. Figuring out when to take a piss. He'd enjoyed that side of things once—conception, pulling it all together, choosing a crew. Nowadays he let the ebb and flow of jobs take him. He wasn't as sharp or as hungry as he used to be. Stuff fell into his lap, or didn't. Some cat got out of Dannemora and wanted back in, or another dude was cooking up a big score.

Maybe Pepper wasn't as sharp these days, but the quality of hood they turned out now? He was sharp enough. No, he hadn't made ribs in a while but it came back quick.

Waiting and watching on Carney's dime. He found his old stash of tiny notebooks he used for planning jobs. The good weather helped. Those weeks in June were hot but it barely rained at all. The first two days Pepper borrowed Tommy Lips's Ford Crestliner, but lucky for him it turned out Duke was a walker, one of those short guys who had a complex about size and had to rooster-strut everywhere. Little head poking up over a car's steering wheel probably made those bully taunts come back. Lucky because Pepper hated Tommy Lips's Crestline, it was a fucking lemon.

The days passed. A new version of this corner of 125th had sprung into being when he wasn't looking, with a lot of old hangouts erased and sleek cafeterias and electronics stores and record stores popping up. Not the most sentimental of men, Pepper nonetheless allowed himself a reminiscence of his last visit to the Mill Building. Or he tried to reminisce. Pepper had definitely dangled the mope out the window by his ankles (black wing tips and black socks held up by garters) and threatened to drop him on Madison Avenue (the window had an eastern exposure), that much he was sure of. He recalled the man's name, Alvin Pitt, and that he was an osteopath by profession, but for the life of him Pepper couldn't get a handle on why he was bracing the guy. He was at a loss. Perhaps when this job was over, he'd pay Alvin Pitt a visit, ask the man himself what the fuss had been about.

Weekdays at noon Duke departed to dine with muckety-mucks of equal rank. Pepper recognized some of them from the papers: judges, lawyers, politicians. They ate at famous Harlem places Pepper had never set foot in, chowing down on lobster thermidor at the Palm and beef Wellington at the Royale, and drinking brandy at the Orchid Room in the Hotel Theresa. Then it was back to the Mill Building. The banker belonged to the Dumas Club on 120th Street, which observation proved to be a variety of shitheel factory. Duke's rooster-strut wobbled after a Dumas Club visit, so Pepper assumed there was a rich man's happy hour going on. Then it was back home to Riverside Drive, one of those monument buildings with a sleepy doorman and service entrance with a broken lock. Once Duke returned home, he was in for the night.

That was it, except for a twice-weekly rendezvous with a hooker named Miss Laura who worked out of a floor-through at Convent and 141st. Once Pepper got Duke's schedule down, Carney put him on the girl.

"Yeah, but what do you want me to do to the banker?" Pepper asked. He was at a pay phone in the lobby of the Maharaja Theater on 145th and Broadway. Currently on the marquee: *Doctor Blood's Coffin* and *Creature from the Haunted Sea*. It had been a glamorous vaudeville house back in the day. Now its most prominent virtues were the bank of pay phones in the lobby and the dark auditorium beyond. A convenient venue for freelance individuals in which to conduct business.

"Nothing," Carney said. "Just watch the lady on Convent."

Lady. "Someone else is taking the banker out?"

"No. I'm getting the lay of the land."

Pepper hung up, opened the phone-booth door. The light went out. The Maharaja had gotten run-down lately, now that he looked at it. This time of day the lobby was mostly junkies and hookers. Pushers and johns. Anyone in the auditorium was either getting sucked off, sucking off, or tying off, cinematic triumph of *Doctor Blood's Coffin* or no *Doctor Blood's Coffin*.

Did he have to find another place? Or was everywhere like this now—shabby and sad and dangerous? Last time Pepper was here he observed two gray rats fucking in the popcorn, rutting in that greasy yellow case. Maybe he should have heeded that sign.

The phones still worked and there was never a line. He'd be back.

Pepper adopted a regular table at the Big Apple Diner, a better-than-average uptown hash joint on Convent. Good grub, the waitresses were nice, with a view of 288. He wasn't surprised when the pimp showed up for the trick money and it turned out to be Cheap Brucie.

Cheap Brucie was the kind of cat who set up his girls in apartments, with regulars. He'd been plying that particular trade a long time, since before Pepper returned from the Pacific theater. The man was ageless; his women put on miles quick. Pepper'd heard more than one story about him dumping bodies in Mount Morris. Six years ago he saw Cheap Brucie cut one of his women across the face, three A.M. at the Hi Tempo Lounge. Unzipped her cheek. One of those long nights that would've gone longer if not for that shriek. Sobered you up quick.

Miss Laura had a couple of appointments a day. Her johns brought her things he watched her shove into the garbage cans later: big bouquets of flowers, red boxes of candy from Emilio's. The ones getting their ashes hauled twice a week, like Duke, tended to be better-dressed. The better they dressed, the emptier the hands.

Sometimes Miss Laura stuck her head out the third-floor window to watch them walk away, wearing an expression of incandescent rage that made Pepper stare into his coffee.

* * *

In early July, Pepper dropped by the furniture store. Marie clocked him as he crossed the showroom. He nodded at her and she turned away, startled by his stolid affect.

Carney flipped the blinds in his office. He looked thinner, or off, like he hadn't had a proper sleep.

"Nice safe," Pepper said.

"What's wrong with it?"

"Apart from how small it is?"

"Yes."

"It's an Ellsworth, and I'm always happy to see an Ellsworth. But you don't want to own a safe that makes a thief happy."

That set Carney sulking for the rest of the meeting. "I went by her place on Convent, sat in the diner," he said. "Duke's visits, it all checked out."

"Course it did," Pepper said. "You think I make shit up?"

He paid Pepper for his work and said there was a new person for him to look at—Biz Dixon. "He's a friend of my cousin Freddie."

Pepper shrugged.

"We grew up together," Carney added.

Pepper was acquainted with Biz Dixon and had a low opinion. He was part of this new breed of Harlem hood: hotheaded, feral, ever-trifling. A couple of years back, Corky Bell hired Pepper for security at the big poker game he ran every January the weekend after New Year's. Corky Bell liked to have some straights at the table, and you couldn't get them to come if they're going to be menaced by lowlifes. It was a three-day game, an effortless gig, everyone behaving, except for the year Biz Dixon showed up.

Corky hired the Saturday-night bartender from the Hotel Theresa. He had a generous pour, as you'd expect in a gambling room. Roast beef on rye with Russian dressing circulated, and come sunup, eggs. One year Corky had Sylvester King come in and do an a cappella version of his hit song "Summer's Romance." They were cousins, that's how he pulled it off. Plus Corky did a little shylocking and a short set covered one week's vig on the loan for King's new pool in Long Island. The pool was kidney-shaped, Corky said, with a small box on a timing mechanism that emitted aerosolized jasmine, a known aphrodisiac.

This white accountant down from Connecticut, name of Fletcher, kept taking Dixon's money. Fletcher didn't say nothing when Dixon started riding him—*Why'd you stay in with a*

six, Why do you play such shit cards—which riled the peddler
to no end. The accountant was a civilian, slumming it uptown
like those Park Avenue white girls in Mel's Place every weekend.
Crooks and civilians need to congregate every once in a while to
reinforce their life decisions. Corky Bell's game was one place
where that happened.

If Negroes like Biz Dixon didn't mess things up, that is. To be
honest, there was a needling quality to the way Fletcher said
"Three kings" that last time and pushed his glasses up on his
nose, but nothing out of bounds. Dixon threw his scotch in the
man's face and leapt. Pepper intercepted and dragged him out
into the street by the collar. Dixon was steaming. The peddler
had a guy with him, but Pepper figured they must have heard
about this or that thing he'd done, because they rabbited up and
walked away. Fletcher tipped him a hundred bucks when the
game broke up, which Pepper used to buy an electric blanket.

"I know Dixon," Pepper said.

"Does that mean you're out?"

"Don't mean I'm out. Means that nigger can't see me is all." He
sawed his knuckles across the stubble on his jaw. Duke and Miss
Laura were connected; Pepper didn't see where the drug peddler
fit in. "What's he got to do with Duke?"

"I have to take care of one thing before I can do another thing,
and I have to do something else before I can do that."

Pepper wasn't getting paid enough to work that one through.
Moreover: didn't care. He split, but not before one last look at
the Ellsworth. He shook his head.

He borrowed Tommy Lips's car for the next stint. Dixon would
recognize Pepper, despite the years and the enemies accrued in
the meantime, so he brought in Tommy Lips. Given the number of players to keep dibs on, he'd need a sideman to spell him.
Tommy Lips left a visible brown outline of his body on his reclin-
ing chair when he rose to shake Pepper's hand. He appreciated
the work and made it known ad nauseam.

Thus commenced a couple of days of cruising around Harlem tailing the drug peddler. Dixon was a pretty boy, high yellow, fit from sparring in the yard or whatever at Dannemora. Pepper couldn't comment on the recreational outlets at the prison as he'd never had the pleasure. Dixon kept up the regimen and applied equal diligence to his hair, which shone in loose whorls.

Carney told him that Dixon hung his hat at a tenement on Fifth Avenue, and from there Pepper shadowed the man to a series of haunts. His mother's place on 129th, two girlfriends' pads on Madison and 112th and 116th, respectively, and a succession of mediocre chicken joints and Chinese places. He had a meal with Freddie. Pepper made a note of it.

Then there were Dixon's work movements. To a man, his crew was drawn from the same clan of young men you encountered uptown these days, spiteful and dumb. Botched somehow. At the Maharaja they showed these juvenile-delinquent and hot-rodder movies featuring angry young white kids. They didn't make movies about their brown-skinned Harlem versions, but they existed, with their gut hatred for how things worked. If they were good people, they marched and protested and tried to fix what they hated about the system. If they were bad people, they went to work for people like Dixon.

"Look at them," Tommy Lips said. "I hate them. Tuck in your shirt!"

The young hoods were slovenly, doubtless. Tommy Lips abhorred their comportment and envied their vitality in equal measure. He'd been out of the game ever since a cop billy-clubbed him upside his head. Blackout spells and trembly hands ever since. He was fine for babysitting work, though, if talkative. "It's downright indecent," Tommy Lips said.

Pepper followed Dixon's employees—pushers and half-assed muscle—until he identified the man who was the least incompetent and the most busy. According to the bartender at the Clermont Lounge, the industrious, jug-eared Spanish guy was

184 | COLSON WHITEHEAD

named Marco. He supervised the lower-level pushers at Dixon's main spot on Amsterdam and 103rd. Steady white customers, it being a subway block. Bedraggled college kids and working stiffs with a secret habit. City employees with the shakes. Another two days of tailing Marco and they identified the stash house, two blocks up. Also off Amsterdam, in the basement apartment of a beaten-down townhouse.

"These jackals taking over," Tommy Lips said one afternoon. A pile of garbage next to where they'd parked had black flies bedeviling them. "You been on First Ave lately?"

"Get me a tank, maybe I roll up in there," Pepper said.

"I been taking these correspondence classes," Tommy Lips said. "Shoulda done it years ago. I could have been set up somewhere, out of this place."

"You don't say."

Following his two targets back-to-back, the banker and the peddler, Pepper had to say they were in the same business. There were obvious junkies in Harlem, swaying, grooving to some inner refrain, and then there were citizens you'd never know were on junk. Normal people with straight jobs who strolled up to Dixon's men, copped, then split to their warrens. Then there was Duke. Every day Duke hustled, doing his own handoffs in restaurants and club rooms, pushing that inside dope: influence, information, power. You couldn't tell who was using what these days, their drug of choice, but half the city was on something if you had your eyes open.

Back in Carney's office, Pepper read from his tiny pad and delivered his report to the furniture salesman. He mentioned the chicken-spot meetup with Freddie.

"He wasn't working for him." Carney said it like a declaration to make it one.

"Not that I saw."

Carney nodded. "They grew up together."

Pepper had nothing to add. "Now what?" These ribs were cooked.

"That's it," Carney said. "Nothing else." He paid Pepper what he owed him for Dixon.

Couple of days later an old crony brought Pepper in on a job in Baltimore. That took him south for a few weeks. Crabs on the Delaware shore to treat himself. He didn't know if Rose still lived there, but it turned out she did. Twenty years is a while. They were both older, fatter, and sadder —"which is the general trajectory"—and that was a nice couple of days.

First night back, he's in Donegal's and lookee here, Biz Dixon's bust is on the TV news, *Report to New York*. Mayor Wagner and this stiff from the junk squad and a bunch of cops posing before a table stacked with bricks of heroin. In flickering black-and-white. Happy as pigs in shit.

Legwork for cops.

Pepper asked the bartender for the goddamned phone.

That motherfucker had him doing legwork for cops.

SEVEN

In early September two seemingly unrelated items appeared in New York City papers. One small, the other more widely covered and consequential.

The smaller item concerned the arrest of a Harlem pimp named Thomas Andrew Bruce, also known as Cheap Brucie. "No stranger to law enforcement," Thomas Bruce was arrested in a sting operation at a local nightclub and charged with promoting prostitution in the fourth degree. The story rated three paragraphs in the *Amsterdam News,* the only paper to mention it.

The bigger item, days later, concerned the disappearance of prominent banker Wilfred Duke, late of Carver Federal Savings. "There's been no word," Mrs. Myrna Duke, the missing person's wife, told one reporter. "Not a one." Mr. Duke was a well-known Negro businessman, and his disappearance made the white papers downtown.

Few people understood the link between those two stories. Three of them—Ray Carney, Miss Laura, and Zippo—were inside or near 288 Convent Avenue on Wednesday, September 6, at nine-thirty P.M. The meeting had been hastily arranged.

Detective Munson had told Carney that he'd give him a heads-up when they were going to pinch Cheap Brucie. The deal that Carney had proposed in his office weeks before—the drug dealer for the pimp—neared closure.

But Munson didn't call him in advance. The pimp was arrested late Tuesday night, and Munson called Carney shortly after three P.M. the next day. "I've been busy, what can I tell you?"

Carney rubbed his temple and paced his office. Now he had to scramble. "When does he get out?"

"Tomorrow earliest, he gets bond. I don't know."

Beyond the office window, Marie circulated in the showroom, recording the serial numbers of the Argent display models. She waved. Carney waved back.

The detective exhaled loudly into the receiver. "You don't sound appreciative. You did me a solid, I got you back."

From Carney's vantage, Munson was not the only one who'd benefited mightily from the raid on Biz Dixon's places of business.

A few weeks prior, the detective told Carney that no one in the 28th Precinct was inclined to touch Dixon, the kind of ice he was spreading around. Given the quality of his product, Dixon was fronting for an Italian gentleman who was circumventing his clan's narcotics prohibition and didn't want his name out there. But a Dixon bust might play better elsewhere, Munson opined, with other parties. At Centre Street, under pressure from Wagner to produce results for Governor Rockefeller's antidrug initiative. With the Narcotics Bureau itself, where they were keen to arrest a crook who wasn't paying tribute, or enough tribute, or had a rival who'd pay to have them kneecapped. Even the mayor, put to the test by his primary challenge next month. To punish Wagner for splitting from the machine, the Tammany bosses were pulling out the stops for their man Arthur Levitt. The mayor could use a friendly headline.

On August 31, a week before the primary, the junk agents raided Biz Dixon. Twenty-two arrests for possessing narcotics with intent to sell, selling to policemen, and other narcotics misdemeanors. Fourteen thousand dollars in cash confiscated, with who knows how much more pocketed by the cops on the scene. So what if in the end the product seized was no record-breaker, and the dope on the table had to be supplemented with contraband from other busts so it looked good for the cameras? It made the papers and the nightly news. The pictures turned out swell. They'd look nice in a frame and hung on the wall against the industrial sick-green paint of a municipal office.

What did Munson get out of it? Carney could only speculate what made the deal attractive to the detective in the end. Burnish his reputation as a player. Appease Dixon's competitors who gave him envelopes. At any rate, he retailed the Dixon info to Narcotics, they followed up with undercover buys and their own surveillance, and everything was copacetic.

"They want to know who my informant is," Munson told him. "Let 'em speculate. This week they love me. Next week? But this week they love me." He said he'd honor the arrangement and get Cheap Brucie picked up.

"You want to know why," Munson said.

Carney said he was curious, yes.

"He cuts women. I'd never take money from a fucking pimp, or cover for one," Munson told Carney, "and I got no respect for guys who do." Which sounded too pat. It wouldn't be the first time that self-righteousness covered for a self-serving impulse. A few years later—when the game had changed, and the stakes, and a long-term relationship with a fellow you understood was an invaluable asset—Munson admitted to Carney that Cheap Brucie had a guy in the precinct looking out for him, and Munson hated this guy for stealing his lunch out of the icebox one time. Egg salad sandwich he'd been looking forward to all day. "Motherfucker has the nerve to call himself a cop."

Maybe it wasn't envelopes the city ran on, but grudges and payback.

Carney got off the phone with the detective. It was three-thirty P.M. If Cheap Brucie got sprung tomorrow, they had one night to pull it off. It was Wednesday, not Tuesday or Thursday, the days Duke typically had his appointment at 288 Convent Avenue.

Miss Laura was determined, Carney knew. She'd pull it off if she had to drag it on her back, up Broadway all the way from the Battery to the Cloisters.

* * *

Carney informed Rusty and Marie he'd be out the rest of the day.

"Okay, boss," Rusty said. "It's looking better today."

"Yeah, it does," Marie seconded.

He touched the lump under his right eye. The day had been so hectic he'd forgotten about his black eye.

Last Friday, the furniture salesman had stepped out of his apartment building's vestibule and was immediately felled. He crashed against the front door and slid down. Pepper had socked him magnificently. He was not enthused with the purpose to which Carney had directed his labor.

"You got me doing legwork for cops?" Pepper said.

Carney was dizzy. Across the street two teenagers stopped dribbling their basketball to gawk. Carney looked up at the crook and tried to sit up. The last time someone socked him like that, it had been his father. For what, what did he do wrong that time, he couldn't remember.

"If you weren't Mike Carney's son I'd choke the shit out of you," Pepper said.

Then he was gone. The right side of Carney's face pulsed with heat. He staggered back upstairs. Elizabeth was out with the kids. The area around the eye was livid and discolored. What would he say? All the junkie shit going down these days, he opted to blame it on the drug trade. Some druggie punched him in the face, yelling something, kept going, didn't even try to take his wallet. *Someone should do something about all these pushers.* An enactment of how decent people felt these days: things are off-kilter, the world is overtaken by shadow.

His eye closed up the first day. The skin bulged, turned purple and motley-toned. He couldn't open the eye for twenty-four hours. Carney was a sight; Rusty handled the customers for the Labor Day Weekend Savings Bash. Two days after the sale, they nabbed Cheap Brucie and the clock started ticking on the Duke job, whether he was ready or not.

Before Carney went up to Convent Ave, he paused to take in his sign. CARNEY'S FURNITURE. If he were arrested, would they seize the store? He'd spent so much time trying to keep one half of himself separate from the other half, and now they were set to collide. But then—they already shared an office, didn't they? He'd been running a con on himself.

Miss Laura met him at the Big Apple Diner. That's how he knew the caper was almost over: She agreed to meet him at the greasy spoon. Today's waitress was the third nested Russian doll, with identical features on a diminished scale. The magnitude of disdain for Carney remained the same. When he sat down, the waitress asked Miss Laura, "You know this guy?"

She said, "Not really." The women chortled.

"The waitresses . . ." Carney said.

"They're sisters," Miss Laura said. "What's that?" Meaning the black eye.

"I got punched in the face."

She pursed her lips in disdain. Then rubbed her fingertips in the pay-me gesture. He forked over twenty bucks.

Before they figured out how they were going to play it, Miss Laura had to cuss him out for the time they'd lost. Carney blamed it on Munson and let her vent. Underneath her irritation, she was afraid. Had been for a long time. The man could be out as soon as tomorrow, and needed girls to take out his wrath on. She'd roll over on Duke, but only if Carney took care of Cheap Brucie first—that was her demand that day in July when they did the deal. *Get Cheap Brucie out of the picture, and I'll do it.*

Sometimes when Carney jumped into the Hudson when he

was a kid, some of that stuff got into his mouth. The Big Apple Diner served it up and called it coffee. "How do we get him here on a Wednesday?" he said. "At night."

"That's the problem."

"Tell him you're in trouble? You'll tell his wife?"

She shrugged. "He don't care if I'm in trouble or need money. And he don't care about his damn wife." She tipped her cigarette into the tin ashtray. "You can't threaten him because it only gets him hot and bothered—trust me."

He looked up at her apartment. If they pulled it off, that's where it would go down.

She said, "I'm going to tell him to come because I want him."

"Just that?"

"Just that."

There was the problem of Zippo. Carney had to track down Zippo and tell him it was on.

"You know where that nigger's at?" Miss Laura asked.

It was a good question. The photographer was mercurial.

Carney brought Zippo in on the Duke job last. It was clear that he needed someone to take the photographs. He purchased the Pathfinder because Polaroid advertised it as easy to use. More important, the film didn't need to be sent out to be developed. One look at the pictures he planned to take and they'd call the vice squad.

Practice runs with the Polaroid proved him useless. "Some people are good at some things and not others," Elizabeth said. Meant in the nicest way. She and the kids were patient with his various attempts to be one of those capable fathers in TV and magazine ads, capturing the major and minor life moments. He failed before the entrance of the furniture store, with the family name emblazoned above; in Riverside Park, as the serene Hudson whispered past; in front of the old fire watchtower in Mount Morris Park, after guiding his family past the place where he'd dumped Miami Joe's body in a Moroccan Luxury rug.

He needed to bring on another hand.

It'd have to be Zippo.

Zippo—part-time check-kiter and full-time purveyor of boudoir shots and blue movies—knew Freddie from around, but Freddie was scarce. Linus had bailed Carney's cousin out of jail when he got picked up with Biz Dixon for mouthing off. Freddie didn't call Carney or his mother for help; he called the white boy. He checked in with Aunt Millie once he got out, to tell her that he was okay, and disappeared underground again.

Elizabeth had been horrified to hear he'd spent a night in the Tombs. The city jail was notorious. "Oh, that's a terrible place!" Carney hoped it hadn't been too rough. The last thing Carney wanted when he came up with the setup was to see his cousin hurt. How could he know that Freddie would get entangled in it? It was bad luck is all—though it'd be swell if Freddie took it as a sign to straighten up and fly right. Hardheaded as he was, something good might come out of it.

One of Carney's regulars—he had a magic well that produced new Sony portable TVs, apparently—was buddies with the photographer and arranged a meet at Nightbirds. How many times had his father met his cronies in this place? To plan a job, or to celebrate one.

Zippo arrived with his limp-dishrag posture, lanky and loose, the sleeves of his blue button-down shirt too short. Carney hadn't seen him in years. He still rolled with that odd energy of his, defiant and jumpy, like a Bronx pigeon.

"You have a camera these days?" Carney asked. Last he'd heard, a model's irate boyfriend had put Zippo out of business.

"That was a temporary setback," Zippo said. "If you call an opportunity to take stock and really think about how you can make your life better a 'setback.'"

Carney had never heard jail described that way. It came back, how Zippo veered every which way, like a drunk driver peeling down the street at three A.M. One person one second, and another the next. *Deranged competency* is how Carney put it later.

"I'm back to work," Zippo said. He checked over his shoulder to prove his discretion. "You and the missus want some pictures taken—"

"My wife is not—it's something else. It's the stuff you do, boudoir stuff."

"Right, right."

"But one person is asleep."

"Sure, there's a whole market in that. Ladies pretending to be dead. Men pretending to be graves. Cemetery scenes . . ."

To curtail further explanation, Carney explained the job in detail. The photographer had no qualms once he named the mark.

"I hate that fucking Carver Federal," Zippo said. "You know they put my name on a list?" He'd busied himself with ripping a coaster to bits and now made a mound of white shreds.

How old was Zippo—eighteen? Nineteen? Too young for this job?

"It might be in flagrante," Carney said.

"In flagrante, out flagrante, you're the boss." Zippo emphasized his superiority to the assignment. "When I was younger, I was more 'fine art,' if you know what I mean." Certainly not the first Nightbirds customer to wax over the promise of bygone days, and not the last. "I wanted to be one of the great chroniclers," he said, "like Van Der Zee. Carl Van Vechten. Harlem life, Harlem people. But my luck has always been rotten. You know that. Any chance I get, I piss it away. Now it's tits. And people pretending to be dead."

"I think you'll like the money," Carney said.

"It's not the money," Zippo said. He scraped the coaster detritus into his hand and asked when it was going down. They did a deal for the photography and the processing.

Now the job had snuck up on them, without warning. Five

o'clock. The phone number on the business card he gave Carney was out of service. On the back, Zippo had penciled in an address. He took a taxi.

Photography by Andre was located on 125th and Fifth, above a flower store. The stairwell creaked in such a way that if it collapsed, no one could say there'd been no warning. Carney knocked on the studio's door and a nervous middle-aged woman rushed past, her face turned so he couldn't identify her.

The studio was one big room, with a ratty couch and chairs by the door, and then the shooting space with lights on stands, a reflector, an umbrella. Toward the back, assorted props and illustrated backdrops leaned against one another. A beach scene of blue skies and blue water half covered a library backdrop of bookshelves crammed with leather volumes.

Zippo was unfazed by Carney's presence. A black cat ran to his feet and he picked it up and held it to his chest. "Just finished," Zippo said. "Little lady's husband is in Germany on an air force base and asked her to send some photos to remember her by."

"Have you been smoking that stuff?"

"She was so uptight, I thought it'd loosen her up," Zippo said. "And it did! To give oneself to the camera, it's a complicated dance. Society burdens us with these hang-ups—"

"It's tonight," Carney said. "It's on for tonight."

Zippo nodded solemnly. "I got to lock up. This place ain't mine, its Andre's. That's why his name is on everything."

Carney and Zippo walked four blocks to the lot where Carney kept his truck. He got a feeling it was a pickup-truck night, a try-to-outrun-bad-luck night. Might he need the truck bed? Carney didn't like the notion of dumping bodies in the back of his truck, deceased or not deceased or any which way. Once is bad luck; twice and it looks like you're getting accustomed.

The photographer lugged a big vinyl bag over his shoulder. It had already been packed when Carney showed up, even though Zippo couldn't have known it'd go down tonight.

"Oh, I had a feeling," he explained. "Half my art is trusting my instincts."

Zippo fiddled with the radio and found a beatnik DJ wandering the lower bands, mumbling desultorily. They parked across the street from Miss Laura's apartment, where Carney could see her window from the driver's seat. The open curtains meant she was alone, according to their signal. He told Zippo to stay put and walked over to Amsterdam for a pay phone.

"He says he's going to try to come over," Miss Laura told him.

"Try? He is or he isn't."

"That's it. He said he had a meeting."

He updated Zippo when he got back to the truck.

"Waiting," Zippo said, "always waiting. I do work sometimes for this white divorce lawyer—Milton O'Neil? He's on all those matchbooks? The job is to catch them in the act. There's a lot of waiting."

"Zippo."

"Yeah?"

"You still light fires?"

Zippo's most famous fire was the one that consumed the empty lot on St. Nicholas. Some rags in the garbage caught, it all went up, and the whole neighborhood came out to watch the firemen do their thing. The primitive glow of the fire and the hypnotic fire-truck lights capered across the abandoned buildings and vacant faces and rendered them beautiful. Zippo was fourteen, fifteen. His mother's uncle lived in Riverdale and had money from a patent, those toothbrush mounts set into everybody's bathroom tile above the sink. A real immigrant-makes-good story. He paid for Zippo's treatment.

"I lit fires because I didn't know back then it was enough to see it in my head," Zippo said. "I didn't have to do it. That's why people dig my boudoir photographs. Seeing it can be the same thing as doing it."

"That's what you've learned?" His patronizing tone, usually

reserved for Freddie, cast Zippo as a lost soul who needed to get wise.

"I wasn't going to bring it up," Zippo said, "since it's none of my business, but since you're asking me shit that's none of your business—what happened to your eye? Your eye is all fucked up. You look like shit."

"I got punched in the face," Carney said.

"Oh, that happens to me all the time," Zippo said.

* * *

At a quarter past eight, Wilfred Duke, wearing a light brown pinstripe suit and whistling happily, rang the buzzer to the third-floor apartment of 288 Convent. Her thin hands drew the curtains shut.

The furniture salesman and the photographer waited. It was the first night Carney had skipped the first sleep since June. In the coming days, he tried to determine when the Duke job actually got underway. Did it begin with the arrest of the drug dealer, that endgame maneuver? With the return of dorvay, and Carney's nocturnal scheming all those summer nights, or the day the banker committed an offense that called for payback? Or had it been summoned from their natures, deep in their makeup? Duke's corruption. The Carney clan's worship of grudges. If you believed in the holy circulation of envelopes, everything that went down happened because a man took an envelope and didn't do his job. An envelope is an envelope. Disrespect the order and the whole system breaks down.

"Let's go," Carney said. He shoved Zippo. The man was asleep.

Zippo looked up at her window and the curtains thrown wide. "I had a dream I was sitting in a truck," he said.

Miss Laura buzzed them in. As he rounded the landing to the second floor, Carney thought: She killed him. Duke's lying on that four-poster bed with his brains spilling out and now he and

Zippo have to help her cover it up. If she hasn't already called the cops and split out the back and left them holding the bag. It had been her setup all along, not his.

Carney was relieved to see Wilfred Duke on the shiny red sheets, arms spread wide, mouth open and chest quietly rising and falling. He was still dressed in his pinstripe suit with his wing tips on, though his shiny yellow tie was wide, as if his head were being slipped into a noose. He appeared to smile. Miss Laura had her arms crossed, her gaze fixed on the banker. She took a sip from her can of Rheingold.

"Okay," Zippo said. He rubbed his hands together. "It's a graveyard scene? That's not really a burying suit."

"Enough with the cemetery stuff," Carney said. "I was clear about that. We have to pose him, though."

"This fucker," Miss Laura said. The knockout drops were good for a couple of hours. "I gave him a double dose," she said. "To be sure."

"You don't want to poison him."

"He's breathing, ain't he?"

"You heard of Weegee?" Zippo said. "You've seen his stuff even if you don't know his name. He did crime-scene—"

"Zippo, can you help me with this leg?"

Miss Laura leaned against the fireplace, contemplating Duke and tapping ash on the Heriz rug.

Carney, weeks before, had suggested they confine themselves to a few shots of Duke in bed with his arms around a suggestively dressed Miss Laura. A few scandalous poses would suffice. Enough to shame and disgrace, excommunicate him from a segment of Harlem society. Lose some business. Nothing too distasteful. She agreed. Then she thought upon it.

"That's not who he is," she told Carney in their next meeting. "I think we should show him as he really is."

"What's that?"

"It should be a bunch of pictures showing different sides of him, like in *Screenland* when they have Montgomery Clift for pages and pages in different scenes."

"We'll be pressed for time," Carney said.

"Different scenes and props, I think."

"That's—"

"That's how we're doing it," Miss Laura said. "After all this thinking you put into it? This is what you want," and she took charge of the choreography, the way the wheelman attends to the getaway, and the vault is the lock man's remit.

It was time to get to business. Miss Laura stubbed out her cigarette. "You ready?"

"Can I put a record on?" Zippo asked. She waved her beer can toward the Zenith RecordMaster. He dropped the needle on *Mingus Ah Um*.

Zippo opened his bag of equipment. Laura went for hers.

The Burlington Hall company out of Worcester, Massachusetts, had been in the furniture business since the mid-eighteenth century and was revered the world over for its peerless craftsmanship and exquisite details. It's said that Prince Afonso of Portugal had one of their canopy beds hauled five hundred miles through swamps and across ravines, over mountains, to his vacation residence on the Amazon, so that his heir would be conceived on the most luxurious bed in one of the world's sacred places. His wife was barren it turned out, but the prince and his wife enjoyed the most magnificent slumbers of their short lives. If Francis Burlington, the founder of the company, could see the array of erotic paraphernalia that Miss Laura stored in their 1958 lacquered armoire, with its regal silhouette and masterful cabinetwork, he would've been appalled.

Or pleasantly delighted. As a salesman, Carney knew better than to make assumptions about a stranger's tastes. He tried not to speculate what the objects were used for, or where. They hinted at a domain beyond the missionary, off his map. He removed Duke's shoes as Zippo worried over his lenses and camera, and Laura plotted the order of events.

"Where's that from?" Zippo asked. "I saw something like it in *Crispus Catalog.*"

"It's from France," Miss Laura said.

Pop. The flashbulb's combustion was an unsettling crunch, the sound of a monster splintering bones. Miss Laura and Zippo's mundane conversation—*Hold his head up, Can you lift that leg*—maddened Carney. Was this his normal world now? He pressed the lump under his eye until it hurt.

Pop. Carney traced the line between the Dumas reception early in the summer and this evening of lewd payback. The petty thieves, drunk burglars, and nutjob criminals he'd transacted with since he started selling the odd TV and gently used lamp were no preparation for his ragtag crew tonight. Is this what revenge looked like, the grotesque choreography underway in Miss Laura's pad? Did it feel like revenge? It did not feel like revenge to him.

Zippo said, "He's actually very photogenic."

Pop. Miss Laura's skin glowed. Now, she was what revenge looked like: fierce and full of purpose, alien to mercy. Humiliation: that's the word Elizabeth had used to describe Carney's Dumas rejection. Duke could do what he wanted because he held the money. Foreclose on your property, sit on your business loan, take your envelope and tell you to go fuck yourself.

Pop. That's how the whole damn country worked, but they had to change the pitch for the Harlem market, and that's how Duke came to be. The little man was the white system hidden behind a black mask. Humiliation was his currency, but tonight Miss Laura had picked his pocket.

"What I really want to get into," Zippo said, "is movies."

Carney ducked out after ten minutes and hung around in the hallway. When Zippo called him inside, the banker was asleep under red satin sheets, the armoire shut and latched. Miss

Laura had changed into blue jeans and a dark blue gingham shirt. A big red suitcase lay at her feet. Cheap Brucie had introduced her to Duke. When the banker woke, he'd complain to management. She surveyed the apartment and said, "This shit is done."

Zippo finished packing his equipment. "I'll make some nice, pretty prints," he said. "And then bring them to the guy at the newspaper."

"We'll start there. See what happens."

"And leave him up here like that?" Zippo asked.

Miss Laura made a dismissive noise.

"He can sleep it off like we discussed," Carney said. "Sometimes you wake up and sleep has taken you to the darndest places."

Zippo jetted off once the trio hit the street, rounding the corner to 142nd, softly crooning. "My truck's over there," Carney said. He reached for the suitcase but Miss Laura rebuffed him. She dropped it in the truck bed and clambered into the passenger seat.

Carney started up the truck and gave one last look at the apartment, at the window with curtains wide. Damn. We should have put a little Napoleon hat on him.

EIGHT

It was a warm, resplendent Saturday afternoon in September. Elizabeth's plan was to fetch Carney at the store around noon and for the four of them to head to Riverside Park for a picnic. Unleash the kids upon the Claremont Playground. It'd be nice to do something together on a weekend for a change. "You're the boss. The store will be okay."

Carney checked his eye in the office bathroom. It was looking better. Good enough for the picture. When he came out the delivery men were ready for him to sign for the safe.

"Built to last, that one," the foreman said.

"Outlast us, anyway," Carney said.

The Hermann Bros. safe resembled a piece of military ordnance, lethal in its black imperturbability. He spun the five-spoke handle; it flowed like water. The shelves inside were bare, but if he wanted to get the walnut drawers lined with something soft, there was no shortage of places on 125th that would oblige.

It was in the perfect spot, describing a triangle with the Collins-Hathaway sofa and sling-back chair. Unlike those two, the Hermann was not going to be upgraded every year. It took weeks of searching until he found the dealer in Missouri who had two in the corner of his warehouse. Made the Ellsworth look like a pygmy. He gave the delivery guys a few bucks to take the old safe with them.

A man should have a safe big enough to hold his secrets, Moskowitz had told him. This would do for now.

Elizabeth and the kids arrived and he corralled Rusty into taking a picture. Rusty knew his way around the Polaroid Pathfinder, had one himself. Coney Island was a favorite trip for him and Beatrice and he had several beach shots tacked up above his desk. Rusty walked Carney through the process step-by-step as he posed them out front. "You have to wait," he said. "You can't pull the backing off too soon."

"I have to be more patient," Carney replied.

It turned out wonderfully. Carney and Elizabeth stood side by side, May and John in front. May mustered a serviceable smile. John's wide-open eyes betrayed the strain of standing immobile, but you had to really look to notice it. Behind them, beyond the plate glass, the fall season's floor models were barely visible in shadow, like lithe animals emerging from tall grasses. The sunlight transformed the sign's letters into a regal proclamation.

Marie picked up a suitable frame a week later and the photograph remained on the wall of his office for many years. The reminder of this day gave Carney a boost when he felt rotten.

"See?" Rusty said. "It's easier than you think."

Carney thanked him and they walked west to the park.

"How is your father holding up?" Carney asked.

"It's not good," Elizabeth said.

To be sure, these were times of tribulation for much of the Negro elite. The *Harlem Gazette,* Duke's local nemesis, was very fond of the photographs from Miss Laura's apartment. Once again, you didn't have to sell people on fucking over Duke; the proposition sold itself. The *Gazette* published three of the photos in Friday's edition, front page, and teased another release for Saturday: BANKER'S BIZARRE LOVE NEST. The naughty stuff—and Laura's face—was covered with black stripes, which let one's imagination compose its own salacious truth.

It was natural for a fellow to lie low after that, especially one as vain and controlling as Wilfred Duke. The last time he was seen was on Thursday, when he left his Mill Building office. Candace, his secretary, reported nothing out of the ordinary.

The *Gazette* published what came to be called the "Safari" series on Saturday. The accompanying articles quoted disgruntled Carver customers as they described how Wilfred Duke had ruined their lives, stolen their homes from under them. The photographs, even obscured, proved a neglect of mental hygiene; the customers' words testified to a moral corruption overall.

On Monday the newspapers covered Duke's disappearance, and on Tuesday they reported that Duke had embezzled the funding capital for the charter of Liberty National. Duke had raised more than two million dollars from early investors, most of them upstanding members of the Harlem community, his friends and business partners and club buddies for decades. How much the banker absconded with was not immediately evident; an early accounting suggested he'd made off with most if not all of the seed money. The cops sent out an APB over the wire. The Dukes owned a property in Bimini; Bahamian authorities were on the lookout.

Carney and his family waited for the light to change. "He and Mommy might have to sell the house," Elizabeth said. "He tied up all their money in Liberty and they were already overextended. A lot of their friends put their money in, it was so surefire. Dr. Campbell told my mother they might have to file for bankruptcy. It's just so stupid."

"Who's stupid?" May asked.

"Your grandfather and his friends," she said.

Carney said, "You're pals with someone for so many years, you think you know them."

"Of course he took their money," Elizabeth said. "He's always been a crook."

"It's a big deal to break out like that and start your own thing," Carney said. "I should know. He must have been under a lot of pressure."

In Miss Laura's apartment that night, the execution of the plan had made him queasy. It didn't feel like revenge, it felt like debasement; he had descended rungs into the sewer and become another shabby player in the city's sordid theater. Pornographers, hookers, pimps, peddlers, killers—these were the fellow members of his new ensemble. Add to that: embezzlers.

But this—this felt like revenge. Sustaining, without flaw. It was the sun on your face on a Saturday afternoon, it was the world smiling briefly upon you. He hadn't foreseen Duke lamming it, but was not disappointed with this turn. Not just one man, but a whole lot of them, where it hurt. It was unfortunate that the banker would never know it was his setup, but that was the deal from the get-go. Had Pierce invested? Carney should ring and see if he's available for lunch. He'd have information that wouldn't be in the papers. Who got hit the hardest, who's on their last legs. It had been too long since they'd had a meal together.

He wondered where Miss Laura had made it off to. The night of the job, he'd dropped her at Thirty-Sixth and Eighth as instructed. Port Authority or Penn Station. Did buses and trains run this late, or was she going to spend the night in a hotel? If she had wanted him to know, she would've told him.

"I couldn't have packed a bag if I knew he was out there," she said, "ready to jump out and cut my throat. He makes you watch what he does to other girls, to advertise what he can do to you." She lit a cigarette with a brass lighter. "He'll have too much on his plate to look for me. And I won't be the only one who runs once they find out he's locked up." She wasn't talking to Carney; it was not clear whom she addressed. She checked her face in the rearview mirror and got out to grab her suitcase. He joined her.

Here it was: the last envelope. He gave her the five hundred bucks and she stuffed it in her bra.

She said, "I checked you out, you know." Just them on the street corner, in one of those New York City eddies that clears the stage for a minute. "After that first time we met. I thought, now what does a man like him have against Duke? Then I said to myself, he ripped you off like he does everybody else. That's why you're mad."

"He did."

"I asked myself, what am I gonna get out of this? What do I want out of it?" She waved her hand at the dirty city heaped up around them in concrete and cold steel. "Can't stay here and can't go home. Which leaves everywhere else." She looked at him. "You go," she said. So he did.

Miss Laura was right about Cheap Brucie having his hands full. Once the pimp made bail, he fixated on one of his girls to blame for setting him up. Emboldened by his arrest earlier that week, she went to the cops and they picked him up again, this time for battery. This news via Munson. Brucie wasn't getting out for a while.

Carney hoisted John onto his shoulders. The boy covered Carney's eyes and he pretended to totter, *Oh no!* He was grateful to Elizabeth for proposing this outing. He wasn't getting home for dinner every night, but the four of them still ate together more often than they had before. It was nice. The night of the job he stayed awake through the first sleep, working the job, and when he got home from dropping Miss Laura off he was too energized to sleep. He finally went down near dawn and when he woke he was back on schedule, in sync once more with the straight world. Cast out from the forgotten land of dorvay, as if he'd never been there. What had they meant, those dark hours? Maybe it was a way to keep the two sides of him separate, the midnight him and the daytime him, and he didn't need it anymore. If he ever had. Maybe he'd invented a separation where none existed, when it was all him and always had been.

When they passed Nightbirds, he checked if Freddie was sitting there at the bar, wisecracking. He didn't see him.

As his little boy tugged his ears, Carney added up the cost of the setup. The initial five hundred to Duke, that went into the overhead with the rest of the envelopes. He was out the cash to Pepper, Miss Laura, and Zippo. Tommy Lips and the car. Throw in Rusty's commissions, the ones he wouldn't have had to pay the man if he'd been around the office. By Carney's inner accounting—if not in the actual books—was there any way to write off the money for the job as a business expense?

Even a half-assed audit would reveal his sins. Black eye aside, it had been all pleasure.

COOL IT BABY

1964

". . . maybe don't play the
same number all the time.
Play something else, see what
happens. Maybe you been
playing the wrong thing this
whole time."

547 Riverside Drive faced the park on a stretch that was quiet more often than not. Until they moved, the Carneys had no inkling of how shallow the elevated train had kept their sleep. As with many things in the city—traffic noise below, quarrelsome neighbors above, a dark walk from the corner to your front door—its effect was unmeasurable until it was gone. The train was like a bad thought or bad memory in that way, a persistent poke and constant whisper. In the spring, the baby pigeons hatched on the roof of 547 and a prodigious cooing woke the household most mornings, but who wouldn't prefer that to the elevated, prefer new life over the screech of metal.

It was a third-floor apartment opposite the north end of the small hill where they'd stuck Grant's Tomb. Instead of the Hudson River, their windows overlooked a splash of oak leaves for most of the year, and a scrabbly brown slope the rest.

"You call that a seasonal view," Alma said. She'd been pouting ever since John had refused "a hug for Grandma." In general John was compliant when it came to grown-ups' unearned demands for affection, so Carney took it as a sign of good character.

"In the winter all those green leaves will be gone," Leland said.

"Yes," Carney said. "That's what happens with trees." He made a quick prayer for Elizabeth's return from the kitchen with the cookies. He asked his in-laws how they were enjoying Park West Village, the complex off Columbus that they'd moved into.

"We love it," Alma said. "There's a Gristedes opening up."

It was their third apartment since they'd sold the Strivers' Row house. They left the first because the block transformed into a drug bazaar once the weather changed. They'd toured it on a snowy afternoon and it had seemed sleepy enough.

The second apartment was in a nice clean building on Amsterdam. Next door to a judge and down the hall from a pastor. Six months into the lease, the Joneses were alarmed by an odd smell. They assumed a mouse had expired in the walls. A reddish-brown liquid dripped from the ceiling and sent them running to the super, who after a quick investigation identified the substance as the upstairs neighbor's putrefying remains. Such unchecked seepage through the substandard flooring pointed to larger structural issues in the building, on that point everyone agreed. The Joneses stayed at the Hotel Theresa until they landed at Park West Village. As for the upstairs neighbor, he had chased away his friends and family over the decades and the city buried him on Hart Island one unexceptional Sunday afternoon.

There had been plenty of relocations and pullings-up of stakes recently. Leland moved his firm from Broadway and 114th to a more affordable space on 125th. Carney and Elizabeth finally made proper use of the apartment fund and split for the river and the boulevard of Carney's aspirational dreams. The building was integrated, with a lot of black families with children moving in. Elizabeth had made two friends already. Historically, turnover had been low, with little wear and tear to speak of in the individual units. The common areas were well-lit and well-maintained. There was a laundry room in the basement with a bank of brand-new Westinghouse machines, an active tenants' group, and of course the park was right there.

The furniture store remained where it was, an anchor on 125th and Morningside, and continued to flourish in areas above-board, and below.

The new living room had plenty of space for the kids to sprawl. On the thick Moroccan Luxury rug, May flipped through her *Richie Rich* comics and disjointedly hummed Motown tunes while John harassed a Matchbox fleet with the toy brontosaurus. This year Carney went Argent with regard to his home furniture, opting for the three-piece sectional with the kiln-dried hardwood frame and Herculean blue-and-green upholstery. As he sat on the couch with his legs extended and his ankles crossed, taking in the room and the greenery outside, Carney grudgingly allowed himself a contented moment. He rubbed his fingertips across the tweed cushions to calm himself as his in-laws prattled.

At last Elizabeth arrived with the cookies. The kitchen in the new place was more hospitable than the last one, granting a survey of an uptown battalion of rooftops as opposed to the dead-end air shaft. Marie had been sharing recipes, and this had to be one of hers, so thoroughly did the aroma bend them to its will. Elizabeth gave Carney a smile to reward his forbearance.

The children jumped up for dibs on the best cookies.

"He get that at the World's Fair?" Leland asked. The little dinosaur.

Carney said yes. They'd taken the subway to Flushing to check out the exhibition last May. "This is what they call 'Queens,' guys." The publicity machine had plugged it so much that it was bound to disappoint, and the editorial pages had wrung their hands over how the city'd pay for it, but the whole production was top-notch. Years from now May and John would look back on it and understand they'd been a part of something special. Sinclair Oil had handed out plastic versions of their brontosaurus mascot at the Dinoland pavilion. John slept with it under his pillow.

"We'd still like to take them," Leland said. "Max and Judy said that Futurama was something else." May and John squealed. The fairground was too vast, too stuffed to take in on one visit. The grandchildren provided an alibi for Alma and Leland to mix with the commoners.

"That's fine," Carney said.

"If they haven't looted the place," Alma said.

"I don't think burning down the World's Fair was high on their list, Mommy," Elizabeth said.

John said, "They burned down the World's Fair? Why?"

"Who knows what they're liable to do, those student activists," Alma said.

"You're against the protest movement now?" Elizabeth said. "After all those benefits for the Freedom Riders?"

"It's not the students I mind," Leland said, "so much as the shiftless element that attached themselves. Did you see what they did to that supermarket on Eighth, next to the AME church?" His ascot was never less than ridiculous and the July heat turned it pathetic. He panted by the window and sipped his lemonade. "They looted everything one day, picked it clean like vultures, and torched it the next. Why would you do that to your own neighborhood store?"

"Why'd that policeman kill a fifteen-year-old boy in cold blood?" Elizabeth said.

"They said he had a knife," Alma said.

"They say they find a knife the next day and you believe him."

"Cops," Carney said.

"I'd like to go to 'It's a Small World' again," May said, and Elizabeth changed the conversation.

The riots had petered out. It had been hot—ninety-two degrees—when they started, and the kindling went up quick. Wednesday's rain extinguished the marches and upset in Harlem, and the violence in Bedford-Stuyvesant died down the next night. Everyone was afraid that another incident or confrontation—by police, by a protester—might spark another round.

That next eruption is why they talked about the riots as if they were gloomy weather. Far off now, but turn your head and it's upon you.

Carney said he had to go to the office to take care of a few things and excused himself from his in-laws' visit.

* * *

The walk to work was longer from the new place, but it allowed Carney to savor a few calm blocks before reinsertion into the Harlem mania. Once you walked under the elevated—look up to see the slats cut the sky like prison bars—and crossed Broadway, you were back in the hustle.

At the corner of 125th, next to the subway entrance, Lucky Luke's Shoe Repair was a blackened ruin. Had it been the best shine? No.

A hulking man in stained yellow dungarees yelled at Carney as he approached, and he steeled himself. Then Carney recognized him—the gentleman had purchased a used dinette set last year, layaway. Jeffrey Martins. Carney waved and grinned. Modern life had put them out of touch with the primitive friend-or-foe sorting but it came back quick. In these aftermath days, folks appraised strangers to see where they fell on the spectrum of outrage. Did their expression say *Such strange days, don't you think?* or their balled fists communicate *Can you believe they're going to get away with it again?* Had the person before you triple-locked the apartment door and waited in the dark for it to be over, or slashed a cop's face with a bottle? These were your neighbors.

Some blocks were untouched and it was the Harlem you recognized. Then you rounded the corner and two cars were overturned like fat beetles, a cigar-store Indian stood decapitated before a line of shattered front windows. The entrance of a fire-bombed grocery store gaped like a tunnel to the underworld. Sable Construction vans idled outside the addresses of their priority customers and dayworkers tossed drywall and fire-hose-soaked insulation into dumpsters. The sanitation department had done a bang-up job of cleaning up the sidewalk trash and debris, which made the stroll more unsettling, as if the ruined addresses had been shipped in from another, worse city.

As Carney walked down 125th, he got to thinking about the grand pavilions in Flushing, Queens. A few miles away, the World's Fair celebrated the wonders on the horizon. Sure, Carney dug all the gee-whiz stuff in Futurama—the sleek moon bases and slowly twirling space stations, the undersea headquarters—but more amazing were the demonstrations of what humanity had already accomplished. In one room Bell Labs had Picturephones that showed you the face of the person on the other end of the line, in another mammoth computers talked to each other through telephone wires. The Space Park showcased full-size replicas of the Saturn V rocket, the Gemini spacecraft, a lunar landing module. Here were impossible objects that had been to outer space—and come back safely, traveled all that distance.

You didn't need to journey far, certainly didn't need three-stage rockets and manned capsules and arcane telemetry, to see what else we were capable of. If Carney walked five minutes in any direction, one generation's immaculate townhouses were the next's shooting galleries, slum blocks testified in a chorus of neglect, and businesses sat ravaged and demolished after nights of violent protest. What had started it, the mess this week? A white cop shot an unarmed black boy three times and killed him. Good old American know-how on display: We do marvels, we do injustice, and our hands were always busy.

Harlem was calm again, or as calm as Harlem ever got. Carney was relieved the protests had ended, for many reasons. For everyone's safety, of course. Only one person had died, a miracle, but hundreds had been shot, stabbed, billy-clubbed, or otherwise smacked in the head with two-by-fours. He'd called Aunt

Millie to check on her—Pedro and Freddie weren't around—and she described the scene at Harlem Hospital as a battlefield. "It's worse than Saturday-night craziness—times ten!"

Apart from the long shifts she was doing fine, thanks for calling.

And he was glad the riots were done for the sake of his fellow merchants. The obvious targets were raided, decimated: supermarkets, liquor stores, clothing stores, electronics shops. They stole everything and then grabbed a broom to steal the dust, too. Carney knew firsthand how hard it was for a Negro shopkeeper to persuade an insurance company to write a policy. The vandalism and looting had wiped out a lot of people. Whole livelihoods gone, like that.

Most of the destruction lay east of Manhattan Ave; Carney's Furniture was outside the border. Furniture stores were low on the list of loot-able establishments, given the portability issue— but of course any savvy neighborhood resident knew that Carney sold TVs and handsome table lamps, and what about that irate dude who'd been refused credit and hungered for revenge? Can't carry a sofa on your back, but you can throw a bottle of gasoline through a front window. Which was why he and Rusty spent four nights in the front of the showroom, cradling baseball bats they'd bought at Gary's Sports down the block. Security gate rolled down, lights out, on sentry duty in the exquisite embrace of their Collins-Hathaway armchairs, whose virtues the salesmen had not exaggerated over the years, no not at all.

Half the Negroes in Harlem had that story about their grandfather down South, the one who spent all night on the front porch with a shotgun, waiting for the Night Riders to fuck with his family over some incident in town. Black men of legend. Carney and Rusty sipped Coca-Cola and upheld the tradition of the midnight vigil. In most of those stories, the family packs up and flees North the next morning, their Southern term brought to an end. On to the next chapter in the ancestral chronicle. But Carney wasn't going anywhere. The next morning he pulled up the gate, flipped the sign from CLOSED to OPEN, and waited for customers.

Business was slow. It was a good time to be in plate glass.

Most important, Carney welcomed the peace because he had a big meeting lined up, one he'd been trying to engineer for years: a face-to-face with the Bella Fontaine company. Lord knows what Mr. Gibbs, the regional sales rep, had seen on Walter Cronkite or *The Huntley-Brinkley Report.* Pillaged storefronts, cops tackling miscreants, young girls with batty smiles chucking bricks at news photographers. Making Mr. Gibbs fight his way through pandemonium was a big ask. Especially given that Bella Fontaine had never taken on a Negro dealer before.

Wednesday morning, Carney had talked Mr. Gibbs out of canceling his trip uptown. *Do I sound like I am on fire? We are open for business.* Carney was small potatoes; if not for Mr. Gibbs's meeting with All-American on Lexington, in white midtown, and with some Suffolk County accounts, he never would have boarded the plane from Omaha. Uptown was burning but business in white Manhattan proceeded as usual.

The NEGRO OWNED & OPERATED sign was still in his window, next to the sun-yellowed TIME PAYMENTS NEGOTIABLE. Carney smiled—from one angle, maybe the two signs went together. Marie had stenciled the "Negro Owned" one and brought it from Brooklyn the Monday after the boy was killed. "So they leave us alone," she said. When the protests jumped to Bed-Stuy, Carney told her to stay home to look after her mother and sister. He and Rusty could manage. Marie agreed, after a round of sobs and apologies. Thursday appeared to be the end of it and Marie showed up for work the next day on time, as if nothing had happened.

No harm in leaving the sign, in case.

* * *

"No sales," Rusty said. "People are taking a nice long look at the Argent sofa, though. They're flipping over the herringbone."

"I noticed."

Five years ago, Collins-Hathaway could do no wrong. Now the customers were going Argent, with those clean lines and jet-set emanations. Take that Airform core, zip it up in the new Velope stain-resistant fabric—they really knocked it out of the park. "You know the Manhattan Project, where they brought in the world's top scientists?" Carney asked his customers. "That's what Argent did, but with stain-resistance instead of the A-bomb." That was usually good enough for a sample bounce on the cushions.

Carney told Rusty to go home early. Now that Rusty had two kids he was less eager to lock up, and the nocturnal stakeouts had made for a long week. On Tuesday, out of riot-night boredom, Carney gave him a new title: associate sales manager. Knowing his boss wouldn't get around to it, Rusty went ahead and ordered the name tag. While he awaited its arrival, he taped an interim version onto a Pan Am Junior Captain pin he'd obtained somewhere.

"What do you think?"

It looked okay. "It looks great," Carney said. Business was slow anyway.

Elizabeth had bought some books for Rusty's little ones and Carney handed them over. "What'd you, loot these?" Carney had asked when she pulled them out of the shopping bag. That would be a sight: Elizabeth climbing into the window display, stepping over broken glass to grab some shit. Wouldn't put it past her, if she'd been born a few blocks over.

Rusty thanked him for the gift and then it was a dead two hours except for cop cars drifting by like slow death out there.

Carney settled at his desk after he locked up to work on a pitch for the new *Amsterdam News* advertisement. The old one was getting hoary and on riot watch he'd ruminated.

The Argent sectional . . . Carney preferred to be hands-on with advertisements, but there was resistance. The newspaper's in-house man Higgins laid out the ads and he was a stubborn sort, with an imperious streak one associated with the lowest rungs of New York City civil service. "Is this the message you want to send to the public?" As if Higgins were acquainted with the whole history and contemporary reality of home furnishings. One time Carney used the word *divan* and it turned out Higgins had a cousin named Devon, and the assistant accounts manager had to break up the scuffle. Bottom line: A man has a mind to place an ad and possesses the means, you run the ad. Save the censorship for the front page.

Carney grew punchy.

Designed with today's Rioter-on-the-Go in mind . . .

After a long day of fighting the Man, why not put your feet up—on a new Collins-Hathaway ottoman.

Presenting the new Collins-Hathaway Three-Point Recliner—finally a sit-in we can all agree on!

Someone thumped on the Morningside door. None of his regulars had arranged a meet, but it was Saturday evening and a fellow might want some money in his pocket for the night ahead. Carney slid back the cover and looked out the keyhole. He let his cousin in, making sure that no one came up behind.

"What's up?" Freddie hadn't been this scrawny since seventh grade—he had existed as a chicken-armed creature until puberty. His skin was sheened, his red-and-orange-striped T-shirt sweated through. He clutched a leather briefcase with gold-tone hardware and a tiny clasp lock.

"Where you been?" Carney said. He put his arm on Freddie's shoulder to test that he was actually there.

Freddie wriggled loose. "I wanted to check in and see how you were doing—how all you were doing." He claimed the club chair and leaned back. "People up to some madness the last few days."

"We're fine," Carney said. "The kids. You talk to Aunt Millie?"

"I'm heading there right after I see you. Surprise her."

"She'll be surprised all right."

Freddie cradled the leather briefcase to his chest. Gentle, like he kept a rooftop coop and the briefcase was his prize flier. Carney asked him what it was.

"This? I know, right! Listen, I have to tell you how I found out what was going down—I was in it! It was Saturday night, you know, the big one."

Freddie had trekked to Times Square to see *The Unsinkable Molly Brown*—his partiality for Debbie Reynolds was durable and verified—and on the ride uptown a weird vibe swallowed up the train. Everyone jumpy, looking around. The heat sent people barking at one another. Since the murder, the news had been running stories about flocks of youth rampaging through the subway, harassing white people, threatening motormen.

"It was nine o'clock," Freddie said. "I get out of the subway to look for a sandwich and the streets are full of people. Raising their fists, waving signs. Chanting, 'We want Malcolm X! We want Malcolm X!' and 'Killer cops must go!' Some of them hold pictures of the killer cop like, Wanted: Dead or Alive. I'm hungry—I don't want to deal with all that. I'm trying to get me a sandwich."

The Congress of Racial Equality had been out in front since the boy was killed, organizing a rally on Friday, and another on Saturday at the 28th Precinct. "Someone said they were at the station house doing speeches, and I thought to myself—maybe I'm an activist. Why not? You know I like those little CORE girls, all serious and shit, talking about change. Last time I was in Lincoln's I started rapping with this girl from CORE. Looked like Diahann Carroll? Could have been her sister. But she wasn't having it. Says she wants herself a college man and I said, I went to college—"

"UCLA," Carney helped out.

"That's right—University of the Corner of Lenox Avenue!" The old joke.

Freddie followed the crowd to the station house on 123rd, where a CORE field secretary with dark horn-rimmed glasses and a red bow tie listed demands: Police Commissioner Murphy must resign; set up the long-requested civilian review board. "Got these Negroes out there yelling 'Killer! Killer! Killer!' this way, over that way this young brother has a bullhorn going, 'Forty-five percent of the cops in New York are neurotic murderers!' It was a ruckus—I should have stayed in the subway, all this going on up here. And you know those cops ain't having it. They got barricades up, herding people. Wearing those helmets because they know people are going to fuck over them. Fucking cop pulls out the special cop bullhorn and tells us, 'Go home! Go home!' And everybody shouted back, 'We are home, baby!'

"This old lady elbows me in the stomach, we're packed in. Hot. All these angry Negroes in one place, and they are pissed—but all I want is a sandwich. I start heading back up to 125th and people are all buzzing, saying the police have beat up and arrested some CORE people. That was that! Boom—it was on! Knocking over the barricades. Niggers on the roof raining down shit on the cops—bricks, soda bottles, pieces of roof. Rocking cars, throwing shit through windows.

"I'm like, how am I going to get my sandwich in all this mess?

"On 125th, everybody's closed or closing up early because of the unrest. That Cuban place with the pickle they put on the meat is closed. Jimmy's, the Coronet's got its lights out. That's when I really got hungry—you know how you want something more when you know you ain't going to get it? Negroes are wrapping chains around those security gates and then pulling the gates off with their cars. Then they break the glass and step inside. I'm a

simple man. Put something between two slices and I'm happy.
But how am I supposed to get a motherfucking sandwich with all
that going on? People running up and down, screaming. I'm like,
damn, this riot stuff will cramp a brother's style."

Freddie had no recourse but to split uptown and hit Gracie's
Diner. "Got my ass a turkey sandwich, finally. And it was good,
too. But that was some wild shit, man," he said. "You don't want
to be out in that, hell no. Me and Linus decided to ride it out at
our place."

"Ride it out." Drop out of the world and get high for a few days.

"Beats getting beat upside the head. What'd you do?"

Carney said, "Elizabeth and the kids stayed inside mostly.
Their day camp was canceled—it's on the same block as the station house, so it was in a hot spot. I was here. Rusty was with me
a lot." He told Freddie about the vigil. A mob marched past going
east, then returned into view stampeding in the other direction,
followed by a gang of white cops. Back and forth. In the end, the
store was unscathed, as Freddie could see. "So what's in there?"
Carney asked again.

"This? I need you to sit on this for a few days," Freddie said.

"Freddie."

"Linus and me, we pulled this rip-off and it got some people
mad. These heavy dudes. And now we got to lay low for a spell.
Can you do that for me?"

"What is it?"

"There's a lot of heat, that's all I can say."

"You're nuts," Carney said. They had extra cops cruising the
neighborhood to keep a lid on, prowl cars and cops on corners,
and Freddie is walking around with a Madison Avenue briefcase
that obviously wasn't his. Was it drugs? He wouldn't bring that
into his place, would he? "What are you getting me into?"

"I'm your cousin," Freddie said. "I need you to do it. I don't
have anyone else."

You couldn't hear the subway from 125th and Morningside, but Carney heard this train. Following its cursed schedule and already pulling into the station and opening its doors whether you were ready or not. "Okay."

"What else is that thing for?" Meaning the safe.

"I said okay."

"I'll be around in a few days to pick it up."

"I said okay."

Carney spun the handle of the Hermann Bros. safe and slid the briefcase inside. He closed it and rapped on the dark metal for effect. "Where will you be?"

Freddie gave him the address of an SRO way uptown on 171st Street, room 306. "I'll pick this up in a few days, Ray."

"What if I open it?"

"You don't want to do that. Something might fly out."

Carney slammed the Morningside door behind Freddie. He regarded the safe.

It came to him: *A comfortable sofa outlasts the day's news—it's built for a lifetime.*

Carney knew Mr. Diaz, the owner of MT Liquors, from meetings of the 125th Street business alliance. He was a Puerto Rican immigrant, gentle-natured except on the topic of crime. He despised druggies, purse-snatchers, and muggers. Public urination was a personal crusade, arguing from the anti position.

When they smashed his front window on Saturday night, Mr. Diaz replaced it the next day. He replaced it when they smashed it the next night. Never mind that the store had been cleaned out and there was nothing to steal but the empty, busted cash register. They broke the window again. He replaced it. They smashed it four times and four times he replaced it. Was he a monument to hope, or to insanity? He was a man grasping after an impossible solution. How long do you keep trying to save something that has been lost?

TWO

The next day was Sunday. The plan was to pop out after lunch and check out this season's Bella Fontaine line at New Century down in Union Square. Get a feel in person, beyond the catalog, a laying on of hands. All-American on Fifty-Third was closer, but he didn't want to be recognized. For fear of sabotage, or ridicule, for fear their enthusiasm over the product would make him feel rotten if things fell through. The company decal was a spiffy item—BELLA FONTAINE AUTHORIZED DEALER encircling an image of Poseidon erupting from the sea, clenching a gold trident. In his mind's eye he'd already stuck one in his front window, on the left as you walk in. For everyone to see.

Bella Fontaine had been on a hot streak ever since *Life* magazine ran those photographs of Jackie perched on their settee in the sunroom of the Kennedy Hyannis Port compound. Carney had dug their stuff since the '56 Home Furnishings Association convention. It was the first and last time he attended the HFA's annual shindig—too many white people, too many toupees and plaid sports jackets—but the rush of the convention floor that first day remained. It was like venturing into Futurama at the World's Fair, that same boggling wonder and plenty. "Bold yet avuncular minimalism." Scandinavian modern and the new plastics. He wended his way through the booths and exhibits—last year's Miss Montana in a bikini, perched on a St. Mark patio set—until he arrived at Bella Fontaine's display. Bring on the sunbeams and heavenly chorus, for surely a divine apparition has manifested inside the Bridgeport Convention Complex off Interstate 79.

Bella Fontaine's Monte Carlo Collection gently twirled on the rotating platform, the birch finish of the dining-room set aglow under the fluorescent tubes. The sleek drop-leaf table; the roomy, multi-door sideboard; the slim hutch with the beveled edges and hidden cocktail station—they subverted notions vis-à-vis domestic entertaining. The company tagline was a lullaby from a kingdom of luxury: *Furniture that looks beautiful, feels beautiful, stays beautiful—furniture for a whole new way of life.* Carney whispered those words into May's ear when she was a baby, to calm her colic. *Start with two pieces and add on later.* It usually worked.

The chatter and hustle of the convention floor started up again. Carney approached the rep to snag a promo catalog. The rep was a pink-faced white man in a powder blue suit who greeted him with a familiar look of racial contempt. "We don't cater to Negro gentlemen," he said, and turned his back to attend to two portly men with Texas accents.

Eight years later, Carney had finagled a face-to-face with Mr. Gibbs. All across the country, one observed signs of racial progress; perhaps the home-furnishing industry kept pace with the changing times.

Carney was halfway to the downtown subway when a man grabbed his arm and said, "Hold it, brother."

The grip was light. The tone held Carney fast. The man was slender, with red-brown skin like he hailed from the islands. When Carney turned to look at him, he twisted Carney's arm around behind his back, painfully. He wore James Bond sunglasses and a blue-and-white Hawaiian shirt over a white tank top. Not lacking a certain style.

Carney had never been robbed. His low profile helped; no one knew exactly what kind of volume Carney carried. The crooked side of the business remained discreet and off-hour. He cut off the crazies and junkies as soon as their natures expressed themselves. Moskowitz knew what he was pulling in on the high end, but not the rest, the coins and whatnot he laid off on separate brokers across the boroughs. Compared to your typical, flashy uptown crook, Carney looked like, well, a furniture salesman.

Munson the cop perhaps had an inkling. One night the detective, drunk, had come upon Carney at Nightbirds and proposed a toast to Carney's health. "To the biggest nobody in Harlem." A compliment on staying out of the fray, or a comment on how much he was making?

"If you say so," Carney had answered, and sipped his beer.

But this wasn't Munson putting the snatch on him. The stranger steered Carney to the corner. None of the passersby noticed anything amiss. Would he force Carney back to the office, make a play for the safe? It was Sunday, so Marie wasn't working. But Rusty was minding the store, and he might start something that got them killed.

"Over here," the man said. A lime green Cadillac DeVille vibrated at the crosswalk. He opened the back door and ushered Carney inside the sedan, sliding in after.

Delroy was at the wheel, so this was a Chink Montague production. Unless the man was freelancing. Or had gone to work for the competition.

"Say hello to Chet the Vet," Delroy said. He pulled away, up Broadway.

Chet the Vet flashed gold canines.

"Tell 'em about the war, Chet."

From his age, Carney gathered he'd been in Korea.

"Fuck a white man's army," Chet said.

"They call him Chet the Vet because he went to school to be an animal doctor. For a month."

"It wasn't for me," Chet allowed.

"Delroy," Carney said, "what's happening here?"

"Have to ask the boss."

Carney met his gaze in the rearview mirror. The hood averted his eyes.

* * *

It had been five years since Chink Montague sent Delroy and Yea Big around the furniture store to recover his girlfriend's stolen jewelry. The purpose of the visit had been intimidation; its result was a promotion, once Chink started steering business in Carney's direction for a cut. Delroy and Yea Big dropped by for the envelope every week, and five years was a long time. At a certain point, an outside observer might characterize them as a species of colleague.

Carney and Delroy, anyway. Some kids throwing a football around one January morning discovered Yea Big in Mount Morris Park, sash-cord wound around his neck. Missing for a week before melted snow gave him up, with the frozen dog shit and cigarette butts. That was last year, at the start of the war between Bumpy Johnson and Chink Montague. Bumpy Johnson got out of Alcatraz in '63 on mandatory release and had an idea to reclaim the empire he'd lost eleven years before. Jerry Catena, an underboss in the Genovese family, backed his play, while Chink operated under the auspices of the Lombardis, making their conflict a proxy war over Harlem's rackets. That Chink was Bumpy's protégé gave the conflict a biblical flair.

"They got us dancing puppets," Delroy told Carney when he came around for the envelope. He'd been up for days. He ran a finger along the scar in his cheek as if scraping invisible peas out of a pod. "We kill each other and these guinea motherfuckers sit back and laugh." It made for a hot couple of weeks until they called a truce and carved up the neighborhood like the messy butchers they were.

After Yea Big's death, Delroy came for the envelope solo. He and Carney were linked now—fellow puppets, crooked confederates, and fellow residents of Harlem, USA, God bless. They shared milestones. Delroy was Carney's first customer when the furniture store reopened after the expansion; the hood needed another dinette set for his latest girlfriend. Some men commemorated a new romance with the gift of a sparkling necklace or a pair of smart earrings from their preferred jeweler. With Delroy, it was dinette sets. "These gals, they don't even know how to set a table proper. How you going to feed your man, you ain't even got a goddamn place to eat?" The logic was sound. For a stretch, Delroy's romantic life was particularly fruitful and he bought three Riviera! by Collins-Hathaway pedestal tables in one year. Carney cut him a break on the last one.

Did Chink think Carney was shortchanging him? Or had someone set him up?

Delroy parked on 155th and Broadway, across from Sid the Sud King. The mascot on the sign was a Mr. Clean knockoff, a bald-headed Negro flexing in a white T-shirt. His grin broad and psychotic. Chet the Vet tugged Carney out of the car and led him into the laundromat.

DRIEST SPIN IN TOWN. White foam pushed against the washers' portholes in a lazy slosh. Old ladies parceled coins and old men wearing their last clean drawers shuffled around the grimy coin-op. The place was a misery, a death ward for old Maytags, the machines rocked and bucked so. *Is there anything you can do, doctor? . . . Could be days, could be weeks. It's in God's hands now.* Every nickel shook the washers closer to the nearest junkyard. Or empty lot, more likely.

The July swelter plus the heat from the mammoth dryers made the room unbearable. You couldn't hear a word above the machines and the fans that shoved the hot air around. Which was probably the point.

LAST WASH 7 P.M. Today it sounded like a warning.

Chet the Vet steered Carney into the office, past the vending machine that dispensed boxes of Salvo, Biz, and Instant Fels.

The back room was dim and most of the light came from the door to the alley. Chink Montague sat in a wheeled, green leather executive chair, one leg crossed over the other, his hands interlaced. Gigantic diamond rings bulged on his fingers like warts.

Chink Montague had made his fearsome reputation with a knife, but no longer conjured the image of a fleet, balletic slasher. People still remembered the audacious sadism of his first campaign, after Bumpy Johnson got sent to Alcatraz. That initial bloody exercise in ambition had served him well over the years, but he'd learned other means of control. Take the publicity trick with the hams. Bumpy had started the Christmas goodwill giveaway, handing out turkeys to the Harlem needy from the back of a truck. Chink followed suit, tossing out free hams the day before Easter, sometimes to people who were unaware that he'd killed their husband or son. Or were too hungry to care. These days he was more likely to hold court than to press steel to some mope's throat, presiding over his minions at the Hotel Theresa bar or buying a round for everyone at one of his clubs, the 99 Spot or the Too True.

And this place, behind one of the city's innumerable fronts, where the operators of power worked their levers and pedals. Sometimes business wasn't business unless rubes and squares walked outside, oblivious to how they were getting fucked over inside.

The manager of the laundromat was a scrawny man in a saggy undershirt painted with sweat stains. Launderer, heal thyself. He leaned against the bathroom door and scratched his neck. Chink Montague snapped his fingers and the man scurried away.

The mobster explained that he was getting the floors refinished at his office upstairs at the 99 Spot. "Contractors," he said. "They promise and promise it's going to take not so long, and then you have to double it. It's hot in here today, but I like the sound of the thumping machines. Like someone's getting worked over in the next room."

A customer hollered through the door to complain that a machine stole his money. Chet the Vet stuck his head out. Whatever his expression was, it ended the dispute.

"First time we met," Chink told Carney, "I was telling you to find something. People told me there was a new fence uptown, keeping his head down."

"I try to stay out of things," Carney said.

"And I was helping out a young starlet—Miss Lucinda Cole. She's in Hollywood now. You seen any of her movies?"

"That one about the orphanage, with the singing."

"*Miss Pretty's Promise*. She wasn't bad at all in that. Should have been the lead, but they have their own way of thinking." He smiled to himself. "I could tell them a thing or two about who she really is, anyone wants to listen."

There was a poster of Sid the Sud King above the desk, him standing in a genie pose, as if he'd zapped the clean into the clothes of a mom and her two kids, who smiled grotesquely. The yard was one of those you saw in articles about those new Long Island developments, like Levittown or Amityville, that didn't sell or rent to Negroes. Carney thought, Do I need a mascot?

"Never did find that property of hers," Chink said, "but you and me started our association, so good came out of it, right?"

Carney nodded.

"You pull a big score, you best give me a taste. And if it turns out someone needs a fence, I might send him by that furniture store on 125th. Something falls into my lap and I think you're the one to call, I call you, right?"

Their arrangement had paid for the expansion of Carney's store and for the move to Riverside Drive. Carney and Chink had only talked face-to-face once before, six months after the Theresa job. Yea Big and Delroy swung by for the envelope and brought Carney out to a cherry red Cadillac parked outside. Chink was in the back. He rolled down the window, looked over his sunglasses, and gave Carney a once-over. "All right, then," the mobster said, and the Cadillac pulled away. *All right, then* was a binding contract, signed in ink or blood, take your pick.

"It's been profitable," Carney said. "And your end has always been reasonable. I hope you've been satisfied."

"That's why I told Delroy and Chet to be polite. This guy sells couches, bring him by the laundromat and we'll have a chat." He rolled up his sleeves. "It's about your brother. He's been messing around and I'd like a word."

"Cousin."

Chink glared at Delroy. "I thought you said it was his brother," Chink said.

"Cousin," Delroy said.

"That right?" he asked Carney.

"Yes."

"I want to talk to your cousin."

"Right."

"Not 'right'—where? Where's he at?"

"I haven't seen him for months," Carney said. "He's hanging out with a different crowd. Just talked to his mother because of the riot—she hasn't seen him either."

"His mother," Chink said. "What do you think about it? All that running around everybody did last week?"

"It's the same old thing. They get away with it, and then people want to be heard."

"Know what I think? I think they shouldn't have stopped. All these angry niggers up here. Everywhere. They should have burned the whole neighborhood down and then kept going. Midtown, downtown, Park Avenue." The mobster mimed an explosion with his hands. "Torch all that shit."

"Bad for business," Carney said. "At least in my line—home furnishings."

" 'Bad for business.' " Chink Montague rubbed his jaw. "You know anything about playing a number? Putting some money down? I see these suckers, I take their money, I know they want to burn shit down. I say, maybe don't play the same number all the time. Play something else, see what happens. Maybe you been playing the wrong thing this whole time."

He nodded at Chet the Vet and Delroy. "You see your cousin, you tell me first. I want him." Chink turned to the desk and struck up a lovelorn humming of "My Heart Is a Pasture (Theme from *Miss Pretty's Promise*)."

Out on the street, Carney started for the Cadillac. Chet said, "Boss didn't say nothing about chauffeur service."

"I'll see you in the car," Delroy told Chet the Vet. The erstwhile veterinary student spat into the gutter and crossed the street.

Delroy checked over his shoulder and waved Carney close. "I'm going to tell you something," he said, "because you gave me a break on that dinette that one time for Beulah. And I want you to listen. I've seen that nigger pitch a bitch, I've seen him at war. I've seen him cut a nigger's eyelids off for blinking too loud. When he talks like that—weird and calm—shit is right and proper fucked up. You see your cousin, you better step up. For everybody's fucking sake."

* * *

The Cadillac turned east. Carney waited for it to disappear. Then he cut over to Amsterdam and walked up to 171st, where he switched back to Broadway.

It had been years since Carney visited this stretch of Broadway. Since he stopped buying used furniture. Why did Freddie choose to lam it up here? Because he wasn't going to run into anyone from the old days. Although he'd been doing a good job of keeping out of sight, downtown with Linus. Then Carney saw it—the old movie theater, the Imperial. With the nickel double features. He and Freddie would spend all day inside, watch the double— cowpoke nonsense usually—and then look at each other: Let's do it again. No need to speak. They rarely made it through four movies, as some dirty old man usually came lurching up the row to try something, whereupon they ran out screaming and laughing into the street.

Shuttered for years from the looks of it. "The Theater Where People See Cinema." Giving the hard sell there. The SRO was right across the street.

He had to get the briefcase out of his safe, whatever it was. Carney had considered jimmying the cheap lock but he was too good at imagining outlandish contents: heroin, gold bullion, strontium 90 in a lead case with Russian lettering. Holding it one night was enough to fulfill his family obligation. Freddie had to get his ass downtown and take it away and not come back until the heat was off.

What kind of loony bird rips off Chink Montague? Or rips off someone with enough juice to mobilize Chink on his behalf? It was Freddie who'd put Carney on the mobster's map with the Theresa job, and now he had returned him to Chink's attention by fucking up once more. *I didn't mean to get you in trouble.* That was fine when they were kids. Adult trouble was more permanent than Aunt Millie smacking you with a hairbrush or his father taking off his belt. He could still make it downtown to Union Square to check out the Bella Fontaines if he wrapped it up quick.

There had been no reason for Carney to notice the west side of Broadway and 171st, all those times he came to the Imperial. Cafeteria, tobacco store, hair salon, the insignificant front door to 4043 Broadway. It was called the Eagleton—like his childhood home, it was a building that didn't deserve a name, despite the ambitions of its architects. Fate has a way of striking places with lightning so that you can never see them the same way again. Carney reached for the knob—in raw spots the metal door was gray beneath the red paint—as a short white man with a long, gnarled beard barged out of the SRO, one hand holding his brown trilby fast to his head.

"Watch it," the man said, scowling. A mottled canvas bag was slung over his shoulder and his elbows sawed back and forth as he zoomed toward the subway. Carney stepped inside the lobby. A thin, inexplicable layer of grease covered the lobby's chartreuse walls, as if he were exploring a five-story chicken place. The front desk was empty. Carney heard a toilet flush; he beat it up to the second floor before the clerk returned.

There were six rooms on every floor. On the second floor, one resident watched *The Andy Griffith Show* at high volume, the next one blasted a Ford commercial, and a third man merely screamed about "them."

Room 306 was silent. A breeze sucked in the door an inch. Through the crack, the mirror leaning against the wall relinquished few details. "Freddie? Linus?" He pushed in.

They had only been there a few days, but his cousin and his pal had made a nest. The sheets on the twin bed were a grimy bundle, and a makeshift bed on the floor had been gathered from frayed couch cushions. In one corner Freddie and Linus had built a trash pile of soda bottles, beer cans, and grease-soaked wax paper; flies zagged above it in deranged loops. They'd lugged their clothing uptown in pillowcases, which sat half deflated by the window.

"Freddie?" Carney said, loudly, to alert anyone in the bathroom before he tried the door.

But Linus was beyond listening. He was scrunched in the bathtub in an odd position, on his side, as if he had been trying to break through the cast iron with his back. The overdose had turned his lips and fingertips blue. Against the white of the bathtub, dingy as it was, they appeared purplish.

THREE

Elizabeth threw off the sheet and walked to the bathroom. "You're keeping me up with all the sighing."

Carney sighed all evening and into the wee hours, often mouthing "Mother of fucking God" as a chaser. He regretted his jokes about Freddie's friend the last few years, the beatnik putdowns and Bowery bum comments. Linus's family had locked him up in the nuthouse, doctors had tied him down and sent a million volts through him. He slunk into a drug hole, where he died. Carney's derision had been a way to let off steam, to express disappointment in and worry over his cousin. Now he thought about the poor man and his last view of earth: the groove of rust worn from the tub's leaky faucet, like the ooze from a wound.

Did you go quick when you died like that? He hoped it had been quick.

Had Freddie returned from a chicken run, or scoring, and discovered his friend's corpse, or had he awakened to the scene in the bathroom? He must be scared. And sad. On top of his fears about blowback from whatever job he and Linus had pulled. An unlocked door in a building like the Eagleton, ajar—they would have called the cops by now. Some down-and-outer pops in to see if anything's lying unattended and gets a big surprise.

No one could identify Carney except the man he bumped into at the Eagleton's entrance, the crotchety dude with the beard. What does that man do when he returns and sees the cops milling about, or hears about it in a few days—speak up or keep it zipped?

When Elizabeth returned she slipped her arm around his chest and pressed her face to his neck. "You're going to kill them tomorrow."

"It's a lot." When he tried to focus on the Bella Fontaine meeting, orchestrate the visit, the floor gave way and he tumbled into room 306 again, hand reaching for the bathroom door.

"You'll be making history." They chuckled.

"I don't think First Negro to Become an Authorized Dealer for Bella Fontaine is going to make the papers. It's not like I'm doing a million things with a peanut."

"What?"

"George Washington Carver."

"George Washington Carver. Just because nobody knows doesn't mean it's not happening. You worked your butt off."

"Trying to keep up with my wife," Carney said. He squeezed her hand. Black Star Travel had opened two satellite offices in the last year. With Dale Baker, the president of the firm, spending half the year in Chicago and Miami, someone had to run the home office—and Elizabeth got the nod. It was more money and fewer hours once they staffed up, which the kids liked, and so did Carney.

Elizabeth brought home enough that from time to time Carney considered dropping the fencing line altogether. They didn't need the cash, not really; any sober analysis rendered the side untenable. They certainly didn't need the risk. With Freddie drawing him into crooked complexities once more, walking away made more sense than ever.

"I'll try to sleep," he said. And was immediately embroiled again. Let's say Freddie comes for his briefcase and moves to Timbuktu. Someone's watching the furniture store, they report to Chink that Freddie came by and Carney didn't speak up. He suffered the momentary image of a torture chamber, basement of the laundromat: splash a bucket of water on the floor to wash the blood down the drain. Meet Freddie for a handoff somewhere else? What if he's being tailed? Back in the basement chamber, naked bulb swinging over a table covered by sharp, gleaming tools, cartoon-colored cartons of detergent piled to the ceiling. Carney was in a fix.

Carney was about to fall asleep when it occurred to him that Linus's overdose was not an accident. "Mother of fucking God," he said, out loud this time. Elizabeth put a pillow over her head.

Where was Freddie?

He grabbed a blanket from the linen closet and spent the rest of the night on the couch.

* * *

For all the worry that the man from Bella Fontaine might cancel, that the protests might prevent it from proceeding, the meeting was on. Events had left little time to prepare. Carney had Rusty and Marie arrive a half hour early for a run-through. Rusty delivered his Argent and Collins-Hathaway pitches while Carney listened for holes. Mr. Gibbs doubtless maintained a mental conception of how a Negro furniture salesman walked and talked, of what the store would look like; he and Rusty would show him that he didn't know shit. He was ashamed at his relief that six years in the city had sawed the edges off Rusty's hick accent.

Marie had stopped bringing in baked goods last year, but this morning she blessed the store with a tray of caramel apple cookies topped with chopped pecans, "like they eat out there, or so I've heard." Out there meaning Nebraska. If this was the kind of treat they went for, Carney thought, who knew what other primitive customs the whites out there claimed as their own?

Carney tidied his desk and stiffened when Linus's cold, contorted body appeared in his mind. He shook it off. He'd seen a dead body in this very room—Miami Joe. But the bathtub—it reminded Carney of a picture of a womb, the way Linus was curled up and pressed against the cast-iron sides. "You guys ready?" Carney called out.

Marie gave him a thumbs-up, like an ace pilot in a war movie.

Mr. Gibbs arrived at five minutes after eleven.

He was younger than Carney had imagined, slim-built, freckled in a band across his nose and cheeks. Gibbs kept his brown hair in a close, hayseed crew cut, and he wore a white short-sleeve shirt with a dark brown tie. He gripped a black satchel in his right hand and hooked his seersucker jacket over his back with his other hand.

Carney welcomed him. "Hot enough for you? How's the weather in Omaha?" In the back of the store, Rusty leaned over Marie's desk, the two of them engaged in a fake conversation.

Mr. Gibbs smiled and looked over his shoulder at 125th Street. Carney wagered he'd seen more Negroes in five minutes than he had in his whole life.

The sales rep had a friendly manner as he recounted the dull details of his semiannual trip out East. A simple phone call took care of most client relations, he said, but it was good to put names to faces. "You know how it is, Mr. Carney."

"Call me Ray."

"Nice operation you got here," Mr. Gibbs said. It was paramount to visit prospective dealers in person, for obvious reasons. For the right fit. Bella Fontaine had a corporate personality; sometimes certain personalities didn't mix as well as others. And of course there was the problem of geography, he said. You didn't want to turn local establishments into rivals so that they're cannibalizing one another's business.

The euphemisms made Carney dizzy and he'd have to check with Elizabeth over whether the cannibal thing was a slur.

Mr. Gibbs asked how long he had been in business and Carney gave him the lowdown. The seed money had been a "dedicated savings plan," instead of a bunch of his father's stolen money hidden in an old tire. The importance of repeat business, maintaining the customer relationship, intimate knowledge of the neighborhood. Carney alluded to last week's unrest—"The city may change, but everybody needs a fine-quality sofa"—as a segue to opine on the waves of Southern transplants. "They're here for good. They're raising a family and like any other family, they need to furnish their house."

Carney had taken Gibbs on a small circuit around the showroom and now directed him into his office. He was about to redirect his pitch to the specific virtues of Bella Fontaine, and then take a brief foray into racial harmony, when Marie distracted him.

Two white cops—they had to be cops—lumbered toward Carney's office.

"Please, sirs, you have to listen," Marie said. They breezed past her.

Rusty asked the men if he could assist them. The cops materialized in the doorway of the office, with sour expressions. They were simultaneously doughy and sturdy, like TV wrestlers, moving quicker than you'd think, given their lumpy physiques. "I'm Detective Fitzgerald of the 33rd Precinct," the taller one said, "and that's my partner Garrett. We're investigating a death that occurred last night uptown. A deceased person."

Also like TV wrestlers: They liked to lay it on thick.

Which would have been fine if Mr. Gibbs had not been present.

At Carney's request, the cops displayed their badges with petulant resignation. The cow-faced one, Garrett, appraised Mr. Gibbs as if he'd stumbled on a narcotics transaction. Mr. Gibbs's mouth fell open and he started blinking rapidly.

Fitzgerald pulled out a notebook. Garrett checked his watch and exhaled loudly.

"Look, I'm in the middle—" Carney said.

"I should be going," Mr. Gibbs said, rising.

They stepped aside to let him pass.

Carney trailed the regional sales manager across the show-room. Marie and Rusty stood by the maroon Collins-Hathaway armchair, dumbfounded. She covered her mouth with her palm.

"Perhaps this visit was not meant to be," Mr. Gibbs said. He weaved through the floor models. "Last week. The unpleasant-ness."

"This is—" Carney began. He stopped.

He wasn't going to beg this white man for a goddamn crumb. Fuck him. Fuck the cops, too.

Mr. Gibbs walked two yards onto the sidewalk and stared into the Harlem hurly-burly. His shoulders slumped. "How do I get out of here?"

"Rusty!" Carney yelled. As the associate sales manager deliv-ered Mr. Gibbs into the embrace of the New York City Taxi Com-mission, Carney returned to the detectives. There would be plenty of time for rage if he made it past this new, unscheduled interview.

Carney sat at his desk and the detectives loomed in the door-way. Fitzgerald did the talking while his partner used his X-ray vision to scan on the sidelines. "A young man died last night in a transient house on 171st," Fitzgerald said. "The Eagleton? His name was Linus Van Wyck. We believe you knew him?"

"Van Wyck?"

"Like the expressway."

Carney was confident in his salesmanship, especially on his home turf. Today's specials: surprise and sadness and curiosity. Yes, he knew Linus, he was a friend of his cousin Freddie. "What happened?"

"If we knew, do you think we'd be here? Your cousin is Freder-ick Dupree?"

"Yes."

According to the building manager, the detective said, Freddie was the last person to see Linus alive. "He was picked up a while back on drug charges—did you know that?"

Because Freddie had been eating a meal with Biz Dixon when the police arrested the drug peddler. The arrest Carney had set up. Carney shook his head. Garrett prowled the office. He bent to peer at the items on the bulletin board, inspecting.

"The case was dropped," Fitzgerald said. "Didn't say why. Is your cousin a user of narcotics?"

"Not that I know of."

Fitzgerald peered up from his notebook. "What about you?"

"What about me? I met Linus once."

Garrett stood before the safe and gave an idle tug on the handle. It didn't budge. "When was that?"

"Years ago."

"Your father was Michael Carney?" Fitzgerald said.

"We weren't close."

The detectives looked at each other. "Rough character, he's the one I'm thinking of," Garrett said. He dislodged some food in his back teeth with his tongue. "When's the last time you saw Frederick Dupree?"

Carney answered their questions. Once it was clear that the man at the Eagleton hadn't fingered him yet, he dummied up. He'd dummied up his whole life, covering for Freddie. All of it practice for this: Chink Montague, the cops.

Who else was coming for Freddie?

Garrett stiffened. "What's that?" he said.

"What?" Carney said.

"That." He pointed into the showroom.

Carney didn't have a lot of cop customers, as far as he knew, but they usually went for the decorative accent pieces for some reason. In the two months the Egon sculpture had hung on the wall no customer had ever remarked upon it. The metal sunburst was four feet in diameter, with three layers of copper spikes that radiated from a polished brass center. The perfect finishing piece for a contemporary living room, or so Carney said to himself. But nobody bit, even after Marie affixed the sale tag. Detective Garrett asked him to put it on hold for him until Wednesday, payday, plus he had all this overtime due from the riots.

"We still want to hear from your cousin regardless," he said. "This Linus character came from a big Park Avenue family. Did you know he was from money?"

"Only met him the one time."

"Freddie sees this rich kid slumming it, maybe he can make a quick score," Garrett said. "There were items that were stolen, according to his family. Missing."

"And this family, they've got connections," Fitzgerald said. "In fact—" He stopped himself. He closed his notebook. "You see that cousin of yours, you tell him to come by the station. And you call us—you don't want to get mixed up in this."

"Good riddance," Rusty said once the policemen departed. He and Marie did their best to cheer Carney up.

Carney told them it was a minor setback. Then he called Mr. Gibbs's hotel and left a message that he doubted would be returned.

* * *

The decor of the Dumas Club hadn't changed in decades, save for the absence of the full-length portrait of Wilfred Duke which had hung in the library. A brass light had conferred upon Duke a dependable, stately glow. Following the "unfortunate incident," as the members referred to it, anonymous parties removed the painting one wintry night and burned it in the street with kerosene.

Wilfred Duke—and the money he embezzled—had yet to surface, although Patrick Carson, dentist to Harlem's elite, swore he caught a glimpse of the disgraced banker at a New Year's Eve revel in Bridgetown, Barbados. Carson hurried through the crowd but was unable to catch up with the man. A faction recalled Duke mentioning Bajan ancestry at some point, which lent credence to the tale. A private detective was dispatched but nothing came of it.

The membership had changed, however. The bankruptcies, assorted ruinations, and multitiered reversals of fortune caused by Duke's betrayal had necessitated a campaign for new blood. As the recently installed vice president of the club, Calvin Pierce made sure the prospective members represented the variety of Harlem's vanguard. Raymond Carney, local entrepreneur, was delighted to receive their invitation. He was accepted without mishap.

Carney's father-in-law remained on the rolls but had stepped down from club leadership. As one of the old dogs, a Duke crony, Leland was viewed with suspicion by most of his fellow Dumas gentlemen. He didn't drop by as often as he used to.

The evening of the Bella Fontaine debacle, Carney arranged to meet Pierce for a drink. Carney was the first to arrive. As was his habit now, he fiddled with his Dumas Club ring while waiting on something. He ordered a beer.

At six o'clock, the lounge started to fill up. Carney tipped his beer glass at Ellis Gray, who offered that strange leer of his, as if they were partners on the same swindle. Now that Carney was on the inside, he appreciated the extent of the club's sovereignty over Harlem. A conversation, a wink, a promise inside these walls expressed itself magnificently, permanently, on the streets beyond in individual lives, in destinies across the years.

Take last week's protests, for example: They altered the energies in the room. Bloviating across the way was Alexander Oakes, Elizabeth's childhood neighbor. He continued to work his way up in the prosecutor's office; his bosses made sure he stood next to Frank Hogan, the Manhattan DA, during press conferences about the boy's killing. Just a matter of time before Ol' Alex turned to politics—he was that type. Oakes sat by the fireplace with Lamont Hopkins, who ran the uptown branch of Empire United Insurance. In the coming weeks as Hopkins accepted and rejected claims, he would shape the next version of Harlem. When it came to cleaning up and rebuilding, Sable Construction was still the go-to construction company in Harlem. Its glad-handing owner, Ellis Gray, was a regular fixture at the weekly Dumas scotch tastings and at this moment traded Polish jokes with James Nathan, who was in charge of business loans at Carver Federal and thus decided which entities took over the demolished spaces, which operations received a bailout, separating the drowned from the saved.

Small men with big plans, Carney said to himself. If this room was the seat of black power and influence in New York City, where was its white counterpart? The joint downtown where the same wheeling and dealing happened, but on a bigger stage. With bigger stakes. You don't get answers to questions like that unless you are on the inside. And you never tell.

Pierce stirred Carney from his reverie with a tap on the shoulder. He sat in the red leather club chair opposite and signaled for his usual drink.

"I saw you on the TV," Carney said.

"Busy days," Pierce said. He loosened his tie. Cases like James Powell's were the specialty of Calvin Pierce, Civil Rights Crusader; you rang him up once you got off the phone with the undertaker.

The boy had been killed five days prior, in Yorkville, East Side in the Seventies. A white building superintendent named Patrick Lynch was hosing down the pavement and asked some students to move so they wouldn't get wet; Robert F. Wagner Middle School was holding summer classes down the street. When the kids refused to budge Lynch said, "Dirty niggers, I'll wash you clean," and sprayed them with the hose. In retaliation, the kids threw garbage cans and bottles at him, and a couple of curse words, which attracted more of the summer students to join in the taunting.

Lieutenant Thomas R. Gilligan, thirty-seven, was off duty and out of uniform, checking out TVs in an electronics store. He went to investigate the commotion and stopped James Powell, a ninth grader who had joined the mob of angry students. Powell was unarmed, according to witnesses. Gilligan maintained that the boy flashed a knife. He shot him three times.

Two days later, Harlem erupted.

Pierce told Carney, "You have the people who are angry. Justifiably so. And then there's the police force. How are they going to defend this shit? Again! And city hall and the activists. And in the way back of the room, you can barely hear a little voice, and that's the family. They've lost a son. Somebody has to speak for them."

"They're going to sue?"

"Sue and win. You know they ain't going to fire the bastard." Sermon crept into his voice here. "What kind of message will that send—that their police force is accountable? We'll sue, and it will take years, and the city will pay because millions and millions are still cheaper than putting a true price on killing a black boy."

"That was good," Carney said. One of Pierce's better tirades. Nearby members had glanced over and returned to their companions when they saw it was Pierce doing his shtick.

"You got to keep stuff like that in your back pocket," he said, "city like this."

They caught each other up on their children and wives. Pierce's wife, Verna, was hot on Lenox Terrace—two of her friends had moved in and wouldn't shut up about it. The amenities, the famous people in the elevator. "One thing she hates is people showing off," Pierce said. "How's Riverside Drive treating you?"

"Let me ask you something," Carney said. "You ever heard of the Van Wyck family?"

"Van *Wick*? You mean *Wike*?"

"Like the expressway."

"It's pronounced *Wike*, but yeah. They've been players in this city since back in the day. You're talking some stone-cold original Dutch motherfuckers. As in, charging the Lenape Indians rent on their own land type shit."

"Oh."

"Yeah," Pierce said. "Robert Van Wyck was the first mayor of New York City, back in the eighteen-whatevers. And they still wear it like that—like royalty. Last time I saw the Yankees, they brought old man Van Wyck to the scout seats behind home plate, practically carried him on a litter like a maharaja." He took out his cigarette case. "Got a hand in everything—politics, banking—but real estate is their main bag. Van Wyck Realty, that's what the VWR stands for, on those little plaques on half the buildings in midtown." He checked out the room and leaned in. "What's up?"

"It came up."

"They dropped in to look at some couches? They strike me as more downtown shoppers." Pierce didn't press. He removed a Chesterfield King and lit it. VWR were known for making their money off everybody else's moves, Pierce said. According to lore, Thirty-Fourth Street was dead when they broke ground for the Empire State Building, but Van Wyck saw what was coming and put up his own office building across the street. "Look at it now." They missed out on the main Lincoln Center contracts, but carved out a big residential complex on Amsterdam, ready for their piece when the arts center was finished.

"They're sneaky."

"Sneaky gets you paid around here." He raised an eyebrow in reference to their fellow Dumas members. "It wasn't my case—I had just started at Shepard—but there was this wrongful death suit we handled one time. Seemed cut-and-dried, criminal negligence. Unsafe conditions at a building site—crane topples over and crushes two men. And it's a VWR operation, near the UN building. They were looking at an excruciating settlement.

There was a VWR employee who was set to testify that his boss had ordered him to bribe the inspector and that he'd done the same at other sites, for years. We had him in the bag for months leading up to trial."

"And?" Carney's neck got hot.

"He doesn't show. Wanted to do his civic duty or whatever. He's a solid citizen, happily married—poof. No sign." Pierce paused to let the situation sink in. "Washes up in New Jersey three weeks later, throat cut so bad his head is barely hanging on. Like a Pez dispenser. Junked the case, obviously. That's that. I'm not saying that anything nefarious happened, only saying what happened." He gestured for a refill. "One thing I've learned in my job is that life is cheap, and when things start getting expensive, it gets cheaper still."

It was Linus's, from the L.M.P.V.W. embossed on the leather. A gift from someone who'd once believed in his prospects. Carney popped the briefcase's latch with the letter opener his downstairs neighbor had given him as a college graduation gift. Because she saw that he had no one to look out for him and pitied him, or because she believed in his prospects.

Inside the briefcase were some personal papers, miscellany of private importance—a Valentine's Day card from one Louella Mather, a 1941 Yankees Double Play baseball card featuring Joe DiMaggio and Charley Keller—and the biggest cut emerald Carney had ever seen. The gem was set in a diamond-studded platinum necklace and flanked by six smaller, equally splendid emeralds on either side; held up by either end of the necklace, the center stone was the head of a gorgeous bird of prey, the smaller stones curving up like wings. Carney shut the briefcase and took a step back. When he'd joked that it contained strontium 90 he had not been far off; he had been bathed in ancient radiation.

His phone call from Aunt Millie Tuesday morning forced him to finally open it. He had slept poorly again. When Aunt Millie rang at six A.M., he had drifted off. They let it ring the first time. When Elizabeth answered the second time, Carney heard his aunt squawk from the other side of the bed: Her house had been ransacked. He dressed.

Aunt Millie had been sobbing; he recognized the puffy eyes from Pedro-related squabbles. But she had stopped and progressed on to Angry Millie, the Terror of 129th Street. As she told it, she got off her late shift at four A.M. and returned to shambles. "You know if I hadn't been at work," she said, "I'd have kicked that little nigger's ass. Come in my house. Come in my house and make a mess like this." Aunt Millie permitted a quick, reassuring hug, which made her flinch, for she did not want to be reassured. She wanted to fight.

Whoever had tossed the place had been thorough. They had slashed the cushions, pulled the dime novels off the living-room shelves, pried up the squeaky floorboard in the hallway to see if it contained secrets. The kitchen was a horror—every container bigger than a Campbell's Soup can had been emptied and rooted through. Flour, beans, rice, and pickled pig's feet made a repugnant mound on the old checkerboard kitchen tile. In the bedroom, Carney slid the dresser drawers back into place as Aunt Millie gathered up ungainly armfuls of clothes.

She could have kicked the ass of a druggie or the ne'er-do-well nephew of her upstairs neighbor—her mastery of her weapon of choice, the hairbrush, went unchallenged—but whoever had done this was not some two-bit crook. They had a purpose. They were completists. Looking for something in particular.

A rotten feeling reared up as they toured the mess; she beat it back. Aunt Millie struggled over what they might have taken. "Why would they do this?" She clutched Carney's arm, whispered, "Do you think Freddie is mixed up in something again?"

"I haven't seen him," Carney said. "I haven't heard anything." His standard response now to all the interested parties, who increased by the hour, or so it seemed.

"Like father, like son," Aunt Millie said. "Into the world somewhere." Pedro was a rover. When Carney was young, Freddie's father spent maybe a third of the year in New York City and the rest somewhere having his adventures. His own father, Carney gathered, had made a performance of being dependable and legit when he wooed Carney's mother. Pedro had been a rolling stone when he met Millie and never made a show of being otherwise. Neither Aunt Millie nor his cousin had ever expressed any emotion over Pedro's "travel," and Carney had learned at a young age not to inquire about it. It was one of the few times his mother had scolded him. "Other people got their business, you got yours."

Freddie idolized Pedro. You knew when he was in town because it was all Freddie talked about, and when he was down South, it was as if his father didn't exist. On and off like a switch. Until Freddie became a teenager, and chasing girls became more important—or following Pedro's ladies'-man ways became a means of worshipping the man. From Freddie's dishevelment these days, it seemed women were no longer his foremost priority.

Aunt Millie picked up a table lamp and set it right. "At least you didn't take Mike as an example," she said.

Carney nodded. He made sure there was no one hiding under the bed or in the closet. "These druggies," Carney said. "They have to get their sick kicks somehow."

Gladys from next door appeared with a broom and Carney said he'd ask Marie to pitch in with the cleanup. His aunt and his secretary went to the movies occasionally, when Rock Hudson's name was above the title. It wouldn't be terrible to have Marie away from the office. Too many unexpected parties dropping in these days.

He went straight to the store, beeline to the safe. He had feared discovering packets of—what? heroin? reefer—in the briefcase. The emerald necklace was worse; drugs explained themselves. Freddie had stopped coming to Carney to fence jewelry or gold, and he'd never showed up with anything near that quality. Had he and Linus ripped off Linus's family, taken the literal family jewels, as the cops insinuated? Or was that some separate beef between Linus and his relatives, and Freddie and his friend had ripped off some heavy players who were after payback? Even if Carney returned the briefcase to his cousin and told him to fuck off, he was still in somebody's sight for being close to Freddie. It was too late: Carney was in.

* * *

Munson beckoned from the sidewalk.

Carney locked up the store. It was half past noon. From now on, Rusty and Marie were on paid leave from Carney's Furniture; opening hours were whenever Carney felt it was safe to leave the front door open. By way of explanation, he blamed the lack of foot traffic after the riot and exaggerated the likelihood of another round of violence. "I'll see you when things get back to normal," he told his employees.

It relieved him more than he anticipated to have them safe.

The detective sat on the hood of his dark brown sedan, lighting a Winston with the smoldering end of the previous one. Carney hadn't seen him in daylight in a long time. The cop was pale and puffier, threadbare from the mileage. His face maintained the record of his boozing, rouged and speckled by popped capillaries. Free meals from local merchants and shady clients had ruined his build.

He was in his customary carefree mood. "I figured you'd be calling," Munson said. "Why don't you ride along while I pick up the mail?"

The mail: his recent coinage about his envelope route. "Neither rain, nor sleet," Munson said as Carney slid into the passenger seat. "Riots though, they'll throw you off schedule."

"We're all in the same boat."

"You don't want people to think you have a forgetful nature. I got to collect before they think it's their money and they spend it." Munson tilted his head toward the furniture store. "You made it out okay."

"Most of it was this way." Meaning, east on 125th.

"Yeah, I was there." He drove one block and parked outside a hole-in-the-wall newsstand Carney had never stepped in. Grant's Newspaper & Tobacco, across from the Apollo. For years, the dingy red, white, and blue streamers across the storefront had snapped ferociously on winter-swept mornings, and hung limp on hot days like this.

"Buck Webb on vacation again?" Carney said.

"Yeah, gone fishing." It was Carney's standard joke: *Where's Buck?* Since Munson's shakedowns—one assumed—fell outside his official police duties, Carney rarely saw Munson's partner. Buck was probably off tending to his own envelopes.

Munson said he'd be out in a sec and entered the tobacco store.

The marquee of the Apollo promised the Four Tops, but a big white CANCELED sign crossed the ticket window. Look at him, sitting in the front seat of a cop's car. He wondered how many black boys Munson and his cronies had worked over and then tossed into the backseat on the way to the station house. Carney's fingers slid on the vinyl: EZ wipe. Munson's line of work was not the kind where you wanted fabric upholstery.

"You ever play in that game?" Munson said on his return.

Carney didn't know what the cop was referring to.

"Grant—Grant's son, now—has been hosting one of longest-running craps games in Harlem in the back. You never threw in?"

Carney rubbed his temple.

"One block away and you never got in on it?" Munson said. "No, you ain't the kind. Grant's kid told me he kept the game running the whole time of the riot. No one wanted to leave, and when they did, someone was always knocking, trying to get a piece. All hell breaking loose out here, back there business as usual."

Carney bought his newspapers elsewhere; Grant's run-down

facade discouraged outsiders, as intended. A whole gambling operation back there—Freddie probably knew about it. The cop's car had made Carney into a country bumpkin, like his own street didn't belong to him.

Munson drove another block and stopped short of Lenox. The detective darted into Top Cat Dry Cleaning. The place had been there as long as Carney could remember. He'd never patronized this place, either; Mr. Sherman's up the street was more welcoming. Perhaps he'd known Top Cat wasn't legit in some way, in his bones, and he'd avoided it because of his solid-citizen side. To disavow the crooked inclinations of his nature.

Munson got back in the car and said, "He takes numbers for Bumpy Johnson."

"You take your piece from Bumpy and leave him high and dry, too?" Carney said.

A man lurched toward Munson's car as he exited a Checker cab. The detective honked. "I was waiting for you to say something like that," Munson said. "Look, I fucking apologize. Take a gander at my Fucking Apology Face—it's like Medusa, you only ever see it once."

With that, the detective gave Carney his account of the riot days, as a prelude for why he failed to run interference with the homicide detectives.

"I knew shit was going to blow up," Munson said, "the second I heard about it on the radio. Kid got shot? Heat wave like that? That ain't a powder keg—it's the munitions factory." Munson was set to go on vacation—down to Rehoboth in Maryland with some buddies who came up with him on the force. One of them had an uncle who owned a bungalow off the beach. Word had it there were some local ladies who liked to have a drink now and then. "He said this one gal likes to dance in the altogether, does a whole show where she wears cha-cha heels and sings Patti Page songs." Then the kid got shot and nobody was going nowhere.

The first two days, Munson ran a surveillance team that made the rounds of Negro groups—the churches, the NAACP—to get a handle on their response. CORE, of course, loud as they were these days. "Two of my men are college types, look like Jewish civil rights agitators, and the other two are young Negroes who walk around with copies of *The Fire Next Time* in their back pockets. You hear old-timers grumbling about the number of Negro cops, but who else is going to go inside? Some fat, red-faced Mick who hasn't done a day's work in years? Me? My guys take a seat and no one's looking at them twice." He paused. "I know you're not political, that's why I'm telling you."

There were known activists and agitators who required a once-over. Downtown wanted to know if they were exploiting the situation, fanning the flames. Munson's team attended the CORE protest at Wagner Middle School on Friday afternoon and popped up at the funeral home on Saturday afternoon, mixing with the crowd, identifying the players. Nodded their heads at the common sense from Black Muslims holding forth on a corner of 125th. Files were added to. Files were opened. "Had to make sure nobody was getting ideas." Munson said his wife helped paint the protest signs. She taught art to first graders.

"The ideas, we already got," Carney said. "Too late for that."

Munson shrugged. "Harlem, Harlem, Harlem," he said. He started the car. "Then Saturday night happened." Once everything blew up on Saturday, Munson was in the trenches with everyone else, putting out flare-ups, rousting the troublemakers. "With one of those dumb helmets on my head so I don't get my brains turned into scrambled eggs."

Needless to say, it delayed mail service, the circulation of envelopes. Five days later things were still not back to normal, as Chief Murphy and his lieutenants hustled to prevent another round of protest and vandalism. If it had been a normal week, Munson would have heard about homicide detectives from Washington Heights coming down to the 28th to investigate a body. "Come into my house, you best say hello," he said. "I would have talked to them first, informed my colleagues that you were a solid citizen. As one can plainly see from your furniture showroom. And I would have given you a heads-up."

"I had an important meeting—they busted it up."

"They had a Park Avenue corpse, what do you want? That's the other part." This time he parked outside Beautiful Cakes, half a block down 125th. The store was a cherished punch line of Elizabeth's, as every demo plastic cake and confection in the window was adorned with dust and attended to by dead flies. Look farther into the gloom and the baker's smoking a cigarette and cutting her nails.

Where'd you get this beautiful birthday cake?

Beautiful Cakes, of course!

Munson darted inside after bowing for a young woman steering a baby carriage. She had a prodigious ass. He let her pass, smiling, and winked at Carney.

Gibbs. Carney hadn't heard from the man since the aborted meeting. The hotel switchboard took his messages, which went unanswered. Bella Fontaine headquarters in Omaha only offered that he was out of town on business. When Carney got back from Aunt Millie's apartment, he rang up Wilson at All-American, to see if Gibbs had made it to their sales meeting. Carney had to endure some Condescending White Man humor about uptown mayhem. "Heard you had some weather the last few days . . ." Once that was out of the way, the midtown salesman offered no insight. "No, he didn't mention anything. How'd it go? He's a straight shooter, isn't he?"

What was Carney going to tell Gibbs, anyway? *The dead man was my cousin's junkie partner, but it was an accidental OD— unless it wasn't—and as you can see the foot traffic on 125th Street is quite impressive.*

The white cop dallied longer in the bakery than he had in his previous stops. Carney remembered Pepper taking him on his hunt for Miami Joe, the fronts and hideouts the crook had exposed during their search for the double-crosser. That time, places Carney had never seen before were suddenly rendered visible, like caves uncovered by low tide, branching into dark purpose. They'd never not been there, offering a hidden route to the underworld. This tour with Munson on his rounds took Carney to places he saw every day, establishments on his doorstep, places he'd walked by ever since he was a kid, and exposed them as fronts. The doorways were entrances into different cities—no, different entrances into one vast, secret city. Ever close, adjacent to all you know, just underneath. If you know where to look.

Carney chuckled and shook his head. The way he phrased it, like he wasn't a part of it. His own stores, if you knew the secret knock, were hip to the password, granted you entrance to that criminal world. You could never know what was going on with other people, but their private selves were never far away. The city was one teeming, miserable tenement and the wall between you and everybody else was thin enough to punch through.

Munson returned, burping and rapping his chest with his fist as if stricken with heartburn.

"Cakes," Carney said. "Let me guess—it's a whorehouse?"

Munson said, "You don't want to know, Carney. Which reminds me of the other reason you're on your own with Fitzgerald and Garrett."

"A minute ago you were sorry and now I'm on my own?"

"You read the paper today?"

"What makes you think we read the same papers?"

Munson reached back for the *Tribune.* He flipped to page 14 and gave it to Carney.

Police are investigating the death of Linus Millicent Percival Van Wyck, of the Van Wyck real estate dynasty. Van Wyck, 28, a cousin of Robert A. Van Wyck, who served as New York City's first mayor in 1898, was found dead in a Washington Heights hotel Sunday night . . .

Hotel—that was a kindness. Raised in Manhattan, a graduate of St. Paul's School and Princeton University, and last employed by the law firm Betty, Lever and Schmitt. Some fancy old-school outfit, Carney gathered, worthy of a monogrammed leather briefcase. How long ago? Before Linus met Freddie. *The exact cause of death has yet to be determined, but authorities have characterized it as suspicious in nature. Any information . . .* The picture accompanying the article depicted a teenage Linus with a crew cut and a smug, yacht-club grin.

Millicent Percival—enough to turn even the hardiest among us to narcotics.

"That's the public version," Munson said. "What you don't see is the mayor getting chewed out in his office by the Van Wyck family counsel. Your cousin's friend—he's Park Avenue. Was." He shrugged. "And now they're applying pressure. Applying pressure like, when I step on a cockroach with my shoe I am applying pressure. Mayor's office rings up Centre Street to chew them out, and then the commissioner makes his own call, to his own men, all pissed off. Shit rolls downhill. They want Van Wyck's friend and what he stole."

Van *Wike*—Munson pronounced it correctly, as Pierce had. "Stole what?" Carney said.

"You tell me."

It hit him: Munson had been interrogating him this whole time.

"Why not walk?" Carney said. "Why are we driving one block, parking, going another block. It's dumb."

"I have a car—what am I going to do? Walk around like some asshole? I don't understand the question."

"I'm out." Carney turned over the newspaper and reached for the door handle.

"Hey—Mr. Furniture."

"What?"

"This shit is heavy, no joke. I don't want to be your cousin right now. Don't want to be you either."

Carney opened the door. Munson said, "You hear about Sterling Gold?"

Sterling Gold & Gem was a venerable jewelry store on Amsterdam, ten blocks up. The dusty orange bulbs in the sign out front blinked on and off to simulate movement, like a greyhound dashing around a track. Young lovers knew the engagement rings and wedding bands out front, while the drawers of uncut stones and hot merch in the back catered to a more disreputable clientele. Given his insulting rates, the owner, Abe Evans, was a fence and shylock of last resort, but he had a policy where he granted delinquent accounts a one-week grace period before his muscle came over to break a leg or appendage of the client's choice. No one had heard of such a marketing gimmick before, this à la carte maiming, although one time in Nightbirds Carney overheard a man declare it a hallmark of an offshoot of the Estonian mob. Fancy that.

"Someone broke in and busted up the joint," Munson said. "No—not looters. Happened last night. Trashed, it's a big mess, busted-up display cases, alarm goes off, but get this—Abe Evans says nothing was taken." The detective clocked a portly man with a porkpie hat who walked behind Carney's shoulder, then returned his attention.

"So what's the point?" Carney said.

"You tell me," Munson said. "Maybe the point is to send a message to illegal operations that someone is lifting up the rock to see what scurries out. Someone with money and a lot of reach is saying, I'm looking for what's mine."

Carney slammed the car door. The three blocks back to the store was faster on foot.

The front door to the store was unlocked. The lights were out, but the door was unlocked. It wasn't Rusty or Marie, come back to get something.

The baseball bat was in his office, next to the safe. He crept along the wall to the back of the store. He paused by the Argent recliner and listened. He called out.

Freddie yelled from the office, "Hey, Ray-Ray!"

His cousin sat on the sofa eating an Italian sandwich from Vitale's, bottle of Coca-Cola resting on the safe. Chink Montague, homicide detectives, and rich people's hired muscle looking for this motherfucker and he's eating a goddamn sandwich in his office.

"I have a key," Freddie said. He chewed. "Remember when May was being born and you had to rush to University Hospital? Before Rusty came on. You asked me to lock up. Gave me the key."

Carney said, "That was seven years ago."

"You never asked for it back so I assumed you wanted me to hold on to it. Why are you looking at me like that?" Freddie grinned. "Be glad you never gave me the combination to the safe."

FIVE

Linus came up with the score in St. Augustine, far as Freddie could tell. "It wasn't like him to stick to one thing," Freddie told Carney. "He had ideas—this day that and tomorrow something else." For an "eraser key" on typewriters, and a special cap on medicine bottles to prevent them from being opened by little kids. A junkie word-of-mouth system tracked which doctors were soft touches for morphine scrips and which drugstores sold needles no questions asked—what if there were a "Yellow Pages for Dopeheads" that listed this week's shady or clueless docs and pharmacies? The schemes were far-fetched or abundantly flawed, were shared once and never mentioned again. The heist was different. "Linus kept bringing up the setup, turning it over in his head the whole drive back.

"By then we were like brothers," Freddie said. Carney took it as the insult it was intended to be, and it pleased Freddie to get under his cousin's skin. When was the last time they'd hung out like this, just the two of them? Like the old days. Now as then, it was Freddie's job to fend off the silence. Too much silence and you might get to thinking about things. Freddie the storyteller, Carney the straight man, the audience. It worked for a long time.

The front door of Carney's Furniture was locked. The blinds in the office window overlooking the showroom were shut. Carney's office was the captain's cabin in a sub: *Run Silent, Run Deep.* The world didn't know what was going on down here in the dark and those below were blind to everything topside.

This wasn't Freddie's first trip underwater. The submarine was his pet analogy for periods of exile from decent society, ever since his trip to the Tombs three years ago. The steel bunks bracketed into the gray cell walls reminded him of the crew quarters in *Voyage to the Bottom of the Sea,* albeit less vermin-filled and overcrowded. Four cots for six men. Freddie curled on the cement floor, with its soaked-in piss. Forty-eight hours in jail nearly wrecked him. Nightmares seized him still, alive with grim, half-forgotten details: roaches scrabbling into his ear like it was some insect Cotton Club; a maggot swimming in the foul, mess-hall oatmeal, twisting on his tongue.

All his life he'd heard about the Manhattan House of Detention from guys dumb enough to get caught. Freddie never understood fools who bragged about doing time—why advertise your stupidity? Then he got busted. The storytellers had undersold the wretchedness. His first trip to the chow line a guard bashed him upside the head with a blackjack. Freddie buckled and dropped to the grimy floor. Years later he woke with a ringing sometimes. Why? Freddie hadn't heard the officer call his name. He staggered with his tray and sat down to a dinner of stiff baloney on moldy bread. Two tables over, one slob bit off this other guy's earlobe for hogging ketchup. Bad meals all around.

Later, in his submarine cell, he stopped swatting the rats—rats boiled forth at night—when one of his cellmates warned him that "hittin' 'em puts them in a biting mood."

He hadn't told Carney about those two days and never would. Freddie called Linus to bail him out because he was too diminished to abide a lecture. Linus wouldn't scold him that it was his fault for eating chicken with Biz Dixon (as if Biz were the only crooked man they knew). Linus wouldn't tell him that it was Freddie's fault for mouthing off to the junk squad when they arrested Biz (as if a man could rebel against his nature and not sass a cop).

Linus bailed him out and they celebrated the remainder of Labor Day weekend by smoking reefer and drinking rum, and that worked out so well they carried the performance over another week, and another. The men had been close before the Tombs, but the arrest confirmed that they were fellow sailors on the same freakish tour of duty. Dive! Dive! Into that silty narcotic gloom. Stationed on the next submarine, Linus's apartment on Madison: the USS *Bender*.

"I'm sorry you got picked up," Carney told him. He separated two slats in the blinds and checked out 125th Street. All clear.

"Wasn't your fault," Freddie said.

The rest of that fall and winter was a mumble. Linus retained a lawyer who got the case dropped. Freddie crashed on Linus's living-room couch most days, until his lease ran out and he moved in full time. They woke, grazed around Greenwich Village and Times Square, got high, made fun of TV soap operas, put their feet up in movie houses and occasionally snorted a little something, and come nightfall ricocheted through various coffee shops and cocktail bars and basement oases, propelled by debauched momentum. Pissing against tenement walls, sleeping until noon. If Freddie got somewhere with a girl, a college girl or typist three drinks in, Linus disappeared at the right time. The next day Freddie either magically manifested on the couch when Linus padded out in his weird, archduke pajamas, or he popped up later in the afternoon, returning from his mission with a sack of doughnuts. They got along fine.

Sometimes Linus drove them out to Jersey in his Chevy Two-Ten to bet on the horses at the Garden. Linus was part owner of a thoroughbred named Hot Cup, a birthday gift from his great-uncle James, who was a scion of derby culture and thought you weren't a man unless you had a piece of a racehorse. Hot Cup's lofty pedigree notwithstanding—his father, General Tip, was a legend in championship jism circles—on the track he was an oddly distracted specimen, listless and morose. Much like his part owner, Hot Cup was well-bred, well-raised, and utterly incapable.

These ventures and others were underwritten by the Van Wyck family, who mailed checks on the second Friday of the month if Linus upheld the meager duties of his office: show up groomed and presentable for family functions and society benefits; visit the law offices of Newman, Shears & Whipple to sign where they told him to sign. *Good to see you, Mr. Van Wyck.* "The work is for the birds," Linus said, "but you can't beat the hours." He kept his nice clothes at his parents' apartment, got into his uniform for work, and slipped back into beatnik attire when he punched out.

One day Linus split for his grandma's ninety-sixth birthday and didn't come back. He rang three days later from the Bubbling Brook Sanatorium in Connecticut; his family had hijacked him when he stepped off the elevator and dispatched him for another round of psychological treatment. Zap! Periodically the Van Wycks scooped up their wayward son and carted him off to a succession of licensed facilities, an archipelago of mental recalibration centers dotting the tri-state area. Linus's first long stint was during his Princeton days. The dorm proctor caught him sucking some townie's dick or vice versa, Freddie couldn't remember which. Zap! Zap!

Freddie didn't care about Linus's proclivities. Linus knew he didn't swing that way and never tried anything. "Far as I remember," Freddie said. He shrugged. "We were loaded most of the time."

The Madison Avenue apartment was small and quiet without Linus. No one to shove the trash into the hallway chute, to laugh at his jokes when he made fun of white people on TV. Hanging with Linus reminded Freddie of the old days, when it was him and Carney running wild. Aunt Nancy had passed, Uncle Mike was who knows where, his own mother doing a double at the hospital, Pedro in Florida: That left the two boys and whole days to cram full of feverish schemes. Then Big Mike came back and took Carney home and it was over.

Before long Freddie was staring at Linus's living-room rug and tracing his missteps, recent and not so recent. The fucked-up haze of lost seasons. Those stretches of pleasurable but aimless loafing, running numbers for murderers, his brief but momentous incarceration. The Theresa job and the guns and hard men it brought into his life. The black water of his thoughts flooded the submarine compartment, he scrambled to the hatch and sealed it off . . . but then his toes went cold again and he looked down . . .

Freddie sighed and shuffled for two weeks and then accepted Linus's abduction as a sign from Jesus or God or the Big Whatever that he should make a change. He decided to clean up. He got his own place in Hell's Kitchen on Forty-Eighth Street, two floors above a chop suey joint. Linus had his sanatoriums; Freddie's version of mandatory shit-getting-together was enduring a series of square jobs. Like a chump. Or a monk performing grunt work to prove something to the empty sky. Stocking shelves in a Gristedes over on Lexington, operating the register at Black Ace Records on Sullivan, selling sneakers at a sports outlet on Fulton Street in fucking Brooklyn. Of the three, Black Ace was better for meeting girls.

"I was pulling a Ray-Ray," Freddie told his cousin. "Keeping my head down, keeping it boring." Like when Carney was in college studying and Freddie couldn't get him out of his apartment. "I got so jealous when you told me you wouldn't be coming out," Freddie said. "I was all by myself. And when you were done and graduated, you had something." What did Freddie have to show for all those nights?

He hit the books. Not schoolbooks but dime novels: *Strange Sisters, Violent Saturday, Her Name—Jezebel*. Stories where no one was saved, not the guilty (killers and crooks) and not the innocent (orphans scooped up at bus stations, librarians inducted into worlds of vice). Each time he thought things would work out for them. They never did and he forgot that lesson each time he closed the covers. So optimistic as he plucked the next one from the spinning wire racks. The novels passed the time, as did the pawnshop TV and the occasional girl in a rumpled skirt. His type? Barely beating back the darkness.

During his occasional visits, Aunt Millie complimented him on his healthy glow. "You have a girlfriend keeping you happy?" Freddie dropped in on Carney and his brood, keeping his clean living a secret as he had his crooked living. He liked it when May and John called him Uncle Freddie, like they knew his secret identity.

"I'd ask what you were up to," Carney said, "and you'd go, 'Doing my own thing.' Why didn't you say?"

"I was doing my own thing," Freddie said. "That's why they call it that."

The mission: reemerge when he had his shit together. Freddie imagined a loud gong would tell him when it was time, reverberating, shaking pigeons loose. Spook half the west side of Manhattan. He took up a pipe and on warm nights perched on the fire escape overlooking Forty-Eighth, puffing, the iron scaffold a periscope that allowed a view of the sleepy-churning Hudson while the saxophone of Ornette Coleman barked and bleated on the hi-fi, wringing the city's death rattle from its harrowed throat. In his own period of isolation, his cousin had cultivated ambitions—starting a business, settling down with a nice lady. Now that Freddie stopped and thought about it, he was at a loss: All he knew was that he didn't want to be who he had been. Climb over the windowsill, flip the record, return to the periscope. Scan the horizon.

It all ended when he ran into Linus outside Cafe Wha? and like that they signed up for another tour and the ship sank into the black water and it was as if the world had never known them.

After a month he was back on Linus's couch. By now Linus was on the needle, using every day. Freddie had a snort now and again, but he'd seen too many people gobbled up to indulge without fear. One time—they were heading uptown on the subway at two A.M.—Freddie shared stories about Miami Joe and the good times on their circuits of Harlem hotspots. He didn't mention the heist, or Arthur's murder, or Miami Joe's not-quite Viking funeral in Mount Morris Park, but he did say that Florida sounded like a righteous sort of place, the way the mobster had described it. "You've never been?" Linus asked.

To Florida? Hell, he'd never been south of Atlantic City.

The next day they were on the highway. New sub, same duties. *Four hundred meters and closing.* Freddie's submarine was anywhere he was cut off from the lives of normal people: a city jail; bouncing around in a debauched bubble with a buddy. Now it was a burgundy 1955 Chevy Two-Ten sinking through the treacherous fathoms of the Jim Crow South. *Stay off their sonar, don't make a sound.*

The trip down was fine. They stuck to big cities, where it was easier to cop if you had the eye. "Linus was like an Indian scout when it came to dope." Ran aground in St. Augustine—flat tire. "It's the oldest city in America. Some Spanish motherfuckers claimed that shit in the 1500s. It's on all the trinkets." The old dude in the garage was cool and they were fixed up in no time but it was the first sunny afternoon in a spell. They decided to flop at the Conquistador Motor Lodge and bivouac for a few days.

Linus rented the room while Freddie waited in the car, per their road-trip custom. Freddie bought some cheap trunks at the five-and-dime across the street and cannonballed into the pool. The manager's wife burst out of the office waving a bent curtain rod and told him to get his nigger ass out of there. When they went out for breakfast the next morning, the pool was as dry as a bone.

"What a disgusting little fucker!" Linus said. He wanted to call the police, or the newspapers. His family had connections with CBS in New York.

Freddie told him to wake up. Instead of leaving town they leased a furnished bungalow four blocks from the water. They were a shaggy duo by now. By way of explanation for renting to weirdos, the landlord offered that her son had run off to San Francisco. Look, the weather was better, the sky was bigger. The bartender at a Negro bar on Washington did a little peddling on the side. They decided to wait out the winter in St. Augustine.

Afternoons they passed the flyswatter back and forth and played gin rummy, nights they partook of the limited menu and always went to bed less hungry.

Freddie dimly recalled some race problem from the news last summer. It turned out St. Augustine was smack-dab in the middle of the rights movement. "If I had known," Freddie said, "I would have told Linus to keep on driving—drive on the fucking rims. These teenage kids—fourteen, fifteen years old—had a sit-in at the Woolworth's, and the judge gave them six months in reform school. Some dudes got beat up for protesting a mother-fucking Klan rally—and the deputies arrested them for getting beat up! One night we were drinking beers in this one spot and the KKK marched up the street, all brazen. I'm from New York, I've never seen that shit before. Niggers really live like that down there? KKK walking around, no big deal?" Freddie sighed. "You can't go anywhere these days without stumbling into a hotbed."

The Southern Christian Leadership Conference made their usual fuss all winter, the NAACP. On the street, those fucking crackers mistook him and Linus as part of the college-kid contingent who came down to protest, when anyone could see they were way too ragged. "Give me a break, man," Linus told the grocery clerk who ordered him off the premises. "I'm just trying to buy some mixers."

The last straw was when they heard Martin Luther King was going to visit. King, cracker cops, the KKK. "I said, Time to split,

Linus. He said no problem—his family had cut him off anyway and he had to return to New York to dance for his money." Plus the bartender at the bar got busted for statutory rape, bye-bye connection. Freddie checked the weather. New York City was warm again. "I was making time with this kindergarten teacher, she was nice, but what are you going to do—argue with Mother Nature?"

They weren't over the Georgia line before Linus brought up the setup. "I'd told him about the Theresa thing, back when," Freddie said.

"The whole thing?" Miami Joe in a rug?

"We were brothers. I told him everything." Freddie didn't apologize. "He'd ask me questions: How'd you keep track of who was on duty? What about the elevator operator? Pulling the job in his mind. Knocking over his own family, he was stuck on it. Who knows what it meant for him—he wanted to stick it to them, he wanted the money, the thrill. They owed him. And his allowance wasn't going to cover it."

"Did you see Pedro when you were down there?" Carney asked.

"It didn't occur to me."

Linus rented a pad on Park and Ninety-Ninth Street, overlooking the subway tracks. Eleven blocks up the ave from his parents but a different city. At some point he started writing stuff down. The names of doormen, which elevator man had a bladder condition, how many doors between the service gate on the street to the back stairs. Laying off the dope. "Enough to keep from getting sick," as he put it.

Freddie looked away from Carney to shove the feeling down— Linus in the tub, Linus cold and still. Carney sat back in his chair and gave him his time.

"We didn't, you know, sit outside with a stopwatch and track all the comings and goings," Freddie said, "but we were thorough. I didn't see any holes in it. Turns out it's a lot easier when you're breaking into your own house."

They sketched out the setup but put it off. Excuses: Some theater types Linus knew from college were having a rent party; they were too hungover; it looked like it might rain. "Then the kid got shot. By the cop. There were police all over, but they were worried about shit popping off uptown." The radio said they dispatched a hundred cops to the CORE demonstration at the dead boy's school and were deploying teams all over Harlem to put down any disturbance. Park Avenue and Eighty-Eighth Street was as open as it was ever going to be.

"Let's do it tonight," Linus said. It was Friday afternoon. His mother and father had a fundraiser for polio survivors and would be out until eleven P.M., easy. "They keep the liquor flowing to loosen the checkbooks." The Van Wycks' old housekeeper, Gretchen, used to live in the apartment—when Linus was little he'd slip into her gassy bed on bad-dream nights—but she passed three years prior. The new girl lived in the Bronx and left at seven P.M. The plan called for Linus to ride up with the elevator man at eight-thirty, hop down the fire stairs, prop open the alley door, and leave the service gate open a whisper.

At 8:41 P.M. on Friday, July 17, Freddie started his trip uptown. Freddie stuck out on Park Avenue for obvious reasons, so killing time leaning against a phone booth was out of the question. He sat at the counter at Soup Burg on Seventy-Third and Madison, contemplating the small orange bubbles of fat on the surface of chicken noodle soup until his watch said it was time. *The Action Watch for Active People.* On the way up he pondered the big imponderable of the day: Was Linus capable of not fucking this up? Freddie had seen the man sloppy, nodding out, observed him puke himself and shit the bed. Last summer he found Linus twitching and blue and overdosing and had to drop him off in front of Harlem Hospital—a cop stopping him at the wheel of a white man's car would have meant his ruin. Did Linus have the heart and balls to pull off a job like this? His family will know he ripped them off—was he ready to cash out? If the service gate didn't budge . . .

He took the long way up Lexington, rounded the corner, and didn't break his stride when he pushed the service gate. It was unlocked, ajar half an inch, and he was in. It was 9:01 P.M.

The Van Wyck residence was a duplex on the fourteenth and fifteenth floors. The walk up the fire stairs was a miserable hump but Linus waited at the back door. His gleeful expression reminded Freddie of other capers: when his family accidentally sent his check twice and they went out for steaks and shrimp; that time they walked by the Cha Cha Club during a delivery and snatched a box of schnapps. Tonight's take was bigger. So was Linus's smile.

The back door opened onto the kitchen. Freddie had been in these big six-room, seven-room spreads before. Above Ninety-Sixth they were cut up into three apartments, and below Ninety-Sixth they were dark warrens, dusty and rife with cat hair and books, the apartments of the parents of college chicks he picked up downtown. The Van Wyck residence was so complicated it needed two floors to tell itself and twice as many rooms. Twelve feet floor to ceiling, paneled walls, parquet floors in Masonic arrangements. Here was a floating mansion.

Noticing Freddie's reaction, Linus said, "Check this out." He pulled back a heavy, mustard-colored curtain in the dining room. "On nights like this . . ." The humidity transformed Park Avenue, the moisture in the air bestowing warm halos to the lights on the street and in the rows of apartment windows. It made the street less stuck-up. Inexplicably kind, like a white cop who cuts you slack for no reason you can figure. Park Avenue creeped Freddie out: The buildings had an attitude, a comfort in and assurance of their own power. They were judges, decreeing that all that you called your own, what you fought for and dreamed of, was merely a cheap imitation of what they possessed. Tonight the street looked kind. From that angle, anyway.

"I was thinking about how you used to talk about Riverside Drive," Freddie told Carney, "how much you love it. The edge of the island, looking out across the water, like putting it all in perspective. There's us, there's water, and then there's more land, we're all a part of the same thing. But Park Avenue, with those big old buildings facing one another, full of old white people, there's none of that feeling, right? It's a canyon. And the two sides don't give a shit about you. If they wanted, if they so decided, they could squeeze together and crush you. That's how little you are." That night, he conceded, it was gorgeous.

Linus led him through the apartment. The paintings on the walls were what they called modern art; the rest of the decor was Rich Mummy.

The safe was in the library. The books on the shelves and inside the glass cases were dignified and elegantly bound. As Linus moved around the large, walnut executive desk, Freddie got a gander at one line of volumes. A lot of *The Complete Letters of Sir Baron St. So-and-so, Vol. 6* and nary a *Jailbait Kitties* or *Murder Was Her Right* in sight.

Behind the desk hung a portrait of Robert A. Van Wyck, first mayor of the newly incorporated New York City. It was hinged. Push, click, and it swung to reveal the round door of the wall safe.

"What kind?" Carney asked.

"Fuck should I know."

Linus knew the combination. His father had let him play with the safe when he was younger and allowed him to store baseball cards. His father being Ambrose Van Wyck, the patriarch, the shadow drawing everything within the icy cape.

"Everybody says Van *Wick*," Carney said.

"That's dumb. It's Van Wyck."

Linus asked Freddie to hold open the briefcase as he scooped. "I thought there was more," he said.

Then Freddie got a load of the necklace. "I had a heart attack," Freddie told Carney. "You should see the size of the thing."

"I have."

"Oh."

At 9:31 P.M. the night of the robbery, Linus's father said, "Put that down."

Van Wyck the Elder stood in the doorway in his pajamas. The same kind as Linus's favorite pair—red with white piping, monogrammed, but less faded. His father was in his seventies, Linus being a late addition to the dynasty. Skinny, shriveled all over, above the shoulder blades downright scrotal, but he had mean blue eyes and Freddie remembered Linus's story about the time he'd said "Can I?" instead of "May I?" and Ambrose took off his loafer and slapped him across the face with it seven times.

He held a glass of milk. Ambrose Van Wyck kept his beechwood walking stick one story below in the foyer umbrella stand. He didn't use it in the house, which was unfortunate because he dearly wanted to poke his son in the chest with it, to punctuate each syllable of the diatribe rising in himself. The sight of his son used to cause him pain—wincingly so—but that had been years before. He was at peace with his son's failure now. Gnaw on a disappointment long enough and it will lose all flavor. Linus would never occupy Ambrose's corner office on the twenty-fourth floor, sit for a conference-room portrait to hang next to those of his ancestors. Ambrose's partners' sons—that cohort of Aryan dipshittery—were in place to steer VWR into the future and with Ambrose's death the firm would cease to be a Van Wyck concern. So be it. The man-child before him was a technicality; Ambrose Van Wyck regarded the structures as his true offspring. The skyscraping pillars, bustling office hives, global HQs, mixed-use complexes blocks wide and so full of families that they were villages unto themselves. When Ambrose looked out of the dining-room window onto Park Avenue and beyond, he recognized his own features in the white brick apartment houses and silver deco steeples, found his face returned to him in the pitiless steel and concrete of the city. The birthmark of the clan was a brass plate bolted by the lobby entrance, affirming paternity: VWR. This man before him? A stranger he might come across on the subway. If he took the subway. Which he didn't. It was a filthy cage for filthy people.

As for his son's companion . . . Ambrose had lived in this apartment his whole life and in all his seventy-five years, as far as he knew, this was the first time a nigger had set foot in it.

"You're here," Linus said.

"When I heard we were sitting with the Laphams, I was staying home, of course."

This was some blueblood vendetta shit, Linus explained later. His mother had had an affair with the husband, or his father had had an affair with the wife, perhaps both things had occurred simultaneously or one had happened later in retribution, and his father was still sore over how it'd shaken out.

"I thought I heard something," Ambrose Van Wyck said. "I should have guessed. I'm too tired to deal with your foolishness right now. Put that back and wait in your room until your mother gets home."

Linus hesitated, then closed the safe. "We're leaving," he said.

There are things a parent can utter to a child that should not be heard by others. Verdicts and spiky assessments, pettiness masquerading as principle and magnified by time, grudges that have taken root in the bones. A witness can render these things indelible and real in a way that they wouldn't be if there were no one else around. No, it's best not to hear your grown friend talked to the way Ambrose Van Wyck addressed his son. The humiliation splashes everywhere. You'll get it on you and it'll become your own bad time, the bloody resurrection of your own childhood sadnesses. In two minutes, Freddie was five years old again, back on 129th Street, cowering under the kitchen table as his father enumerated his mother's shortcomings with sadistic flair.

A specific reference compelled Linus to lunge, putting an end to Ambrose Van Wyck's harangue: "It's like that day on Heart's Meadow all over again." The glass of milk fell to the carpet. It would not be accurate to say that the two men fought or wrestled. "More like they gripped each other's upper arms and shook." Linus held back so as not to hurt the old man, and the old man despite his fury was too old to give the conflict much gas. It was a low-key battle, a mutual trembling. Freddie crept past them into the hallway. In a limp rush, Linus overcame his reticence, pushed, and the old man tumbled into a large, red leather club chair, panting.

At 9:41 P.M., Linus and Freddie ran down the back stairs.

At no point did Ambrose Van Wyck acknowledge Freddie's presence.

The riots hadn't started yet but the night was full of sirens. A scuffle on a subway platform, kids running wild in a cafeteria: the preface to the next night's unrest. In the original plan, Linus's family wouldn't know of the theft until the next day at the earliest. They wouldn't immediately tie it to their rascal son, so the thinking went. Now the head start was gone.

They packed up some clothes at the Ninety-Ninth Street apartment. "Where to?" Linus asked.

Freddie thought of the Eagleton first thing. Miami Joe had asked him to pick up a gun from one of the residents once, for a job. He didn't tell Freddie what it was, but its heft in the brown paper bag made an announcement. Freddie shook all the way down the stairs—and out on the street. The Imperial was right there. "We used to hang there every day," Freddie said.

"The rats," Carney said.

"Loving that popcorn."

The association with the old movie palace made the SRO stick in Freddie's head. It was a natural place to lam it. Freddie got the bed. Linus slept on the floor, with the briefcase and his wadded-up robe for a pillow. When Freddie woke the next morning, Linus was gone, with the briefcase. Had he gone to score? Back to his family to beg forgiveness? Either way Freddie was too jazzed to stay inside. *The Unsinkable Molly Brown* was the first ad he saw in the movie section on the way downtown. Plus it had Debbie Reynolds. Freddie had already told Carney the rest—Saturday night, the first night of the riots.

Back at the Eagleton, Linus was on the nod, leaning against the wall, sitting on the briefcase so that he'd wake if anyone tried to grab it. In the run-up to the robbery, Linus had talked of his grandmother's diamond necklaces, gem-encrusted bracelets, a box full of gold coins, a variety of pirate treasure that had passed through the safe. The only notable item they'd walked away with was the emerald necklace, and between the cops, the crazies, the protest days, unloading it was unworkable. The emerald was too big for the fences Freddie knew, Abe Evans and the Arab. "I wasn't going to bring you in, don't worry."

They had to lie low until the heat was off. And 171st and above felt safe—from rioting Negroes with pitchforks, cops, and "my father's men," which Linus had never mentioned before. Private detectives? Ex-army guys? "They do work for him, make sure things get done." After a brief scout, Freddie and Linus found an Irish bar on 176th that catered to marginal clientele, and a Greek diner with decent grub and broken tabletop jukeboxes. They made forays.

Monday afternoon, Freddie had an itch at the back of his mind and called Janice, their next-door neighbor on Ninety-Ninth. She was relieved to hear from him—Linus's apartment had been broken into and robbed. The subway roared in the earpiece as it passed outside Janice's place, like suspense music—crazy violins—in an action picture. The super had called the cops after discovering their front door hanging on one hinge. Freddie told her they were behind on their installment payments to the Britannica company, they play for keeps.

The submarine's hull failed beneath the tons of pressure.

Seawater geysered from joints, the depth gauges cracked and died, the whole vessel lit by a sickly red light: going down. The break-in freaked out Linus, still panting from the robbery and the fight with his father. They needed a safe place to stash the briefcase, he said, and had already chosen where: Carney's. "Hell no," Freddie said. "I wasn't going to get you involved, but he said it was the best play." He smiled reluctantly. "He liked you. Whenever I complained about some shit you said to me, or some fight we had back in the day, he'd say you were only looking out for me. And that he wished he had someone like that."

Freddie got choked up and went into the bathroom. Carney checked out the showroom again. No one had seen Freddie enter the store. Or they had seen him, had called for reinforcements, and were waiting to break in or to snatch Freddie when he walked out.

Freddie returned. Handing off the briefcase to Carney improved their moods. Even with Washington Heights as a boundary, their Saturday night was something out of the old days, like when Linus sprang Freddie from the Tombs. They hit each place when it started taking off and left before it got dead, and found like-minded hedonists and lushes at every stop. "It wasn't a full-moon night, but it was like we were the full moon, making everybody act crazy."

"First big night after the protests," Carney said. "People were ready to cut loose."

"You got to ruin that, too?"

Freddie went out to the Greek place for breakfast Sunday morning and gave himself permission to sit and enjoy the paper like a normal citizen. "Fooling myself." Gone long enough for Linus to OD. "He'd been laying off while planning the job, like I said, but once we got uptown, he was back with gusto." Freddie was hitting the booze so he didn't feel he had a right to say anything.

"Do you think it was an accident?"

"Fuck you."

"I didn't mean he did it on purpose," Carney said, "but was someone else in the room when you were out." He told Freddie about Aunt Millie's apartment getting tossed, and the homicide cops who came around the store, getting orders from above. "You stirred somebody up."

"No one would do that to Linus." They sat with the implications. "I don't know what to do," Freddie said.

"You have to split. It'll take money."

Freddie nodded to the safe. "It'll take that." The emerald.

"I got it," Carney said.

He needed help, however. He needed Pepper.

SIX

Pepper folded his newspaper flat when Carney appeared in Donegal's doorway. He nodded at the bartender, who shambled to the other end of the bar, by the street. The bartender wore a sleeveless undershirt gone yellow. It exposed his massive arms and the bawdy Betty Boop tattoo that started on one bicep and continued on the other. Labeled BEFORE and AFTER below his elbows.

Carney gestured to the stool. Pepper granted his permission. He hadn't changed his uniform; the faded dungarees might have been the same pair he wore the first time they met, after the Theresa, a dark speck of Miami Joe's blood on the hem.

"Buford thought you were serving papers," Pepper said. "Policy is, officers of the court get the bat he keeps under there, in case."

"You look the same," Carney said.

"You got some more legwork for cops you need done?"

"I didn't see it that way."

"No other way to see it."

Carney was about to say that he'd been doing the community a service by yanking a weed like Wilfred Duke, but three years on he was comfortable with the fact it had been revenge. "I didn't think of the larger picture when it came to you, that is correct."

Pepper cracked his neck. "It was nice to see all

those upstanding Negroes get theirs, I have to admit. That dude really run off with all their money?"

"They say he's in Barbados. Has some family down there."

"Bajan niggers will rip you off in a New York minute," Pepper said.

Outside, Donegal's green neon sign had given Carney a twinge. Now that he was inside he was sure he'd been there many years before. The grotesque, disembodied grin floating on the GOOD BEER WITH GOOD FRIENDS sign. The dusty jar of hard-boiled eggs that contained the same hard-boiled eggs from decades before. Pepper had been one of his father's running partners so it made sense. Carney had carried this fantasy idea of Donegal's from Pepper's talk of the place, when he'd already seen it. He'd envisioned gunsels in zoot suits, block-browed experts in blunt force trauma, but the Wednesday-afternoon crowd looked like the bickering geezers who played chess in parks, trading pawns and grievances. Although in Donegal's they drank from mugs instead of flasks.

Carney had been a child—had his father left him there while he conducted some business? *Watch my kid while I break this guy's legs?* Perched on a stool, his head barely clearing the cloudy varnish of the bar. Very young, if his father hadn't left him in the apartment. Where was his mother? Anyone who could clarify things was dead.

"You used to come here with my father," Carney said.

"Plenty. This was where—" Pepper cut off the anecdote. His smiles were rare and he terminated this smile precisely. "The bartender in those days was a crook," he said, "like us. So if we finished a job late he'd open up and celebrate. Dawn coming in through the windows there. Newspaper trucks rumbling. That was Ishmael, before he got shot. He's been dead, I don't know, ten years?" His expression soured. "What do you want? Trying to sell me a couch?"

Carney didn't make the same mistake he made last time. He

gave Pepper the rundown, from Freddie's friendship with Linus and his rich family, to the interrupted robbery and everything that happened after it. The crook knew about the Theresa, the Duke job—no one else had as much dope on Carney's other life. No reason not to come clean.

Carney finished. Pepper scratched his neck, looked at the ceiling thoughtfully. He said, "Like the expressway."

"A lot of people think it's *Wick*."

Pepper shrugged. A gun battle broke out on the afternoon movie, a Lee Marvin picture, and everyone in the bar stopped talking to check out the TV. For tips? To critique? The getaway car sped off and Donegal's patrons returned to their affairs. "Using the riots," Pepper said. "If I had something cooking, I would have done the same thing. Everybody running around like chickens with their heads cut off, you can pull a job."

"People weren't acting crazy over nothing. They had good reason," Carney said.

"Since when do white people care about reason? They gonna put that cop in jail?"

The bartender looked up from his racing form. "Put a white cop in jail for killing a black boy? Believe in the fucking tooth fairy."

"Buford knows what's up," Pepper said.

"Newspapers talking about 'looting,'" Buford continued. "Should ask the Indians about looting. This whole country's founded on taking other people's shit."

"How'd they fill their museums? Tutankhamun."

"Right? I'm glad they stood up," Buford said. "I'm saying a week later it's like it never happened." He decamped to the other end of the bar again and relit his cigar.

Like it never happened? This struck Carney as pure cynicism. For instance, after the riot of '43, the pants his father had looted from Nelson's had lasted two years before the knees gave out. That was something.

They saw things differently, him and Pepper, but Carney had come to Donegal's—risking a punch in the face—because the man had another angle on how the world worked. Which is what Carney required at the moment. Five years after the Theresa, another necklace had brought them together, one that made Lucinda Cole's look like it rolled out of a gumball machine. "I'd like to hire you for security," Carney said. "In case anyone else comes knocking."

"Sounds like someone might, one or another," Pepper said. "Look, you don't want my advice. You're not an advice-taker and I don't give a shit. But—cut him loose. He's a loser. It's already done."

"It's not done. He's splitting."

"Trouble'll find him again. Your father would say, fuck him. Even if he is family. Even if it was you."

"That's why," Carney said.

Pepper grimaced and gestured for another beer. "What are you going to do with the loot? The shit from the safe—who are you going to lay it off on?"

"I have a guy who can handle it."

"Deals with that heavy shit." Pepper sipped his Rheingold. "If he deals with that heavy shit, he covers his ass. What if covering his ass means hanging niggers out to dry?"

"He's solid."

"Nothing solid in the city but the bedrock."

He took the questions to mean that Pepper was in. Pepper did not disabuse him of that assumption.

Carney mentioned a figure. Pepper said he had a mind for something from the store.

"Whatever you need. What's your current home situation?"

"Situation?"

"With regards to furniture—eat-in kitchen? Do you have a separate place for dining?" Carney knew not to say, *How often do you entertain?*

"Do I look like I want people knowing what my house is like?"

"A couch, then."

"That flips back when you put your feet up, with a lever."

"A recliner."

"That's it—a recliner." They did a deal for the security and miscellaneous manhandling.

Carney laid down some bucks on the bar for Pepper's beer and stood to go.

Pepper said, "He used to say that you were going to be a doctor, you were so smart, but that you were smart enough to know you make more money being crooked."

"Who'd want to be a doctor?" Carney said.

* * *

The shade outside their apartment, down the hill from Grant's Tomb, provided a cool retreat from the day's heat. Traffic was light on Riverside. When Carney tried to relax in his living room after a long day at the store, the squeal of the kids in the park below usually set him on edge, but today they were a token of normalcy. Gangsters strong-arming him into sedans, white cops disrupting his business, riots and real estate barons and what have you—it was nice to pretend his world remembered the old, stable orbit.

Then Pepper said, "I'm here," and Carney's planet went awobble again. He handed Pepper the keys to the furniture store, as they had arranged. Ever since the Donegal's meeting earlier that afternoon, the image of Pepper sitting at his desk on watch duty had made him chuckle. *You'll take the matching ottoman and fucking like it.*

"You got your boy on ice somewhere?" Pepper asked.

"Out in Brooklyn," Carney said. Freddie's new hidey-hole was a rattrap off Nostrand.

"I don't want him underfoot."

Neither did Carney. Would Freddie appreciate his efforts when

Carney packed him into the train, or bus, with all that get-out-of-town money? Before the bus pulled out of Port Authority—maybe the Newark Greyhound depot was a better bet—and Freddie disappeared Out West, would he give a proper thanks, or see it as something owed him?

The goddamned park squirrels had been brazen all summer—that was a whole nother story—so that's what Carney thought the pressure on his leg was, a squirrel. "Daddy!" John said, wrapping his arms around his thighs. From the dirt on their clothes and the scrape on John's knee, it looked like Elizabeth had taken them on a playground excursion.

Carney introduced Pepper as a friend of his father—a mistake, as Elizabeth invited him to join them for dinner. She insisted when Carney made an excuse. "We have plenty." She was disappointed the leftover pot roast (often dry, per statistics) usually went unconsumed by her family and welcomed help in polishing it off.

Pepper didn't put up the fight that Carney expected—a residue of politeness or curiosity—and that was that. The crook extended formal handshakes to May and John, like they were bank managers reviewing his loan application.

The smell of the cooking meat filled the hallway outside the elevator. "Damn," Pepper said, in pleasure, and he did not apologize for the blaspheming in front of little children because it did not occur to him. Pepper didn't speak as Carney showed him around the apartment, until they reached the living room and he gave his verdict: "Nice setup." He registered the rooms' dimensions and checked out the angles from the window as if appraising the defensive and offensive possibilities of a hideout. Elizabeth went to get the pot roast out of the oven.

The children, as they often did before dinner, lazed on the rug with their comics and toys, occasionally sharing with the grown-ups an urgent non sequitur. Carney normally leaned back in his spot on the Argent sofa but he didn't want to appear too casual

in front of their guest, who might judge his middle-class indul-
gences. Pepper took his time before he finally sat in the armchair. He crossed his arms.

For the most part, the men sat in silence. At one point, John
brought over his souvenir program to show it off and Pepper
said, "World's Fair—what will whitey think of next?"

Elizabeth told May to get the good napkins and they sat down
to eat. She had cooked the roast with potatoes and carrots and
made cornbread earlier in the day. Elizabeth nodded in approval
as Pepper helped himself to a healthy serving. Carney brought
two cans of Schlitz to the table.

"How did you know Raymond's father?" Elizabeth asked.

"He knew Grandpa?" May said. Having experienced the one,
she was curious about the other.

"From work," Pepper said.

"Oh," Elizabeth said.

"Not that," Carney said, before the broken kneecaps grew too
vivid. "Remember I told you my father used to work at Miracle
Garage sometimes."

"The garage," Elizabeth said.

"I wouldn't work with Pat Baker," Pepper said. "More crooked
than a country preacher."

Elizabeth squinted at Carney but let it drop. "What sort of
work do you do now?"

Pepper looked at Carney. Not for a tip on how to respond but
to communicate that his rate had gone up. Carney might have to
throw in a side table, to hold a beer or a bowl of grapes. Pepper
said, "Odd jobs."

"Can you pass the potatoes?" Carney said. "Just how I like
them."

Despite the slow start, Elizabeth got more out of Pepper than
Carney ever had. Where he lived now (off Convent), where he
grew up (Hillside Avenue in Newark), if he had a lady he liked
to take out on the town (not since he got stabbed in the gut,

mistaken identity, long story). John moved over to sit on May's lap and asked their guest his favorite color. He said, "I like that shiny green that parks get around here in the spring."

To Elizabeth, he was another colorful character from Carney's Harlem, a place not entirely congruent with her Strivers' Row version. Pepper was one of the stranger walk-ons she had encountered, but she tended to enjoy that variety more.

Elizabeth put her elbows on the table and laced her fingers. "What was Raymond like?" she asked. "When he was little?"

"Much the same. Smaller."

"Whenever Pepper came over," Carney said, "he always brought me something—a stuffed animal, a wooden caboose. It was very sweet."

John cackled at this, picking up on the absurdity, then the rest of them. Pepper's downturned mouth straightened into a tight line, his version of amusement.

Elizabeth said that the phones at the office had started ringing again. Business with out-of-town clients had remained the same, but the New York City calls went to zero the week of the protests. "No one wants to go on vacation when the house next door is on fire," she said.

Carney told Pepper that Elizabeth worked for Black Star Travel, which they then had to explain, as Pepper was "not one to vacation much."

On the one hand, it was everyday word of mouth, what people shared in the neighborhood for mutual survival. *That cop Rooker who hangs out on Sixth is out to get black people. Don't show your face on the Italian block after seven o'clock. They'll snatch your house for a late payment.* But Black Star and other travel agencies, the various Negro travel guides, took that crucial local information and rendered it national and accessible to all who needed it. On the wall at Elizabeth's office they had a map of the United States and the Caribbean with pins and red marker to indicate the cities and towns and routes that Black Star promoted. Stay on the path and you'll be safe, eat in peace, sleep in peace, breathe in peace; stray and beware. Work together and we can subvert their evil order. It was a map of the black nation inside the white world, part of the bigger thing but its own self, independent, with its own constitution. If we didn't help one another we'd be lost out there.

That was how Carney put it to himself, as his wife gave Pepper her standard client pitch. Pepper took in Elizabeth's spiel patiently. He chewed, savoring, squeezed in between John and May like an eccentric uncle. He was a relative, this crook, part of his father's clan. Carney raised his Schlitz and made a toast to the chef. It was Wednesday night, family supper, both sides of him at the table, the straight and the crooked, breaking bread.

SEVEN

She grabbed his arm and startled him—Sandra from Chock Full o'Nuts. He was headed for the subway, downtown to Moskowitz's. The emerald in his leather satchel made him suspect everybody on the street had X-ray vision. On the lookout for a gunman or an anvil-chinned heavy with a five-o'clock shadow, he didn't catch the waitress's approach.

Outside of the coffee shop, Sandra was just as chatty and vivacious. She asked after his family; he had shown her pictures over the years, courtesy of his Polaroid Pathfinder. Sandra told him she'd made it through "all that drama last week okay." Some roughneck had lobbed a brick through the Seventh Avenue window of the restaurant so they boarded up the place until the protests subsided. They were back in business now. "People need their coffee," she said.

Carney apologized for being too busy to come by. She touched his arm again and said they weren't going anywhere.

A few minutes later he was on the subway, humming the shop's theme song: *Better coffee a millionaire's money can't buy* . . . What can a millionaire's money buy: everything else. Cops and city hall and faceless thugs to do your bidding. Carney recalled the fear of those days after the Theresa job, the fear that Arthur's killer might come for him, his family. Now Freddie and Linus had unleashed trouble of another magnitude, pissed-off rich people who were as bent as gangsters but didn't have to hide. They did it out in the open, notarized their misdeeds or engraved them into bronze plates for building facades.

Sure, when this was over he'd return to Chock Full o'Nuts for a nice, solid cup of coffee, but he had to get this racket going first. Pepper had signed up, so Carney was spared the tricky business of hitting up one of his customers on the fencing side to see if they had a name. He was not impressed with Harlem's thugs overall. Whether you were talking construction, poetry, or women's pumps, the Walt Whitmans, the Peppers, of a given field were hard to come by. It was no different in the violence-and-mayhem trade; the majority of practitioners were average or subpar. Carney was grateful Pepper had forgiven him, even if he suspected it was only out of an old obligation to his father, ancient blood-oath shit.

After their initial discussion of the job, Pepper hadn't tried to talk him out of helping Freddie. Carney had enough doubts with outside encouragement. The debacle of Bella Fontaine and Mr. Gibbs aside, Freddie had brought danger close again. When they were children, when he'd brought down parental wrath and they sat in the bedroom waiting for the belt, Freddie would croak out a pitiable, "I didn't mean to get you in trouble." It never occurred to him that things would go wrong, that the caper would go sideways and there would be consequences. There were always consequences.

Carney didn't have to do it anymore. Freddie was a grown man. What to call this operation: the Freddie job, the Van Wyck job? Maybe it was the Carney job, because he wanted to prove that he could move a big rock like that, stick it to the rich bastards again. Rich white bastards this time. This wasn't a broken radio some strung-out loser had grabbed from a widow's apartment. This necklace was mythic, a piece out of legend.

He scored a seat on the train. Carney pulled out the flyer and unfolded it—he'd rediscovered it in his wallet when he bought tokens. Last week in the middle of the protests, this young woman, college kid, had stopped him as he surveyed 125th Street. It was Monday morning and Carney was getting his first real look at the weekend carnage. She wore white slacks with a green-and-white-striped top. Given the uneasy mood on the street, her cheer and purpose were a declaration of principles. She grabbed his wrist and tucked a leaflet in his hand:

> INSTRUCTIONS:
> ANY EMPTY BOTTLE
> FILL WITH GASOLINE
> USE RAG AS WICK
> LIGHT RAG
>
> TOSS
> AND
> SEE THEM RUN!

When he looked up she had vanished. Who'd print such a thing? It was dangerous, the product of a demented mind. Back at the office he folded the flyer and tucked it away. He wasn't sure why.

The white lady next to him on the subway read it over his shoulder. She frowned. That's why you shouldn't read over people's shoulders. He returned the paper to his wallet. No harm in keeping it. As a talisman or a crooked hymn kept close for reference.

Back to the setup: Freddie was lamming it in Brooklyn, Pepper minded the store in case anyone showed up. Next up was Moskowitz. Did the man have enough cash in that Hermann Bros. safe of his or did Carney have to wait a few days? He had kept it cryptic on the phone; that plus the uncustomary afternoon meeting would warn the jeweler that it was serious.

In midtown there was no indication that New York City had

been besieged one week prior. The black city and the white city: overlapping, ignorant of each other, separate and connected by tracks.

Moskowitz's was busy—Carney passed four customers as he went up the stairs. Ari, the nephew who sat next to Carney during his lessons, nodded hello and excused himself from the young couple gawking at the diamond necklaces. There was another man by the Ventura display buying something for his mistress. One of Moskowitz's more engaged lessons had dissected the differences in posture when a customer was buying something for a wife versus a mistress, and how to adjust one's sales pitch. Ari rapped on the office door and stuck his head in, then waved in Carney.

Moskowitz stood at the window, taking in the manic boil of Forty-Seventh Street. Two fans were trained on his executive chair, they swiveled to and fro and nudged the hot air. The jeweler let down the blinds and greeted Carney with his usual reserve.

"It's a lot this time," Carney said.

"I gathered," Moskowitz said. "Your uptown associates getting ambitious?"

Carney didn't like the tone. He opened the satchel and set the Van Wyck necklace on Moskowitz's desk blotter next to the overflowing ashtray.

The jeweler withdrew. "Put it away," Moskowitz said.

"What?"

"I had to see it, but I don't want to look at it. You know why."

Carney returned the necklace to the leather satchel.

"It's too hot," Moskowitz said. "People are inquiring. You must know that. I couldn't move that five feet."

"You had a visit?"

"Anybody who can move that knows not to touch it. Toss it in the East River and don't look back. I'd say return it and ask forgiveness, but I don't think it would be forthcoming."

You might say it wasn't a rosy picture. "That's it?" Carney said. "It's best you don't come back."

Ari waved goodbye as Carney departed. Carney didn't notice.

It had gotten hotter outside. Carney wiped his neck with his handkerchief in the middle of the sidewalk stream. You can have all sorts of craziness in your head and people will walk right by you as if you are a normal person. Moskowitz. He'd been threatened. Had someone linked the two of them or had they come at him because he handled heavy weight?

At the corner of Seventh Ave, Carney heard his name. The intonation was that of a dispassionate clerk, engaged but too overworked to offer more than the perfunctory. "If you have a minute, Mr. Carney."

The man was tall and thin, with sharp features—Carney thought of museum statues cut from cold white stone. Hermes, the God of Speed. Or was it Mercury? May had brought home a book on Roman gods from the library. This guy looked like he relaxed at home with a chalice and one of those laurel-wreath crowns around his head.

He shook Carney's hand as if they'd been doing business for years. "The name's Bench—Ed Bench. I'm with the law firm of Newman, Shears & Whipple." He gave Carney his card. Heavy stock, dignified typeface.

Carney said he didn't understand.

"I represent the Van Wyck family." He tilted his head. "I'm here with Mr. Lloyd."

Presenting Mr. Lloyd, the muscle, neck and head a solid column atop his barrel chest. Carney doubted he'd taken the bar exam. The man's right hand was in his jacket pocket, pointing a revolver at Carney. He wore a fake, dumb smile to camouflage him as one of the tourists gee-whizzing at the Big City.

"Let's walk, Carney," Ed Bench said. Carney looked back at Mr. Lloyd, who kept pace, gun at an angle, same smile. Carney's heart pounded and the street noise—the honking and backfiring and cussing—doubled in volume, as if by radio knob.

"How's your cousin, Carney?" Ed Bench said.

"I haven't seen him."

"That's unlikely. We hear you're like brothers. Do anything for each other. Can I have that, please?"

Mr. Lloyd coughed for emphasis. Carney handed over his satchel.

Ed Bench performed a quick look-see for confirmation. He said, "The rest?"

"That's it. If somebody's saying something else, they're wrong."

"The other items. I'm referring to the other items."

The DONT WALK sign at the corner of Forty-Ninth and Seventh kept them put. Carney tried to get a handle on what was happening. Had they followed him from uptown? Straphanging two feet away while he dreamed of wheeling and dealing? This Van Wyck lawyer—the one who handled their dirty stuff, he supposed—was more concerned with the other things Linus had swiped from the family safe. Carney had been so distracted by the fact of the emerald he hadn't gone over the papers thoroughly.

"I don't have them."

"Carney," Ed Bench said.

Mr. Lloyd jabbed the nose of the pistol into Carney's back.

Ed Bench made a gesture and Mr. Lloyd backed off. The lawyer led them to the opposite corner. "A hundred years ago," he said, "this was a cow pasture—all of this. Midtown. Times Square. Then someone had an idea, and built, and bought more land, and built. Some things pan out. Some things don't. The Van Wycks didn't build here on Seventh Avenue. They built there." He pointed toward Sixth. "The one on the east corner. If this was a cow pasture, that was a mud puddle. Now look at it. You don't have to be first. Second is fine. If you have an eye for what's going to pan out, second is fine."

Carney spied a patrolman across the street, drinking a Coca-Cola through a straw with bovine serenity. For a moment, he entertained the ridiculous proposition of a Negro calling a cop to complain he was being threatened by two white men.

Ed Bench saw the policeman give a sympathetic frown at Carney's plight. "You're a smart man, Carney. An entrepreneur. I wonder if you've recognized your current venture isn't going to pan out." The lawyer showed his teeth. "Have you considered what will happen? To you? Your family?"

Moskowitz had tipped off the Van Wycks and sold Carney down the river. They visit the jeweler's store, brace him, and tell him to give a heads-up if the necklace appears. Because whoever has that emerald has the briefcase and the rest of its contents.

Back when Buxbaum got pinched, Carney and Moskowitz had sweated over whether or not he'd squeal. Buxbaum, weak sister or no, had kept his trap shut. He was still up at Dannemora, doing time. Moskowitz, the old gentleman, the professor, was the one who ratted him out in the end.

Fuck this.

Ed Bench said, "Hey!"

Johnny Dandy starring Blake Headley and Patricia De Hammond had been running on Broadway at the Divinity Theater since Memorial Day weekend. Critics had meted their blows and yet. The dialogue and action were so shrouded in euphemism, so opaque in meaning and intention, alternately dull and worrisome, that no one could decide what the play was about, if they understood it, let alone enjoyed it. Was this tragedy or farce? Such a faithful reflection of existence proved irresistible. Every night a pantomime of modern life unfurled before a sold-out house. *Dandy*'s run was cut short when Blake Headley slipped a disk; his understudy's inert line readings broke the spell. The play was never produced again, save for an avant-garde attempt in Buenos Aires that closed during the first intermission (arson). Its author moved to Los Angeles and made a name in

TV Westerns. Every afternoon the matinee ended at 3:42 P.M., ejecting hundreds of distracted theater mavens into an already congested Forty-Ninth Street.

South Ferry 306, which claimed as its domain fourteen miles of the IRT line between South Ferry and Van Cortlandt–242nd Street, was scheduled to pull into the Fiftieth Street station at 3:36 P.M. but was delayed after a signalman reported a figure shambling among the tracks at Herald Square. Subsequent investigation determined the shape in question to be an addled raccoon. It happened sometimes, a wrong turn. The train screeched into Fiftieth Street at 3:45 P.M., nine minutes behind schedule. The station's Forty-Ninth Street exit was convenient and popular. A train car collects specimens, the station releases them from captivity. Men and women stepped from the cars, bumped turnstiles, and mounted stairs to feed the maddening flux of Broadway.

Carney ran, availing himself of this confluence. He ran as if Freddie had stolen a comic book from Mason's display racks and Old Man Mason himself pursued them down Lenox with a machete, he ran as if he and his cousin had dropped a fist-ful of firecrackers into the aluminum garbage cans outside 134 West 129th and rattled the whole street. He ran like a kid con-vinced that the whole grown-up world with its entire grown-up might was going to beat him silly. There were people and cars. He danced and darted and zipped through, weaving around frumpy salesmen and limping matrons, threading himself between slow-walking rubes and briskly moving sophisticates as if he were a piece of celluloid navigating the rollers of a gigantic movie projector, lost footage from a B movie.

He shook Ed Bench and Mr. Lloyd after two blocks—not the God of Speed after all—and kept going another ten, although not as fast, trotting some, for he was out of shape. They'd finished construction on another segment of Lincoln Center and the south entrance of the Sixty-Sixth Street stop was open again.

The necklace was gone, like that. Yes, you can have all sorts of craziness in your head and people will sit right next to you on the train as if you are a normal person. He felt safe on the train, all the way up, until he got to the store and saw Pepper.

* * *

Pepper hadn't been himself lately. It probably had something to do with getting stabbed in the stomach on the Benton's rip-off. The job had started fine. A routine hijacking, trailer full of overcoats, sleepy Sunday night. Dootsie Bell brought him in on it. In former times, Dootsie Bell had been an ace stickup man. Prompt, with a bogeyman voice that kept the squares in check. Then he went on the needle and the only cure that took was the Bible. Sure, a little Jesus is good for some individuals but you don't want *Do unto others* riding shotgun on a job. Dootsie had assured Pepper the driver was tied up tight. The blade got him deep.

A week in the hospital on this dopey ward. Chumps rotated in and out. The day after he returned to the apartment on 144th, the boiler quit. The landlord gave him excuses for weeks until Pepper gave him an or-else. Hard weeks, the kind where you realize you've engineered it so that nobody has anything on you, and that means nobody has anything for you: help, a kind word. He had plenty of time to think about that and decided he wouldn't change a thing about how he'd lived his life, but going forward a man was allowed to make changes if he saw fit.

His gut bothered him worse than he'd admit. He couldn't work. The first job that came his way was a payroll rip-off, a glass factory in New Brunswick. Working with Cal James—his girl's cousin worked there and had the inside dope. Half an hour into casing the place for security patterns, his stomach started twisting and he passed out in the car. Somehow he got back into the city and had to spend a week in bed. Sorry, Cal. He didn't sign up for anything after that. A voice kept saying, *Are you sure you want to do that?* His commonsense voice that had saved his hide many times. It was out of his hands.

He spent a lot of time at Donegal's. Used to be he walked in and there were men he liked, or at least had worked with—they had something in common. These days he didn't know where everybody'd gone. Jail, the graveyard, sure, but besides that. There were no pension plans for retired safecrackers, for heisters and hustlers. Looking around Donegal's, he realized everyone in the bar was a washed-up crook—too old to play the game anymore, brains scrambled after ten years in the joint, or so luckless that no one would work with them. Those guys, plus him. Which is why he was glad that afternoon when Carney walked in. Sometimes Big Mike's face lurked in his son's face, in the eyes and the frown, and his friend was returned to him.

They were in Donegal's one night, him and Big Mike, and Pepper was sharing some thoughts about the nature of the universe. Big Mike said, "You know what your problem is?"

Pepper said, No, please tell me.

Big Mike said, "You don't like anybody."

Pepper told him, I like plenty of folks, I just don't like people. He liked Big Mike. Any resemblance between father and son was dispelled pretty damn quick when the furniture salesman opened his trap, but it was nice to see that glimmer. However briefly. Pepper'd work for the man, if he wasn't going to take his advice and cut his loser cousin loose. Pepper's convalescence had confirmed the void in his life. A recliner would fill it handily.

He was on the clock as soon as he hit 125th Street. Pepper rolled up the store's grate and flipped the keys in his hand after the one for the front door. Behind him, a reedy voice asked, "Why's he got his store closed all day?"

It was not a customer. The sunglasses and hepcat demeanor fit Carney's description of Chet the Vet, one of Chink Montague's thugs. Pepper ignored him and unlocked the front door.

"You igging me? I'm talking to you."

Pepper faced the man, with the resignation of a man discovering his toilet is still busted after the plumber had left.

"Who are you?" said Chet the Vet.

"I'm the night man."

"I'm looking for your boss."

"I'm here."

Chet the Vet squinted into the gloom of the store. He took stock of Pepper. The man's attitude bewildered him. "I'll come back," he said.

"Store ain't going nowhere."

Chet the Vet took off. He glanced back twice, and twice turned away quickly from Pepper's glare.

Guard duty commenced with an egg salad sandwich and a milkshake from Lionel's on Broadway. Wednesday night was quiet, allowing him to contemplate the relative merits of the Argent recliner and its advertised smooth hydraulic action. A fine piece of furniture overall, he decided, although he preferred upholstery with a little more texture.

The Argent was a bite of the forbidden apple. The next day he took advantage of watch duty to peruse some of the man's promotional material. Get a sense of what was out there, recliner-wise. His sentry station was Carney's office, with the lights out. He had the blinds open a fraction, allowing him to see into the showroom and out to the street, but not the other way around. He held the catalogs up to his face in the dimness. Locking wheels, stainproof, lever action. There was one newfangled model had a built-in TV tray that flipped up over your lap, which he reckoned might come in handy if he ever got a TV set.

Had it been three years since he stopped using this place as an answering service? The furniture looked different—changing with the popular tastes—but Carney had kept the place up and running. He'd done a good job. His father would be proud, even if it was a straight job. Like his father in one way, and not like him in another. Which is why he didn't hold a grudge for the thing with Duke and the drug peddler and the cops. Big Mike had never been able to resist some payback, and he'd passed that down.

He stretched. There was something in the back pocket of his overalls. One of the activist leaflets they were handing out last week on 125th:

COOL IT BABY

THE MESSAGE HAS BEEN DELIVERED

We have been screaming for jobs, decent schools, clean houses, etc. for years.

Some folks just wouldn't listen.

We've been telling them that all hell was liable to break loose unless Negroes saw real progress.

Some folks just wouldn't listen.

Today everybody's listening—with both ears.

The Message Has Been Delivered

This young brother laid it on him, a sit-in type wearing one of those African shirts they're selling nowadays. "You have a look," he told Pepper, like he was some Southern hayseed who had to be educated about the ways of the Big City. Pepper's heat vision sent him scurrying. *Cool it baby.* Ain't nobody listening. Do you listen to what the roach says before you step on him? He almost tossed the leaflet in the trash, but returned it to his back pocket instead.

At 3:32 P.M., two white men strolled up to the front door. Customers turned around on seeing the CLOSED sign, but these two cupped their eyes and pressed their faces to the glass to see inside. They were clean-cut young men, in gas company uniforms that were not theirs. They weren't meatheads, like a lot of muscle, panting after a few punches. These dudes were fit and clean, like astronauts. That new generation. Half his age. Pepper grabbed the spot in his belly where the knife had gone deep. It already hurt from the fighting he was going to do.

They split up. One astronaut, the redhead, walked to the corner and looked up Morningside, to the side door of the office. The blond astronaut walked the other way, to the wall between the store and the bar next door. They returned to the front door, conferred, and left.

Five minutes later they were back. The redheaded astronaut bent down to pick or pop the lock on the grate and rolled it up while the other pretended to consult a clipboard. On a job, wearing the clothes of a waiter or porter gave Pepper free passage among white people. Same way a white man in an official-looking uniform in a Negro neighborhood can get into a lot of places, no sweat. A cop uniform sends one message, a utility man's another, long as they're not there to turn off the electricity. The redheaded astronaut picked the front door without a fuss and his companion wheeled a metallic box over the threshold. Acetylene torch, most likely.

Once inside, their movements turned slow and they entered the hunt. In tandem: one step, pause and survey, another step. The redhead taking Carney's office and the blond heading for Marie's. Halfway into the store, the blond let go of the box and the both of them reached for their pistols, Colt Cobras. They continued toward the back of the store with predatory attention.

Pepper was at a disadvantage in that he was not armed. His last gun had been the throwaway he used in the hijack, and he'd last seen it on the floor of Dootsie Bell's Cadillac before Dootsie dumped him in front of Harlem Hospital. Pepper had a meetup with Billy Bill scheduled that evening to buy a piece. What he had on hand now was a baseball bat and a hunting knife.

The bat to start. Pepper popped the redhead below the rib cage with the head of the baseball bat, then brought it down with gruesome force on the base of the man's skull. He'd left the office door ajar and pounced when the man got in range, had the astronaut seeing stars. There were scarce seconds before his scream attracted his partner. Go for the gun or use the fallen astronaut?

The Colt Cobra had bounced and skittered on the floor—where? The sounds of its passage had muffled, so across the rug. No time to scramble for it.

Pepper pressed the hunting knife to the redhead's throat when the other one appeared in the doorway. His body was half shielded by the redhead. A certain kind of man would have fired anyway, but the blond wasn't that breed.

"Move on back, buddy," Pepper said. The redhead yelped as Pepper increased the pressure on his neck. "We're getting up, right?" They rose. Pepper sensed the man trying to figure out his opening. He steered him a foot closer to the entrance. The astronaut moved deliberately, to force an opportunity. Pepper reached out to slam the office door shut and rammed the man into it. He hit the button on the doorknob to lock it.

The astronaut elbowed Pepper in the stomach, then slugged him in the jaw. Pepper had been protecting his stomach where he got stabbed, angling his body, and it gave the man his chance. The other man tried the lock, then rammed his shoulder into the door to break it down. The redhead tackled Pepper and brought him down.

The office window shattered inward before the weight of the Collins-Hathaway ottoman the other astronaut hurled against it. The blinds were twisted up. The rug: Pepper saw the butt of the fallen pistol. So did the redhead. They crawled over each other to get it. Pepper got there first and twisted and fired at the shape in the office window. He missed. He brought the butt down on the redhead's cranium.

Last time it was bloodstains on the man's rug, this time his window.

The window gaped. "Cool it, baby," Pepper said. "Anything pops up, I'm shooting it." He got ahold of the redheaded astronaut and continued to address the man's partner. "You get on back to the front window. I'm coming out with this motherfucker." He instructed the redhead to open the office door.

It was odd—the white man's silhouette against the 125th Street scene, which proceeded as if their violent drama did not exist. On the opposite sidewalk, a teenage girl tried to master her Hula-Hoop. The gunshot hadn't attracted the stepped-up police patrols. So far.

From the way he aimed the gun, the blond astronaut's ambitions lay in the vicinity of a headshot. Maybe two in the belly as a chaser.

"You can drop that," Pepper said. "Unless you want to leave him here."

The astronaut bent low to place the gun on the floor and put his hands up.

"Now get the fuck out of here," Pepper said.

The message had been delivered, as the young people of Harlem liked to say.

* * *

Carney saw the broken glass and ran to his office phone. Elizabeth didn't answer. At the store, the park, no telling.

"I know a guy who'll buy the torch, you don't want it," Pepper said.

"The what?"

"Over there. They were going to torch the safe." He paused. "No, J.J. got pinched. I'm sure there's another guy."

"Look, I have to get home."

He removed Linus's briefcase from the Hermann Bros. safe. Pepper told him to leave the safe open. "So they wouldn't bust it open if they came back." Carney took the cash—Freddie needed it now that fencing the necklace was no longer on the table.

He had a quick look at the papers inside the briefcase. Blueprints for a big office complex on Greenwich Street downtown—important, perhaps, but hardly irreplaceable. Beneath the blueprints were legal documents, real estate stuff with Linus's name on them and the family corporation. One of them granted

Mr. Van Wyck power of attorney over his son. Was that what it was all about? Later, Carney could figure out what had the Van Wycks so uptight. Now he had to check on his family.

As Carney locked up, Pepper asked if he still had his father's truck. It would come in handy, he said. They got the truck out of the lot and beat it to Riverside Drive.

It hit Carney anew: The necklace was gone. He had handed it over, like that. And they didn't even care about it. He honked the horn at the red light. Elizabeth and the kids. "They're okay," Carney said.

"Maybe."

"Freddie." The way Carney used to say it when they were kids and he'd put them in line for an ass-whipping. *Freddie.*

"I'll sit on your house tonight in the truck," Pepper said. "Tomorrow I'll bring on another guy to watch your family."

A big pothole rocked the truck, one of those craters with its own zip code, and Pepper winced. He laid his palm on his belly, below his heart.

"They work you over?" Carney told him he looked like crap.

Pepper mumbled something about spacemen.

When they got to the apartment, Elizabeth was lying on the couch and the kids were pinching each other. "Pepper," she said.

"Helping me move some furniture," Carney said, "since Rusty is out." He'd explained the closure of the store by telling her that Marie and Rusty deserved a break after last week, plus people were too unsettled to think about home furnishings.

Elizabeth made a joke about being his secretary, too, since Marie was off.

"What do you mean?"

She got the message pad. "You got a call from Ed Bench. He said he gave you his card?"

Carney called the lawyer from the phone booth around the corner.

They had Freddie.

EIGHT

He took Park down. It made sense to him, to trace the line of soot-streaked uptown tenements to where they terminated abruptly at Ninety-Sixth and became the world-famous regiments of grand residential buildings, which in turn gave way to the corporate behemoths in the Fifties and below. Park Avenue was like a chart in one of his economics textbooks illustrating a case study of a successful business, Manhattan street numbers on the x axis and money on the y. *This is an example of exponential growth.*

"It's Fifty-First," Carney said.

"That's what you said," Pepper said.

Carney still wasn't used to seeing the Pan Am Building looming at Forty-Fifth Street, cutting off the sky. They keep going up—the buildings, the piles of money.

The orange safety cones were where Ed Bench promised, halfway between Fifty-First and Fiftieth on the west side of the ave. Pepper moved them and Carney parked.

Across the street was 319 Park, behind a plywood fence festooned with posters for the new Frank Sinatra record with Count Basie. The building was more than thirty stories high, clad in light blue metallic panels. The panels stopped halfway up; construction was still ongoing. Far enough along that the elevator worked and the fifteenth floor had a floor in place, according to the lawyer's instructions.

When Carney had stepped out of the phone booth, he recounted the conversation to Pepper. The bloodless voice, the calm declaration of facts. They had nabbed Freddie outside his mother's house.

"I told you he'd fuck it up," Pepper had said.

"Yes," Carney said. Knowing his cousin, he wanted a glimpse of Aunt Millie to tide him over. If Moskowitz had been quick with the necklace money, Freddie would have beat it on a bus without seeing her.

Ed Bench told him to bring "Mr. Van Wyck's property" to a certain Park Avenue address at ten P.M. His cousin would be returned in exchange. Ed Bench handed over the phone to Freddie, who had time to croak "It's me" before the lawyer took the receiver back.

"On their turf," Pepper declared. "They control the scene."

"Will they do it?"

Pepper grunted. What were they capable of? They had ransacked Aunt Millie's, vandalized Sterling Gold & Gem, come to his place of business with guns. They had not killed Linus— Linus would have given up the location of the briefcase if they'd braced him. From Pierce's account, they'd murdered the witness in a criminal suit before he could testify. If Pierce was to be believed. The question remained: What would they do to Freddie, and would they return him?

"I'm starving," Pepper said.

"What?"

"We should eat before," Pepper said.

"He didn't say bring somebody."

"Did he say don't bring somebody? We're old friends, me and those Van Wyck dudes."

They drove to Jolly Chan's on Broadway. It was getting dark, every day as summer contracted it grew dark earlier. Dinner service at the restaurant was in full swing. At the door, a young woman in one of those long Chinese dresses welcomed "Mr. Pepper." She had an air of brusque confidence and led them to where Pepper and Carney had sat last time, pulling out the table so that Pepper could take his preferred seat. Back to the wall, as Carney's father used to say, so nothing can sneak up on you. Carney hadn't appreciated the wisdom until recently.

"Chan died," Pepper said. "That's his daughter. She runs the place now." He ordered fried chicken and fries, Carney pork fried rice. A young boy with untied shoelaces deposited a pot of tea on the table and quickly bowed.

Carney opened the briefcase. What did Van Wyck want? He examined the power of attorney. Linus had signed his rights over to his father three years ago. In and out of the booby hatch, dope problem—smart play is to take your son out of the family business. Had Linus been looking for the document, or did it happen to be in the safe? With his death, it was void—his family had control of his estate. Unless he had a will, but did young men get wills drawn up? If you had money, maybe.

"What's that?" Pepper said.

"Love letters," Carney told him. He held up the Valentine's Day card from a girl named Louella Mather—the handwriting and the date said she and Linus had been kids at the time—and a letter.

Carney read out sections to Pepper, summarizing. The thing was out of Elizabeth's dime novels, the ones with a white lady in a flowing dress running from a cliff-side castle, candelabra in hand. Young Miss Mather expounded upon the night with Linus on the patio, the bonfire at the beach. "Counting down the days until we can see each other again on Heart's Meadow." Heart's Meadow—it reeked of gazebo confessions in splintered moonlight. Romantic letter aside, Linus and the young lady didn't end up together, he knew that.

A woman in shiny red hot pants strolled by on the sidewalk and distracted Pepper, which Carney took as an indication to stop reading. He was returning the letter to the yellowed envelope when he noticed the folded piece of paper. It was new and didn't belong with the old letter. The heavy white office bond contained five rows of numbers, typewritten. Carney held it up to Pepper.

Pepper grunted.

"What is it?"

"From the number of digits, numbered bank accounts," Pepper said.

Carney looked them over again. "How do you know?"

"Where do you think I keep my shit?" Pepper said.

Carney couldn't tell if he was joking or not. Money stashed abroad. Laundered? Tax evasion? Is this why they were chasing Freddie down? The last item in the briefcase was the 1941 Double Play baseball card featuring Joe DiMaggio and Charley Keller. But it'd be ludicrous to go through all this for a baseball card.

Pepper and Carney killed time in the Chinese joint. Instead of offering prophecies or lucky numbers, the white slips inside the fortune cookies advertised United Life Insurance. Pepper left an inordinate tip.

They walked over to Carney's truck. Carney had gotten a new paint job for the Ford but the sounds it produced when he turned the key betrayed its age. He had stopped selling gently used furniture years ago and mostly used the truck to make the rounds of the swap meets, to off-load old coins or watches on specialists. Given the way his business was going, and Elizabeth's, they could afford a new car, a sporty but practical number, but he liked the truck because it felt like a disguise. The kids could still squeeze in the front seat and it made him happy to have the four of them in a line, chopping his hand to restrain them at a sudden stop.

Pepper said, "Still runs." He closed the door.

"It's a good old truck." He decided: Get a proper car for the family at the end of the summer, before May and John got too big. And concentrate on the job at hand.

When he and Pepper left the furniture store that afternoon, Pepper had put a steel lunch box by his feet. Now he opened it up and took out the two Colt Cobras inside. "They dropped these," he said. He checked them.

Carney pulled out his own gun. "From Miami Joe," he said. He'd found it under the sofa a few months after Pepper killed the man in his office. It had remained untouched in the bottom drawer of his desk, beneath a copy of *Ebony* with Lena Horne on the cover, until today.

Pepper was unsurprised. "Know how to use it?"

There had been one time in high school when his father was out and these rats had been squealing for hours behind his building. That anyone could hear it and not go crazy was inconceivable. He knew where his father kept his gun. On the closet shelf where his mother had kept her hat boxes, Big Mike had a shoebox with bullets and knives and what Carney later figured out was a makeshift garrote. And this month's gun. The day of the rats it had been a .38 snub nose that sat like a big black frog on Carney's thirteen-year-old palm. It was loud. He didn't know if he hit any of the critters, but they scattered and Carney lived in fear for weeks that his father would find out he'd been in his stuff. When he opened the shoebox months later, there was a different pistol inside.

He told Pepper he knew how to use it.

Pepper grunted. He put one of the Colt Cobras into a pocket inside his nylon windbreaker.

Now that they had arrived at the Park Avenue meet, Miami Joe's gun seemed silly. For the last five years, Carney had told himself that if anything bad went down, there was the gun from under the couch for protection. Secret security, like get-out-of-town money you keep in a shoe just in case. But they were on Park Avenue. One of the most expensive streets in the world. The building Van Wyck had chosen for the handoff was worth tens of millions of dollars; it was a token of the man's concentrated power, the capital and influence that scaffolded his greed. As for Carney, he had a dead man's gun and a worn-out crook who was too cheap to buy new pants.

"Ready?" Carney said.

"I was checking out the Egon one."

Carney looked at him.

"The Egon recliner with the EZ-Smooth Lever Action. In your office, the catalog. And a standing lamp."

"Of course," Carney said. "It's usually four to six weeks."

A tiny latch secured the plywood doors in front of 319 Park, next to a sign that read VAN WYCK REALTY: BUILDING THE FUTURE. Pepper and Carney moved beyond the fence and the sounds of the city magically hushed. The bronze plate was already up: VWR. White tape crisscrossed the newly installed glass of the lobby entrance. Dusty cardboard covered the floors and gray clouds of plaster mottled the walls.

A white security guard sat on a folding chair by the bank of elevators. He removed his reading glasses—he had been scratching at a book of word jumbles—and regarded Carney and his partner with irritation. His hand dropped to his waist, in the vicinity of his holster. He pointed to the glass case containing the building directory, where white letters floated on an expanse of black felt: SUITE 1500. The lone occupant.

Inside the unfinished elevator, a bare plate awaited the inspection certificate. Still time to turn around. "How do you know which bank?" Carney asked.

"Was wondering when you'd ask," Pepper said. Weary. "You like this heat?"

Carney thought, Let Freddie lie in the bed he made. And then what? Raid the maybe bank accounts and run off to an island somewhere like Wilfred Duke? It was a short-lived fantasy, a brief excursion between floors: Elizabeth would leave his ass in a second when she found out about his crooked side. Call the cops herself if thugs came knocking on Leland and Alma's door looking for them.

The elevator produced a crisp, cheerful ping and opened its doors.

The hallway of the fifteenth floor was carpeted in red, sturdy pile and a series of faux-marble panels ran its length. The ceiling lights, Carney noted, were encased in those Miller globes that had caught on in office buildings. A thin brass arrow pointed to suite 1500.

"High up," Pepper said. "The last time I was above the tenth floor . . ." He pulled out the Colt Cobra from his windbreaker. Carney had left his gun in the glove compartment after telling Pepper about it. He wasn't going to use it so it didn't make sense to bring it. In due course, the stupidity of this argument made itself evident.

The lights were on in reception. No one present. Ed Bench yelled, "In here, gentlemen," from down the hall. It smelled of paint, so fresh that the pale green walls looked like they'd smudge on you from a foot away. Chest-high dividers cut the big rooms into individual work areas, but the desks, chairs, and everything else were missing. Businesses had moved into Pan Am before it was finished, Carney remembered. There was so much urgent business to be done that the buildings couldn't keep pace, the money pushed on ahead. Next week these rooms and sub-rooms would be full of men in pinstripe suits barking into receivers.

A different sort of deal had to be concluded before that.

The door to the conference room was propped open, and inside waited Ed Bench and two men in gray flannel suits with skinny lapels. From Pepper's description, the two men were the astronauts. Ed Bench was seated at the big oval-shaped table, a white telephone with an intercom system by his elbow. There were twelve empty seats. The table and chairs were from Templeton Office's new fall line of business furniture. Not even out yet, as far as Carney knew. Outside the glass wall to the street, the new midtown skyline—ever changing—marched in silhouette.

Pepper nodded in greeting to the two astronauts, who made no response. They flanked Ed Bench and had their guns trained on Carney and Pepper in the doorway. The astronauts were more at home in the tailored suits than the gas-company costumes; this corporate warren was their natural habitat.

From his reaction, Ed Bench had been briefed on the couch salesman's bodyguard, but could not resist raising an eyebrow at his rustic attire.

Pepper kept his gun on the redhead. He had a particular dislike.

"My client was glad to have the necklace back," Ed Bench said. "He'll be pleased you brought the rest of his things."

"Where's Freddie?" Carney said.

Ed Bench gestured at the briefcase. "Everything inside?"

"The man asked you a question," Pepper said. He checked the office behind him for party crashers. The partitions made it impossible. "Can we quit with the jibber jabber?"

The eyes of the two astronauts communicated that they waited on a pretext.

"You parked where I told you?" Ed Bench said, lowering the temperature.

Carney said, "Yeah."

Ed Bench dialed a number. He said, "Okay," and hung up. "If you go to the window, you'll see."

Pepper said, "Go ahead," and kept his gun level. Carney moseyed over. His father's truck was directly across the street.

"He'll be along," Ed Bench said.

"Van Wyck," Carney said. "He must be broken up about his son."

"Linus had a knack for getting into trouble. He hung out with a bad element."

Below, two men emerged around Fifty-First Street. They carried a limp figure, which they deposited in the truck bed. They withdrew. Perhaps it was Freddie. The person did not move.

"What's wrong with him?" Carney said.

"He's alive," Ed Bench said.

The blond astronaut made a sound.

"Mr. Van Wyck took a dim view," Ed Bench said.

Pepper said, "Fuck is that?"

"Introducing his son to narcotics. Laughing."

Introducing—that wasn't true at all. "What do you mean, laughing?" Carney said.

Ed Bench registered Pepper's new posture. "When they robbed the apartment. Linus and Mr. Van Wyck had a scuffle and he fell. And Linus's friend laughed." He stroked his chin. "He took a dim view."

For the first time the redheaded astronaut spoke: "So we tuned him up."

Later, Pepper explained it was the principle of the thing: Let white people think they can fuck all over you and they'll keep doing it.

That was two months after the night on Park Avenue. Summer had burned off and autumn crept in like a thief. They were in Donegal's. Carney had stopped by to see how Pepper was enjoying the Egon recliner and pagoda standing lamp. Carney said, "You said with the riots, what was the point? Everything keeps on the way it is, so all the protests were for nothing."

Pepper said, "I am right in that. Grand jury had nothing to say about that cop, did it? He's still on the job, right? But as it pertains to me shooting those dudes . . . maybe you start small and work your way up."

TOSS

AND

SEE THEM RUN!

That night in 319 Park, Pepper started small by shooting the redheaded astronaut in the mouth. Instinct compelled the redhead to fire his .38. He missed. The blond astronaut shot at Pepper and got him in the meat above his left hip before Pepper shot him once in the face and twice in the gut. Pepper fired two more rounds into the redhead to put him down, for the man flopped weirdly on the conference table as if electrocuted. The final bullet put an end to the flailing.

"Spinal column," Pepper said. "Makes them go buggy like that."

From his reaction, Ed Bench had never seen two men shot to death close up. Pale by pedigree, he grew more so. Carney had seen Pepper kill a man before, so seeing him kill two held little novelty, but he didn't have the psychological burden of wondering if he was next. He rushed over. "You're shot, man," he said.

Blood unspooled from Pepper's fingers. "I got to get a look at it," he said. Meaning the wound. "We should wrap this up."

Carney put the briefcase on the conference table. "Do what you want," he told the lawyer.

"You sure?" Pepper asked.

"I am." There was no other ticket back.

"Shit, take the guns at least," Pepper said. "Have this fool shooting at us."

Carney did as instructed, not that Ed Bench was in any condition to chase them down. He stared at the redheaded astronaut's body. Blood had sprayed on Ed Bench's shirt and face. The lawyer's mouth worked silently. If attended to promptly, the new space-age fibers in the Templeton Office carpet prevent stains.

Down the hall the elevator was waiting. How many people worked in the neighboring buildings and might report the shots? Carney hadn't checked if any offices with line-of-sight on the conference room had their lights on. "Is it bad?" Carney said.

"It's a gunshot wound." Pepper left bloody whorls on the LOBBY button. He wiped away the print.

The lobby guard jumped out of his chair when the elevator opened and scrambled to the opposite elevator bank. He did not interfere. How far did the sound of gunfire travel? No cop cars waited on the other side of the plywood. Pepper hobbled into the street. He allowed Carney to give him a hand. They traversed the median that separated the uptown and downtown lanes, stopping only to let a gray Rolls-Royce pass. The passengers made no indication of seeing them.

Freddie lay in the truck bed, a heap in bloody clothes. He croaked when Carney appeared and put his hand on his chest.

"Give me the keys," Pepper said.

Carney did so and climbed into the back. The ladies had always loved his cousin, especially in his glory days before he was drinking and drugging too much. *Pretty boy*—Pedro had passed that down to him the way Big Mike had passed down crookedness to Carney. Those young women would not recognize Freddie now, the way they'd worked over his face.

They had to get to the hospital. Carney had given Pepper the keys distractedly and it was only when the truck lurched forward that he realized the man intended to drive with a bullet in his side. Had the slug gone through him? Were the cops close? The hospital was how far? The truck swung a U-turn and Carney got down low with Freddie and slipped his arm under his cousin's head. Carney's arm wettened. They were both on their backs. Looking up, Park Avenue was a canyon, like Freddie had said, cliff faces of buildings racing against the dark sky. It reminded Carney of when it got so hot, those summer nights years ago, that he and Freddie would take a blanket and lie on the roof of 129th Street. The day's heat radiated out of the black tar but it was still cooler than being indoors. Beneath the vast and eternal churn of the night sky. The eyes adjust. One night Freddie said the stars made him feel small. The boys' constellation knowledge stalled after the Dippers and the Belt, but you didn't have to know what something was called to know how it made you feel, and looking at the stars didn't make Carney feel small or insignificant, the stars made him feel recognized. They had their place and he had his. We all have our station in life—people, stars, cities— and even if no one looked after Carney and no one suspected him capable of much at all, he was going to make himself into something. The truck bounced uptown. Now look at him. It wasn't a bronze plate on a skyscraper, but everybody knew the corner of 125th and Morningside was his, it had his name on it— CARNEY'S—plain as day.

The truck rear-ended the car parked out front, fast enough for a nice jolt. The lights from the entrance to Harlem Hospital washed over them. Pepper helped Carney get his cousin out of the truck bed. Two young orderlies appeared with a stretcher.

"You're what, not coming in?" Carney said.

"I was just there. I need a break." Pepper took two steps uptown, hand tamped to his side. "I know a guy." He took two more steps.

Carney trotted alongside the stretcher into the hospital. He grabbed Freddie's hand. Freddie stirred. His head lolled. "I didn't mean to get you in trouble."

NINE

It took Carney a year and a half to make it downtown to the construction site. Lord knows he'd been busy. Was Marie going to come back to work when her baby got big enough? Her husband, Rodney, was the type to consider a woman bringing home money a threat to his manhood. The new girl Tracy was learning the ropes but she was no Marie, who knew when to zip it and when to politely avert her eyes. It wasn't clear what Tracy's reaction would be when she realized there was something hinky going on.

Lunch hour on Rector and Broadway. The office workers spilled out and sloshed around the avenues. Curbside hot dogs, Automat specials, bloody steaks for big shots at their reserved tables. Why today? The contract with Bella Fontaine, for one thing. Mailing the contract to Bella Fontaine's Omaha headquarters brought back everything about that sticky July. The killing of James Powell and the riots, and then the dangerous urgency of the following week—the heat that came down and what happened to Freddie. Signing up with Bella Fontaine after eighteen months of renewed pursuit of Mr. Gibbs made those events into a mirage.

He reconsidered: The consequences remained, but the reasons had turned spectral, insubstantial. Harlem had rioted—for what? The boy was still dead, the grand jury cleared Lieutenant Gilligan, and black boys and girls continued to fall before the night-sticks and pistols of racist white cops. Freddie and Linus were gone, their heist unwound as if it had never happened, and Van Wyck kept throwing up buildings.

Freddie hung on for two months in a coma. Pressure on the brain. His last words: "I didn't mean to get you in trouble." He had been jealous of Harlem Hospital, Carney knew, for the hours it had deprived him of his mother, the double shifts and night shifts over the years. He liked to think Freddie sensed and savored the warmth of her hand those final days and nights that the hospital reunited them on the fourth floor. There was no running out to the night spot, no lying about where he'd been. No vanishing acts. Pedro came up when he got the news. He stuck around for two days after the funeral and then split back to Florida.

Death took Freddie from Carney and mourning returned to him a visitation, an invisible companion who shadowed him everywhere, tugging at his sleeve and interrupting when he least expected: *Remember what my smile looked like, Remember when, Remember me.* Its voice grew quiet and Carney didn't hear it for a while and then it was loud again: *Remember me, This is your job now, Remember me or no one else will.* At times it seemed the grief was powerful enough to shut down the world, cut off the juice, stop the earth from spinning. It was not. The world proceeded in its mealy fashion, the lights stayed on, the earth continued to spin and its seasons ravaged and renewed in turn.

Munson came by for his envelope two nights after the visit to 319 Park. Given the heat on Freddie, the authorities accepted Carney's story that he'd showed up at the store, beaten half to death by someone he'd crossed. Munson didn't indicate whether he believed the story or not, merely relayed that there was no interest in pursuing it further. Via the *New York Post,* Centre Street let it be known that the Linus Van Wyck case was closed:

death by misadventure. Carney handed over the envelope to the detective and their business resumed.

Delroy, too, visited the office for Chink's envelope like everything was copacetic. Whoever had put their foot on Chink Montague's neck had relented. Things were awkward between Carney and Delroy—beyond the coerced protection-money aspect—until the hood started seeing this Jamaican gal with a lackluster dining situation. Carney was happy to move another Collins-Hathaway dinette set, ten percent off for loyal customers.

August arrived. Carney didn't know if it was over, if Van Wyck was done with him. Business deal concluded, blood on both sides, aggravations mounting—these things were usually enough to terminate a mob war, and they appeared to end the hostilities in this case as well. Mr. Van Wyck got what he wanted, after all. Carney lost sleep for a long time afterward, but come morning Elizabeth was in bed next to him, the kids were making noise down the hall, and his world was intact. For now. When Pepper came by to pick out his recliner, Carney asked him if he thought they were done. Pepper had lost weight during his convalescence, but retained his malevolent aplomb: "I'd take a dim view if it wasn't."

Carney arrived at Barclay and Greenwich. At the intersection, a Checker cab clipped a green sedan and the drivers leapt out into the street to bully each other. Two red-faced white guys making like jungle apes. Carney followed the plywood fence around the corner to Barclay, where it was calmer. The sign on the fence around the construction site announced VAN WYCK REALTY: BUILDING THE FUTURE. A big yellow crane hoisted a large section of steel tubing through the air. It wobbled like a surfer and disappeared below the fence.

Carney made his way to the tiny window in the plywood. He'd always thought of those site windows as kid stuff—May never let them pass one without making him lift her for a glimpse of the hidden operation. Here he was, pressing his nose to the glass.

The hole went four stories deep, deeper than he'd ever seen. Underground parking? Or is that how far down you have to go to get these big skyscrapers up these days? A simple fact of physics. All that dirt and rock were already accounted for. Read those articles about the city's Battery Park scheme and you know it'll take a million tons of landfill to expand the footprint of the island that much. They had to dig down ever deeper to build ever higher, then make more island to fit the other stuff they wanted to put up. It was a racket, the whole thing.

Across the street the New York Telephone Company Building hunkered in art deco splendor, a graceful, granite rebuke to the steel-and-glass upstarts around it. The peasant structures formerly occupying the construction site had posed no threat to its dignity. A row of unremarkable three-story commercial buildings, they had been vestiges of the old downtown. Carney had looked it up: According to the Hall of Records, Linus Van Wyck had owned three of them since 1961: Barclay Street numbers 101, 103, and 105. The Van Wyck corporation acquired them on August 2, 1964, eight days after his death, the same day that it closed on six adjacent properties on Greenwich. This time next year, the consolidated parcel would be the home of a fifty-six-floor office building, the most ambitious VWR project to date. Open for business well before the World Trade Center was completed and poised to take advantage of the megadevelopment one block south. The World Trade Center was going to transform the city, if you believed the hype from Rockefeller and the newspapers in Carney's pocket.

Nice to get in early. You don't have to be first, the Van Wyck philosophy went, merely have an eye for what's coming down the road.

Carney only had city records and Freddie's secondhand info to go on. The family business puts the property in Linus's name as a tax dodge—listening to his father-in-law gloat about screwing over the government had taught Carney about rich people and how they hold on to their money. To keep his allowance, Linus signs where they tell him to, and the power of attorney keeps things cool through his various hospitalizations. Was the break-in about getting that piece of paper and freeing himself, with the jewelry angle to get Freddie to help him out? Or did Linus only realize what he had once he got uptown to the Eagleton, and then try to use that leverage? Rings up Dear Old Dad and makes a threat, light extortion with a side of childhood grudge. Then his overdose—how did that change things?

Say Pepper was right that the numbers in the envelope referred to overseas bank accounts. Judging from the timing of the Greenwich Street deal, maybe VWR needs the money they've stashed in order to pull it off. *Heart's Meadow.* Ambrose Van Wyck puts the account numbers in an old love letter that reminds him of how things could have gone differently for his son. Reminds him of the shape of Linus's life if he'd dug women instead of men— and all the things his boy might have built for himself.

Maybe it was all over a baseball card, a 1941 number featuring Joe DiMaggio and Charley Keller. Worth some money if you were a fan, meaningless to everyone else.

It was like trying to decode a mystery from childhood, like why a man leaves his young son alone on a stool in a run-down bar. Anyone who knew the story was dead or wasn't talking. That left the repercussions and your feeble attempts to make sense of it.

A patrolman dispelled the confrontation in the intersection. The angry drivers went on their way and traffic resumed. Carney looked at his watch. Time to wrap this up.

While he was downtown, he wanted to see Aronowitz's place one last time. For old times' sake. He'd seen the protests on the local news. Irate citizens marching between the big bins of radio parts before the courts ruled against them: NO EMINENT DOMAIN FOR PRIVATE GAIN. SAVE DOWNTOWN. Stenciled prayers on cardboard. Carney was too late, as he discovered when he turned onto Greenwich. They'd already knocked it all down.

The neighborhood was gone, razed. Everything four blocks south of the New York Telephone Building and four blocks east of the miserable West Side Highway had been demolished and erased for the World Trade Center site, down to the street signs and traffic lights. This was the aftermath of a ruinous battle. Block after teeming block of Radio Row, the textile warehouses and women's hat stores and shoe-shine stands, the greasy spoons, even the indentations in the sidewalk where the struts of the elevated tracks had been riveted to the concrete—rubble. The buildings of the old city loomed over the broken spot, this wound in itself.

It was unreal to have your city turned inside and out. He felt unreal those days of the riots when his streets were made strange by violence. Despite what America saw on the news, only a fraction of the community had picked up bricks and bats and kerosene. The devastation had been nothing compared to what lay before him now, but if you bottled the rage and hope and fury of all the people of Harlem and made it into a bomb, the results would look something like this.

The wrecking balls had moved on to their next unravelings. The dump trucks and construction trailers dotted the broken plain, waiting for the next phase—excavation. More dirt and more rock to make more island for more buildings. One day they'll fill in the rivers altogether and everything will be just more Manhattan.

Aronowitz & Sons had shuttered long before. Carney had dropped by to say hi once—he hadn't needed the man's services in years—and a TV shop had taken its place. ELECTRIC CITY. Purple neon lightning bolts for emphasis, blinking. The new owner, a fast-talking man with a honking Bronx accent, had assumed Aronowitz's lease but had no information on where he'd gone after he handed over the keys. "He didn't look that healthy," the man said.

"He never did," Carney said.

Carney gave the WTC site one last look. The next time he was here it'd be something totally different. That's how it worked.

He headed for the train. He had to have a quick chat with his rare-gem connection, telephone out of the question. The man's office was on Ninetieth off Second and the subways were a mess today, water main explosion on the East Side.

Then it was off to meet Elizabeth. There was an open house for a place on Strivers' Row and he wanted to take a look. Distress sale. Riverside Drive was nice, but it was hard to turn down a chance at Strivers' Row. If you could swing it. It was such a pretty block and on certain nights when it was cool and quiet it was as if you didn't live in the city at all.